Stephen Kimball

D·E·A·T·H
D·U·T·Y

A SIGNET BOOK

Signet
Published by the Penguin Group
Penguin Putnam Inc., 375 Hudson Street,
New York, New York 10014, U.S.A.
Penguin Books Ltd, 27 Wrights Lane,
London W8 5TZ, England
Penguin Books Australia Ltd, Ringwood,
Victoria, Australia
Penguin Books Canada Ltd, 10 Alcorn Avenue,
Toronto, Ontario, Canada M4V 3B2
Penguin Books (N.Z.) Ltd, 182–190 Wairau Road,
Auckland 10, New Zealand

Penguin Books Ltd, Registered Offices:
Harmondsworth, Middlesex, England

Published by Signet, an imprint of Dutton Signet,
a member of Penguin Putnam Inc.
Previously published in a Dutton edition.

First Signet Printing, April, 1998
10 9 8 7 6 5 4 3 2 1

 REGISTERED TRADEMARK—MARCA REGISTRADA

Printed in the United States of America

PUBLISHER'S NOTE
This is a work of fiction. Names, characters, places, and incidents either are
the product of the author's imagination or are used fictitiously, and any
resemblance to actual persons, living or dead, events, or locales is entirely
coincidental.

BOOKS ARE AVAILABLE AT QUANTITY DISCOUNTS WHEN USED TO PROMOTE PROD-
UCTS OR SERVICES. FOR INFORMATION PLEASE WRITE TO PREMIUM MARKETING
DIVISION, PENGUIN PUTNAM INC., 375 HUDSON STREET, NEW YORK, NEW YORK
10014.

For my mother and father,
the U.S. Foreign Service's finest

ACKNOWLEDGMENTS

I would like to thank William Daniels of the U.S. Department of State's Citizens Emergency Center for his gracious responses to my questions about the work of his office. I am also grateful to Gary Sheaffer of the State Department's Consular Affairs Office for sharing his insights into the Foreign Service. For so generously providing invaluable details about the State Department and the Foreign Service career path, I am especially indebted to James Bermingham.

Carol Buckland read an early version of the manuscript and made many excellent suggestions for character and plot development. Chuck Harman and Frank Desiderio helped with important details about Washington, D.C., and Prince George's County, Maryland, the principal settings of the story. The Fleet Management Division of the U.S. General Services Administration provided helpful information about the federal government's motor vehicle fleet.

At Dutton Signet, Ed Stackler, my editor, encouraged the novel from its earliest stages and thoughtfully edited the manuscript for style and content.

My literary agent, Marian Young, deserves special thanks for her unflagging support and uncommon grace. Howard Sanders and Rich Green put icing on the cake.

As always, thanks to Cindy, Peter, and Michael.

★ PROLOGUE ★

The lone foreign woman at the reception desk of Beijing's Great Wall Sheraton Hotel shifted her feet uneasily, trying to shake off the unsettling feeling of being watched. The young concierge behind the desk had been struggling with the hotel computer system for nearly ten minutes, typing in one command after another on his keyboard in an effort to get her a room assignment. Finally he stopped typing and waited, clearly hoping a room would come up on his screen. He smiled contritely at her. She returned his smile, but hers was tense and strained, given out of pure politeness.

As she waited, the woman fought the urge to look behind her at the crowd milling in the lobby. Finally she allowed herself a glance. Her eyes tracked around the vast room that was crawling with men, mostly European and drunk. They choked the entrance to the Atrium bar, some shouting and laughing boisterously, others barely managing to stand up. The polyglot din competed with loud rock music—at least ten years old—that blared from the bar and filled the lobby. The Chinese staff wisely stayed off to the side, their faces registering neither approval nor disapproval as they took in the frenzy around them.

Scanning the crowd, the woman caught eyes staring at her. They belonged to leering unshaven faces and appeared in fractured bursts, like images in a slide show. She shuddered and looked away. No wonder she felt as if she were being watched.

The sensation had begun more than an hour ago when she'd cleared customs at Beijing airport. It grew as she made her way through the airport terminal and sought out a taxi. She knew that it wasn't unusual for An Quan Bu—the Chinese secret police—to tail foreigners. On one visit to China the woman had even come to recognize the agent following her, a familiar face throughout her stay.

Tonight at the airport she was careful not to let on that she suspected anything. She ducked into a rest room on the pretense of washing up. On leaving, she managed to steal a casual glance around her. But there was no one to be seen. Inside the taxi on the way to the hotel she kept watch on the traffic around her, trying to discern if anyone was following. Again, nothing.

Now, still waiting for her room, she turned back to the concierge. "Are all these people guests?" she asked in perfect Mandarin. She almost had to shout above the racket.

The concierge looked up quickly, obviously surprised at the quality of her accent. "Most of them," he answered back in Chinese. "They've been here almost a week now."

"What's going on?"

"Oh, a convention at the Exhibition Center across town. All the hotels are full." He gave her a convention brochure that said "French Light Weaponry" in Chinese, French, and English. The logo in the middle was an automatic assault rifle surrounded by a ring of ammunition. The woman shook her head; the French would sell arms to anyone.

The concierge's face showed relief when the assignment finally flashed up on his screen. "You'll be in room 1232, up above the noise." The woman smiled gratefully and took the key the concierge held out. She waited until he returned her black American diplomatic passport, a courtesy extended to foreign representatives.

"Should I call a bellman?" he asked.

"No, thank you," she said. Tipping was frowned on in China, and the woman did not want someone carrying her bags if she couldn't give him something for it. Besides, she knew the way already, having stayed at the Great Wall Sheraton several times before. It wasn't her first choice of Beijing hotels, others having more Chinese charm or better locations near the U.S. Embassy over on Xiu Shui Bei Jie. She'd gotten her travel orders just a week ago and had to take what she could get. The one advantage she saw to the Great Wall was that it was near the road to the airport. She didn't plan to stay long.

She picked up her only bag and scanned the lobby. *Damn.* To get to the elevators, she would have to cut through the thick queue of men waiting to enter the bar. There was no other way. As if preparing for battle, she tightened the belt on her black trench coat, put her head down, and strode quickly toward the elevators.

The line of men parted reluctantly as she made her way through it. The odor of colognes was overpowering, hanging dense in the air. She excused herself in German, hoping none of the men around her spoke it. There were muttered come-ons in several languages, and hands reached out for her as she passed, but she shook them off and kept going.

At last she made it to the bank of elevators, where she pushed the up button. She cursed to herself as she realized that only one of the elevators was in operation. Behind her, men continued to shout their catcalls and lurid invitations, but she kept her back to them and her eyes fastened to the lights of the slowly descending elevator.

Suddenly two men seemed to materialize from nowhere on either side of her. She kept her fear in check and calmly glanced at each of them, one tall, wearing a long brown leather coat, the other shorter and heavyset in a black nylon jacket. *Get down here*, she urged the elevator silently.

"What airline you with?" the tall one said to her in a British accent with a faint trace of cockney.

"I'm not with an airline," she said curtly, looking him straight in the eye. He had stringy yellow hair and bad teeth.

He shrugged. "Doesn't really matter now, does it, luv?" he said. The other man laughed lewdly, expelling a vapor of gin and peanuts. "So how's about us coming up for a drink?"

She slowly shook her head, feeling heavy-legged and drowsy. She watched as the elevator light blinked on. "Actually I'm waiting for my husband," she said, half turning toward the reception desk. "He's the big man carrying the rifle case."

Both men spun around to look into the crowd. The elevator door slid open, and the woman hopped in and hit the close button before the men realized what was happening. Their curses faded with the other lobby noise as the elevator ascended.

"Good riddance," she muttered, and dropped her bag on the floor between her feet. She leaned back against the elevator and rubbed her eyes. It'd been a while since she'd had to deal with such obnoxious behavior in China. For a moment she worried that she might run into those two idiots in the morning, but it was a large hotel, and she would be up well before them to make an early appointment.

The woman wondered why the embassy had been so merciless this time, scheduling her for an 8:00 A.M. meeting. She'd been in the air nearly twenty-four hours, not including a four-hour layover in Tokyo. Years ago she tried taking a mild sedative to help her sleep through the long transpacific flight but only wound up with a headache from it. So now, resigned to catching up on her sleep when she got back home to Washington, she read and dozed on the plane.

She hoped she could get at least some rest tonight to be able to function at her meeting. Nowhere in her travel orders was it clear what the meeting was about. In fact, this entire TDY—temporary duty—was something of a mystery. The orders came straight from the

Secretary of State's office in a classified memo. No way she could avoid it even though she'd busted her hump for the past several weeks preparing for the Secretary's visit here that wrapped up a few days ago. With a young daughter back home, a trip was the last thing she needed right now.

The elevator ground to a screeching stop, and the door slid open to the twelfth floor. The long corridors were empty and silent as she searched for room 1232. She found it at the end of the hall. A Do Not Disturb sign in four languages hung from the doorknob. She held it in her hand, studying it. Why was it there on the outside of the door? she wondered. Suddenly a sharp sound behind her caused her to jump. She shook her head when she realized that it was only the elevator, being summoned to another floor.

She slid the key into the doorknob and turned it. Inside, the room was unexpectedly bright from the light of the full moon pouring through the open window. She heard the door click shut behind her and felt for a light switch on the wall. She flipped it on, but nothing happened. No light. She tried the table lamps on the dresser and nightstand, but those didn't work either.

"Damn." She sighed. What was next?

Her first thought was that the hotel had an electrical blackout—it wasn't uncommon in China—but the lights had been on in the hallway when she came in. That meant her room, or maybe a group of rooms, was out of power. Or maybe the maid had forgotten to plug the lights in after cleaning.

The woman tossed her bag onto the bed and wearily bent down to look at the wires. Feeling for the switch-plate, she muttered, "Uck," as she felt her hand enclosed by tacky cobweb. She yanked it back quickly, loose shreds of dirty web dangling from her fingers. Furiously she wiped her hand on the bed ruffle.

Well, at least she'd ruled out the wires as the problem. They were plugged in right where they should have been. She decided to try one more thing. Steadying the dresser lampshade with one hand, she moved her other hand up to the bulb. When she reached the top, she gasped out loud. Nothing was there! There was no bulb. She checked the nightstand lamp. There was none there either.

What was this anyway? The woman knew of hotel staff stealing room TVs and linens, but that was out in the provinces. But lightbulbs? In Beijing? Absently she wiped away cobweb on her trench coat as she pondered what to do next.

From the darkness close behind she heard a door creak slightly, and she turned toward the bathroom. Then she heard another sound, like someone spitting, and felt a sudden bolt of pain searing her neck. She reached for her neck but panicked as she suddenly felt her chest tighten, her breathing constricted. She opened her mouth to scream, but her vocal cords were dead.

She flailed her hands, clawing at the darkness, searching for something to hold on to. Her legs grew wobbly, and she began sliding to the floor. As she did, her fingernails dug into the flowered wallpaper, tearing long grooves in it.

Gasping for air, she pushed herself away from the wall and seized the back of a chair. The room was gyrating, and she clung to the chair. She looked up and saw someone staring at her, a woman with wild eyes and a ghoulishly contorted face. There was something protruding from the side of her head. Was it a needle? How could it have been a needle? It seemed to glow metallic in the moonlight, an S-shaped stream of blood bubbling from beneath it.

Then in horror she realized she was looking at herself in the mirror.

Another face slowly appeared from the shadows behind the woman. It was a man's face. First the eyes—dark and angry under heavy eyebrows—then the nose, twisted. It wasn't a Chinese face, but European or American. What was that in his hand, some kind of tube? He held it close to his mouth, like a woodwind instrument. He watched her, his eyes steady.

Who are you? the woman tried to say. But she couldn't manage it. The room was spinning faster, out of control. She felt her strength draining from her limbs, her brain and senses failing. The fabric on the chair began to slide beneath her clutching fingers. Her eyes fastened on the man's face. The edges of his mouth turned up in a slight smile as she lost her grip and dropped to the floor.

CHAPTER
★ ONE ★

"How many ways can an American die overseas?"

Kate Verdi, junior death officer in the State Department's Citizens Emergency Center, froze in her seat as she heard those words that struck terror in hearts throughout the office. They were spoken by her boss, "Calamity" John Dietz, and they could mean only one thing: Dietz had a fresh death case he was looking to dump on someone.

Verdi carefully peered around her computer monitor and spied Dietz as he stalked the other end of the office. He bustled around his secretary's desk, muttering to himself, and riffled violently through a stack of papers there, like a hound after a holed fox. All around him heads disappeared behind files, office doors were being closed, and one lucky bureaucrat whose desk was near the rest room casually escaped into it.

Ever so nonchalantly Verdi adjusted her monitor, keeping it between Dietz's line of vision and her. Normally she would be the last in the office to shirk an assignment, but one thing she didn't need right now was another death case. She was rushing to finish her work so she could make opening pitch of an Orioles game up in Baltimore, a good forty minutes from Washington. Worse if she hit rush-hour traffic.

She first had to pick up Nonno, her grandfather, out in Seat Pleasant—a Maryland suburb—and then fight beltway traffic on her way to Route 95 to Camden Yards. His eightieth birthday was next week, and the tickets for box seats behind the Orioles' dugout were her present to him. Besides, Mussina was pitching, the hated Yankees were in town, and the Os needed to take this series to gain ground on the Yanks before the players' strike everyone was expecting pulled the plug on the 1994 season. She *had* to be there. It was already past four, and opening pitch was at five-thirty.

Before she could sneak away, Verdi had three cases that needed her immediate attention. They concerned extraordinary events in the lives of the people involved in them but were merely routine for the Citizens Emergency Center, the office at the State Department that handles the deaths and other catastrophes Americans suffer overseas. It was all gritty, thankless work, hardly the stuff noticed by the diplomatic press corps or the Sunday TV pundits.

In the first one Verdi was typing out a cable to the State Department's country officer for Singapore, bringing him up to speed on the son of a prominent American lawyer who'd been arrested there for trying to buy drugs from an undercover narc. She called the case the Singapore-Ass-in-a-Sling, and it'd been handed to her this morning, marked "Highest Priority." A note was attached, informing her that the senior U.S. senator from Connecticut, the lawyer's home state, was *personally* interested in it.

Verdi had already wired bail money—a king's ransom—from the boy's father, who was too busy on a big case to fly out there himself. She'd also arranged temporary legal counsel for the boy through the American Embassy until Dad could dispatch a team of his own lawyers. She'd been told to have the embassy pull out the stops and keep a lid on it. They were working overtime on this one.

She knew that any other American kid busted in Singapore, one without money and connections, would be in a jail cell right now, peeing in his pants. But this was no ordinary kid: He was a fortunate son, and the system was being bent in his favor. To Verdi, it bit the big one, but that was the way it worked. She fully expected to get a cable sometime soon telling her the boy had mysteriously jumped bail and was on a plane bound for the United States. And that would be the end of it.

Verdi stared bleary-eyed at her computer screen, the white words melting away from the blue background field. Another file on her desk, an international child abduction case, competed for her attention. Before she could leave, she had to draft a memo to the embassy in Damascus, Syria, where the child had been taken by its father. This was the first case of this kind Verdi had seen since starting in CEC three months ago.

The third was a death, requiring a casualty message to the next of kin. Verdi, following procedure, tried calling the family several times throughout the day, but no one answered. So now she had to work from her *Foreign Affairs Manual* to draft a telegram, one she knew would be opened by shaking hands and read in disbelief. It would be read over and over and might well be folded up and slipped into a Bible, to be passed on from one generation to the next. It had to be right.

Leaving the lawyer's son for a moment, she toiled away at the telegram, careful to avoid the thoughtless mistakes commonly made in these kinds of messages, like a misspelled name or a reference to a deceased son as a husband. Fortunately for Verdi, she didn't handle death cases all the time. It only seemed that way.

It is unfortunate at this sad time that we must also immediately call your attention to the urgent need for making necessary arrangements. The law requires disposition of remains (either cremation or burial) within 48 hours unless the remains are to be shipped outside this country. The next three paragraphs explain the options you have for making your decisions.

"Think you'll make your game?" Parker Harrington asked snidely from the next desk, his voice sounding as if it had come through his nasal passages and out his nose. Verdi looked over at him, but he was hidden behind the *Washington Post* Style section opened in front of him, obviously unworried that Calamity John would swoop down on him. He was either terribly sure of himself or stupid; Verdi wasn't sure which.

"How'd you know about that?" she asked, annoyed.

No response from behind the paper, but Verdi saw Harrington's shiny tasseled loafers shuffling restlessly over the institutional-grade brown-gray carpet, standard federal issue. She knew Harrington was at the end of his rotation as a death officer, having been here the requisite three years, and couldn't wait to get out. He already had pictures of Morocco—his top choice for his next post—tacked on the cork board next to his desk.

Verdi looked below her desk at the bright orange tickets poking out from the top of her purse, a beacon in the darkness. She could almost taste the sudsy beer and hear the roar of the crowd. *Concentrate*, she ordered herself, and she went back to her casualty message. Suddenly a shadow passed over her desk, and Verdi felt her stomach in her throat as she looked up into the dark, bespectacled eyes of Calamity John Dietz.

"Death Officer Verdi," he said, nodding curtly, "how many ways can an American die overseas?"

Verdi swallowed hard and prodded her memory. She thought—crazily, she knew—that by giving Dietz the right answer, she might somehow avoid the death case he held in his hand. "Two hundred ten?" she said hesitantly.

Dietz's mouth turned up in the slightest of grins— the sure sign of a wrong answer—and he plopped

down in the chair next to her desk. He waited, knowing it would increase the tension, maybe even get her
to say something she shouldn't. But Verdi knew his
game; as anxious as she was to leave, she would let
him make the first move.

"Actually, that's the closest anyone's gotten this
month," he said finally. "I've seen two hundred seven
since I've been here, going on seventeen years."

"Do I get a prize?" she said, giving him a big smile
and a direct look with her dark eyes, hoping for a
break.

Dietz ignored it all. "I've been accused of counting
too liberally, you know. For example, I would count
being gored by a bull at, say, Pamplona separately
from being gored by a wild boar. Generically the
deaths are the same, but to me, being gored by a bull is
entirely different from being gored by a boar. What do
you think?"

That depends on the boar, doesn't it, Calamity John?
Dietz was being even more coy than usual with this
assignment, prompting Verdi to be wary of what was
coming. She always found Dietz tough to read, and
now was no exception. He was Civil Service and
therefore a lifer in his job, unlike the Foreign Service
officers such as Verdi, who rotated assignments in different offices at State and around the world. Early on
Verdi had noticed how her fellow FSOs talked about
the Civil Service, as if they were of some lower caste.
But Verdi, who had had respect for others drummed
into her since she could remember, did not share this
attitude.

Not that Dietz didn't deserve it once in a while. For

whatever eccentric charm he put on display, he was a heartless bastard among heartless bastards. He ran the office like a prison guard. Verdi sensed a trace of sadism in him, a *Schadenfreude* inappropriate to his position. The book on him was that he was of the same mold as the college chemistry professor who liked to see students flunk his course. His nickname came from the gusto he brought to his job as administrator for the misfortunes of his countrymen. No one would call him Calamity John to his face, but he was almost certainly aware of the name. Verdi recognized his intelligence and experience but found him a conundrum in terms of his motivations, which seemed to be so unlike her own.

For Verdi, being a death officer was part of the whole process of getting her ticket punched, a stepping-stone to better things. Apart from the satisfaction she got from doing her job well and helping others, she went the extra distance and pulled in top evaluations because she knew her performance would determine her next, and future, Foreign Service assignments. But Dietz was here to stay. What drove him? Verdi wondered. What satisfaction did *he* derive from this grim job? And what did he want from her now?

Verdi took in a breath. "You have something for me, Mr. Dietz?"

"I most certainly do," he said with some relish. "A wet one. *Wringing* wet," he added ominously.

Verdi tried to keep her face impassive but found it harder to do so. In the office parlance a wet one was the victim of an accident or violent death, usually leaving a gory corpse. Although Verdi would not have to identify the body, she knew she would have to work hard to artfully convey the cause of death to the next of kin without dwelling on the violence. She'd done it before. What was the big deal here? She wished he'd quit jerking her around and get to the point.

No such luck. "How long have you been with us now, Kate?" he said. His voice sounded nasal, as if he had a cold. For a moment she thought he might be spending too much time with Parker Harrington.

"A little over three months," she answered, her eyes narrowing slightly at the question.

"Three months," he said, sitting back and chewing on that revelation for a while. "And how long have you been a Foreign Service officer?"

"Into my third year."

Dietz pulled a handkerchief from his pocket and sneezed into it. "Your first assignment was in Asia," he said. "Indonesia, was it?"

"Yes," she said, as recent memories came back, pleasant memories. "I did consular work at the embassy in Jakarta. It was a small staff, just—"

"So," he said, homing in on the kid in the back of the chemistry class, the one who never raised her hand. "You're still on probation as an FSO, is that correct? Untenured and unconed?"

Nervous heat began to crawl over Verdi's shoulders and prickle her neck. Her attention was on full alert. With her blue-collar roots, Verdi did not take talk of her probation lightly. Her father was a plumber, and her mother did laundry and made meals for the parish priests. Money was always tight, and a job, after one's soul, was one's most sacred possession, jealously guarded. Although she didn't buy into the Generation-X orgy of self-pity, she knew that at twenty-seven she could be stuck in nowhere assignments for years if she didn't watch out for herself.

A cone was one's area of expertise as a Foreign Service officer—political, economic, consular, or administrative, in that pecking order. Used to be you were coned when you became an FSO, but now that distinction came with tenure at the end of your fourth year. If you made it, that is. Many didn't, as Verdi was acutely aware.

Her instinct was to deflect Dietz's cross-examination. She tilted her head and smoothed her hand over the top of her desk. "Yes," she said, smiling, even though her cheeks were flushed with heat. "Untenured and unconed. But the food in the cafeteria more than makes up for it."

Dietz frowned, not seeing the fear he was expecting. "I have a case here," he said, thumbing at the edge of the file and watching her like a crocodile. "It's going to take a significant degree of diplomatic skill to handle. Personally I would have chosen a more seasoned officer for it."

Verdi, feeling the sting of his belittlement, was tempted to pick up the gauntlet and take the case. Instead she cast an obvious sidelong glance at Parker Harrington, who had somehow lost his newspaper and was now spellbound by a death file. He picked up the phone and began dialing. *Probably just calling his home number,* Verdi thought sourly.

"Well, Mr. Dietz," Verdi began carefully, "I appreciate

your considering me for the case. But I'd understand if you gave it to a more senior officer. Especially today, because I have some pressing personal business to attend to this afternoon, outside the building, I mean."

Dietz grinned again, showing teeth this time. "That's very big of you. But I'm afraid you're stuck on this one. You have to do it. In fact, this case came to me through some ... irregular channels, with specific instructions that one Katherine Verdi handle it."

Dietz leaned closer to her. An odor of Aqua Velva and lunch meat seemed to rise off his shoulders. "Tell me, Kate, who do you know in the Office of Foreign Service Career Development and Assignments?"

Verdi blinked. "Uh, there's an admin officer I knew in Jakarta assigned to that office. He's just back; we had the same tour. But I haven't seen him since I left Indonesia."

Dietz looked at her skeptically. "This ... request here is pretty high-level. It has Kendall Holmes's name on it, the director of the Career Development and Assignments office. I doubt your admin friend can pull those kinds of strings."

Verdi tried to hide her surprise. Kendall Holmes: Now that was a name she knew. In fact, anyone in the Foreign Service with the slightest concern for his career had better know it. Holmes—director of the all-important office responsible for placing Foreign Service officers in their domestic or overseas jobs—was one of the most feared people at State. Getting on his bad side could put one stamping passports in the middle of a jungle somewhere.

Dietz was pleased to see from the look on Verdi's

face that he'd impressed on her the gravity of the situation. "In all my time here"—he went on—"I've never gotten a case from that office. How would you explain it?"

Verdi shook her head. Dietz certainly had a point, for a change. What would Career Development and Assignments be doing assigning death cases? And why would it put *her* name on it, of all people?

"It gets stranger," he said, pushing the file into her hands. "The decedent is no less than a deputy assistant secretary—name of Patricia Van Slyke—in Beijing on a TDY. She died in a fall in her hotel room shower."

Verdi frowned as she realized why Dietz called it a wet one. Questions flipped through her mind, foremost of all: Why wasn't Patricia Van Slyke's office brought in on the return of her remains?

"Maybe you can figure out why Career Development, instead of Van Slyke's bureau, tasked this to us," Dietz said, anticipating Verdi's question. "I have no idea whom to liaise with at Career Development. Maybe you can call your friend over there and find out."

Verdi thought of Chester Lundquist—whose name she purposely kept from Dietz—now toiling in Career Development and Assignments. Chet had been her first friend in Jakarta, a place entirely alien to any she'd seen before. Chet, who'd toured in Asia before, took her under his wing, showed her around, was always there for her. But then things changed as he began making painfully oblique romantic overtures to her—that is, until Antonio came into her life. She wondered how Chet was doing and whether he'd speak to her again.

Dietz pulled her from her reverie. "Get on the horn to Beijing, Verdi," he growled. "Immediately. Find out what you can, and get precise instructions. You'll see in the file the family's been notified. They're local—Great Falls, Virginia, I think. But the remains require disposition.

"One more thing," he said, drawing closer to her. "This case gets top priority. The seventh floor wants it wrapped up quickly and by the numbers. They also want it kept out of the papers. Until this is resolved, there are no other cases. There will be no screwups or solecisms, am I clear?"

Verdi nibbled at the flesh inside her bottom lip. "What about the lawyer's son in Singapore," she said, "the friend of Senator Ramsey?"

"Give that to me. I'll put someone else on it."

The Van Slyke case *must* be important for Dietz to take a case off her hands, Verdi thought. She gave him the file but left the cable on the computer. She would give it to him later. Something else occurred to her, an opportunity.

"And my orientation course at the FSI tomorrow," she said hopefully, "the one you wanted me to take?" If she could get out of the dreaded course at the Foreign Service Institute, where the department held its language training and area studies courses, there might at least be some good in getting this case.

Dietz frowned at the annoyance. "Better go or they'll be on my back. Just come back as soon as it's over. Don't stick around for the wine and cheese after."

He slowly rose from the chair with great effort and looked toward the window, rubbing his back. "Sky's getting dark," he announced, watching her from the corner of his eye. "Your baseball game will probably be rained out anyway."

Verdi's head shot up. *How did he know about the game?* She looked over at Harrington, with whom she had seen Dietz talking sailing, Dietz's obsession, at the office coffee machine. Some serious male bonding had been going on here, and she was now getting the short end of it.

But Harrington was gone. So was Dietz, who'd left the Van Slyke file on the chair, still warm where he'd been sitting.

CHAPTER

★ TWO ★

"Yes, I'll wait," Verdi said to the Marine guard who'd picked up her call to the Beijing embassy. She knew that it was about 4:00 A.M. there and that she'd be dragging someone out of bed.

Verdi kept herself from looking at her watch or the clock on the wall. Knowing the time would just make her nervous and possibly rush her through this call. Aware that everything she did on this case would be carefully watched and recorded, she gave herself as much time as she needed. As soon as she finished this, she'd call Nonno and work something out with him.

A man's voice came on, sounding groggy but intelligent. "Yes, hello?" he said.

"Yes, this is Katherine Verdi in the Office of Consular Services, Citizens Emergency Center in Washington."

A pause. "Norm Price, duty officer. What can I do for you?"

Uncertain of Price's ability to understand much of anything right now, she began slowly. "I'm a death officer, Mr. Price, asked to handle the shipment of the remains of an American citizen." She waited for him to acknowledge.

"Go ahead, please," he said.

"I've just been assigned this case. You're probably aware of it. A senior Foreign Service officer on TDY in Beijing died in a hotel room accident on July ninth. Her name was Patricia Van Slyke. The family has asked OCS to handle the shipment and disposition. My deputy director suggested I give you a call to see if you had anything for me on Van Slyke, especially the current status of the disposition."

"Van Slyke, did you say? Mmm, don't recognize the name."

Verdi almost dropped the phone. How was it possible that he'd never heard of her? "What?" she said.

"I said, I don't recognize the name."

"Yes, I heard you, thanks." She thought for a moment. "Mr. Price, this is a highly sensitive case. Patricia Van Slyke was Senior Executive Service, deputy assistant secretary for East Asian and Pacific Affairs. I can't imagine why you wouldn't know she'd been there."

"Miss Verity, the Secretary of State was through here a week ago on his tour of the Pacific Rim. People have been going in and out of here like Grand Central."

"But certainly you must—"

"Hold, please," he said, and went off the line for several seconds. Static hummed and buzzed through the line.

He was back in less than a minute. "Still there? Yeah, I'm looking through the TDY roster right now, but she's not on it. It hasn't been updated since the Secretary's visit, and you said she's been dead for just a couple days, isn't that right?"

"Yes, three days," Verdi said, speaking loudly over a loud rush of static. "She died on July ninth, last Saturday. Maybe there's something in your shipping records, a waybill or diplomatic clearance to transport remains?"

"Hold," Price said, and went off the line again. "Yeah, I found it," he said, back on the phone, sounding relieved. "Just as you said. It says the remains of Patricia Van Slyke have been committed to diplomatic courier and shipped on July eleven. Hmm, that was two days ago, or yesterday for you."

"What?" Verdi said, prickly heat rising up her neck for the second time in an hour. She had visions of Patricia Van Slyke's casket lost in a warehouse somewhere or being routed to Australia. "Does it say where they've been shipped?"

She heard papers being ruffled. "Yeah," he said, and began reading: "Trans World Airlines flight number 1167 out of Tokyo. Arriving TWA freight hangar, Dulles International Airport. ETA 11:05 p.m., Tuesday, July 12, 1994."

"But that's tonight," she said, the prickly heat spreading to her face. "No specific instructions, no funeral home?"

"There's something else," Price said. "It says here the remains are to be picked up by a representative of the Department of State on behalf of the family. To clear customs and deliver the remains to a funeral home of the family's choice."

"A representative?" Verdi said, the heat spreading over her body. "Who?"

Silence on the other end.

"Mr. Price?"

"I'm looking. There's nothing here, Miss Verity. I guess you're the representative."

A long slow breath whistled between Verdi's teeth. She tried to collect her thoughts.

"May I make a suggestion?" Price said. "Call the family—says here they live in Virginia—and ask them where they want the remains to go. Pick up the remains at Dulles yourself; that way you'll know they got in safely."

Verdi gritted her teeth. "Mr. Price, I rent a one-bedroom apartment in a walk-up building. I don't think a casket will fit in there very well."

Price didn't laugh. *Don't any of these people have a sense of humor?* Verdi thought.

"Didn't you know?" he asked quietly.

"Know what? I got this case five minutes ago. Obviously I don't know much."

"The remains were cremated. They'll arrive in a small wooden crate that'll fit easily in the back of a car. Besides, you could have the people from the funeral home there with you at the freight hangar."

"Great." Verdi sighed, sitting back in her chair.

"Anything else?" Price said.

Verdi sat up and spoke quietly into the phone. "Mr. Price, do you have any idea what Patricia Van Slyke might have been doing there? Or who might have sent her out to Beijing?"

"No idea," Price said. "I never even knew she was here."

Verdi touched her temple with one finger and massaged it slowly. "OK, Mr. Price, thank you very much."

"You're welcome," he said. "Can you give me the correct spelling of your name? For the log."

She spelled it out for him.

"Sorry about mispronouncing it," he said.

"No problem," she said, and they hung up.

Verdi stood up to stretch and surveyed the office. Everyone was gone except for Boris Kubanyi, his back to her across the hall, two offices over from hers. Kubanyi was a Foreign Service officer nearly twice her age who'd been in the office even longer than Dietz. No one seemed to know how long he'd been there or much else about him. Verdi had briefly considered suggesting to Dietz that he give the case to Kubanyi but realized she'd never seen him speak to Kubanyi, much less assign him anything.

Verdi herself had never heard Kubanyi speak to anyone. She'd smelled the booze on him and noticed him stepping out of the office throughout the day, apparently to get a drink or three. The word on him was that he had burned out on death cases years ago, and no other office had wanted to take him. Now he was putting in his time, showing up most days, waiting for his pension.

She stepped into the hallway in search of the northern Virginia telephone directory to look up Patricia Van Slyke's home number. For some reason it had been left out of the file. At least the family had been notified. She spied the directory on top of a secretary's desk and went over to pick it up. As she did, she groaned when she saw streaks of rain across the window pane in the office next to hers. Lightning flashed in the slate-black sky, followed by a low rumble of thunder. The view from the window was due north, toward Baltimore.

"Damn Calamity John," she muttered. "He had to be right."

CHAPTER
★ THREE ★

The storm raged through the evening and into the night, grinding Dulles air traffic to a halt. Verdi, soggy and restless on a bench in the TWA freight hangar, could hear the rain pelting the thin walls of the building. Her ball game was rained out; at least she'd get new tickets. She'd called the airlines before she left for the airport and was told to expect brief delays in incoming flights. Taking no chances that she'd miss the arrival of Patricia Van Slyke's remains, she'd gotten there precisely at 11:00 P.M. It was now 1:23 A.M., and still no word on when the flight was getting in.

Verdi had spoken with someone at the Van Slyke residence who gave her the name of a funeral home. The funeral director told Verdi he'd send someone out to the airport immediately. Honestly believing her head would explode if she stayed in the office a minute longer, Verdi left after speaking with the funeral director. She drove around in the rain, stopping at a fast-food place and, later, killing time at a bookstore before heading out of town to Dulles.

The TWA hangar was nothing more than a huge open room separated by blocks of freight skids on a bare cement floor. The only sign of life came from the TV in the freight supervisor's office back behind a particle board counter, a string of sitcoms blowing off canned laughter. The night supervisor, an ancient man with a pompadour of white hair, poked his head out of the office on her arrival, asked her what she wanted, and told her the flight was delayed two hours. He pointed vaguely at a bench and never reappeared.

Verdi's eyes were tired, her stomach was queasy, and her butt sore from the hard bench. With no one from the funeral home showing up either, she was resigned to taking Patricia Van Slyke's remains home with her, if they ever came in.

"If you're going to be staying at my apartment, I might as well get to know you better," Verdi said to Van Slyke's file. She opened it again for what seemed the hundredth time. On top was the standard form OF-180, Report of the Death of an American Citizen Abroad. Verdi scanned it. Name: Patricia Van Slyke. Place of Death: Beijing, People's Republic of China. Cause of Death: Died from a fall in a hotel room shower as declared by Lao Yu-lin, Beijing Notary Public. Disposition of the Remains: Cremated at Feng-Tai Crematorium, Beijing, on July 10, 1994, at 4:35 A.M. and returned to her family. And behind the OF-180 was the official death notice, written in Chinese, and a brief translation. The words *massive blunt trauma* jumped out at her.

"Poor woman," Verdi mumbled.

Stapled to the back cover was a sheet of paper with some personal information about Van Slyke: She was divorced and had a daughter who stayed at home in Virginia with Van Slyke's mother. Her ex-husband was in San Jose, California, an office number next to his name on the form. Van Slyke's family had been notified, as Dietz said, but there was nothing in the file about the shipment of her remains: how and when it was to be done. Maybe that was what was bothering her.

Someone had placed in the file a summary of Van Slyke's personnel record. It was impressive; she had credentials to die for. Clearly Van Slyke was not only on her way but was already there. At forty-four, she was deputy assistant secretary for East Asian and Pacific affairs and SES—Senior Executive Service, the archbishops of the Foreign Service. Except for possibly Russia, China was State's most important client country. And Van Slyke had been just a heartbeat away from the top job in her bureau. Verdi counted about two dozen commendations and awards Van Slyke had earned in just this job. What was next for her? Assistant Secretary? A major ambassadorship?

Verdi was even more impressed with Van Slyke's education and previous positions and what they said about her. She had gotten her bachelor's and master's degrees in political science from City College in New York, not some hotshot Ivy League school or Foreign Service factory. After college she started out at the embassy in Laos as the Vietnam War was winding down. Things were still hot there, but Van Slyke volunteered for the assignment as a junior political officer. For years she shuttled back and forth between Washington and Southeast Asia, always assigned to difficult posts, before working her way up to heading the China and Japan country desks.

Verdi knew what Van Slyke was doing: building her career by taking the tough jobs no one else wanted. Verdi sensed in Van Slyke a kindred spirit, a woman who'd come up the hard way, who earned her success rather than have it handed down to her as a birthright. Verdi knew that such women could be shrill, especially to other women, but her respect for the dead made her give Patricia Van Slyke the benefit of the doubt.

But other than those three or four pieces of paper, there was nothing else in the file. It was remarkably spare of documentation, especially given Van Slyke's prominent position in the State Department. Normally the death of someone of her stature would have generated flurries of cables between the embassy and Washington, not to mention numerous expressions of sympathy from the Chinese government. Verdi would have also expected to see evidence in the file of an investigation of some kind, however cursory, by the embassy or Chinese authorities. After all, the woman died in her hotel room under arguably suspicious circumstances. The file should have been thick as a beach novel.

In fact, there was no evidence that anyone above the functionary consular level at the embassy had had anything to do with Patricia Van Slyke. But how could that be? She was a distinguished Foreign Service officer, a high-level diplomat. Verdi flipped through the file one more time, searching for something, a clue. A clue to what?

She closed her eyes and leaned her head back against the paneled wall. She tried to nap to pass the time, but she was too keyed up to unwind. Her conversation with Calamity John and his reference to the seventh floor, the Secretary's office, teased her, tantalized her, with possibilities. Here she was, a rookie FSO with a high-profile case just dumped on her lap. She'd been singled out to handle what was obviously a very sensitive assignment. The department heavies would be watching, Dietz was telling her in his not-so-subtle way. It was hers to ace or screw up.

Other things about the case tugged at her, drew her in. For instance: What brought Van Slyke to China for this trip? The file didn't say. Neither did Norm Price, the consular officer she'd spoken with that afternoon. How could a Foreign Service officer of Van Slyke's rank just slip into the embassy unnoticed? And why was Verdi's office called in to handle it, by Career Development and Assignments, of all places?

But the question that loomed largest in her mind was: Why Verdi? What possessed someone to choose her, *by name*, to handle this case? Verdi, who had worked nearly three years as a blackjack dealer in Atlantic City to pay off college loans, believed she had few illusions left about life. People rarely granted favors out of pure kindness. She knew this case offered opportunities, but she was also wary of a trap. But who would set her up? And why?

Her eyes snapped open as a door slammed, ringing off the cement floor. She turned to see a young man standing in front of her, his black raincoat buttoned up to his chin. He was short, maybe five-five, and the rain had plastered his red hair across his head. She might have almost giggled at his comical appearance if it weren't for the objectionable way he was staring at her.

"You Miss Verdoo?" he said, his voice reminding her of Truman Capote. "Looks like you're sleeping on the job."

"Who are you?" she asked crisply.

He wiped a deathly white hand down the side of his dripping coat and held it out to her. "Gary Pemburton, Pemburton Funeral Home. You been waiting here all this time?" He laughed, low in his throat. "You didn't really have to. The remains've been here over an hour. I just spoke with the customs inspector. He's on his way over now to sign off on them."

Verdi groaned, realizing that if only this obnoxious little undertaker had bothered to call her, she could have been somewhere else all this time. Almost anywhere would have been better. So now she had to sit here and wait with Gary Pemburton.

"Some rain," Pemburton said, brushing up against Verdi's legs as he took a place next to her on the bench. His breath smelled of medication. "I hear we're in for weeks of it."

"Mmm," Verdi said, nodding and glancing at her watch.

"I've dealt with people from your office before,"

Pemburton said. He squirmed a bit on the bench. "You been there long?"

"Three years," she said, taking the broader view and hoping it would head off what she feared was coming from him. "When I called this afternoon, I spoke with someone else named Pemburton."

"That was my father," he said, looking down at her legs. She was still in her work clothes. "So, where you from? Let me guess: Michigan. Seems everyone at the State Department is from Michigan."

Verdi shook her head. *Where was the goddamn customs inspector?*

"So where then?"

She looked at him. "Seat Pleasant."

Pemburton's eyes narrowed as he tried to connect the name with the place. "You mean the Seat Pleasant in Maryland?" he asked, grimacing. "But that's Southeast Washington. I wouldn't even drive my car through there."

Verdi looked him in the eye. "Yeah," she said, "we might not let you out if you did."

Pemburton looked away. "Listen," he said, rubbing his hands together. "You get out much? Reason I ask is that I know this new place in town—"

Oh, shit, Verdi thought, *here it comes*. Just then the door opened, and a man in oilskins came through, carrying a small pine crate he set down carefully on the counter. He turned toward them and said, "Both of you here for this?"

"No," Pemburton said, eyeing the crate, anxiety spreading over his face. "I'm here for the Van Slyke remains."

"That's it," the man said, pulling papers from an inside pocket.

"No, there's some mistake," Pemburton insisted. "I'm supposed to pick up a casket."

Verdi stood up. "The remains were cremated," she said. "I spoke with Beijing this afternoon. It was all set."

Pemburton turned to face her, his eyes even with her chin and his lower lip quivering. "This—this is outrageous," he said, his voice rising an octave. "The family never authorized cremation. They're—they're Catholic. They're expecting a body. Do you have any idea how upset they'll be about this?"

"Calm down, Mr. Pemburton," she said as she searched the file for her notes. "I was told specifically that a cremation had been ordered."

"Will one of you sign for this so I can get out of here?" the man in oilskins said.

"I—I hope you're prepared to take responsibility for this!" Pemburton screamed at Verdi. "This is a very serious matter. The funeral home could be sued, lose its license."

"Problem out here?" It was the night supervisor, shuffling out of the office.

"Here, I'll sign for it," Verdi said, taking a pen from her purse.

"I don't believe this," Pemburton huffed at Verdi, flailing his arms. "I get dragged out here in the middle of the night in the pouring rain, for what? And people wonder why the government's gone down the tubes."

He turned toward Verdi. "Well, here's your reason. It's run by incompetents who can't even handle something as simple as shipping a body. They send this—this bimbo, who manages to muck the whole thing up. They screw you while you're alive and screw you when you're dead."

Suddenly stress and fatigue ganged up on Verdi. She moved up to Pemburton, her face less than an inch from his. She gave him The Look, letting her eyes go slack, indifferent, and utterly hateful. "Now hear this," she said quietly through clenched teeth, "I'm not a bimbo, and I'm not incompetent. I'm a Foreign Service officer, if that means anything to you, and I make my living by working, not sponging off my daddy's business."

Pemburton's eyes widened in surprise. He took a step back, but Verdi stayed on him. "The order to cremate came from Beijing, not Washington," she said. "Got that? Mortuary facilities aren't always available, local officials screw things up in translation, and you get a situation like this. It *happens*."

"But—but I—" Pemburton stuttered, tongue dry.

"You don't shut up and get that crate out of here right now, they're gonna be taking *you* out in a box. Hear me?"

Backing away from Verdi, Pemburton snatched up the crate and winced as he cracked his knee trying to kick the door open. "The State Department will hear about this," he shrieked, and stomped out, the door slamming behind him.

Verdi steadied herself on the particle board counter and looked toward the door. She was certain her career was in that crate with Patricia Van Slyke.

*   *   *

It took Verdi nearly an hour to get home and another half hour to find a parking space. The streets of Adams-Morgan, the Washington neighborhood where she lived, felt slick and greasy as she dragged herself to her apartment building.

After counting the fifty-eight steps to the top, she pushed open her door, punched on a light, and dropped her coat, purse, briefcase, and bag of takeout tapas she had picked up at an all-night Spanish place three blocks away. It was supposed to be her dinner, but she was too tired to eat. She fell on the couch and closed her eyes.

A bath would've felt good, but she wasn't up to drawing one. Her bed would've felt good too, but she felt immobilized on the couch. She felt pressure in her bladder but couldn't work up the energy to get to the bathroom.

Slowly she rubbed her eyes. Night driving always made them hurt. The muscles in her shoulders were knotted with tension, and a dull pain hammered behind her right ear. Out of nowhere a violent surge of anger flared into her consciousness, and she tried her best to contain it, to corral it into a safe place.

Bimbo. Incompetent. The words stung like a ruler to the back of the legs.

Think you'll make your game?

Personally I would have chosen a more seasoned officer for this case.

Pemburton, Harrington, Dietz. *Who are these fucking men, and what do they want, a defenseless, eyelid-fluttering slice of cream cheese, the kind of woman they thought their mothers were? Well, they won't get it here.*

Verdi wondered what they saw when they looked at her. In this weak moment she imagined it was nothing more than a callow, brittle schoolgirl or, worse, low-rent hoi polloi polished up so she'd be let in the front door but was still not worthy of their respect. She shook her head, trying to clear it of the entire matter. How could she have let things with Pemburton get out of control like that? Why did she let jerks like him get to her? She imagined him now, kicking his cat or talking tough into his mirror.

She groaned when she thought about how she'd have to face Calamity John tomorrow and give him the news about Patricia Van Slyke's remains. Who could have been so stupid as to order cremation without the family's consent? It was unconscionable, a major screwup that put her on track for a head-on collision with basic State Department policy. Someone's ass would fry, no doubt hers. A mean voice inside her castigated her for believing that she'd been given this case for any reason other than to take the fall for it.

She groaned again when she remembered her class tomorrow in Arlington, an orientation program she had to attend, starting at eight sharp. Now it seemed all the more ludicrous for her to go. The image of someone rearranging deck chairs on the *Titanic* as it was sinking came to mind. But Dietz had warned her about the course; she had to be there. She wondered when she could talk to him. Maybe she'd get over to State during lunch.

Verdi's apartment was decorated with souvenirs from Indonesia. On the wall in front of her she'd hung a puppet from the *wayang kulit*—the shadow theater—made from buffalo parchment. It was an exceptionally delicate rendering of Durga, the goddess of death, with her intricate crown, fearsome face, and arms spread wide.

That's me, Verdi thought glumly, *the goddess of death. And not a very good one either.*

She drew her hands away from her eyes and looked down on the floor. Her Walkman was where she'd left it a couple of nights ago. She dropped one hand to the floor, felt around for the Walkman, and scooped it up. Good, there was a tape still inside it. With enormous effort she pulled on the headphones and pushed the start button.

Good, it was an old 10,000 Maniacs tape, turned up almost full volume. Using the last of her energy, she nudged the volume up to the max. She eased back on her pillow and closed her eyes as Natalie Merchant's wonderful voice filled her head. For the few remaining hours of night she fell into a fitful sleep.

CHAPTER
★ FOUR ★

Miles away, in the grim Washington night, Brian Porter was struggling to stay awake as if his life depended on it. His eyelids felt leaden, rusted shut, and the muscles in his face slack and unresponsive. He made an effort to move a hand; he thought it was the left one. But his arm seemed far away, a log adrift in a still lake.

To keep himself conscious, Porter tried to remember where he was, how he got here. He was in a car, that much he knew. The rhythmic rocking of the car over rutted streets helped to deepen his trance. He could recall being late at the office, finishing up a cable to the embassy in Moscow. He remembered leaving the office, looking for his car in the State garage, and suddenly feeling fear as hands went around his mouth and throat, and sharp pain before blackness. After that he lost all track of events.

With great effort Porter forced open one eye and focused it through the tinted window. Overhead, streetlights skimmed by, pulsating hypnotically. He turned slightly and saw the side of a man's face, the driver of the car. The face seemed massive and Buddha-like, a halo of flickering light around it.

"Look, he's coming around," said a voice in the shadows next to him. The voice reached Porter as if it had traveled a great distance, perhaps underwater. The Buddha head turned toward him and nodded, smiling slightly.

Porter was suddenly aware of a vague pain coming from his thigh. He bent his head and looked down at the small puncture in his trousers, an inch above his knee. He found he could move his hand if he didn't raise it and slowly slid it over the puncture, protecting it.

"Know where we're going, Brian?" asked the voice. Porter touched his lips with a numb tongue.

"That's all right. You don't have to answer. We're going for a ride in the country. Place you've probably never been before. It's very quiet there, lonely. It's so lonely no one would notice you there, lying in the woods with a bullet in your head, wild animals having their way with your body. Weeks, months, would go by before anyone would even think to look for you there. By then your bones would be picked clean, just another home for the worms."

Fear crept across Porter's fogged brain. It spread down his neck to his shoulders, seeping over his chest and crotch and into his arms and legs. He moved his

eyes toward the man in the shadows. It was then that
he saw the gun, shiny and blue, even in the darkness.

"Want to know *why* we're going to the country,
Brian? And why you'll be getting a bullet in your
head? You didn't do your share. You didn't keep your
end of the deal. It's that simple.

"You seem to forget, Brian: This is Washington, the
most political place on earth. You don't turn your back
on the people who put you where you are. How do
you think people manage to stay here as long as they
do? Get a favor, give a favor. Forget to give back, and
you can fall faster than you can imagine."

Somehow Porter sensed he knew that voice, had
heard it before in an entirely different context. He tried
to connect the voice to a face but was distracted by the
shiny blue gun pointing at his chest.

The ride began to get bumpier. There were still
lights overhead, but they seemed to get farther apart.
Where were they now? How long had he been in the
car? He looked at his hand still covering the puncture
in his thigh. He willed his hand to move, and it did.
He was even able to raise it slightly.

The voice went on, and Porter carefully returned his
hand to his leg. "I can imagine what you're thinking right now: How can I get out of here? Is the car
door locked? Can I open it? Well, even if you could,
you wouldn't get too far. You might even kill yourself
trying.

"You see, Brian, you have a lot of drugs in your
body right now. Your spirit may be willing, but your
flesh is weak. Best you could do for yourself right now
is make peace with your God. You believe in God,

Brian? Doesn't really matter. Either way, you'll end up a pile of bones in southern Maryland."

Through the corner of his eye Porter was watching the gun. He tried to gauge its distance from his hand and how long it would take to reach it. All he needed was a second to turn it around and fire it at the voice, and then he could take his chances with the driver.

Then the voice changed direction. "Is this the right way, Li?" he said to the driver.

Li turned halfway, and Porter could see most of his face. "Cutting through town. We'll be on the freeway in a few minutes."

"Good."

Using all his strength, Porter moved his hand toward the gun. His fingers wrapped around the muzzle, and he leaned forward with his body, turning the gun toward the shadows.

"Hey!" the voice screamed. "What the—What are you—"

The voice, caught off guard, was struggling. Li, the driver, turned back to look, not smiling now. Porter tried to make his other hand—the right one—move. But it was paralyzed. With his good hand, he worked his fingers toward the trigger, sliding them down, hooking them in.

Porter used the motion of the car to lunge at the gun as he squeezed his fingers as hard as he could. His body shuddered at the sound of two explosions, one after the other. The car fishtailed momentarily, throwing Porter back against his door. He felt massive pressure in his chest, and he gulped for air.

"You stupid fuck!" the voice screamed. "You dumb

shit, look what you've done! Oh, shit, there's blood all over the windows. Li, get us out of here. Get us somewhere dark, away from traffic."

Porter heard the engine roar as the car spun off into side streets, bucking painfully with each pothole. Intense cold seized his hands and feet. His head was tilted against the seat, and his throat was dry as he gulped harder for air. He sensed movement around him and felt someone pressing on his chest.

"You weren't supposed to get shot," the voice screamed from just below Porter's line of sight. "Don't you die on me. Shit, Li, where are we?"

"Fourteenth Street, heading north."

"Move it, he's going fast."

There was more talking, some screaming, but Porter couldn't make it out. He watched the lights flashing overhead and felt the bumps in the road, each one making breathing more difficult. His arms and legs were cold now, pretty much all of him, and his field of vision was narrowing, squeezed in by blackness.

Suddenly there were no lights overhead, and the car jumped violently from deep ruts. Porter heard snatches of the voice: "Stop . . . this place . . . hide . . . there . . . trash." The pressure on his chest eased up, and he felt more movement over him. He felt someone push him, and he caught a glimpse of dark buildings before seeing them roll away. Rolling, falling, sharp pain at the back of his head. And then stillness. Engine roar and smoke smell as he lay still.

Darkness enclosing his field of vision. Above, dark night sky. Very still and quiet, many seconds. The darkness was almost total, only a small window left.

Out of nowhere a face appeared in the window above him. It was an apparition, unearthly, with a black face and brilliant yellow hair. Its brown eyes looked down at him with mild curiosity.

Brian Porter tried to reach out a hand to the apparition, but neither hand responded. He tried to speak to it, but he could only manage a faint gurgling noise. Then the face disappeared, and he was left with the rapidly shrinking night sky above him.

CHAPTER
★ FIVE ★

Concentrate, Clarence Witherspoon commanded himself as he studied the intersection before him. It was just before dawn in the Trinidad section of Northeast Washington. Even for D.C., it'd been a wild night. It was also sweltering, the kind of oppressive, muggy heat for which Washington was famous, that seemed to drain the life out of people. Steam rose like dry ice off the oily street made slick by the thunderstorm, giving the place the look of a graveyard from some old grade B movie. Witherspoon didn't have much concentration left in him.

A light breeze blew up around the cops and technicians combing the scene for evidence, a task rendered ludicrous by the incredible amount of garbage billowing into the intersection. Witherspoon, a detective sergeant with the D.C. homicide unit, tried a trick his former partner, Tom Galvin, had taught him: When studying a crime scene, blot out the TV cameras, the lights, the swarm of police activity, and imagine the scene as the killer saw it. He closed his eyes, clearing his head of extraneous thoughts, and opened them back onto the intersection. But the crime scene was parsimonious, yielding none of its secrets.

Witherspoon sipped his coffee, deathly pale from nondairy creamer. The coffee held four heaping teaspoons of sugar that helped keep Witherspoon going through the busy late-night shift. It was in a cardboard cup that was beginning to soften and take on the shape of his grip. Witherspoon was tired, and the coffee merely made his stomach angry. He tried to shake off his discomfort and focus on the business at hand. There was something about this place he felt he had to understand or appreciate. The question seemed to be: Was it pure coincidence that made this the scene of the murder he'd been called in to investigate, or was it something else, something not yet revealed to him?

He was on his third call of the night, all of them gang-related. Until now, he concluded. This one, at the intersection of Orren Street and Simms Place, was different from the others in a way he didn't like at all.

The victim was a white male, mid-thirties, shot twice in the chest at close range. He had no ID on him when the uniforms arrived on the scene. Maybe he'd been robbed before he was shot, maybe after. No way to tell.

What Witherspoon particularly disliked about this murder was the attention he knew it would stir up. A white John Doe shot in black Washington, the papers and TV would have a field day. The mayor's office

would get its nose into it, the Chamber of Commerce
too. Hell, even Congress if the man was a Capitol Hill
staffer. Not only that, four hundred black murders a
year barely got noticed in the press, and this white one
would make the front page tomorrow, guaranteed.

Clarence Witherspoon, forty-eight-years old and
black, had learned long ago never to think he'd seen it
all on the streets of Washington. In his twenty-six
years on the D.C. force, he'd hauled in pimps, killers,
and congressmen, and sometimes couldn't tell the difference among them. He'd delivered babies and found
them dead in Dumpsters, been shot twice and once
administered mouth-to-mouth to save the life of the
man who shot his partner, brought groceries to families whose fathers he'd arrested, and seen his city turn
into a hell because of drugs and children with guns.

Washington just wasn't the same anymore as when
he was coming up. Used to be, a homicide'd have a
motive he could understand: a fight over a woman or
a card game. Now he'd be hearing things like "I
wasted him because I didn't like the music he was
playing." Stupid things.

Here he had a dead white guy in a black neighborhood at least five miles from anywhere most white
people'd go, even in the daytime. First assumption:
He was looking for drugs. Witherspoon had checked
the victim out already and even walked through the
scene in search of plastic bags, crack pipes, or other
telltale signs of a drug market. But the absence of
paraphernalia, and the victim's nice Brooks Brothers
clothes, did not add up to a dope deal gone bad. Not

to say that people in Brooks Brothers didn't do up, but why would he come into Trinidad?

Even if he had a bad drug habit, there were lots of markets around the city closer to where he'd hang out, like Capitol Hill, Georgetown, the Virginia suburbs. Trinidad was too black, too foreign and threatening, for most of white Washington. Prostitution was another possibility, but Witherspoon knew of no action around in this neighborhood. Someone looking for that could do much better around the big hotels downtown. The only other attractions around here were Gallaudet College, the national school for the deaf, and Mount Olivet Cemetery a few blocks away. Witherspoon didn't see this guy at either place, especially this time of night.

Taking in the intersection, Witherspoon was struck by only two things. First, the lighting was dim, almost nonexistent, but brighter in the streets that fed into it. The streetlights had been broken or just went out and were never repaired. He knew that the National Guard had been through this neighborhood, using big spotlights to scare away the dealers. Of course the dealers came back like cockroaches soon as the Guard pulled out. And now spotlights set up around the intersection by the investigators illuminated the alleys and hidden cavities around it.

The second thing was the trash, mounds of it. Where was it all coming from? Witherspoon set his coffee down on the roof of a police cruiser, pulled a small dime-store notebook from his breast pocket, and scribbled down his observations.

An unmarked Ford with a detective's removable bubble on top hissed through a nearby alley roped off from the intersection and pulled up behind a forensics van and an ambulance. Witherspoon watched as the driver stepped out and smoothed out his suit and straightened his tie. That would be Carl Chance from Fifth District public affairs, always ready to get his face on TV. Chance waved at Witherspoon and picked his way through the intersection, mindful of his Italian calfskin loafers.

Paramedics pushing a squealing gurney beat Chance to the victim. "Wait till I give the word," Witherspoon said quietly to them, and took a sip of coffee.

"You still drinking that 7-Eleven shit?" Chance said, coming up on Witherspoon's side.

"Chance," Witherspoon said, turning to face a man a full head shorter and a good sixty pounds heavier. Carl Chance stood there grinning, his round eyes locked on Witherspoon's coffee cup. He was dressed for a big night on TV, sporting an Armani double-breasted suit, a red pin-striped silk shirt and matching handkerchief, and one of those wide ties with a design that looked as if somebody's kid had dropped something on it. Word on Chance was that he had started as a uniform and after a few months on the job nobody wanted to ride with him anymore. So, true to form for the D.C. government, somebody went and made him a public affairs officer.

"Don't you know about the coffee bars, Clarence?" Chance said, louder than he had to and looking around for the TV cameras. "You can get a nice cup

right off a street vendor now. There's one down
Dupont Circle opens five-thirty every morning. Me, I
go for cappuccino myself with a little dusting of cinna-
mon on top. Usually I get two.

"Now you," he said, peering over the top of Witherspoon's cup, "I see you like it light. You'd go for caffè
latte. About equal portions of coffee and milk. And
they'd put in as much sugar as you like."

"Awful early for you, isn't it, Chance?" Witherspoon said, taking a deep drink this time.

But Chance wasn't listening. He was already thinking about a statement he could make to any reporter
who'd listen about the mayor's new crime initiative.
Witherspoon heard that Chance was angling for a promotion in the department and was using a woman in
the mayor's office he was dating to get it. But the deal
was that he had to mention the mayor as much as possible whenever talking with the press, it being an election year.

"So," said Chance, "what do we have here?"

"A white John Doe," Witherspoon answered, "early
to mid-thirties, shot twice in the chest at point-blank
range. No murder weapon, no evidence, no apparent
motive."

Chance moved forward a half step toward the victim without getting too close. The John Doe's face was
turned away, and his hands were submerged in trash.

"White, huh? That'll make my job a hell of a lot
tougher. What do you like?"

Witherspoon made a motion with his head and
shoulders. "It'd be a guess."

"Drugs?"

"You know of any markets around here?"

"You mean right here? Closest one I know of is about five blocks away, up around Fenwick and West Virginia Avenue. But maybe it's moving down."

Witherspoon kicked an empty can of Valvoline from the street into a pile of rubber foam stuffing hemorrhaging from a broken couch. "Look at this place, Chance," he said. "What dealer would want to work here, in a dump like this? Nobody, not even the little kids fresh out on the streets. The smell, the rats. Bad for business.

"And look, no traffic to speak of coming through here. Neither Orren nor Simms is a through street on this block. Hard to imagine anything going down here to get caught in the middle of."

"You're right about that smell," Chance said, suddenly aware of his surroundings. He pulled the silk handkerchief from his pocket and held it in front of his nose. "This heat sure doesn't help."

Witherspoon shook his head at Chance, his smile disappearing when he gazed down on the corpse. "I've seen two drug hits already tonight. We must've found a hundred shell casings at each of those scenes from street sweepers, TEC-9s, AKs. Hell, dealers can't shoot. Best they can do is point their pieces and hope they'll hit something."

He nodded toward the ground. "This guy here was hit in the chest at very close range with two shots. Powder still on his shirt. Not the work of dealers."

"So what do you like?" Chance said again through the handkerchief.

Witherspoon shrugged. "Maybe a carjacking. None was found here, and I don't know how else this guy could've gotten here except by car." He looked up toward the eastern sky, a red wash bleeding into gray. "Or maybe it was something else, something I'm missing."

"Carjacking," Chance said, scraping something from the bottom of his loafer. "Haven't heard of any of those around here."

"Mmm," Witherspoon said, thinking about those bullet holes. They were very close together, so close, in fact, that to an untrained eye they might have looked like one big hole. Somebody was steady with his gun, as if he'd done this before.

But this shooting just didn't feel right to Witherspoon. Nothing fitted, nothing connected with his experience. He'd seen enough shootings to know. He finished his coffee and slipped the cup in his jacket pocket, then laughed lightly.

"You got a joke you want to share?" Chance said. "I could use one about now."

"No, no joke," Witherspoon said, beginning to stroll. Chance had to hurry to keep up. "It just occurred to me how useless it was for me to save my cup in my pocket. With all this trash here, I mean."

"Oh," Chance muttered breathlessly, either not getting or not appreciating the irony.

Witherspoon drew up and seemed to gaze off into nowhere. "You got a flashlight on you?" he said.

Chance looked at him. "No. Why?"

"That wall over there," he said, pointing toward a

warehouse hidden in the shadows. "I want to see what's on it."

"*On* it? What the hell for?"

Witherspoon sighed, much too tired to explain basic police work to Chance. "Check for graffiti," he said anyway. "See which crews hang here. Maybe they'd know something about this hit."

The street gangs—crews they were called—marked their turf by spray-painting their names in distinctive styles around a neighborhood they claimed. Tagging, it was called. Like dogs leaving their scents, Witherspoon thought. In the L.A. barrios the graffiti were known as *placas*. The Delta unit, an elite group of detectives and officers over in the Seventh District, kept a file on crew graffiti. Witherspoon would come back later when the sun was up and check out the intersection. He headed back toward the crime scene.

"Hey, Clarence, I meant to ask. How's Tom doing?"

Witherspoon looked down, an image of his ex-partner in a hospital bed wasting away from cancer surfacing in his mind. "About the same. I saw him last night and spoke with Ruthie. She said he was hoping to go home yesterday but the doctors want him to go through another round of chemo. Doesn't look good."

Both men stopped walking and looked up as a TV transmission truck eased as far up Simms as it could get to the murder scene. A camera crew began to emerge from the back.

"Hup," Chance said, stuffing the handkerchief back into his pocket. "I'm on. Hey, Clarence, after I'm done here, I'm going down to Dupont Circle for my cappuccino. Why don't you join me?"

"No, thanks, Chance."

"OK, talk to you," Chance said, and hustled off to intercept the TV crew before it could interview a uniform and cut into his time.

Witherspoon watched Chance for a moment and then returned to the victim's body, still sprawled over the curb. The police photographers were done shooting it, and cops and technicians were beginning to come in from around the intersection, their surgical gloves crackling as they peeled them off. The paramedics hovered over the body like vultures, waiting for Witherspoon to give the word before taking it away.

Witherspoon bent down over the body, taking it in for the last time. *What do you see, Clarence?* Once Tom Galvin had told him that the most revealing aspect of a person's clothing is his shoes. What did the victim's say about him? They were black wing tips, with more than a little wear on them. Establishment shoes. Taken together with the victim's suit and rep tie, Witherspoon guessed he was a lawyer or a mid- to upper-level bureaucrat in the federal government. That narrowed it down to forty percent of Washington. The guy could just as easily have been in Washington on a job interview and taken a very wrong turn. *Look closer.*

No jewelry on the guy, no watch. Witherspoon checked his ring finger. That was interesting: A small white mark—a tan line from a ring—encircled the finger. Why would he have taken it off? Maybe he didn't want someone to know he was married. Or someone took it from him. Was it before or after he was murdered?

Carefully, respectfully, Witherspoon lifted John Doe's right arm, stretched over his head. *What's this?* Something Witherspoon missed before, a label or something on the dead man's sleeve.

Witherspoon looked up at a technician packing a bag. "Hey," he said, "borrow your flashlight for a minute?"

The tech handed it over, and Witherspoon trained it on the sleeve. "All right," he whispered, grateful for small breaks. Right there at the end of the sleeve was a monogram in a fancy pyramid shape—BLP—all but covered by ash and oil stains. He placed the arm at the man's side and stood up.

"OK, I'm done," he said, and the paramedics immediately went to work, zipping up the body and unloading it onto the gurney. On the way back to the ambulance the gurney squeaked a little less with the body on it. The ambulance started up and began to move out, the driver not bothering to run the siren or the lights. The departure of the body was like a signal for everyone to leave. Car doors slammed in rapid succession, and Witherspoon watched the exodus that followed, leaving him alone in the intersection.

He looked down at the chalk outline on the street, a twisted afterimage of the corpse now on its way to the morgue for examination. Traffic noise rose from the surrounding streets, the first wave of the Washington rush hour. Witherspoon glanced at his watch and pulled his notepad from his breast pocket. He read his meager notes: "7/14/94—Orren and Simms/ Trinidad—John Doe—WM, mid-thirties—carjacking?

Murder scene: dark from bad lighting; lots of garbage—
Did killer try to hide victim's body? Why?"

Witherspoon thought a moment, clicked his pen,
and wrote: "BLP??"

CHAPTER
★ SIX ★

A bad night's sleep and not enough of it, Verdi thought sardonically as she sat in the back row of her orientation seminar at the Foreign Service Institute in Arlington. She was on her fourth cup of bad coffee from the vending machine outside and had the latest *Baseball Weekly* open behind a notebook. She felt so crappy she didn't even feel like reading the headlines.

It wasn't enough that she was exhausted. The course she was taking was even deadlier than advertised. It really was geared to people just back from overseas assignments or new to the area, offering tips on such things as house hunting and schools. The instructor—a semi-retired Foreign Service officer in a sleeveless sweater and steel-frame glasses—prowled around the classroom, covering the material and serving up occasional factoids about the State Department that clung to Verdi's consciousness.

The department employs some 25,000 people, including 9,500 Foreign Service officers reflecting a broad range of backgrounds, expertise, and interests to meet the challenges of a changing world.

About three and a half million U.S. passports are issued annually at thirteen domestic passport agencies and more than 255 diplomatic and consular posts. In addition, six million visas are granted to foreign nationals at U.S. posts abroad.

Each year the Citizens Emergency Center monitors the cases of 6,500 Americans arrested overseas, responds to 200,000 welfare and whereabouts cases, and assists in the disposition of remains for an estimated 4,000 citizens dying in foreign countries.

The instructor mercifully announced a break, and Verdi was the first among the class to stream outdoors for a few minutes of fresh air. The sunshine, brilliant in the clear air from the night's storm, stung her bloodshot eyes as she stepped outside. Shielding her eyes from the glare, Verdi looked around for a place to sit and caught sight of a free bench.

She was careful with her coffee as she navigated through the crowd to the spot. As painful as the sun was in her eyes, it felt wonderful on her skin as she leaned back against the bench. She left her coffee on top of her *Baseball Weekly* while she watched her classmates mingle on the patio. They bore the signs of State Department noblesse: well dressed but not flashy, confident and insouciant, and possessed of a certain social ease and grace. She guessed that some of them had trust funds and most had been to the best East Coast schools. They were like a tribe. Verdi knew them well, having studied their ways at Georgetown. It took her a while and a few additions to her wardrobe, but eventually she could pass herself off as one of them. The question was: Did she want to?

The group mingling on the patio was a mixture of new, trendy FSOs and old-line career officers. But they all played the same game: networking future assignments, trolling for contacts that might propel them into choice jobs somewhere down the road. Verdi looked on with a mixture of envy and scorn as business cards were swapped, names and numbers scribbled on backs of notepads. To her, this was the Foreign Service at its worst, when human relations were reduced to their most basic what-can-you-do-for-me level. She imagined a pack of scavengers circling one another in some ritual of dominance.

Even though the whole business seemed terribly unsavory to her, she knew this was how the system worked. You were either on the inside, working and hustling your way toward the top, or on the outside, bouncing from one assignment to the next, letting others make the calls for you.

Where did she fit in this nest-feathering game? she wondered as she took tentative sips of the scalding coffee. With the Van Slyke cremation debacle sinking in, right now she felt about as far on the outside as she could get, waiting for the ax to fall. Oh, she knew nothing would happen to her immediately, that no one would suddenly show up and throw her out on the street. What *would* happen was that she would begin to see a gradual change in her case assignments, from frontline emergencies to Mickey Mouse cleanup after the fact, the kinds of things Burnout Boris was getting. Come tenure review time she would have a tidy little portfolio that her panel would rate "lackluster," the kiss of death.

Moping over her future, Verdi decided to do something about it, to call Calamity John right now and explain the whole thing. Maybe Pemburton hadn't gotten to him yet and filled his head with crap about her incompetence. Or maybe something else was breaking in the office she needed to know about, something about the Van Slyke case.

Rising slowly, Verdi spied a man she hadn't noticed before, stretched out on the lawn with what appeared to be the sports section of the paper open on his lap. Didn't he care about getting wet? she wondered, still watching him. He was off away from the group, his back to a tree, drinking tea with the bag still in it. Discreetly she appraised him: early thirties, longish hair blown back by the breeze, rumpled shirt with tie loose and askew, hiking boots, and surfer sunglasses hanging on a band around his neck. He looked more like Peace Corps than State Department. Somehow sensing her presence, he looked up from his paper, and their eyes met. Verdi, the undisputed stare-down champion of her family, looked away first.

Inside on the phone, good news from the office: Calamity John was out today with a cold. That meant Verdi could talk to him before Pemburton could, and she could blow off the rest of this class and get back to work.

There were two phone messages, one from Nonno—probably about their plans for the rain date game—and the other from Lorna Demeritte.

Lorna. Verdi carried small memories of her from their days rooming together at Georgetown, like the fresh-cut flowers Lorna always kept in their dorm room, an extravagance Verdi found amazing, or Lorna's frequent "to-do's," as she called them, little parties to which she'd invite the more socially well-connected students, with Verdi thrown in as contrast. Lorna was now an up-and-comer in State's Bureau of Legislative Affairs, her career moving at the speed of light. She was probably calling to set up another get-together of her little group of State Department friends, all highly placed Foreign Service officers representing different quarters of the department. Since returning from Indonesia, Verdi had been invited to three of the gatherings but had attended only one. She'd felt out of place with Lorna's friends and saw the group as another example of crass networking.

Outside, Verdi fished through her bag for her car keys. The people from her class began filing back into the building. Verdi smiled at them with secret pleasure, knowing she wouldn't be joining them. Then she thought of the man on the lawn. She looked around for him, but he was nowhere to be found.

CHAPTER
★ SEVEN ★

Back at the main State Department building, Verdi worked her way slowly down a corridor, heading for the cafeteria. She wasn't particularly hungry but was still tired and thought she should eat something to keep up her strength. Verdi was still on the fourth floor, where her office was, which was also home to many of the country desk offices. As she passed by the offices, she took in their names: Macau, Tibet, Finland, Togo, Brazil, and on and on. It hadn't been long ago, when Verdi was a green recruit to the Foreign Service, preparing for her first overseas posting, that she'd walked these hallways and gaped in wonder at those names.

Like the character in the James Joyce story "Araby," Verdi could feel the romance of the names drawing her in, evoking memories of pictures in her seventh-grade geography book she stared at for hours, of wonderful places she promised herself she'd someday visit. And the people she saw in those offices: seasoned officers, serious and purposeful. She had to remind herself she was one of them.

There was still a part of Verdi that felt that way, but she feared she was using up her chips too fast and was at the top of a downward spiral to the twenty percent heap, that unlucky group of junior FSOs who end up with a handshake and a push through the back door after their four years of probation. She knew the cremation wasn't her fault, but that wouldn't matter if she were seen as part of a disaster, a major screwup. Who would stand up for her when the hammering began on the gallows? Calamity John? Hell, he'd be the one tying weights to her ankles before they dropped the trapdoor.

Her head down, eyes on the linoleum floor, Verdi saw the shiny black wing tips coming around the corner a half second before she ran smack into them—*shit*—a convulsion of arms and legs locking, flying, papers mushrooming into the air, a sharp pain in her cheek. Verdi ended up on her ass, feeling a welt rising on the side of her face and looking at the top of a silver head bent down in front of her.

"Are you all right?" she mumbled to the head, not sure if she herself was OK.

The head looked up, two ice blue eyes glaring into hers. He must have been in his early sixties, with a tennis tan, a hawk nose, and strong brows knotted in anger. He opened his mouth to say something but only scowled and went back to collecting his papers.

"Let me help you," Verdi said, working her way to

her knees. Her head felt woozy. Clearly she'd gotten the worst of it.

"No, don't," he growled, gathering in the last of them. "I had them in careful order before you came along." People milled around to help, but the man shooed them away. A woman helped Verdi to her feet and asked her if she wanted to go to the medical unit. Verdi shook her head and thanked her.

The man stood up, his papers in better shape than his dignity. "A word of advice," he muttered, an edge of menace in his voice. "Walk around this city like that, and you'll end up with a bullet in your back."

She opened her mouth to speak, but he turned and stalked off.

Verdi at the cafeteria salad bar, loading artichoke hearts onto a plate, was wondering what was coming next. It came in threes, her mother always said. The way things were going, it could be anything. Maybe she'd drop her salad on the Secretary of State's lap, she mused, or the President would come through and she'd throw up on him. And then Verdi grimaced as she heard a familiar voice rising above the hum of the cafeteria.

"Katie!"

Verdi turned to see Lorna Demeritte waving at her from a table. So this was the third thing, Verdi thought ruefully. She smiled weakly, and Lorna rose and came to her. In her cream-colored silk suit, long string of pearls, and shoes that looked like ballet slippers, Lorna seemed to float over to where Verdi was standing. Behind her trailed a mane of black hair, clipped back with delicate mother-of-pearl barrettes.

"Now, where have you been hiding?" she boomed, her powerful voice with its Georgia accent belied by her fragile appearance. "I've been trying to reach you for days."

Verdi shrugged. "Hello, Lorna," she said.

"Just as I thought." Lorna chided her in mock disdain. "No excuse. Well, can you at least spare a few minutes before disappearing for another three weeks?"

Resigned, Verdi followed Lorna back to her table. Amazing how little things change, Verdi thought. Here were Lorna and Kate behaving just as they had in college, Lorna dragging Kate to some dull sorority mixer, introducing her around, and leaving her with some Ivy League type she picked out for her.

It'll be good for you, Lorna used to admonish her. *You study too much as it is. I honestly think you're on your way to becoming a nun.*

They were known as the odd couple at Georgetown. Lorna was the consummate social animal from a prominent Atlanta family with big-time political connections. A product of debutante balls, Junior League, the whole upper-crust nine yards, she seemed to look on her career as a hobby, like collecting demitasses, and never seemed to worry about her future to the extent Verdi thought she should.

Verdi, on the other hand, was the hard-core student from the gritty Maryland suburbs, the grind with the partial scholarship, always at or near the top of her class while juggling two or three jobs. Verdi, always the one to go out to pick up pizza for her dorm floor so she didn't have to pay for it. Verdi, who felt for her mother and father on parents' day at the university as they received cursory handshakes from her friends' more fashionable parents before being shunted off to chat with a Jesuit for the rest of the afternoon.

To Verdi, Lorna wasn't so much a friend as one of those people who drift in and out of your life. Through Christmas cards and chance meetings at weddings, they stayed in touch over the years, even when Verdi was out on her own, first as a waitress in Washington and then a blackjack dealer in Atlantic City to pay off her college loans. In the last three years or so Lorna's career had flourished while Verdi's moved at a snail's pace, maybe even going backward, proving the time-honored truism that it wasn't what but whom you knew. Lorna was rising swiftly through the ranks of the Legislative Affairs Bureau as a front-line congressional liaison. She had a perfect life that Verdi envied: a great job, a very respectable FS 3 salary, and her own town house on Capitol Hill.

Verdi was always careful not to show resentment, but in some small part of her mind she attributed Lorna's success to her pedigree, not her ability. To Verdi, Lorna was one of *them*—the refined, the well-bred, who always seemed to gravitate to one another. And now at the State Department, Lorna had found another group for herself, a clique of some of the most accomplished, most promising young Foreign Service officers.

They called themselves the Circle. Verdi noticed they referred to that name only among themselves. She considered the group to be beyond cliquishness. She never saw any one of them without others from the group.

Verdi had met most of them, at Lorna's a little more than a month ago, and it was impossible not to be impressed by them. They all had glittering twenty-four-carat résumés, with strings of frontline assignments in their relatively short time at State. They were among the best and brightest, the rising stars of the State Department. For reasons Verdi couldn't fathom, she sensed Lorna was trying to draw her into the group, to insinuate her into this hermetically tight circle of would-be ambassadors.

"What would your high-powered group want with a lowly death officer?" Verdi had asked Lorna, who just waved her hand and said that Verdi needed to meet some new people.

But Verdi felt way out of their social and professional league, especially now that she was on course for the Foreign Service Dumpster. They could probably help her out of this predicament, but she could never bring herself to ask.

"So you're still hanging out with the same crowd?" Verdi said with a smirk as they came up on the table where the group was sitting.

Lorna turned and gave her a look. "Honestly, Kate. Don't you see opportunity when it's banging at your door? These people can help you."

"Help *me*? You think so?"

Lorna just shook her head and pulled out a chair. "Hey, everyone," she trilled. "You remember Kate, my friend from Georgetown?"

All heads turned toward Verdi, who waved at them and quickly dropped into the nearest seat. Then she was hit with a barrage of attention from people she'd met only once or twice. Polite questions, small talk. Despite herself, Verdi enjoyed it.

"How're they treating you up in OCS?" someone asked in a heavy Boston Brahmin accent.

Verdi looked up to see a man she vaguely recognized with short strawberry-blond hair and tortoise shell-frame glasses. Mid to late thirties, he wore a white shirt so heavily starched it looked as if it might crack and a bow tie the color of lemon sherbet. In the pocket of his shirt was a pipe. Verdi wondered if he ever smoked it. Pure inbred WASP, she thought sourly. She wasn't sure, but she might have met him at Lorna's party. How did he remember that she worked in the Office of Consular Services?

He stuck out his hand, and Verdi shook it. "Jonathan Rashford," he said with his George Plimpton voice. "Tell me, Kate, is that character still there? What do they call him? Calamity John?"

"Still there," Verdi said.

"Where did you get that skirt? I've been looking for something like that for months."

Verdi turned toward the finely cultured voice coming from the end of the table. It belonged to a stunning woman whom Verdi remembered as Alexandra something—with a hyphenated last name. A ringer for a young Cybill Shepherd—with perfect ash blond hair, flawless skin, and an outfit and accessories to die for—she looked as if she divided her free time between Georgette Klinger and Neiman Marcus. And she liked Verdi's skirt!

"Sumatra," Verdi finally managed to answer. "But

I've seen them in a batik shop in Adams-Morgan. I'll get the name of it to Lorna for you."

"That was your last post, wasn't it?" asked Jonathan Rashford.

"Adams-Morgan?" Verdi grinned, and the table broke up.

"Kate is just back from Indonesia," Lorna said, "and is now doing deaths, accidents, all that horrible stuff in CEC. Remember, I warned you about her sense of humor."

"Do you play tennis?" Rashford asked. "I'm desperate for a partner for a doubles match this weekend."

"Sorry," Verdi said, and felt a jab in her arm.

"Why don't you?" Lorna whispered fiercely.

"Death officer," said Alexandra, sipping at mineral water and studying Verdi. "That must be fascinating work."

"Well," Verdi said, looking at the salad untouched on her plate, "our motto is: 'Visit Exotic Places, Meet Interesting People, and Collect Their Remains.' "

They all laughed again and gradually drifted back into their conversations. Verdi turned to Lorna Demeritte. "Help me out here, Lorna," she whispered. "Tell me who these people are again."

Lorna cupped her hand over her mouth and brought her voice down to a whisper. "The man whose tennis date you so foolishly refused is Jonathan Rashford, of the Boston Rashfords. Very old shipping money.

"Harvard, of course, with a law degree from there as well. Fluent in Russian, French, and I don't know what all else. He was DCM in Moscow and staffed

that big task force on nuclear security, the one the Secretary initiated? He's considered *the* State Department
expert on the former Soviet Union. I've had my eye on
him, but I'll share him with you."

Lorna nodded once toward the end of the table.
"The gorgeous blonde in the Chanel coat dress is
Alexandra Rhys-Shriver, a honcho in the China Bu-
reau. She's fluent in Mandarin and Cantonese, and I
have it on good authority that she was a key player in
the most-favored-nation status negotiations with
China, even meeting with Jiang Zemin, the president.
She's on her way to an ambassadorship, for sure."

Lorna shifted in her seat and looked toward the
other end of the table. "Now that man down there, the
one in the leather suspenders, is—"

"Chalmers Mount," Verdi said, nodding her head.

Lorna's eyes widened. "You know Chalmers?"

"Know *of* him," Verdi said, sitting back and recalling a lecture he had given at Georgetown when she
was a student there. It was an analysis of a possible
American response to the then-emerging Maastricht
Treaty of European unity, even laying out the details of
a likely North American free trade zone a good five
years *before* NAFTA. Mount had so impressed Verdi
that she had begun seriously to consider a career
in the State Department, an option she had only vaguely
thought about previously.

She looked at Mount. She hadn't seen him since the
lecture more than four years ago. The years were beginning to catch up with him, gray sprinkling his
temples and light wrinkles at the corners of his eyes.

But he was still handsome and smooth. She didn't recall seeing *him* at Lorna's party.

"What's he doing now?" she asked Lorna, who was picking at chicken salad.

"He's deputy director of Career Development and Assignments," she whispered.

The mention of Career Development and Assignments stopped Verdi in her tracks. Did Chalmers Mount know about the Van Slyke fiasco? she wondered. Did he have anything to do with her being assigned the case? And why would Mount, a hotshot economist, be working in that office?

Verdi looked at Lorna. "Are you kidding? What's Chalmers Mount wasting his time *there* for?"

Lorna was genuinely miffed by the question. "It's a very important post," she said defensively. "He may very well decide your next assignment."

"So what? He's so much brighter than that. It's a total waste of talent."

Lorna shushed her as Mount glanced up at them and then returned to the questions being peppered at him from every side. Verdi smiled when she figured out what they were about. This was the most important time of the year for Foreign Service officers, when the assignments for where they'd be for the next several years were made public. These assignments, which ultimately determined the FSOs' places in the State Department pecking order, were considered even more important than salary raises. The assignments were due to be announced any week now, and Mount knew what they would be.

"Oh, come on, Chalmers." Jonathan Rashford badgered him good-naturedly. "You can give us a hint. At least tell us if we got, say, one of our top three choices."

"And spoil the surprise?" Mount deadpanned. "You'd never let me live it down."

"I hope the assignments will be more equitably distributed than last year's," said Alexandra Rhys-Shriver. "I've studied the '93 postings, looking at the success rate of top choices awarded per cone and tenured versus nontenured. We political types have been getting the short end of the stick, compared with you economics people."

Mount looked away for the slightest second. "I'm not an economist anymore," he said, his mouth tense. Then he smiled. "Besides, you political cones get all the career Foreign Service ambassadorships."

"That's not true," she shot back.

Uh-oh, Verdi thought. *Open confrontation. This should be good.*

"You see more and more people in admin and consular cones getting ambassadorships." Rhys-Shriver went on. "I think there's some kind of preternatural gerrymandering going on. Appeasement of the angry proletariat."

Verdi, herself in a consular cone, felt a twinge of anger at Rhys-Shriver's comment. It was true that in the past the best those in the consular and administrative cones could hope for was a consul general spot or maybe deputy chief of mission, both a quantum step below an ambassadorship. And maybe there had been modest efforts in recent years to correct the situation. But she didn't have to rub it in.

"You sound paranoid, Alex," Mount said evenly. "If you compare ten-year averages, nothing's changed at all. The distributions have remained almost exactly the same."

Rhys-Shriver laughed derisively. "Don't call me paranoid. Why not do a five-year average? Better still, a two-year. Admin and consular cones are being brought up faster. That's fact, not delusion."

"Now, now," Lorna admonished them. "We have a guest here. What'll she think about us?"

"Lorna's right," Rashford said. "We should all follow Chalmers back to his office and let him show us the assignments. That would settle everything."

Everyone at the table roared, and Verdi made motions to leave. As she did, she spied someone in the cafeteria line: tall, wind-blasted hair, hiking boots. Was it the guy she'd seen on the FSI lawn? she wondered. She craned her neck to see over the tables, but his back was to her, and she couldn't see his face. She watched as he disappeared through the cafeteria door and into the halls of the building. Getting up, she felt a hand on her arm. It was Lorna's.

"Before you disappear for another month, Kate," she said dryly, "do you know when Antonio is coming to town? I have to get that appointment you wanted for him on Dana's calendar."

Hearing her boyfriend's name in this context—here in the State Department cafeteria while she was ogling another man—caused Verdi to stop in her tracks. Normally when she imagined Antonio, she associated him with the sea. He would be stretched out on the beach at Denpasar, his body gleaming copper against the white sand. Or feeding her turtle satay in peanut sauce at Gusti's, their favorite Jakarta rijsttafel dive. Or alone with her in his bungalow, with his eyes sealed tight, muscles tense, rolling over her like a wave.

Since she'd been back, they normally spoke a couple of times a week, usually about his visit to Washington, which they'd been planning even before she left Jakarta. Verdi couldn't wait to see him, especially since they'd talked about his transferring from the Foreign Ministry in Rome, where he was now, to Washington or New York. She'd found out that Lorna knew someone on the Italy desk and agreed to act as go-between on a meeting between Antonio and some higher-ups at the Italian Embassy in Washington. But Verdi just this moment realized she hadn't spoken with Antonio in more than a week.

"I don't know, Lorna," Verdi said, sitting again. "I'm going to have to get back to you."

Lorna waved her hand. "Only reason I mention it is that Dana's going out on TDY in November. Lucky stiff, she gets to go to Rome."

"I'll call him tonight," Verdi said.

"I just don't want him to pass through town without my getting to meet him. I'm figuring I won't see hide nor hair of you the entire time he's here."

"You'll meet him."

"Oh, the other thing," Lorna said, nervously twisting a napkin in her hand. "Now don't you say no to this. Next Wednesday Kendall Holmes is having a private luncheon for us in one of the executive dining rooms up on the eighth floor. He won't tell us what it's for. Usually these things are private, but I asked

Kendall, explaining what good friends we are, and he said it would be fine if you came."

"Lorna, I'd love to," Verdi said, smiling.

"You would? That's great. Now, I want you to go out and get a nice outfit for yourself—you'd look great in black or hunter green. I don't want to see you there in one of those batiky things you're always wearing."

"Hmm," Verdi hummed, studying her skirt. "But Alexandra liked it."

CHAPTER
★ EIGHT ★

On a map the District of Columbia appears as an imperfect diamond, bisected at its heart by the Potomac and Anacostia rivers. Impaled on the eastern tip of the diamond is Seat Pleasant, an old Maryland suburb where middle- and working-class blacks, Asians and ethnic whites, many of whom go back two or three generations here, live together, besieged by encroaching crime and drugs. Here Kate Verdi grew up with her two brothers, and here her parents and grandfather, stubborn and set in their ways, still made their home.

Saturday afternoon Verdi was on her way there for Nonno's birthday party, heading due east out East Capitol Street. Looking for the turnoff to Central Avenue, she began to smell oil burning in her car, a 1983 Camaro her brother, a used-car salesman, had passed off on her. With sixteen valves and a V-8 engine, it was much more car than she needed. She guessed it was hot and he'd had to get rid of it. This was the second time this week she smelled oil.

Verdi passed through Capitol Heights, a neighborhood so shabby it made Seat Pleasant look good in comparison. While many of their neighbors moved out for the communities in semirural Prince George's County or elsewhere, Verdi's parents refused to leave, heedless of their children's protests. Every time Verdi came out here she'd see a new group of young men clustering around an intersection, an open-air drug market.

Images of her childhood flashed through her mind: the one-room beauty parlors, May Day processions at her parents' church, and wedding receptions in halls paneled with club pine. Seat Pleasant seemed small to her growing up, claustrophobic. Determined to be more than a plumber's daughter who married the boy next door, she was the best in her class year after year, won a scholarship to Georgetown University, the most prestigious school in the area, and enrolled in the School of Foreign Service. That was her ticket to the bigger world.

Although it was only a half hour drive from the State Department, Verdi considered Seat Pleasant light-years away in every other respect. She knew that for better or worse the city was imprinted on her like a tattoo. It wouldn't scrub off; the best she could do was to keep it covered over with layers of polish and competence.

As much as she tried to avoid thinking about it, Verdi wondered what she would do if the State Department let her go. It wasn't totally out of the ques-

a strange, giddy expression Verdi didn't like. "Kate, listen," she seemed to whisper above the music. "There's someone here I want you to meet. Carmello's just taken on a new partner in his law practice. He says he's very nice, never been married, and he's told him all about you. Now I want you to stay here while I go find him."

"Mom," Verdi protested, but her mother slipped off.

Verdi did too, heading toward the stairs to the basement. She had to shout above the Puccini to greet the well-wishers pushing toward her with their hugs and bourbon kisses. She squirmed her way through the crowd toward the stairs. Just as she reached them, a familiar face—beet red and bald—came stomping up the steps.

"Well, look who's here," he said, his voice ringing off the walls.

"Hi, Uncle Dom," Verdi said, hearing the ice in his glass tinkling behind her as she endured a long hug.

He backed away quickly, and his face grew serious. "Say, what's going on with you guys?" he said.

"How's that?"

"I mean that asshole Saddam," he said, pronouncing the name the way George Bush used to: Sadam. "How come you guys haven't saved us a lot of time and money and put a bullet through his head? I mean, what's going on? He should be dead already."

Verdi watched as Uncle Dom balanced precariously at the top of the stairs. She wanted to sit him down and splash water in his face. From the corner of her eye Verdi saw her mother in earnest conversation with a terribly clean-cut young man in a black suit. Her cousin's new partner! She began her escape to the basement.

"Uncle Dom," she finally said, "the United States is prohibited by law from assassinating foreign officials. Even when—"

"Aaah," he growled, waving his hand and disappearing into the crowd.

Verdi moved quickly down the stairs into the basement, where she heard a baseball game coming from a TV. She knew she was getting close to Nonno. Rounding a corner, she heard a toilet flush, and the door to the bathroom swung open. Out burst her brother Larry, still zipping up.

"Hey, who's this?" he shouted. "I don't believe it. The hotshot from Washington."

Verdi had to smile. Larry, her older brother, was frozen in time, with the same bad haircut, heavy five o'clock shadow any time of the day, and white shirt he always seemed to wear, a vestige of parochial school. The family joke was that Larry had been born in a white shirt.

"So, Larry," she said. "How's the car business?"

"Oh," he said, rubbing a shaving cut on his cheek, "can't complain. Things've been a little slow lately."

"Oh?"

"Yeah, we ran up against a little inventory problem, acquiring a few too many of the utility RVs just before demand dropped on them, so we had to go way out beyond our normal trading zone to balance our stock. Took a bath on a couple trades, but nothing I can't recoup on the right sales with the right customers. Know what I mean?"

"Larry, I wanted to ask you something." She paused. "It's about the Camaro you sold me. You still have a mechanic on your lot?"

His eyes narrowed. "Something wrong?"

"Well, it's running pretty rich. I smelled oil on my way out here."

"Yeah? Give me the keys, and I'll go take a look at it."

"No, Larry, it can wait. I'll just—"

He held out his hands, beating his fingertips against his palm. "Hand 'em over. I stand behind my sales."

Verdi relented and gave him her keys. Larry sprinted up the stairs and out the front door.

"Good job," came a voice behind her, "you got rid of him for a while."

She turned to see Billy, her younger brother, squatting in the boiler room. She hadn't known he was there.

Verdi smiled. "Don't start, Billy. I did not try to get rid of him."

"So what if you didn't? You got the right results."

Verdi took a step inside the boiler room. Billy was busy tinkering at something, some piece of sound equipment she didn't recognize. It looked like a big speaker or amplifier. But he wasn't squatting; he was sitting on something. She looked closer and saw it was a motorcycle helmet.

"So how are you?" he asked.

"Not too bad," she said. "How about you?"

He tilted his head and frowned. "No use complaining."

Billy. Verdi looked at him, darkly handsome in

jeans, black T-shirt, and boots, pack of cigarettes rolled up in his sleeve. When she was growing up, he was her favorite brother: cool, quick, more than a little dangerous. Always in and out of trouble, he was a cause of constant worry for their parents.

"Mom says you're starting your own business."

Billy stood up and wiped his hands with a cloth, his eyes on the sound equipment. "Yeah, I bought a step van a few weeks ago, doing deliveries for a hardware store in District Heights."

"How's it going?"

He shrugged and looked at her. "It's steady work. That's what I'm supposed to be doing."

His smile was bemused, self-deprecating. Verdi knew what he meant. Billy had been out of prison for less than a year after doing time for moving stolen property. He'd been arrested shortly before Verdi left for Indonesia and jailed a few months later after exhausting his appeals. She wrote to him every other day while he was doing his sentence. Now, holding a job was a condition of his parole.

"Nonno in there?" she said, pointing toward the TV room.

Billy nodded. "Go ahead. I'll be there in a minute."

Verdi found Nonno just where she imagined he'd be: in his Barca Lounger in a corner of the room, his feet up, the TV tuned in to a baseball game, the volume up full and competing with Puccini. Nonno paradise.

Verdi frowned when she saw Nonno, always the perfect gentleman, beginning to get up to greet her. He wore an ancient brown cardigan over a flannel shirt buttoned all the way up to his neck. Slippers and brown polyester pants pulled up over his stomach completed the look.

"Sit down, Nonno," she said from the other side of the room. But he stood anyway, and she ran up and hugged him, his arms still strong, but gentle.

"Sorry," he said, pointing at the TV. "All I can get is the Tigers and Angels. Orioles don't play till tonight. Maybe you'll stick around for it?"

"Sure," she said. "Hey, happy birthday."

He smiled, wrinkles blooming around his eyes and mouth. "No one should have to get this old," he said, and laughed.

"I brought you these," she said, holding out an envelope.

Nonno gave her a look. "What's this?" He opened the envelope and read his birthday card before taking out the tickets.

"Thank you, Kate."

"Sorry we got rained out last time," she said.

"You keep these for me, will you? Guy my age might lose them."

"Oh, go on. I thought we could use these weekend after next. The Red Sox are in town. You have any plans?"

"Well, let's see," he said. Verdi, knowing what was coming, slowly shook her head. "I got a marathon to run, a couple of hot dates. The usual."

"I stepped into that one."

"Things OK with you?" Nonno asked, his wise eyes studying her. "You look . . . worried."

"Sure, great," she said, embarrassed she could be so transparent. "Things are fine."

Nonno frowned, not believing her. Then Verdi was conscious of people streaming down the steps into the basement. It was time for Nonno to open the presents that Verdi suddenly realized were spread out on the floor around the Barca Lounger. Then Nonno was enveloped by a rush of cloying bodies.

Strange, Verdi thought, how she could feel so at home and so out of place at the same time. All around her were the people she'd known growing up. In some way pieces of all of them were in her. But part of her didn't really belong with them anymore. They thought about different things from what she thought about, lived entirely different lives. Yet she felt comfortable here, knowing everyone as well as she did and feeling reassured that no one had changed. Where did she really belong? With them or with Lorna Demeritte's fancy friends at the State Department? She really didn't know.

She was pulled from her thoughts by the sound of high-pitched squealing noises. Coming up at her right, Billy was pushing a hand truck loaded with the sound equipment he'd been working on.

"A little room, here, please," he said, wheeling the truck up in front of Nonno.

"What's this?" Nonno said, eyeing the equipment.

"It's your birthday present, Nonno," Billy said. "A karaoke machine."

"A what?"

"Here," Billy said, plugging it into an outlet and switching it on. He picked up a microphone on top of the machine and handed it to Nonno. Just then Larry pushed his way to the front of the crowd, his white sleeves spattered with oil.

"You're always singing in the shower, in the garden," Billy said. "Now the whole world can hear you."

"That thing fell off the truck, eh, Billy?" Larry said, laughing stupidly. Billy shot him a hard look, and Larry looked down.

"Go on, sing something," called someone from the crowd. A few people clapped.

Nonno took the microphone and cleared his throat. Feedback whined through the amplifier, causing children to cover their ears. But Nonno, looking up at the ceiling, getting into the mood, was oblivious. He began to sing, a bit shakily at first, but then his voice, a sweet baritone, steadied and picked up volume.

Verdi smiled when she recognized the piece, an aria from Giuseppe Verdi's *La Traviata*. For as long as Verdi could remember, Nonno had insisted the family was directly descended from "the maestro," as Nonno called him, with no proof whatsoever to back up his claim.

Verdi and all the others filling the basement watched silently as Nonno stood straight and formal, singing the mournful aria as if he were a boy in school.

CHAPTER
★ NINE ★

Hunched over his desk at the Fifth District police station, Clarence Witherspoon wasn't quite sure what was bothering him the most: the stifling heat, the constant drip-drip of the worthless air conditioner, or the impossibly slow pace of the case he was working on. He decided it was the air conditioner, reasoning that if it had worked, he wouldn't feel the heat as much and he could make some progress getting through the stack of missing persons files in front of him.

Futility coated the walls like mildew. Three days after the John Doe had been found in Trinidad, Witherspoon was no closer to solving the case than he had been at the crime scene. At least there he had hope and John Doe's initials. He sent the initials out over all the wires, hoping for a nibble. But nothing popped, not a single lead.

The clock was ticking on him—loudly. As he'd expected, the murder of a white man in black Washington sent shock waves over the city. The mayor, girding up for a tough election race this fall and desperately needing the white vote, was screaming for results. In the midst of all this, and just when it was most needed, the missing persons computer system broke down.

"Damn computer goes down more often than a whore on Thomas Circle," the detectives grumbled. But complaining was a luxury Witherspoon couldn't afford. Rather than sit around and wait for the computer to come back up, he called local police jurisdictions and had copies of missing persons files sent over to him. He had no idea how many there were. A couple of detectives offered their help—that is, until the files began arriving in boxes. Then the excuses began to fly, and before Witherspoon knew it, he was alone again with the case.

It was tough work, going through these files. Witherspoon began with the District and, when that turned up nothing, moved on to Montgomery County, a well-to-do Maryland suburb. He was guessing that John Doe lived in one of the more upscale jurisdictions. So far Witherspoon had found only one missing person with the initials BP, but that was a seventy-eight-year-old District woman missing from her nursing home for more than a month. It also occurred to him to run a DMV check on "BLP," on the outside chance that his John Doe used his initials on a vanity plate. Again, nothing came up.

Even with this fine-comb search, Witherspoon knew that he could be wasting his time. John Doe could easily have been an out-of-towner, meaning that Witherspoon would have to wait until the computers came back up before he could run a national search. A fingerprint check so far turned up nothing, which wasn't surprising, since it sometimes took days before reports made their way to the FBI database.

With a deep sigh, Witherspoon dropped the Montgomery County box to the floor and briefly pondered which of the two other ones closest to him to take. One was marked "Prince George's County" and the other "Northern Virginia." No contest there. Prince George's—sometimes called the Ugly Sister, wedged as it was between more prosperous counties—was an unlikely home for his upscale-looking John Doe. Witherspoon would go with Arlington or Fairfax County in Virginia. With some effort he lifted the box to the table and pulled out a stack.

"At this rate I might make it to Kentucky by midnight," he muttered.

On the table next to the files was a can of Mountain Dew that Witherspoon lifted to his lips, leaving circles of sweat on the veneer tabletop. As he flipped through one file after another, his mind drifted to the medical examiner's report that confirmed the obvious: The victim had been killed by two .45 rounds in his chest at close range, less than three feet. The trajectory of the shots through the body suggested that the killer was about the same height as the victim. Nothing came out of the examination of hair and fiber on the victim's clothing. One thing was interesting: The ME found traces of barbiturates—phenobarbital, to be exact—and large amounts of cocaine in the victim's bloodstream. Two needle marks were found on his thigh, where the drugs had been injected.

The discovery of cocaine fueled the drug-deal-gone-bad theory, but the phenobarbital was an entirely new twist. Why both? Witherspoon wondered. He could understand John Doe taking cocaine, but not phenobarbital, one of the heaviest downers on the market. Hell, he knew people put all kinds of fool things in their bodies. But this didn't make sense. It was almost as if someone had given him the cocaine to cover up the barbiturate. The ME shrugged when Witherspoon suggested this.

"Sure it's possible," the ME said, "anything's possible. Maybe he ran out of barbiturate and took cocaine."

In other words, the ME didn't give a shit.

So Witherspoon slogged his way through the missing persons files, first looking for the lighter ones that hadn't been around as long. For most of them, he didn't even need to read the names. A look at their photos was enough. Among missing persons in the Washington area, middle-aged white males were in the minority. It was a sad business, checking these files. Children, teenagers, old folks, all colors and sizes, each one its own story of punctured dreams and festering pain.

The lighter ones were almost gone for northern Virginia when Witherspoon opened one with a photo of a white male, dark hair, clean cut. He squinted at the picture, trying to recall the face of the John Doe as it lay in the Trinidad gutter. Witherspoon's memory of that face wasn't too clear, since the man was covered with street grime. But he was dead certain as he studied the picture:

This was the same guy. He quickly checked the name: Brian Lovejoy Porter. BLP.

Witherspoon sat back and sipped on his Mountain Dew, briefly savoring the victory. But that was all the celebration he'd allow himself, and he returned to the file. Brian Porter. Age: thirty-eight. Wife: Danika M. Residence: Reston. Reported missing: July 18. That was yesterday. Witherspoon thought for a moment. Brian Porter was killed on Thursday, the fourteenth. Why would he be reported missing just yesterday, at least four days after he'd been murdered?

He read through the file. The Virginia police had called Porter's office and interviewed his coworkers. The state police had also been notified. There was absolutely no indication where Porter had gone. No one noticed anything unusual, no signs of depression or erratic behavior.

Where did Porter work? Witherspoon wondered. He went back to the beginning of the report. There it was, right at the top. How could he have missed it before? Place of Employment: U.S. Department of State.

"Did your husband have any unusual investments?" Witherspoon asked Danika Porter, seated on the living room couch in her Reston colonial split. The room bore signs of a seasoned traveler: Russian icons on the walls, kilims on the floors, and a couple of antique-looking samovars displayed on a credenza.

"No, none I know of," Danika Porter answered, her accent barely obvious. Witherspoon had checked: She was from Holland.

He looked at her. She was a good-looking woman,

reddish blond, fine bones, and a nice smile, he imagined, even though she probably hadn't smiled in days. She was remarkably composed for a woman who'd just been told a few hours ago her husband was killed and buried in an unmarked grave.

"No gambling problem, no outstanding debts?" Witherspoon went on.

"Just a mortgage," she said.

"Mrs. Porter—" Witherspoon began gently—"your husband was found with traces of drugs in his body. Phenobarbital—a strong sedative—and cocaine." Her eyes flickered when he said "cocaine." "Was your husband on any prescription?"

She nodded. Witherspoon leaned closer. "He had a heart condition. He took something once in a while when he was feeling stressed. I don't remember the name, but I can find out."

"Did he have any problems with drugs?"

"No," she said, folding her arms.

"Did he ever take drugs? Like cocaine?"

"No. Brian told me he tried marijuana in college, like everybody else. But he didn't keep it up. He could have used hashish in The Hague when we lived there—it's legal—but he never did."

"He met you there?"

"Yes. Brian was a lawyer for the State Department, assigned to the World Court. He was also fluent in Russian. He worked on many different kinds of things."

"Like the Russian Mafia?" Witherspoon learned from one of Porter's colleagues at State that Porter had been staffing some task force on organized crime in Russia.

"That was one of them, yes."

"Can you explain why you waited three days to report him missing?"

Danika Porter was quiet for several seconds. "Brian and I did not have a . . . conventional marriage. We were very independent. There would be times when he would be working on something and I wouldn't see him for days at a time."

Witherspoon scratched behind his ear. "Didn't he call or at least stop in to change his shirt?"

She shook her head. "He had a foldout couch in his office. Sometimes he came in late and would sleep in the downstairs guest room. He'd be gone before I ever got up in the morning. The only reason I reported him missing was that his office called about him."

Witherspoon took a deep breath. "Mrs. Porter, were there any problems between you and your husband?"

"Problems?"

"Yes. Was your marriage . . . happy?"

"Brian and I had a good sex life," she said, looking him in the eye. "We'd been married only three years. If there was anything going on, it never got in the way of our marriage."

"Do you have any reason to believe anything was going on?"

"No," she said, and left it at that.

Witherspoon nodded and looked down at the notepad in his hand. From experience he knew that the family was usually the last to know if someone was playing around. So far all he had was that Porter was in the office the day he disappeared. He kept his car in the State Department garage. On the day he was killed, a guard remembered seeing Porter heading into the garage for his car about 7:30 P.M. Witherspoon was still waiting to hear from the State Department about getting in to interview the people Porter worked with. But the department was taking its sweet time about it.

Porter drove a Honda Accord, a good car but hardly the type to attract carjackers. Yet carjackers were a vicious bunch, even worse than drug dealers, Witherspoon believed. They'd kill for a ten-year-old station wagon. The Honda hadn't turned up yet, as cars usually did after the thieves had their joy ride. This one was probably in a garage out in Northeast D.C. somewhere, being cut up for parts.

A team of detectives had gone through the house already, looking for clues to Brian Porter's murder. It would be days before anything came out of their search. For some reason, Witherspoon didn't really believe the search would yield any meaningful leads.

"Mrs. Porter, just one last question. Do you know why anybody would want to kill your husband?"

Danika Porter looked up at the ceiling, water pooling in the corners of her eyes. "No, I don't," she said, her voice trembling. "But this didn't have to happen to my husband for me to see what a barbaric country this is. So what if you catch his killer? You'd just put him in an electric chair. That makes absolutely no sense to me."

Witherspoon nodded his head again. The woman was angry, had a right to be. Besides, he really didn't expect to learn much here. He closed the notepad and stood up. "Thank you very much, Mrs. Porter. I hope I can call you if I need to."

"I'm leaving for the Netherlands in two days," she said, not looking at him. "A real estate agent is selling the house for me. If you have any questions, you can call the State Department."

Witherspoon let himself out. Walking down the front steps toward his car, he reflected how nobody but the mayor and he really seemed to care if Brian Porter's killer was brought to justice. He unlocked the door and sat down behind the wheel.

"OK," he muttered, turning the ignition. "Who needs the business anyway? Let's just call it an unsolved carjacking. That'd be just fine by me."

He gunned the engine and drove off.

CHAPTER
★ TEN ★

The State Department building is sometimes compared to a cruise ship, with the cheaper berths on the lower decks near the engine and the lavishly expensive suites at the top. Verdi thought the metaphor worked nicely as she dumbly followed Lorna Demeritte on an impromptu tour of the beautifully appointed diplomatic reception rooms on the building's eighth and highest floor. Verdi's office, down on the fourth floor, seemed far away to her as she took in the incredible antiques, oriental carpets, and historic paintings and prints.

"I can't believe you've never been up here before," Lorna said as she led Verdi through an elegant salon decorated in Federal style. Lorna told her it was the John Quincy Adams Room.

"Is that an *authentic* Chippendale table?"

"Are you kidding? See that desk suite over there? It

was Thomas Jefferson's personal desk, reportedly where he drafted the Declaration of Independence."

"So which room is Chalmers Mount's office?" Verdi joked.

"He might as well have one up here, all the functions he has to attend."

"*Functions?* Lorna, I think you've been in Washington too long. Remember when we used to call them mixers?"

Lorna sighed. "Honestly, Katie." They were standing before a floor-to-ceiling mahogany door embedded with brass studs. "Wait till you see *this*."

"What, George Washington's personal bathroom?"

Verdi caught her breath as Lorna pushed open the door into a room that seemed as long as a football field. The first thing to catch her eye were rows of enormous crystal chandeliers; then she saw the gilt molding on the walls and heavy damask curtains. Wandering into the room, Verdi stared up at the huge gilt seal of the State Department—an eagle, its talons clutching an olive branch and torch—spread across the ceiling. Fluted marble columns lined the walls, their rusty red color reminding her of dried blood.

"This is the Benjamin Franklin Room," Lorna announced. "That portrait way down at the other end above the marble fireplace is of him. Of course, I don't need to tell you he was our first Secretary of State."

"Of course," Verdi answered, the thick carpet like quicksand that didn't want to let her go. As she stood there admiring the room, she had to remind herself that she was in the building with its labyrinth of nondescript corridors and offices in which she worked.

Up here, among the crystal, mahogany, and burnished brass, there wasn't a trace of the State Department's legendary bureaucracy or high technology.

Lorna glanced at her watch. "Goodness, look at the time. We'd better get back to the dining room. Kendall will be there any minute."

"Oh, right," Verdi said, "the luncheon."

She followed Lorna, who hustled her out the door and through a maze of corridors toward the executive dining area on the same floor. She could never have found her way there alone. On the way Lorna said, "You look great, Katie. Are you trying to make the rest of us look bad?"

Verdi had to smile. On Sunday she'd trooped up to Saks in Chevy Chase in search of an outfit for the lunch. After an hour of sifting through the marked-down racks, she saw the perfect dress in the designer section, an elegant black Donna Karan. She nearly passed out when she saw the price tag. It cost an entire paycheck. But she swallowed hard and bought it anyway. Then she had her hair cut, a modified pageboy, a new look for her. She already knew what jewelry to wear; she limited it to a solid gold Italian bracelet, a gift from Antonio.

"I've a long way to go to catch up with the rest of you," Verdi said back.

Kendall Holmes had not yet arrived when they returned to the Daniel Webster Room, a private dining room. Catching her breath from the brisk walk, Verdi sipped at her iced tea and lemon. She was seated at a table between Lorna and Chalmers Mount. Clearly it was set for a special occasion. Sunlight filtering through a window played off the china, crystal, and fresh-cut flowers. Verdi counted four forks and three spoons among the heavy formal silverware at each setting. She resisted the temptation to turn over the china and silverware to check out their pedigree.

Verdi noticed that the members of the Circle were quieter than usual today, even subdued. There was none of their almost trademark bravado or baiting of one another. Even Mount and Alexandra Rhys-Shriver seemed to have set aside their stilettos for the time being, barely acknowledging each other's presence. Verdi attributed it all to nervousness before the arrival of their host and patron, Kendall Holmes, who was now running late.

Verdi kept her eyes down, her hand smoothing the linen tablecloth as a few whispered conversations swirled around her.

". . . anywhere but Bogotá," someone murmured. "You need clearance to use the john there."

"Maybe next week. That's what I heard."

". . . at least an FS two. I've been in grade two years now."

"Did you see the *Post* this morning? I didn't see anything about it."

"I'll die if I don't get . . ."

"Annapolis. You'll call me if you go sailing?"

". . . Vienna, Rome, Prague . . ."

"He wasn't supposed to wake up."

Verdi strained to catch something, some small reference that floated in and out of her range of hearing. She moved closer to Lorna, their shoulders touching.

"Did you read about the Foreign Service officer found dead on the streets in Northeast?" Verdi whispered.

"No," Lorna whispered back.

"Murdered. Shot to death. They don't have a clue who did it. They said it might be drugs. Did you know him?"

"No," Lorna said, and sipped her iced tea.

Just then all conversations stopped as a man briskly strode in: Kendall Holmes. He was tall, sixtyish, with silver hair and a hawk nose. He wore an impeccably tailored black pinstripe suit and white silk shirt that set off his tennis tan. As he glanced at the group, Verdi saw the ice blue eyes that caught the sun coming through the windows. She almost choked when she recognized him as the man in the hallway, the one she'd run into yesterday.

Shit. Just let me die right now and get it over with.

Holmes worked his way around the table, pressing the flesh, swapping pleasantries, and allowing an occasional guffaw. Verdi felt light-headed and sick to her stomach. Perspiration oozed over her brow.

"Lorna," she whispered. "I don't think—"

Lorna, a smile stamped on her face, turned to her. "Kendall, this is Kate Verdi in OCS. You've heard me talking about her."

Suddenly Holmes was in front of Verdi, his hand out and icy eyes looking through her. She commanded her arm to rise and her hand to open. Holmes seized and pumped it. "I've heard a great deal about you," he said, still smiling, studying her.

He doesn't recognize me. I look different to him . . . my hair.

Relief rushed through her. "I've heard about you, of course," she said, flustered. She chastised herself immediately for the lameness of her reply.

That rated a guffaw from Holmes, and everyone else standing about the table joined in. "Well, don't you believe any of it," he said merrily, and moved on to Chalmers Mount and then Alexandra Rhys-Shriver. Verdi was surprised to see Holmes give Rhys-Shriver a peck on the cheek before sitting down next to her. The queen bee, Verdi thought.

Waiters suddenly appeared out of nowhere, filling water goblets, serving lunch. Verdi drank iced tea, wishing it were something stronger. Covertly she sucked in a deep breath and looked up at an oil portrait of Daniel Webster hanging on the wall. She'd long admired Webster ever since high school, when in a debate class she used rhetorical devices from one of his greatest speeches, the 1830 rebuttal to Senator Hayne on the importance of preserving the Union. But now, framed in brooding shadows like a Rembrandt, Webster only glared reproachfully down at her.

So what if Kendall Holmes recognized her? Verdi thought. What was the worst that could happen? She'd be banished from the group? She realized that was precisely what she feared.

Lorna turned to her. "So what do you think?" she said.

"About what?"

"Kendall."

Verdi had to stop and think for a moment. What *did* she think about Kendall Holmes, the man who had assigned her a deathcase that would probably do in her career, nearly knocked her senseless in the corridor and treated her like a criminal for it, and was overlord of this little band of mercenaries? She knew a few words that could describe him, only how would Lorna react to them?

"Kate?"

Verdi snapped her eyes and looked over at Lorna. "Huh?"

"Pity's sake. I asked what you thought of Kendall."

"Uh, nice. He seems nice."

"Nice? Is that all?"

Verdi shrugged and glanced over at Holmes, deep in quiet conversation with Alexandra Rhys-Shriver. He didn't look nearly as intimidating as he had looked steaming at her on the corridor floor.

She let a waiter take away her plate even though she had barely touched her lunch, watching longingly as her poached salmon was carried out. After the table was cleared, another waiter came in with a tray of glasses filled with what looked like champagne. *This is more like it*, thought Verdi.

Lorna leaned close. "Dom Pérignon," she whispered.

Glasses were passed around, and the group seemed to relax. Jonathan Rashford held up his glass out of Holmes's line of sight and inspected it. "Mmm, this stuff again?" he said.

"Oh, *really*, Jon," Lorna said chidingly.

"We used to brush our teeth with it in St. Petersburg," he said, "back when water was rationed and you could get DP for a couple dollars a bottle."

"This would get me brushing after every meal," Verdi said.

They were interrupted by Holmes, standing and tapping his glass with a spoon. "Ladies and gentlemen," he said, and then added, "Did I forget anyone?"

"Well, there're no Civil Service people here," Jonathan Rashford said, nervous chuckles all around.

"Not yet anyway," Holmes shot back, staring at Rashford with mock severity.

Holmes raised a hand, and the group fell quiet. As his eyes bored into the faces looking up at him from around the room, Holmes clenched his teeth, his jaw muscles popping. To Verdi, he looked as if he were a fighter psyching himself up for a title bout.

"Downsizing," he began, spitting out the word as if it were some vile poison. "Reinventing government. Peace dividend. New World Order. This, my friends, is the language of the barbarians at our gates."

Verdi shifted uncomfortably in her seat. She looked at the champagne glass in front of her, coveting a drink from it.

"As you know"—Holmes went on—"the department is now under siege. Since beginning my career here some forty years ago, I have seen only one other period in this great institution's history that rivals the present in disgrace and infamy. That was the McCarthy era, a dark time of suspicion, fear, and demagoguery.

"We hear that Congress is clamoring for us to reduce our ranks. We hear that entire divisions are being eliminated at the stroke of a pen. We hear that international diplomacy runs a distant third behind defense and intelligence in the eyes of the American people in terms of protecting our national security. The mother ship is being assaulted from all sides, and the American Foreign Service, the greatest diplomatic corps in the world, is on the verge of becoming merely a concierge for our embassies abroad.

"But the threat is not only from without the State Department. Even our own internal policies seek to undermine our strength. Merit and achievement as means of advancement are being cast aside in favor of social quotas. The self-proclaimed experts on the seventh floor—the political appointees—are concerned not with shaping foreign policy but with writing our epitaph.

"So, my friends, how can we stop this insidious erosion of the very foundations of the Foreign Service? How do we restore the honor and dignity of our profession? The answers can be found right now, in this room."

His eyes moved from one face to another around the table. Verdi felt her skin tingle as his eyes came to rest on her. "You are the future of the Foreign Service. Each of you has the tremendous responsibility of carrying forward the tradition of excellence that has marked the department since its founding in 1789. Each of you has distinguished yourself in some aspect of the Foreign Service. For those of you further along in your careers, your contributions have been substantial. Those of you just beginning, your contributions will grow over time.

"Of supreme importance to our continued success is your unswerving allegiance to this group. We are being asked to deliver much, to accomplish an unprecedented amount with few resources. It is said that a chain is only as strong as its weakest link. The Circle does not have, nor will it ever have, such a link, only a spectrum of strengths.

"And now to the purpose of this occasion. From time to time one of our number is honored with a special assignment that commands recognition. Today one of you has attained such a distinction."

Holmes paused to pick up his champagne glass. Verdi watched Chalmers Mount as he twisted around in his seat, a film of sweat shiny across his forehead. His eyes were cast down, as they'd been throughout the speech, and he gripped a butter knife he'd kept from the meal.

"Later today," Holmes droned on, "it will be announced through the formal channels that Alexandra Rhys-Shriver has been promoted from her current position as director of the Office for Chinese and Mongolian Affairs to deputy assistant secretary of East Asian and Pacific Affairs. She has also been named a member of the Senior Executive Service."

Verdi was ready to break into applause, but she observed the members of the Circle quietly raise their glasses to Rhys-Shriver, who sat still and stoic, eyes straight ahead, like a soldier receiving a medal. The champagne was tart on Verdi's tongue, almost bitter, as she tasted it. She stole another gulp before putting it down. She noticed Kendall Holmes set his glass aside without drinking from it.

Verdi stared at the champagne bubbles dancing violently in her glass. An uncontrollable shivering crept up her back as if someone had plugged her spine into an electrical socket. Like a wild animal sensing danger, she went on full alert and took in quick, shallow breaths. *What is it?* she wondered. *Why can't I stop shaking?*

"Speech!" Lorna called out, and Rhys-Shriver allowed a slight smile.

"Go ahead, Alex," Holmes encouraged her, taking his place.

Rhys-Shriver rose from her seat and cleared her throat. Watching her preparing to speak, Verdi suddenly understood the reason for her inexplicable anxiety. Alexandra Rhys-Shriver had just been named deputy assistant secretary of East Asian and Pacific affairs, the position Patricia Van Slyke held at the time of her death.

CHAPTER
★ ELEVEN ★

An hour after the reception broke up, Chalmers Mount was in his second-floor corner office, slowly massaging his tired eyes. He'd just gone through the personnel file of a Foreign Service officer applying for an opening in the Paris consulate. It was clear that the officer, a mid-career consular aide now in Dakar, had done her homework. First, she knew that a position would be available in Paris, making several references to it in her essay. Also, she discussed how her experience in francophile Africa would lend itself directly to a post in France. She didn't miss a trick, mentioning the advanced French training she'd taken in Senegal, as well as her volunteer work there on behalf of illiterate children.

This was the seventy-ninth transfer application Mount had seen for this one slot. Each one seemed to be stronger than the one before it. There was a lot of talent out there, in the Washington home office and the many overseas posts. But Mount wasn't concerned about having to explain why he'd put all those applications in the Pending file. If anyone bothered to ask, Kendall Holmes could swiftly offer a ready answer.

Mount tossed the buff-colored manila file to the side of his desk and picked up the crimson one in front of him with the name Verdi, Katherine on it. He flipped through Verdi's file, scanning the quantitative section—test scores, performance evaluations—that was really quite impressive. The file might not have been as deep as others he'd seen, but it had its strengths. Most important to Mount was that it offered enough hooks for him to explain rationally why Katherine Verdi, an untenured junior Foreign Service officer, could get a job coveted by many others above her in the pecking order.

Mount carefully slid Verdi's file into a drawer file, stood up, and began pacing. He was still worked up over the party, unable to block it out enough so that he could concentrate on his work. He found that he needed every ounce of self-control to get through that pathetic display. Imagine, having to watch Her Highness, Alexandra, pretending modesty over a promotion he'd engineered for her. Not that Kendall Holmes would ever acknowledge Mount's role in anything. That was becoming a way of life.

In fact, Chalmers Mount had to get used to a lot of new things, not the least of which was having to subjugate his own career in service to the Circle. Mount had been a rising star in the department, a sure bet for an eventual ambassadorial post, when he met Holmes in Moscow. He would have made it with or without Holmes in his corner. But to this day he couldn't really remember how it all started. Holmes did a favor for him, he did one back, and the whole thing kept escalating until Mount realized he was in too deeply, having swallowed everything, hook, line, sinker.

Even the fisherman and his pole, Mount thought bitterly.

Kendall Holmes. Mount never felt so utterly vulnerable to another person as he did with Holmes. In less than four years Mount's function in life had devolved to that of keeper of Holmes's little stable of protégés, his garden of hothouse flowers. Like Alexandra Rhys-Shriver. Mount hadn't overlooked any of her theatrics this afternoon, like the little kisses she gave Holmes when he arrived, the blush on her cheek when he called her name or the measured quiver in her voice toward the end of her acceptance speech. An Academy Award-winning performance.

He'd also observed Alexandra's sudden interest of late in the Office of Career Development and Assignments, her unprecedented visits increasing in frequency as the date for her appointment review drew closer. Even though she knew her promotion was in the bag, she took no chances, dropping in on Holmes at all hours, brushing by Mount as she made a beeline to Holmes's office. Then he'd have to listen to them in there, tittering like teenagers for at least an hour at a time. A few days ago she actually brought Holmes a tie, saying it would look just *fabulous* on him. The old man ate up every second of it, eagerly letting her wrap him around her little finger.

Mount felt fatigue creeping up his extremities. Although he was used to working late, he needed a break. He stood up to stretch and looked out his window overlooking Kelly Park. There was a tent down there, a pathetic flimsy firetrap infested by indigents. He leaned toward the window, wondering how the police could let them just camp out there. Of course, the D.C. police would let *anything* go by in the city, except a parking violation. Just then a voice caused him to jump, almost banging his head against the windowpane.

"Chalmers?"

Mount looked up into the face of Lorna Demeritte hovering in his doorway. He managed to speak. "Lorna. What a surprise. Come in." She smiled slightly and shuffled in, her head bent down.

"Please sit down," he said, glancing at his watch. What did she want? he wondered. He hoped it wouldn't take long, whatever it was.

"Th-thanks," she stuttered as she decorously tucked her skirt under her and took a seat. "I can see you're busy."

Mount made no effort to contradict her. Instead he sat back, watching her, waiting for her to state her business and leave. Lorna looked haggard, overwrought, although Mount couldn't imagine why. He was generally up on the schedules of everyone in the Circle, and he knew Lorna wasn't especially busy right now. She had only one chore to do for the Circle—nothing requiring much effort—and her job as congressional liaison should have been a breeze right now, since most of Congress was out grubbing votes back home.

"That was a nice little to-do you had for Alexandra," she said. "I was happy for her."

Mount stiffened and crossed his legs, keeping the smile on his face. "Well, that's the way the Circle works, Lorna. We do our share whenever we're asked, and sometimes fortune smiles on us."

She nodded, her eyes locked on her fingers knotted on her lap. "Yes, I suppose that's true. In fact, that's what I wanted to talk with you about. It's, uh, my assignment. The one you asked me to take care of."

She looked up at him. He almost had to look away from the loathsome cast to her eyes, somewhere between fear and self-pity. He wished she were as far from him as humanly possible. Mount knew what was happening and didn't like it a bit. An unwelcome trend was emerging here as more and more of the people Kendall Holmes recruited were coming to him, rather than Holmes, to express their doubts or to unload. This time it took a greater effort than usual to retain his good nature.

"Yes?" he said, more gently than she deserved.

"I—I don't know if I can do it."

He leaned toward her, feigning sympathy. "Why, Lorna?"

"It's not the assignment itself, I guess; it's more the way things are—are turning out. It's not really what I expected. I think what I mean is that I don't think I'm right for the Circle."

Chalmers Mount smiled broadly and held up a

hand. He'd heard this before—in fact, more recently than he cared to remember. But that was an entirely different situation. It'd gotten way out of control before he could do anything about it. Something told him he could handle Lorna Demeritte, that she hadn't completely made up her mind about leaving the Circle. All she needed was a little reassurance, he told himself, a pat on the head.

"You know something, Lorna? I can completely understand what you're feeling."

"You can?"

"Sure. The pressure of leadership. It's to be expected."

"That's not really—"

He held up his hand again. "You're in a difficult position, Lorna. The career track in functional areas like Congressional Affairs is far less certain than in the geographic bureaus. Somebody like Alexandra is on her way to an ambassadorship, with or without the Circle behind her. But with you it's much dicier. It's like a university faculty member in some sort of interdisciplinary field; when push comes to shove, which academic department do you hang on to? Or, more important, which department hangs on to you?"

Mount could see that he was beginning to get to Lorna, her eyes registering a new kind of desperation—fear for her job—that was overcoming the old one. He knew that Lorna had been born into money, so that he couldn't use that on her. She would require an altogether different tack.

"You know, Lorna," he said, moving in for the kill, "I honestly don't think you could go back to where you were before the Circle picked you up, in the State

Protocol Office. You've reached a certain stature where you are now. The people on the Hill know you, call you up for favors, invite you to things, all those lovely parties. Without the Circle that would just disappear."

Lorna's eyes, glazed with tears, stared blankly at him. "But—but you just can't take away a job I already have."

Chalmers Mount shrugged and looked away. "If it were up to me, Lorna, you could just walk away from the Circle and stay right where you are in Congressional Affairs. But I don't think Kendall would take that view. To be perfectly candid, I think he'd take your leaving as a personal insult."

"But why? I've done everything he's asked me."

"This isn't just a favor swap, Lorna. The way Kendall sees the Circle is as an investment in people he trusts, a mutual long-term investment. He's taken a risk on each one of us, that we'd live up to our potential. You just don't give up on an investment when things take a downturn. You ride it out." Mount leaned closer to her. "You've seen how he gets when he feels betrayed," he said ominously. "He has his own personal standard of loyalty and a low tolerance for backsliding."

He smiled reassuringly and picked up a Kleenex box from his desk and held it out to her. The poor woman was completely unglued. Mascara streamed down her cheeks, and her lips were trembling. She took a tissue and daubed at her face.

"Tell you what," he said. "I'll give you a hand with your assignment. Why don't we have lunch tomorrow and talk about it?"

She nodded her head and stood up, folding the tissue now streaked with black. She kept on nodding as she walked out of his office, looking every bit the victim she thought she was.

CHAPTER
★ TWELVE ★

The Citizens Emergency Center was a cavern of darkness as Verdi arrived early the next morning. She reached out her hand to the row of light switches on the wall but withdrew it. The thought of white fluorescent spikes showering over her was about as appealing as having to face Calamity John about the Van Slyke cremation fiasco.

Verdi had had a horrible night, never really falling asleep at all. To make matters worse, she was still coming down from yesterday's champagne buzz. She'd spent the afternoon and much of the evening with Lorna and her crowd after Holmes had left, tossing back toasts to everything from John Foster Dulles to antidiarrheals. Why did she think only *bad* liquor could give you a hangover?

She turned on a desk lamp and opened the *Post* before forcing herself to eat a yogurt and banana. As usual, she started with the sports section. That usually cheered her up, especially if the Orioles won or the Yankees lost. But the Os were idle yesterday, and Verdi had trouble concentrating as she scanned the box scores.

The news of Alexandra Rhys-Shriver's appointment to the dead Patricia Van Slyke's job was haunting Verdi, prickling the edges of her consciousness even while she was concentrating on something else. It had kept her up all night puzzling over the coincidence, if it really was one. Verdi couldn't be sure. No one else at the lunch seemed to be troubled by the whole thing. For all she knew, they had no idea about Van Slyke's death, except from an obituary or some blurb in a State Department newsletter. And the poor woman wasn't even in the *ground* yet. What was the rush to replace her?

Verdi closed her eyes and massaged her temples. *Get real*, she told herself. Anything other than an innocent coincidence was too terrible even to consider. Besides, there was every reason to believe that nothing was fishy here. A Foreign Service Officer died—FSOs do that sometimes—and Rhys-Shriver was the obvious replacement. They both were hotshot China experts, worked in the same division. Who else was as qualified for the job?

And yet. A stubborn voice inside Verdi nagged at her, demanding a credible explanation for Patricia Van Slyke's death. She stepped on the voice, ground it into the carpet, and got up in search of coffee.

"Damn," Verdi whispered when she noticed the light coming from the office at the other end of the hall from her. Why hadn't she seen it when she came in? The office was Calamity John's.

She thought for a moment. At first tempted to turn in the opposite direction, Verdi knew that she had to face the music and now was as bad a time as any. Besides, she knew that managers—especially government ones—hated to be surprised by anything. There was certainly a chance that everything could turn out OK with the Van Slyke case and Dietz would never find out about it. But that was unlikely, and Verdi calculated that she stood to lose a lot less by telling him now than she would if he found out from someone else. And maybe Calamity John was better in the morning, although she didn't see him as "better" at any time of the day.

Verdi drew in a deep breath and peered into the office. She caught Dietz's eye just as his head reared up for a shuddering sneeze.

"Bless you," she said, and he waved her in with one hand as he blew his nose into a ratty tissue with the other. He looked terrible: pallid color, pink, watery eyes, and a chapped and blistered nose from constant sniffling and blowing. Death warmed over, as her mother would have described him.

"Pretty bad one?" she said, not venturing to ask how he was. She wished she were anyplace else but here.

He shrugged. "Still alive," he murmured through blocked sinuses. "What can I do for you?"

Verdi plucked at the skin around her right thumb. "It's about that case you assigned me the other day, the death of Patricia Van Slyke." She paused and waited for a reaction, some sign of recognition that never came.

"There are some, I mean, I've run into some ... complications. It concerns the disposition of the remains. Mr. Dietz, the body was cremated in Beijing and shipped back before I even talked to anyone there.

"I went out to Dulles to pick them up the night before last, and the family's funeral director was there. A real pain. He was all over me about how the family never agreed to cremation and was expecting a casket. So I released the remains to him, but I think you're going to be hearing—"

Dietz raised a hand, and Verdi fell silent. "I got a call last night from someone in the Secretary's office," he said. Verdi suddenly felt her chest tighten.

"I forget the name. He explained the problem and said that Van Slyke's family was hiring a lawyer to sue the department. It's not certain that they'll do it, but you should be prepared to be deposed."

Verdi kept her shaking hands out of sight. "How serious is this, Mr. Dietz?"

"Quite serious. But my advice to you is not to dwell on it. I know that's easier said than done, but you're best served by doing everything by the book from here on out. Maybe it'll just blow over."

Verdi couldn't look him in the eye. She tried to fight down the fear that everything she'd worked and sacrificed for was slipping away. She felt the floor beneath her pitch and yaw like a boat in a storm.

Dietz leaned closer. "I don't know what's happening here, Verdi. I don't know why we were tasked this case, much less why your name was on it. But I do

know one thing, and that is, you need eyes in the back
of your head to survive in this place. Things aren't always as they seem."

Verdi was barely listening. She was thinking of the
pine box containing Patricia Van Slyke's remains. She
realized she had held it for only a moment. It was sur-
prisingly light.

"Would it be OK if I took the afternoon off?"
she said.

Dietz's eyes narrowed. "Everything all right, Verdi?"

*Of course, you heartless son of a bitch. The next sound
you'll hear is my career being flushed down the toilet.*
"Yeah," she said softly, "just an appointment I need to
keep."

Dietz nodded and sat back, watching her. Without
saying another word, she left the office and went
straight to the women's room, where she sat in a stall
until she could breathe normally again.

The sun was unremittingly bright on the crescent
of people, darkly dressed, their heads bowed. They
stood close together at the base of a long, grassy slope
where a small, square hole had been dug in the earth.
A priest in black vestments read a benediction from a
worn prayer book.

Kate Verdi was surprised how well she knew the
words to the benediction. Entire passages came back
to her with all the associations of old funerals she'd
been dragged to as a girl, of grieving women in black
veils supported by grim-faced men, fidgeting children
curious for a glimpse of the corpse, and endless plat-
ters of food at the wake. Verdi, from a large family, had

been to many funerals in her life. She couldn't remember her last one, though.

At the back of the funeral party and off to the side, she was doing her best to remain inconspicuous. She had not shown up for the viewing and receiving line at the funeral home. Nor had she gone to the church for the Mass; she hadn't been in church since leaving for Jakarta and wasn't ready to enter one now. Besides, she didn't want to have to explain herself to the family and risk having them calling the Secretary of State's office again to complain about her being there.

The priest was winding down now, having finished the prayers. Verdi took one last look at Patricia Van Slyke's mother and daughter up in front. It was touching; the girl, who couldn't have been older than ten, was standing straight, holding her grandmother's hand. The priest handed the girl a long-stemmed white rose to place on the mahogany urn box and was inviting others to do the same.

A good time to leave, Verdi thought. Just then she caught sight of a man in a gray suit standing several yards away from the funeral party, partially hidden behind a grave marker. She felt an inexplicable chill ripple over her body. What was he doing there? Why hadn't she noticed him before? He wouldn't have been apparent to most of the others, but Verdi had a clear look at him. He was big, swarthy, with heavy eyebrows and a nose that looked as if it had been broken years ago and was badly set.

He was probably with the funeral home, she thought, until she spied a face she recognized: the little creep from the freight hangar, Gary Pemburton, standing next to Van Slyke's mother, his lily white skin in contrast with his black suit, his red hair blowing comically in the breeze. Verdi gritted her teeth when Pemburton caught her staring at him. Verdi held the gaze until he looked away.

The crowd was breaking up, and Verdi dug in her purse for her car keys. *Where were they, dammit?* She had begun climbing the slope toward her car when she felt someone tugging at her sleeve. She turned quickly to see the anguished face of Patricia Van Slyke's mother.

"You're the one who picked up my daughter's ashes at the airport?" the woman whispered. Her lips trembled, and her dry, bloodshot eyes were fixed on Verdi's.

Verdi drew back. There was an air of hysteria about the woman, something unstable and dangerous. "Y-yes," she managed to say.

"What happened to her over there? I have to know."

"What do you mean?"

The woman stepped closer. "They told me she slipped in a shower. But that's ridiculous. I know it is. Patricia was a dancer; she won trophies for ballroom. She had excellent balance and coordination. It just doesn't make any sense."

Verdi suddenly realized that it must have been Pemburton who pointed her out to the woman. The prick. She was on her guard, knowing that whatever she'd say would figure into the family's lawsuit.

"All I know is what I read in your daughter's case file. The embassy believed that her death was accidental. Otherwise it would have launched a full investigation."

Verdi could tell that her explanation was not satisfying the woman, whose anger and frustration were welling up in her eyes. The woman looked down at the ground, nodding her head. Here it comes, thought Verdi. She steeled herself for physical violence.

But the woman merely looked away and drifted off in search of her granddaughter, who was still at the graveside. Verdi watched as the woman said something to the child, and took her by the shoulders. They stood staring at the urn case laden with white roses.

Verdi was dumbfounded. She'd felt absolutely no malice or anger directed toward her. What about the lawsuit? Pemburton had been right, that the family was Catholic. But Verdi saw no sign that the cremation disturbed the family. The woman never said a word about it.

Feeling drained, Verdi wearily trudged up the hill to her car, parked away from the others. She looked down at the knots of people who couldn't bring themselves to leave. Her eyes swept over the scene, searching for the man behind the gravestone. Where had he gone? she puzzled. She shrugged and turned away, looking for the Camaro.

CHAPTER
★ THIRTEEN ★

Clarence Witherspoon had always liked stopping by Turkey Thicket, a park in Northeast Washington. In the great religion of Washington pickup basketball, Turkey Thicket was Rome, Jerusalem, and Mecca rolled into one. Its courts had produced the likes of Dave Bing and Elgin Baylor and a slew of college recruits who never went all the way. It was the rare weekend any time of the year when its three full courts weren't in constant use.

What Witherspoon liked about the place was the order of it all, the rules being followed. Oh, sure, there were the usual flying elbows and butts-in-the-guts off the boards. But mostly the players here were well disciplined and serious about their game. Turkey Thicket was an oasis of order amid the chaos of the Washington streets.

There were always more than a few fans in the

bleachers watching the action. The few white faces were usually college scouts. Witherspoon, his jacket over his shoulder and his firearm hidden in his belt, sat at the top of a row of stands, his eye on one game in particular. It was an unusual game in that it was five-on-four instead of the usual five-on-five.

One of the "four" was Rico Settles, a young man Witherspoon had busted on a dope charge while investigating a homicide. Rico had lost an eye—years ago in a turf fight over a corner, he said—and today the opposing basketball team fielded only four players to keep things fair. Rico always made a bigger deal out of his missing eye than he had to, Witherspoon had observed.

Whatever Rico lost by way of vision he more than made up for in intensity. Witherspoon watched as he aggressively took over the game, feeding assists and picking cherries on the fast break. A little more than a year ago, when Witherspoon interrogated Rico after arresting him, the detective was impressed with the boy's character and ability to think on his feet. Rico was looking at his third drug conviction, which would have sent him away for a long time. Despite his two priors, Rico was not as hardened as a lot of the kids coming up trying to make a rep for themselves.

Witherspoon agreed to cut Rico a break, provided he went back to high school and kept up his grades. Before committing himself to helping Rico, Witherspoon met with the boy's mother, probation officer, and high school principal to see if he was worth the risk. It wouldn't have looked good for Witherspoon if, after he had spoken up for Rico, the kid had been hauled back in for popping somebody or moving up to big-time dealing. Witherspoon kept an eye on him, checking up to see he was in school and receiving his grades. So far Rico was making it.

The game was breaking up, and Witherspoon stood up by the bleachers so Rico could see him. He didn't want to approach him, knowing that being seen with a cop would at best damage Rico's reputation. At worst it could get him killed. Instead Witherspoon waited until Rico spotted him, and then he ducked into a quieter part of the park where no one was around.

Rico made him wait awhile before he showed up, wary and taciturn. He was carrying a basketball and sporting a baby blue sweatshirt with the word *FILA* across the front. His shorts were cut maybe two sizes larger than he needed.

"Hey, Rico," Witherspoon said, extending a hand.

Rico took the hand and nodded. "So, what's up?" he said.

"How are things?" Witherspoon said.

"You're asking *me*? You know more about what I do than my own mother."

Witherspoon had to smile. "Just protecting my investment."

"Yeah, right."

"As long as you remember I'm keeping an eye on you."

Rico turned his head to give Witherspoon a look at his translucent glass eye. "And I'm keeping an eye on you too."

Witherspoon nodded. Pleasantries over. "OK. Listen, Rico, I could use some help with something I'm working on."

Rico frowned broadly. "Yo, now wait a minute. I appreciated you helping me and everything. And I'm keeping my side of it. It ain't easy, believe me. But our deal never called for any informing. That's bad news around here."

"Now you wait a minute," Witherspoon broke in. "I work with informants. What I'm asking here is nothing like that. You understand me?"

Rico dribbled the ball, slapping at it and gazing off somewhere. Finally he said, "You can ask, but I may not know anything."

"Fair enough." Witherspoon sat down on the edge of a wooden bench. Next to it was a water fountain long out of commission. "Four days ago the body of a white man was found at an intersection in Trinidad. Hear about it?"

Rico shrugged.

Witherspoon went on. "Looked like the man might have been dumped there, he was so covered over with garbage. Shot twice in the chest, point-blank. No signs of dealers or pros in the area. You hear of any car-jackers working the area?"

"No."

"How about crews then? Was somebody sending a message leaving that body there?"

Rico shook his head, smiling. "Cops always think there's a message, like somebody gets blown away and there's got to be a reason for it. People get blown away. *That's* the reason."

Witherspoon stood up quickly, his face close to

Rico's. "But this one's different, man. This one's white, State Department white. And you know what that means. The papers and the TV pick it up big, follow it. Hell, the chief's had a press conference every *day* since this murder went down. Then it comes down on my ass."

Rico turned away, scowling. "It's your problem, man. Not mine."

"I'm making it your problem. How about it?"

Rico jumped in Witherspoon's face. "What you want anyway? Do I look like directory assistance or something?"

Witherspoon held his temper and his tongue. He looked down as Rico stalked in circles, angrily bouncing the ball off the cement sidewalk. It was crucial that Witherspoon not beg or appear desperate. Rico knew Witherspoon wouldn't have come to him if he hadn't really needed the help. He would help him or he wouldn't.

Rico sat down on the bench. "Shit, man, I hope this don't turn into nothing regular."

"Just one other thing," Witherspoon said, and Rico, predictably, groaned. "Two weeks ago there was a shoot-out on an Ivy City schoolyard. Three people dead, all kids. We know it was the Brentwood Crew, but no one's talking. We could use a name on this one."

Rico smiled a disgusted smile. Witherspoon knew what he was thinking and didn't bother to ask. The detective really wasn't interested in the Ivy City shooting. He wasn't even working on it; other detectives were. Tom Galvin used to say that the criminal mind needs to think that it's smarter than others and takes every opportunity to prove it. Witherspoon knew that Rico wouldn't get near that gang killing. Just asking about it could get him shot. But what he gave Rico was something he could blow off while getting him the information he really wanted on the Porter case. Something to save face.

"Anything else?" Rico said.

"That should do it for now," Witherspoon said, finally allowing a smile.

"Right," Rico said coolly, and sauntered off, dribbling his ball.

Witherspoon watched him walk away. Let Rico think he was smarter, Witherspoon thought. Maybe he was.

CHAPTER
★ FOURTEEN ★

"Oh, damn, I forgot the radicchio."

Lorna Demeritte led Verdi around the back of her town house. They'd just been shopping at the Sutton Place Gourmet up on New Mexico Avenue, where Lorna seemed to buy every imaginable kind of trendy cheese and salad fixing. The Circle was coming over tonight, and everything had to be perfect.

"I could put fingernail polish on some cabbage," Verdi offered deadpan. "After all this wine nobody'd know the difference."

Lorna rolled her eyes and pushed open a low wrought-iron gate. Verdi hefted the bags she was carrying full of wine bottles and caught the swinging gate on her hip. She followed Lorna around the side of the town house to the back. The earthy odor of chrysanthemums drifted up from the garden below the deck. Verdi watched Lorna bend down with the two bags in her arms and fish out a key from behind a massive geranium planter.

"High-security building, huh?" Verdi said as Lorna unlocked the patio door and returned the key to its hiding spot.

"If they want to get in, they will," Lorna answered, already inside the house. "Besides, this isn't Adams-Morgan."

"You can say *that* again," Verdi mumbled, gawking at the place. It had been professionally decorated since she'd been here last. Every piece of furniture looked like an expensive antique, and everything on the walls was original art. In stark contrast with Verdi's apartment, Lorna's place was spotless, a cleaning woman coming in once a week, and she'd heard Lorna mention that the garden had been landscaped as well.

"So this is what trust funds are for," Verdi said, but Lorna wasn't around to hear. She set the bags on the kitchen countertop, inlaid with cerulean Spanish tiles, and began removing wine bottles. "OK if I open one?" she shouted. No answer. That would constitute a "yes" in Verdi's household, so she found a corkscrew in a drawer and went to work on one of the bottles.

Lorna had asked Verdi to pick out the wine, and the selection reflected her tastes, which meant heavy on Bordeaux and French cabernets. After the funeral that afternoon and her conversation with Calamity John earlier, Verdi was ready for a drink. She didn't much feel like making nice with anyone. Yet she'd already accepted Lorna's invitation for tonight and would never hear the end of it if she backed out. But there was another, more urgent, reason for Verdi's coming here tonight, even volunteering to arrive early and help with the food.

The cork protecting the St. Emilion gave way with a satisfying contralto *thwop* as Lorna entered the kitchen. "There is nothing friendlier than a bottle of red wine," Verdi proclaimed, holding up the bottle and cork.

Lorna frowned. "Save some for the guests."

Verdi knew better than to come back with a wise-crack. Lorna, whose moods at the store had ranged from sullen to testy, was now bustling angrily around the kitchen, opening and slamming cupboards, com-plaining about every little thing. She would toss off or-ders to Verdi but would never look her in the eye. *What is wrong with her?* Verdi wondered.

She also wondered how she would navigate the con-versation toward her hidden agenda. "What's the occa-sion tonight?" she asked as she cut up fresh broccoli.

Lorna was studying three sets of salad servers, ten-drils of long black hair hanging over her face. "Oh, someone's been promoted."

Verdi looked up. "Again? My God, you people are incredible. Who is it this time?"

"I honestly don't know. Chalmers will tell us when he gets here."

"You mean you're having a party for someone and you don't know who?"

"Chalmers likes to surprise us."

"I've noticed."

"Besides, what's wrong with having a little to-do

for your friends? Tonight I intend to put a full-court press on Jonathan Rashford. Now don't you get in my way."

An image of Rashford surfaced in Verdi's mind: Boston accent, tortoiseshell glasses, and Oxford shirt starched to the consistency of papier-mâché. "Don't worry about me." Verdi took in a deep breath. *Here goes nothing.* "Lorna, you have contacts in the Secretary's office, don't you? For your job, I mean."

Lorna kept her eyes on the salad she was tossing. "Sure. A couple."

"Have you talked to any of them lately?"

"Mmm, a few days ago. Why?"

"Well, I was wondering if my name's come up at all."

"*Your* name? Why, for heaven's sakes?"

"My boss got a call yesterday from the Secretary's office. About me. A Foreign Service officer died in the PRC, and her remains were shipped back, cremated."

"So?"

"The family didn't authorize it. The cremation, I mean. It was a major screwup. The family's planning to sue the State Department."

"Oh," Lorna said, a worried look spreading across her face. "But that shouldn't concern you, should it? The cremation would have been done in China, right?"

Verdi shrugged, gripping the paring knife she was using. The anger she'd felt this morning was slowly turning into numb resignation, but it still had a way to go. "I don't know what to believe anymore. My boss tells me not to worry, but I have a bad feeling about this. Just the other day he was reminding me that I'm still on probation. God, I'm thinking of doing something drastic, like going to law school."

She snatched up her wineglass and drained it in a single gulp. Lorna dropped her salad forks, came over to Verdi, and gently took the knife from her hand. "Listen to me, Katie," she said softly but firmly. "There's nothing that happens in the department that can't be fixed. Remember that. That's what you have friends for."

Verdi suddenly felt tired. "Forget it, Lorna," she said. "I'm sorry I brought it up."

"Why? Why are you sorry? You think I wouldn't help you? I'll speak to Kendall Holmes myself. He'll have this straightened out in no time."

Verdi looked at her. "You'd do that? I mean, why would he? He hardly knows me."

Lorna scowled and went back to tossing her salad. "Honestly, Kate. Since college I've been telling you, you can't make a career glued to a desk. You need to get out and around. With your looks and brains, you could open any door in town. All you have to do is want it."

There it was again, the big Washington C word: Career. What you did was who you were. Whom you knew was what you did. It was sickening to Verdi, even more so since she was on the same treadmill as everyone else.

All her life Verdi had been taught to be modest, self-effacing, to put others before her. But she'd also been told that she could go places, do better than her surroundings. Be ambitious, she'd been told, but keep it well hidden. Stand up for yourself, but don't be pushy. Grab for the gold ring, but be genteel about it. No one ever told her what she'd have to do to get to the top, only that she should make it there.

Verdi stared at a drop of red wine sliding slowly down the side of her glass. At that moment in Lorna Demeritte's kitchen Verdi knew she was facing a crossroads of some kind. The gold ring was hanging in front of her now. Her career was hanging in the balance. To get it back meant becoming one of *them,* those she'd always held in contempt, the manipulative and self-serving.

"So," Verdi said, feeling reckless, "if Kendall Holmes goes to bat for me, do I have to join the Circle?"

Lorna froze in her tracks for a brief second. She turned toward Verdi. "If you did join, it would be the smartest thing you did since coming to the State Department."

"That's not saying much," Verdi said dryly, pouring another glass of wine. "Want some?" she said, holding up the bottle. Lorna shook her head.

"The Circle is very powerful, Katie. Look what it's done for Alexandra."

"All right," Verdi said. "Tell me about the other end of this deal. What did Alexandra have to do for that promotion?"

"She *earned* it, Kate. She's been working at it for years."

"But you just said the Circle helped her. So what is

it, Lorna? Is there some kinky sex angle here you're hiding from me?"

The strain in Laura's laugh was audible. "Kate, if I didn't know what nice people your parents were, I'd've sworn you'd been some kind of deprived child. You see everything as subterfuge. Alexandra had to be qualified to get that job. All we do in the Circle is look out for one another, bring each other on to high-profile task forces and projects, speak up for one another in performance evaluations. Kendall and Chalmers back us up, keeping things smooth in the Career Development Office. There's nothing *sinister* going on here."

Verdi said nothing, her eyes level with Lorna's the way the Indonesians would look at you: inscrutable, nonjudgmental. *Methinks the lady doth protest too much*, she thought. She took in a breath.

"What do you do to join?" she asked quietly.

Lorna laughed again, slightly off-key. "Pity's sake, this isn't a sorority or anything like that. Everybody knows you, and they trust you. All you need to do is say you're with us. Now, every other blue moon Kendall might ask you for a favor, which you'd do."

Verdi smelled blood. "Favor? What kind of favor?"

Just then the doorbell rang and Lorna showed great skill in quickly clearing debris off the counter. "He never asks for anything you can't deliver," she said over her shoulder as she went to the door.

The entire Circle—minus Kendall Holmes—arrived together. They filed in like a line of crows, each pecking Lorna on the cheek. Every one of them, even

Chalmers Mount, made a point of saying hello to Verdi, who was standing off to the side and observing the whole thing. They brought wine and small gifts, and Mount presented Lorna a bouquet of white gladiolus over which she gushed appropriately. When Mount went for a drink, she handed them off to Verdi to put in water.

Back in the kitchen, searching the cupboards for a vase, Verdi peered through the serving port at the guests in the dining room. None of them brought a date, she noticed. And they drew together in a circle and talked quietly, forming a chain-link fence that Verdi wouldn't even attempt to penetrate. Finished with the flowers, she left them in a vase on the counter and drifted out to the garden. She found a seat beneath a fiery red Japanese maple.

A hot breeze was blowing from the west. Verdi put her feet up on a chair and drank deeply from her wineglass. With her eyes closed, she lifted her face to the last rays of the sun. She thought of Antonio, of what she'd do to him when he came to Washington, how she'd lock him into her apartment and throw away the key. Why hadn't he called in so long? she wondered. Maybe she'd try him when she got home, get him out of bed.

Someone had put on music inside, but Verdi couldn't quite make out what it was. With this crowd, it was probably the Boston Pops doing Michael Bolton. Suddenly she had the alarming sense that someone was near. Her eyes snapped open to see Chalmers Mount standing over her, looking down with a crooked smile on his face. Where had he come from so quietly? she wondered. Had he slithered down from the tree?

"Are you the search party?" she asked, shielding her eyes and pulling her feet off the chair.

"Why, were you lost?" His tongue flicked over his lips, and he sat down, casually appraising her. His linen slacks and jacket over a polo shirt looked tailormade. "It's nice out here."

"Mmm," she agreed. "Sun feels good."

"Long day?" he asked.

She blinked at the question. "Yeah, as a matter of fact. They seem to get longer every day."

"Oh?" She shrugged, trying to change the subject, but Mount stayed with it. "You're just back into a rotation at CEC, isn't that right?"

"Yes. I suppose I should say, 'How did you know?,' but I've given up asking that question with you people."

Mount only smiled his Cheshire cat smile, spinning the wine in his glass. "How do you like it? The CEC, I mean."

"It's not bad. You get lots of experience, opportunities to develop diplomatic and administrative skills." She felt as if she were reciting from a book.

"You don't sound too convinced. Or maybe you're trying to convince yourself that you like it."

She leaned toward him, saying, "Not all of us are lucky enough to have the perfect job."

"Luck has little to do with it," he said, spinning his wine more rapidly now. Verdi had to keep herself from watching, it was so hypnotic.

"Look at the Foreign Service," he went on. "It's like

a club you join, only everybody in it wants what you want. It's not enough to be smart and capable in an organization full of smart, capable people. You need that extra push; you need well-placed people you can trust who'll look out for you."

Verdi felt lulled by Mount's low, soothing voice. She considered herself an above-average reader of human faces, but Mount's completely eluded her. It shifted constantly, like a dune in a sandstorm.

"Didn't they tell you about mentors at Georgetown?" he added. "The Circle can help you, in more ways than getting you off the hook with the Secretary's office."

Verdi's eyes widened and she sat up straight. "Is my entire life on display here tonight?"

Mount waved a hand. "Calm down. Lorna told me. She's worried about you. Actually she's worried that you're worried."

Verdi ordered herself to relax. "Let me ask you something . . ."

"Chalmers," he said, nodding.

"Chalmers," she repeated. "Why do you all want me in your group? I mean, it's very flattering, but I don't see what I have to offer."

Mount took in a breath. "Kate, how many people do you think take the Foreign Service exam each year?"

Verdi thought back, recalling that bear of exams— worse than SATs, GREs, and every other test she'd ever taken—that she'd had to pass as her first hurdle into the Foreign Service. She shrugged and said she had no idea.

"About twelve thousand, on average. But in 1990, the year you took it, sixteen thousand and one hundred people were examined, one of our biggest years. As usual, only about five or six percent passed. But did you know that you had the fourth-highest score of that entire group, answering correctly one hundred forty-four out of one hundred fifty questions? The three people ahead of you didn't make it through the BEX, in which you also excelled, making you the highest-scoring officer in your class."

Verdi was stunned. Not only had Mount known her FS exam scores, but he'd even gone to the trouble to see how she'd done on the Board of Examiners test, the grueling hourlong inquisition by three Foreign Service officers given to the few who managed to pass the written exam. She was about to ask him how he knew all this but stopped herself.

"The Circle likes to surround itself with smart people," Mount said. "The best and brightest—an overused term, especially in Washington—is an apt description of the group. You graduated summa at Georgetown, top of your class. Your performance evaluations from Jakarta were glowing. And Lorna speaks highly of you. Not only that, but you're on a consular track where the Circle has no one represented. We need to be . . . diversified."

"Diversified?" Verdi said, tasting the cabernet, dry on her lips.

"Just think of your current assignment as a death officer as useful experience. Temporary, but useful." Mount leaned toward her, his eyes boring into hers. "Kate, there's something else. You've probably noticed that many of us come from, well, privileged backgrounds."

"Try 'aristocratic,' " she said, and they both laughed.

Mount nodded his head. "OK, aristocratic. Or Waspy. You've seen it yourself, probably wondered what you have in common with them. Not surprising, a woman from Seat Pleasant, father a plumber.

"You came up the hard way, worked your way through college, even dealt blackjack in Atlantic City to pay off your loans. That took guts, perseverance. The Circle needs that, Kate. It's in danger of collapsing under its own dead weight. It needs a good kick in the ass. It needs your energy and drive."

Verdi sat back, appraising Mount with fresh eyes. She could feel herself being drawn in by the charisma she'd felt years ago at the lecture. He was getting to her, hitting all the right buttons. And he'd certainly gone to a lot of trouble to find out about her. She wondered what else he knew.

"Kate," he said, "if you could choose an assignment, any one at all, what would it be?"

She swallowed. "You mean besides ambassador to King James's Court? I think I'd be happy with an assistant consul general spot at a major embassy, like Rome. Is that outrageous enough?"

"Not at all."

"You know I'm not up for reassignment for another two years, at minimum."

"It's not unheard of for someone to be sent out ahead of schedule if it was determined that the need was there. Other things can happen as well. Given

exemplary performance and other factors, an untenured FSO could be tenured ahead of schedule, even
stretched."

"Like me?" she said, giving him both barrels of her
dark eyes.

Mount rose from his chair. Shadows from the tree
partially obscured his face. "I'll let you in on a secret,
Kate," he said softly. "For the first time ever, there's
going to be no Foreign Service exam next year, no new
class of recruits. Things are going to get extremely
tight for young officers in the next few years, very few
opportunities for advancement. You're going to need
every possible advantage."

"Like the Circle?"

Mount nodded in the shadows. "Kate, this is the
proverbial invitation on a silver platter. If you refuse,
we won't bother you about it again. So, the Circle. Are
you in or out?"

Here she was, at the crossroads again. She drew in a
breath. "Count me in," she said quietly.

Verdi couldn't be sure, but Mount's face seemed
to contort in a smile. "You're doing the smart thing,
Kate," he said, and turned to go inside.

Verdi sat alone in the gathering darkness for several
moments before following him into the house. Lorna
rushed up to her and made a face as if to say, "Where
have *you* been?" She grabbed Verdi's hand and thrust
a fistful of confetti into it. Someone else handed her a
glass of champagne just before Lorna tapped a spoon
against her glass, calling for attention.

Mount stepped forward and raised a hand. "*Per-
miso*, fellow Circlers. Tonight is indeed a momentous

occasion for us. Not only do we celebrate the ascendancy of one of our numbers, but our ranks grow. Please hold your applause until I'm done. First, let us toast the newest member of the Circle. Ladies and gentlemen, I give you Kate Verdi."

Verdi felt her cheeks flush as the champagne glasses were silently raised. She was aware of Lorna's eyes on her from across the room, of her friend smiling in deep satisfaction. Verdi wished she could have taken a drink with everyone else, but she politely held her glass by the stem.

"Another toast"—Mount went on—"to the latest among our number to feel the dazzling light of success. We have just gotten word that one of our own has been named to the coveted position of executive director of Russian Affairs. And not only that, he will become director of the Secretary's Interagency Task Force on Russian Organized Crime. Let us congratulate Jonathan Rashford."

Immediately a cheer went up, and Verdi was hit with a blizzard of confetti and streamers. The music also went up, way up, and the group began to dance. Without Kendall Holmes there, decorum and restraint went out the window. Through the veil of streamers covering her head, Verdi could see Lorna in a corner, passionately kissing Rashford on the mouth.

Standing there, gulping her champagne, Verdi felt the smile melt from her face. There it was again, she thought, that same eerie tingling up the back of her scalp she'd gotten at the luncheon for Alexandra Rhys-Shriver. Her mind was working, the questions racing through it. What was going on here? Why was she getting this reaction? Where did Jonathan Rashford's promotion fit into it all?

Suddenly Verdi felt someone seize her by the hand and pull her into the mass of dancing bodies in the middle of the room.

CHAPTER
★ FIFTEEN ★

Back at her apartment and among familiar surroundings, Verdi began to feel better. She immediately sought the restorative sanctuary of her couch and Walkman. As she eased back on the soft batik-covered pillows, her eyes surveyed the apartment.

"Shit," she groaned, closing her eyes. Seemingly every surface in the place—floors, tables, counter-tops—was occupied by clothes, tapas cartons, or newspapers. The apartment, like her life, was in chaos, and it suffered profoundly in comparison with Lorna's. She dragged herself up from the couch and got to work, cleaning up.

As Verdi prowled the apartment with a laundry bag, her thoughts were pulled back to the party, especially her conversation with Chalmers Mount. So now she'd finally done it, agreed to join the Circle. It seemed so natural at the time, like walking barefoot on grass. She didn't know what would happen next, but she saw no point in worrying about it.

But the news of Jonathan Rashford's promotion still troubled her. Not that she begrudged the guy his promotion, even though he probably didn't deserve it. Rather, there was something about the position that resonated with her, touching some part of her brain that was sending out warning signals. What was it?

Finished with the clothes, she decided to go to work on the newspapers. She began tying them into bundles she'd throw into the recycling bin downstairs. She finished with the living room and moved on to the bedroom, ruthlessly collecting old *Baseball Weekly*, *Sports Illustrated*, *Time*, and *Washingtonian* magazines and gathering them into stacks.

A newspaper was open on the dresser, and she went to get it. She remembered leaving the paper open on this page so she could read the story again. It was about Brian Porter, the Foreign Service officer found murdered last week. The story had shocked her, as it had others in the department. There was a picture of Porter and below it a caption with his title: executive director, Office of Russian Affairs, U. S. Department of State.

Verdi found that her hands were trembling as she held the paper. And then it hit her: *Brian Porter held the same job that just went to Jonathan Rashford.*

"Oh, my God," she whispered. She felt light-headed, disoriented, and reached out to steady herself. Something was flashing at the corner of her eye, and she realized the signal was blinking on her answering machine on the nightstand. She sat down on the bed and fumbled with the replay button. She jumped as Antonio's voice came from the machine.

"Hello, Kate," he said in his heavily accented English. "It's Antonio. I called before, but you weren't home." Long pause. "Listen, Kate, there's something . . . I need to talk. I—I've been seeing Loretta. She's in Rome now. We've been together, and it's been . . . good."

Another long pause, and Verdi felt her stomach doing somersaults. Loretta was Antonio's ex-wife. They had been divorced just before he left for Jakarta.

"Loretta and I, we've been talking . . . about getting back together. I'm very sorry, Kate. It looks like I won't be coming to the States. I want you to know how much you—you've meant to me. This is very hard to say. I'm very sorry.

"It's that things have gotten better between Loretta and me. She seems to understand things better now, about my job, the travel. This has nothing at all to do with you. You must understand that. I'm very—"

Verdi pushed the rewind button, erasing the message.

"Mmm," Verdi hummed as she studied the label on the carton of Häagen-Dazs chocolate chocolate-chip ice cream. "Now, which has more calories, this or pralines and cream?" It appeared that the chocolate chocolate-chip had 285 calories per serving—beating out the pralines and cream by ten—so she tossed it into her shopping cart and moved on up the aisle.

As Verdi saw it, she had at least two options that

night: Either sit around her apartment and fret and fume, or get out and do something constructive. She decided to put Antonio out of her mind; he didn't deserve the effort, and she somehow had to deal with her troubling revelation about the Circle and Brian Porter's murder. But what could she do? What proof did she have? She scoured the rest of the newspapers in her apartment, searching through stories on the murder for clues to what leads the police were pursuing. But she'd found nothing. She'd have to take a different tack, but what?

With the frustration mounting, Verdi went shopping. She was in an Adams-Morgan version of Safeway, with stuffed pigs' heads, nine kinds of maize, and other Third World specialties. She'd already been through the bakery and the candy and cookies aisle, snatching up only the most fattening stuff she saw. Now she was searching for the magazines so she could load up on everything the store had on sports and fashion. And then it was off to the liquor store for more St. Emilion. It was going to be a total junk food night for body and mind.

Pushing the cart past the frozen foods section, she caught sight of someone spinning through an intersection, a familiar face. In the brief moment she saw him, she took in the unruly hair, jeans, sloppy T-shirt, and baseball cap. The guy from the FSI lawn, the one she thought she'd seen in the State cafeteria. *Could it be?* she thought. *No way. Stuff like that doesn't happen.* She started following him anyway, keeping a discreet distance.

Verdi lost him at the meat section, and after casually

combing a few aisles, she gave up and headed for the checkout. She chided herself for acting so ridiculously, chasing a man around a supermarket. As punishment for herself, she gave up on the magazines. She quickly turned a corner, and her cart banged head-on with another. Standing behind it was a man in a T-shirt and baseball cap, the man she'd been following.

"Damn, I'm sorry," he said, pulling his hands away from the cart and looking surprised. "You OK?"

"Yes, no problem," she said, her hands stinging from the collision. It *was* the guy from the center; she was ninety-five percent sure. He was taller than she'd remembered, and he needed a shave. She noticed that his cap had a Chicago Cubs emblem. National League. Too bad. He looked down at her cart and laughed.

"Something amusing you?" she said.

"That's quite a selection," he said, still laughing. "Are those *chocolate*-filled Twinkies? I didn't know they made them. What, did your cat die or something?"

"I'll have you know that my doctor ordered me to get this stuff," she said, keeping a straight face. "I have a processed sugar deficiency." He laughed so loud that every one of the few people in the checkout lines looked over at them.

What the hell, she thought, and decided to take a chance. She asked, "Have I seen you somewhere before?"

"I don't know," he said, "do you frequent McDonald's?"

"Try the FSI in Arlington. Or the State Department."

His eyes grew wide. They were a nice shade of

brown, she noticed. "Yeah, I work there. Don't tell me you do too."

She nodded her head. "Consular Affairs. CEC."

"No! Office of Foreign Buildings. I'm Jake Wheeler."

"Kate Verdi."

They shook hands and stood for a moment through the awkward silence. *Let him break it*, Verdi thought.

He did. "Hey, you have any plans tonight?"

"You mean other than burying my cat and feasting on this fine cuisine?"

He lowered his voice to a conspiratorial level. "Why don't we ditch this stuff and go somewhere? There's any number of fine fast-food establishments around here."

Verdi smiled. "I know someplace better."

She took him to the Tabard Inn, her favorite watering hole in Washington. The Tabard—a wonderfully venerable Victorian hotel whose dark romantic lounge with overstuffed couches, beamed ceiling, and outsize fireplace—was the perfect place for a seduction. She had yet to try it out.

Verdi and Wheeler talked for hours, barely touching their drinks. She very nearly forgot about Mount and Rashford, Antonio, Calamity John, and the rest of the wreckage that was her life. Wheeler asked her about herself, and like most people she met, he was surprised to learn she was from Washington. But he never blinked when she told him *where* in Washington. She found out that Wheeler was an architect who designed embassies, consulates, and other American buildings overseas. He explained how he came to the State Department from a small architecture firm he'd worked with in Indiana, where he'd grown up.

She got him talking about his family. His father was a bricklayer, and his mother a hairdresser. He was the first in his family to go to college—at one of those huge midwestern universities—and hacked around at odd jobs before going into architecture. He joined the Foreign Service on a whim; he thought it sounded like a good way to see the world.

"So, where were you last?" Verdi asked, noticing they were the only ones left in the lounge.

"Manila. I had a project there, a consular annex. A real slab of a building it was too. Eighteen inches of steel and concrete–reinforced walls and only fifteen percent of the exterior covered with windows. Forget aesthetics. The priority was bomb proofing."

"Like being back?"

He looked at her. "Not much. I miss being out there, in the field. And Washington, well, you come from here . . ."

"Go on," she urged him.

"It's not the city. Actually I like the place physically. It's the people. There's this obsession with careers I just don't connect with. Does any of this make sense?"

Verdi smiled. *You've got potential, Jake Wheeler*, she thought. Plus, he was also one of the few men she'd met at State who didn't have two last names. Only she didn't press it; the wounds from Antonio were too fresh. She just nodded and sat back, enjoying the quiet of the lounge.

"I'm keeping you."

"You're what?" Verdi said, and turned to see him glance at his watch. "Oh."

"Say, do you have any plans for dinner tomorrow?"

"Well, now that you mention it," she said, smiling, "my dinner plans were left back at the Safeway."

CHAPTER
★ SIXTEEN ★

Clarence Witherspoon had seen all manner of people—good, evil, and everything in between—sitting in the heavy oak chair bolted to the floor of the Fifth District station interview room. Usually they tended toward the evil side of the spectrum. But rarely did he get someone like the person sitting in that chair right now.

She'd called first thing that morning, just before Witherspoon had to leave for a downtown court appearance. She said she had some questions about the Brian Porter murder and wanted to speak with the detective in charge of the investigation. He was tempted to give her off to another detective, but there was something in her voice that made him agree to meet her at lunchtime—the time she requested—even though he was still off duty until tonight.

He'd seen her come into the station and immediately

known it was his caller. She was twenty-seven or twenty-eight, a couple of years older than his daughter, dark, nice figure, a real looker. He counted four uniforms or detectives who went up to her asking if she needed any help as she waited on a bench. She smiled and was polite to each of them, he noticed, even though it must've been tempting just to blow them off. After a minute watching her, he entered the waiting area and brought her back.

She introduced herself as Katherine Verdi. Closer up, she was even more striking. She had a model's face, delicate but strong, with deep brown eyes that didn't miss much going on around her. Her handshake was firm, and something about her—her voice, her manner, he wasn't sure what—suggested an inner toughness that he appreciated. But within his first few minutes with her, he could see what it was that he'd heard on the phone with her: fear. The woman clutched her purse and jacket against her chest the way a fullback would hold a football on a fourth and short.

Her explanation for calling him was terse, vague. She claimed to work at the State Department, was a colleague of Brian Porter's, whatever that meant. People in the office were wondering how things were going in the investigation, she said, and she was picked to bring back an update.

Witherspoon was polite, patient, but he didn't buy any of it. He had no problem with the part about Katherine Verdi's working at the State Department. She was smart, that was clear, and polished and well spoken. Besides, if she were a reporter, he could simply pick up the phone and find out easily. But the rest of the story smelled like smoke.

He never let on that he didn't believe her. His instincts told him to go slowly, not to push it. Maybe something would break. He deflected her questions by countering them with questions of his own. Keeping his own voice even, he asked her how Porter's office and family were holding up.

"Fine, far as I know," Katherine Verdi said.

"How about his kids?" Witherspoon asked. He knew that the Porters had no children. But did she?

Katherine Verdi shrugged. "I don't speak with the family. Someone else does."

Witherspoon nodded his head. The woman certainly was smooth. As he studied her, a new line of inquiry occurred to him. He would have to pursue it carefully.

"Miss Verdi," he said, "was Mr. Porter very . . . sociable with his office? Did he go out with his staff, for lunch or drinks after work?"

She only shrugged and looked off into nowhere.

"Did you ever go out with him?"

Frustration registered on her face. "I never socialized with him, if that's what you're asking. Detective Witherspoon, all I wanted when I came here was a little information on the case. So far all you've done is treat me like a suspect."

Witherspoon leaned back in his chair and smiled slightly. No way he was going to get her to say something she didn't want to say. He rubbed at something on the edge of the table. "Where you from, Miss Verdi?"

He was expecting a huffy blast of righteous indignation from her, but she calmly put her purse down on the table and leaned back too, as well as one could in that oak chair. "Not far from here," she said. "Seat Pleasant."

Witherspoon's smile broadened. "Is that right? I wouldn't've taken you for a local."

"I'm not offended."

"Seat Pleasant, huh? I lived not too far from there myself. There used to be a pizza place out that way, off Marlboro Pike. What was its name?"

"You mean Luigi's?"

"Yeah, Luigi's. Is it still there?"

"No, it closed."

"Is that right? Now that's a real shame. We used to order from that place. Best pizza in town. Anywhere, for that matter."

"No argument there. Where are you from, Detective?"

"Naylor Gardens. Alabama Avenue. You know it?"

She nodded. "My mother used to take us clothes shopping at the Sears around there."

"I lived right around the corner from that store. That closed too, you know."

"No, I didn't. That's too bad."

"Yeah," he said, eyes cast down. "Folks around there now have to drive ten miles or so just to do their shopping or go to a bank. Lots of businesses moving out. It's tough."

They sat quietly for several moments. Witherspoon could feel the atmosphere in the room lightening up. Katherine Verdi didn't look as tense as she had when she came in. He even sensed that she was beginning to trust him. What the hell, he thought. He might as well go all the way and tell her the truth.

"We don't know what happened to Brian Porter," he said, sitting up in the chair. "The prevailing theory is drugs. There were traces of cocaine found in his body. But I'm not so sure Porter was looking to score in that area."

"Why?"

"Doesn't figure. There was no drug activity around where we found him. None we know of anyway. What would he be doing there, in Trinidad? Besides, nothing I could find out about Porter suggested he was into drugs."

He looked at her. "But nothing much figures in this case. A white man found dead on a street in Trinidad, covered with trash. No car, no ID, no known enemies. It doesn't figure. To be frank with you, Miss Verdi, *you* don't figure to me."

"And how is that?" she said, the tension returning.

"Listen, I've been straight with you. Put yourself in my place. You call me up sounding scared to death, come in here with some story about bringing back information for your office. What do you know about Brian Porter, Miss Verdi? This is the time to come forward."

Katherine Verdi abruptly stood up and collected her things. "I don't know anything about Brian Porter's death. And I don't appreciate being treated like a criminal."

She turned to leave, and he began following her. "Nobody's treating you like a—"

But she was gone. Witherspoon stood at the station

door, the midday light pouring through, stinging his eyes. He went back inside, looking for a telephone.

"You're sure you're not rushing off to see another man?" Jake Wheeler asked Kate Verdi as he clung to the door of her Camaro. He looked down at his feet, balanced precariously on the curb of Wisconsin Avenue in Georgetown. Behind him was the Indonesian restaurant where they had just had an early dinner.

Verdi, halfway out into traffic, fixed her eyes on him. Pangs of lust rose inside her. She had a nice little fantasy going that was rudely interrupted by horns blaring from the line of cars in the lane behind them.

She leaned toward Jake. "I'm really sorry I have to go," she said lightly into his ear. "It was just something I couldn't get out of."

"The night, she is young," he sang.

She kissed him, just missing his lips. "I had a great time. Call me?"

"Just try and avoid it," he said, and shut the door.

The drive to the Tabard Inn seemed to take forever. Verdi swore at herself, wishing she'd arranged things better. She would dearly have liked to stay with Jake, to share a dessert or another glass of wine. Or maybe even go back to his place. But there was no reason to rush it. Nothing was worth it if it wasn't worth waiting for, Nonno told her.

At the Tabard she found a corner couch in the lounge and ordered a cabernet. Sitting there in the dark, alone in a roomful of happy couples cozying up—some obviously well along on their way to a memorable night together—Verdi was surprised how good she felt. Particularly surprising in that she'd just been dumped by what she'd thought was her boyfriend in the most ignominious fashion imaginable. And, not least, that her career, possibly her life, was veering out of control and she had no clue what to do about it.

There was only one explanation for this irrational happiness: Jake Wheeler. She'd just had a genuinely great time with him at dinner, introducing him to the wonders of rijsttafel and reliving their "cute meet" last night at the Adams-Morgan Safeway. Things got even more animated when the restaurant's owner came out and snapped a photo of them, explaining that the picture would be used on the new takeout menu. Verdi and Jake had a good laugh over that one, imagining their grinning faces under hundreds of windshield wipers and refrigerator magnets throughout the city.

It was tempting to stay, but earlier that day, after returning to her office from her inquisition at the police station, Verdi had called up Chester Lundquist. Chet, her buddy from Jakarta, was now working under Chalmers Mount and Kendall Holmes in Foreign Service Career Development and Assignments. She was a bit reluctant to call Chet, since their parting in Jakarta had been rather less than cordial. But he seemed glad to hear from her and eagerly accepted her offer of a drink.

Verdi squirmed in her seat, suddenly conscious of the fact that she was about to use Chet, to milk him for a big favor. Calculated manipulation was not a strong suit of hers, but this was different. She told herself she wasn't doing this for herself alone.

Chet arrived at nine o'clock, precisely on time. In his

seersucker suit and oversize glasses, he hadn't changed a bit. Verdi and he had been best pals in Jakarta for nearly a year, her grueling, bewildering first year there. He'd helped get her past it until she could really enjoy the place. That is, until he confessed his love for her when she'd already begun her affair with Antonio.

Chet hugged her, and she made no effort to deflect his kiss on her lips. He pulled back and looked at her. "You look terrific, Kate, as always." His eyes narrowed. "But I detect something's wrong. Am I right?"

She sighed. Chet knew her a little too well. "Long day." Where had she heard *that* before?

Chet plopped down on the couch, pointed at Verdi's glass, and held up two fingers to the waitress passing by. He scanned the lounge and the couples quiet in dark corners.

"Nice place, Kate," he said. "You come here often for the floor show?"

"It's not always like this," she said. "So how are you, Chet?"

The waitress brought their wine, and they drank quietly. Verdi flipped through her various stratagems for getting Chet to do what she wanted. None of them was very appealing.

"I am well," he said, "to answer your question. Although I must admit, I'm finding it difficult to recall the last time I saw you. It wasn't the airport in Jakarta, I'm sure of that. You stayed on after I left. When was it?"

Verdi laughed. "You don't want to know."

"Oh, come on. Tell me."

She sipped her wine again and put it down. "The

Marine House. Tim and Della Murphy's going-away party. I think it was the night before you left. It was your going-away party too, wasn't it?"

Chet groaned and touched his forehead. "Don't tell me. It's starting to come back."

"One of the Marines—I can't remember which one—challenged you to a chugging contest. You started with beer and worked your way up to schnapps. It was painful to watch. I think you won, but I have no idea how you made your plane the next day."

Chet was grinning. "To this day I don't remember a minute of that flight. But I think I'm still feeling the hangover." Another long silence. "And how are you, Kate? How is it being back?"

"Oh, fine."

"Very convincing," he said. "Now, tell me what's the matter."

She paused a second. "You're in Foreign Service Career Development, aren't you?"

He looked at her. "Uh-huh. You need a new assignment?"

"Very tempting. What I could really use is some help where I am now."

Chet, sensing an opening, rolled his buttocks over the couch until he was right next to her. "Go on."

"It's a case I'm working on. A Foreign Service officer on TDY died in China. I've been assigned disposition and I haven't a clue why she was there. My boss, a real ballbreaker, is on me to wrap this up. I was ... hoping you could help me on this."

Chet nodded, deep in thought. "Have you spoken

with her bureau? They should know why she was there."

Verdi frowned. "It's one big runaround: No one knows anything, and if they did, they don't want to go on record about it. You know how it gets. Someone must have signed travel orders for her. I just need to find out who."

"Well, that's easy. Come by tomorrow, and I'll check her file in our computer. Travel orders are all in there. Everything."

Verdi picked at the skin around her thumb, her mind racing. All she needed was for Chalmers Mount, Chet's boss, to catch her in that office. "But I'll be in meetings all day tomorrow," she said, "and the next couple of days. They're . . . reorganizing the office. Do you think we could go tonight, like right now?"

She could tell from Chet's face that he was reluctant. "If I take you," he said somberly, "I'm going to want something in return."

Shit, Verdi thought. "What's that?" she said, forcing a smile.

"Dinner, afterward."

"It'll be on me," she said, still smiling.

"Is Van Slyke one word or two?" Chet asked Verdi as he sat down at his computer. At her request, he'd left the office dark, the only light coming from his computer screen.

"Two," she answered quietly. "Both capitals."

Slowly, deftly, Chet began keying in commands, jumping from one personnel directory to another. Verdi carefully watched over his shoulder as he entered codes to get to the more sensitive files. She held herself from shaking. Why was she so nervous? she wondered.

She had no idea what would happen if they were caught here. Given the deep glue she was already in, it would probably do her in, get her permanently kicked out on a security violation. She remembered feeling jumpy as they entered the building and worried that her fear would give them away. Only one entrance was open at this hour, and it was lightly guarded. They had to show their badges and sign in, but the guard barely glanced at them as they did so.

Verdi watched Chet's fingers as he entered another set of codes. "There, that should do it," he said, sitting back. "It'll take a couple of seconds. This system is cross-referenced to all department computer files. That way, when you search a name, you can see everything entered on a department computer with that person's name on it."

"Wow," Verdi whispered. No telling what one could find in there.

"Here we are," Chet announced. "Van Slyke, Patricia."

As Chet pressed the scroll key, Van Slyke's performance audit report flashed over the computer screen. The PAR began with her date of birth and continued with marital status, residence, list of dependents, and other information until it came to her list of assignments, official awards, and commendations. Verdi stopped counting after about thirty awards.

"You don't see many files like this," Chet muttered, obviously impressed. "She sure is something." He began toggling the key, slowing down and reading more carefully.

"*Was* something," Verdi corrected him.

"We're into this year now," Chet said, bouncing his finger off the key, causing the screen to jump each time. "Hmm."

"What is it?"

"Of course. The PAR doesn't keep travel orders. You wanted to know who sent her to China."

"Where would they be?"

Chet shrugged. "We can check her official performance file. That's much more comprehensive than the PAR."

"OK," Verdi whispered, standing up with him. "Did you hear that?"

"What?"

"Sounded like a door closing." She paused a moment but heard nothing else. Chet led her into the outer office, to a long wall of files that appeared beige in the dim light. Verdi glanced over her shoulder, noticing a photocopying machine that filled a far corner. Chet opened and closed two drawers before he dug into the files.

"Here we are," he said, drawing out a hefty file held together by a thick rubber band. "It's a big one."

Verdi stood next to Chet as he pulled off the rubber band and began flipping through the reams of paper. "God," he said, "I should live so long to get a file like this."

"Go to the end, Chet. Let's see who signed off on her orders."

He went straight to the back and pulled a sheet of

paper. "Hmm. That's odd. No name. Hey, see there? Her travel orders were written on the Secretary's letterhead. But he didn't sign them."

Chet was right. It *was* odd. Verdi recalled the words of Norm Price, the duty officer in China: "I never even knew she was here." Someone knew. Whoever wrote those travel orders knew. "Other than the Secretary himself, who would be able to issue travel orders to a deputy assistant secretary?"

Chet shrugged, took off his glasses, and massaged his eyes. "What's the chain of command? I'm sure the deputy secretary could do it, and, let me think, under him but over Van Slyke would be the undersecretary for Political Affairs. And under him are all the assistant secretaries. One of them would be Van Slyke's boss. Hmm, that would be . . . East Asian and Pacific Affairs."

Verdi sighed. "That's a lot of suspects."

"Suspects?"

"Chet, wouldn't it look strange for anyone other than someone in the Secretary's office to be issuing travel orders on his stationery? I can't even imagine the Secretary of State issuing travel orders to anyone."

"Yeah, I guess you're right. Hey, look at the time. I'm getting pretty hungry myself. What about that—"

"Shh," Verdi whispered, hearing keys in the outer office door. She quickly closed the file drawers and pulled Chet to the floor and under a temporary table stacked with piles of papers.

"Hey, I like aggressive women," he whispered. "What's the mat—?"

She pressed her fingers over his mouth and shook

her head. Chet, taking full advantage of the situation, pressed up close against Verdi as they lay there. Actually there was nothing wrong in their being in the office. People came and went from State at all hours. But Verdi didn't want anyone other than Chet to know she'd been there.

She held her breath as lights came on and the sound of jangling keys drew closer. Then a foot in a shiny black leather shoe appeared no more than three feet from Verdi's face. The foot was below black pants with gold stripes running along the seam. A security guard. He was pausing a little bit longer than he should have in front of the tables.

Verdi waited long seconds before the guard moved away and out of the office. She let out a long breath and began to disentangle herself from Chet.

"What's the rush?" he wisecracked. "That's the most fun I've had in months."

"Chet, I have to run. Can I take a rain check on the dinner?"

"Promise?" he said, standing slowly and brushing off his pants. "You know, Kate, while we were lying there, I was thinking of the time we got caught in that monsoon driving through Java, and we had to hole up in a farmer's house. Remember how we had to share the bed of straw for the night, in his barn?"

Chet looked up as the office door closed, Verdi gone.

Minutes later, outside in her car, she tried to catch her breath as she rooted through her purse. She'd just raced down two flights of stairs and managed to compose herself long enough to pass through the security gates as she exited the building. She got out without a hitch.

She was searching for a pen and paper. The pen she found easily, but the only paper she could come up with was a Tabard Inn coaster. When had she taken *that*? It would have to do. In the darkness she scribbled a series of numbers and letters on the back of the coaster and hid it in a pocket of her purse.

Verdi started up the Camaro, which kicked in and rumbled a little too loudly for genteel Foggy Bottom. Pulling out of her space and heading north toward Adams-Morgan, she did not notice the gray sedan with its lights off that slipped into traffic behind her and followed her all the way home.

CHAPTER
★ SEVENTEEN ★

"If I can't get Rabat, I'll take Casablanca." Parker Harrington begged in what had to be his most pitiful voice. "I hear the beaches nearby are nice."

Kate Verdi smiled and shook her head as she dumped nondairy creamer into her coffee. She found a plastic stirrer and turned around to face Harrington, who was leaning against a steel file cabinet, his hands nervously shaking the change in his pocket. "But, Parker," she said, creating an eddy in her coffee with the stirrer, "what makes you think I can get you your first choice, or any other for that matter?"

Harrington took a step toward her. "Oh, come on, Kate. I've seen you in the cafeteria with Chalmers Mount. He's the man. A word from you to him could make all the difference in the world. I don't know what I'll do if I don't get Morocco."

Verdi tossed her stirrer into the trash can. This was

certainly a twist, she thought, Parker Harrington, her senior death officer, coming to her for help. She knew she couldn't really exert any influence on his behalf, even if she wanted to, but she was secretly thrilled that he was sucking up to her like this.

"Well, they say you should never expect your first choice," she said innocently. "It's just not good diplomacy. Now, if you'll excuse me."

She stepped around him, ignoring his expression of pained disbelief, and returned to her desk. There was a stack of files she recognized and a few new ones she didn't. *Won't it ever stop?* she wondered. Then a single name, the title of the file, caught her eye: Patricia Van Slyke. Verdi picked it up and stared at it for several seconds until she spotted Calamity John coming toward her. She slid the file into the drawer in her desk.

"I was looking for you at lunch yesterday," he began, without any undue politeness, as usual. "Seems we have some good news."

"Now that would be a switch."

He lowered his voice. "The Secretary's office called. It appears that the lawsuit against the State Department was dropped. And the investigation on the case, specifically of you, was also concluded. You've been cleared of any responsibility in the Van Slyke cremation."

Verdi felt a lightness in her chest she hadn't known for a long time, an incredible lifting of a burden. Lorna. It had all happened as she said it would. Kendall Holmes and the Circle had come through for her. Maybe she'd been wrong about them.

"One other thing," Dietz said. "None of this will ever appear in your file."

In her moment of relief something occurred to Verdi. "Did you talk to Van Slyke's mother?" she asked. "I mean, personally."

Dietz seemed taken aback by the question. "Why should I? It was all handled out of the Secretary's office."

"Who did you speak with there? What was the name?"

Dietz had to concentrate for a moment. "Fellow named Mudd," he said. "Winthrop Mudd. Why? Is it important?"

She shrugged.

Dietz held his gaze on her for several long seconds, and Verdi looked straight back at him. She knew what he was thinking. He was always watching junior death officers for signs of depression, burnout, and suicidal behavior. It wasn't uncommon in the office to see at least one of those at any given time. Even senior people weren't exempted. More than anything else, Verdi felt embarrassed that the intrigue swirling around her might be starting to show on her.

Dietz drifted back to his desk, and Verdi kept an eye on him as she groped through the drawer for the Van Slyke file. Just as her fingers found it, she stopped. *Leave it alone,* she ordered herself. *Why dig anymore? You're safe now. The Circle's taken care of it for you. Forget about Patricia Van Slyke.*

Too many questions haunted Verdi for her simply to walk away from this. Somehow she was sure that Patricia Van Slyke's mother was a key to the mystery. Why had Van Slyke's mother dropped her suit? Verdi wondered. And what had the Circle done to make her change her mind? Every instinct in Verdi, excepting self-preservation, was drawing her back into the case. She pulled the file and flipped through it.

Having found what she was looking for, she picked up her phone and began dialing the number for Van Slyke's mother. One ring, two, and then a message came on: "The number you have reached, 703-555-6782, has been disconnected. Please check the number and try again. If you need operator assistance—"

Fear slithered up Verdi's back. She tried the number again but got the same message. Her mind began racing. *What is this? The mother couldn't have moved already. I just saw her—what?—two days ago. And she had the little girl. . . .*

A thought flew into Verdi's head, and she flipped through the file again, searching for the number of the Pemburton Funeral Home. She punched it in and waited many long rings. Finally a voice came on, thick, gravelly.

"Pemburton Funeral."

"Is Mr. Pemburton there?" she said.

"Speaking."

Verdi was relieved; it wasn't the hostile gnome but his father. His voice was strong and seemed to jump out at her through the telephone. "Mr. Pemburton, I'm calling from the State Department. I was trying to reach the mother of Patricia Van Slyke, whose funeral your home handled this week."

"Yes, I know. A cremation burial. How can I help you, Ms.—?"

"It's just a routine follow-up. I called her today and

got a strange message, that the phone was disconnected. Can I confirm my number against yours?"

"Certainly. Hold a minute."

Verdi looked around the office. Calamity John was a safe distance away, terrorizing his secretary and another death officer. A few doors away Boris Kubanyi sat stiffly at his desk while he read a file. Verdi wondered what was in it, since he never actually seemed to handle any active cases.

"Hello?" Pemburton shouted, back on the line. "It's a northern Virginia number. Are you ready? It's 703-555-6782."

A sound of frustration issued from deep in Verdi's throat. The numbers were the same. "Mr. Pemburton, did Patricia Van Slyke's mother mention anything to you about moving away or visiting family?"

"No, no, can't say that she did. I wasn't aware there was any other family except for a son-in-law somewhere, in California, I think. I got the distinct impression they weren't very close."

Van Slyke's husband. Of course. Verdi had seen his name in the file. "Thank you, Mr. Pemburton. You've been very helpful."

"Oh, a pleasure."

There it was, on the third page of Van Slyke's bio sheet. Spouse: Donald K. Residence: San Jose, California. And with it, a telephone number. Verdi snatched up her phone and dialed it. She waited, her heart thumping.

"The number you have reached has been disconnected. . . ." Verdi gritted her teeth and studied the number. She called directory assistance for the San

Jose area code and asked for the number for Donald K. Van Slyke.

"I'm sorry," said the operator. "That number is unpublished."

A dead end.

"Shit!" Verdi roared in disgust before slamming down the phone. All activity in the office came to a sudden halt as eyes turned toward her. She smiled thinly. It seemed that everyone, even Calamity John, was staring at her. Everyone, she noticed, except for Boris Kubanyi, his back to her, still riveted on his case file.

CHAPTER
★ EIGHTEEN ★

The hallways of the Vincent Lombardi Cancer Center at Georgetown University Hospital always seemed too bright to Clarence Witherspoon when he went there. He couldn't imagine a single germ—or human frailty—escaping the glare of those lights. He kept his eyes down as he walked, passing families on their way out at the end of visiting hours.

Witherspoon did his best to hide the covers of the magazines he was carrying. They were gardening magazines, with names like *American Garden* and *Green Thumb*, each with a picture on its cover of someone holding up the biggest, most colorful flower imaginable. He cringed slightly as a nurse passed him and smiled, her eyes on the magazines.

He pushed through double doors bearing the words *Concentrated Care* and immediately spied Ruth Galvin, alone in a corner chair. Upon seeing him, she rose.

"Hi, Ruthie," he said, coming closer and taking her in his arms. She clung to him, and he felt the weight of her pain pressing against him.

A head shorter than Witherspoon, Ruth Galvin looked up at him. She was normally a happy, upbeat woman—you almost have to be to be married to a detective—but her husband's long fight with cancer was taking its toll on her. She'd lost a lot of weight, and her clothes hung off her in a sad kind of way. Her usually bright green eyes were now always bloodshot and jumpy from lack of sleep.

"Clarence, it's good to see you."

"You too, you too. How you doing?"

She shrugged and looked away, fighting tears. "I'm all right. I didn't want to give you the news over the phone. The doctors told us this morning: The cancer's taking over his liver now. Just a matter of time, I guess."

Witherspoon grimaced and exhaled loudly, his arms going limp at his sides. "Does Tom know?"

She nodded her head. "He's dozing now. He's been asking for you, Clarence. You've been great, visiting him so often like this."

"Nothing you haven't done for me," he said, smiling. Witherspoon thought back to the time when Ruth came over every day and stayed with Simone, his daughter, who was going through a bad time. Had it already been seven years? He'd just buried Yvette, his wife, killed by a car as she was coming out of her beauty parlor. It'd been driven by a junkie nodding out after a fix who ended up without a scratch and no memory of what he'd done. Witherspoon wanted time to be with Simone, then only fifteen, but the police department cut him only so much slack, especially after his being jumped to detective. Ruth would stop by with videos and pizza, or she would take Simone shopping. Ruth and Tom, always there when he needed them.

Witherspoon squeezed her hand and entered the room. A heavy scent of roses and medicine hit him as he stepped inside. The only light was from a table lamp next to the bed, but it was enough for Witherspoon to see Tom's ashen face and the patches of gray fuzz on his head. Tom wheezed lightly as he slept. Witherspoon heard joints cracking as he sat down in a chair next to the bed.

"Ruthie?" Tom mumbled before one eye opened. He smiled slightly. "Clarence."

"Hey, Tom, how's it going?"

Tom sat up, blinking through the medication. In the light his skin looked more yellow than white. He reached out slowly for Witherspoon, who took his hand gently, noticing his fingernails, dried and cracked from the chemo.

"How do you like my Deep Secrets?" Tom said, voice raspy.

Witherspoon leaned closer, not sure he'd heard right. "What was that?"

Tom nodded toward a vase of roses on the dresser, directly across from him. "Tea Hybrids. I started them last year in the nursery. I tried the Climbing Hybrids before, but they didn't come in so good. The Tea Hybrids, they're hardier. These are called Deep Secrets. They turned out all right, don't you think?"

"Yeah, they're beautiful."

Galvin broke the long silence between them, something he was becoming used to doing since getting sick. "How's business?" he said.

"Too much of it." Witherspoon sighed, thinking immediately of his meeting with Katherine Verdi.

"Something I should know about?" Galvin said hopefully.

Witherspoon shook his head. "Got a case that's busting my ass. White guy found shot in Trinidad, at Orren and Simms. State Department, it turns out. His own wife didn't report him missing until three days after his death. What is it with you white people anyway?"

Tom managed a smile. "I saw it on the news. Good they have you working it. Getting any heat from the mayor?"

"Full blast. She needs the white vote next month. A white murder isn't exactly helping the campaign." Witherspoon looked down at his lap. "Oh, these are for you." Witherspoon put the magazines in Tom's hand.

"Good Lord, thank you," Tom said as he studied the covers, slurring his words a bit. "You take out a subscription?"

"Yeah, right. Next time I'm bringing them in a bag so I don't have to suffer the looks I get." They were quiet for a moment, the words *next time* making both men pause.

"So tell me about the case," Galvin said.

"I thought I got a break this morning," Witherspoon said. "Woman calls me as I'm about to go to court, tells me she knows Brian Porter, the victim. I could tell something was wrong, even above the usual nerves people get when they call the police.

"So I had her come in later. She's there on her lunch hour, from the State Department. Good-looking woman, classy. She was scared, man, big time. At first I thought she was the other woman, you know, coming in to see if we knew about her. Maybe she and Porter were together the night he was murdered. But something about her told me that wasn't going on. Anyway, we played serious cat and mouse for a while. I don't think I got a straight answer from her the whole damn time. I turned up the heat on her a little and she lit out of there so fast my head was spinning. So now I'm having—"

Witherspoon looked up as he heard a sound coming from Tom's direction. He was asleep, a light snore issuing from his nose. Witherspoon rose, gently took the magazines from Tom's hands, and arranged them in a fan on the nightstand. He took one last long look at Tom and left.

Back home Witherspoon stood over the stove, studying the water in a pot. It was just about to boil, tiny bubbles forming around the edges. He debated whether to pour in the pasta—tortellini filled with cheese and pesto—wondering if he should wait until the water came to a "rolling boil," as the directions on the package said.

He was making dinner for Simone, who was at the library, studying for a test. She was in her first year of law school at Howard University, and he was learning that what he'd heard all these years from DAs about law school was true. He hardly saw her anymore. Tonight she would be at the library until nine, come home for a quick meal, and rush out again for her study group, which met until midnight. Then up at six tomorrow to start the whole thing over again.

Witherspoon checked his watch and decided— rolling boil or no rolling boil—to dump in the tortellini. He didn't go in much for this tortellini business; a plate of spaghetti and meatballs was fine by him. But Simone liked it, and he indulged her every chance he got.

His head turned quickly as he heard a light knock on the back door. It wouldn't be Simone; she would use her key in the front door. Still dressed for work, his firearm holstered to his belt, Witherspoon eased off the pistol's safety and wrapped his hand around the butt. There were more than a couple of people in the city who'd probably considered going after him at some time or another. He peered out the window into the darkness. Someone was there on the back porch, but he couldn't make him out.

"Who is it?" he called.

"Rico," came the reply from the dark.

It was his voice all right. Witherspoon put back the safety and swung open the door. Leaning against the railing and appearing slight in baggy street clothes, Rico stayed to the back of the porch, hidden in the shadows.

Witherspoon motioned with his hand. "Come in. I was just putting on some dinner."

"No, thanks. Can't stay long. Listen, I checked into that Ivy City shoot, one you asked me about?"

"Yeah?"

"No one's talking. It was a crew, that much I know. But they're all chilled. They're looking at some big time here, and they know it. You have to call in one of your crackheads on this one, get him to go on a suicide mission."

"Yeah, thanks."

"The other shoot, the Trinidad one. You asked about carjackers, so I checked on it. Nobody I talked to's heard of any working that area. You try and jack wheels in that part of town, no telling who's driving or what they're carrying. Know what I'm saying?"

Witherspoon nodded slightly, his collar chafing the back of his neck. Rico was sweating him, and he knew it.

"OK. A brother with business near that intersection says he saw something going down, night you're talking about. He's on his way home and sees something being dropped out of a car."

"Business, huh? So what did he see, a body?"

Rico shrugged. "Could be. It was dark. Car was in a big hurry to get out of there."

"You get a license number, a description?"

Same shrug, even more indifferent this time. "That's all I got."

"What's the brother's name, Rico?"

The darkness seemed to collapse around Rico, who stood silently for what seemed like hours. "OK, this is what I need. Friend of mine just got busted. Grand theft auto. He was stupid, had a piece on him when they got him. So he's looking at hard time."

It was Witherspoon's turn to sweat Rico. He offered him no help whatsoever. Seconds ticked by.

"So what's it gonna be?" Rico snapped, not liking the treatment. "You help me, I help you."

Witherspoon slowly rubbed the back of his neck. "It's going to depend on your dealer friend, how good his information is. I get anything solid from him, I'll do what I can for you."

Rico held out a piece of paper. "That's the name of my friend, the one who got busted. Dude you're looking for is Stray, his street name. I don't know his real name. He works along Benning Road, that moving market there. Got two priors—possession and intent. You pick him up and offer him a deal, he'll talk."

Witherspoon nodded. "Where'd you hear about Stray?" He turned his head at the sound of someone at the front door.

"Hello, Papa," he heard Simone call. When he turned back to Rico, the back porch was empty. Witherspoon stepped out and peered over the railing into the shadows, training his ears for a sound of Rico. All he could hear was a siren's mournful wail, several blocks away.

CHAPTER
★ NINETEEN ★

Kate Verdi hung on for dear life as Jake Wheeler spun her in a circle and then smoothly led her back into the hop-and-three-steps rhythm of the polka. Verdi dizzily watched other dancers skipping past them, whooping and shouting. Up on the stage the grin stamped on the accordion player's face widened as he picked up the pace, his foot keeping time beneath red knee-highs and lederhosen. He'd announced the song he was playing as "In Heaven There Is No Beer?"

"So this is Blob's Park," she shouted breathlessly to Jake. "You come here often?"

"My first time," Jake shouted back. "Isn't it great?"

Verdi rolled her eyes. Blob's Park, Washington's answer to a burning cultural need for a German beer hall. She remembered avoiding this place like the plague when she was growing up, her parents always threatening to take her here with their friends and teach her to dance. It was midway between Washington and Baltimore, far enough from Seat Pleasant so that the threat didn't arise too often, but close enough that she always made sure she had a ready excuse— like a play rehearsal or a test to study for—in case it did.

Still, the place was fun. Tonight it was even more enjoyable in a perverse kind of way with Lorna Demeritte and Jonathan Rashford in tow as double dates. Lorna had called Verdi just as she was getting ready to go out, complaining that Jonathan and she couldn't agree on which foreign film to see and asking if Verdi minded terribly if they went along with her and her "new boyfriend."

Verdi saw the whole thing as a ploy for Lorna to check out Jake, whom Verdi had described only superficially. She didn't particularly feel like sharing her evening with Jake, especially with two of the most pretentious people she knew, but Jake had picked up on the whole situation the minute he'd set eyes on them, and Verdi could see his devious plan as soon as he suggested they all go bowling.

Lorna and Jonathan swallowed hard but went along, suffering through three games at a bowling alley in Bethesda. It was into their fourth one that Jake introduced the idea of Blob's Park. Verdi tried to dissuade them from going, knowing how much they'd hate it there. But they eagerly jumped at the idea, anything to get away from the bowling alley.

Now, as Jake led her around the dance floor, Verdi

almost felt sorry for Lorna and Jonathan. She caught glimpses of them at their table, glumly drinking beer, avoiding each other's eyes. But it wasn't just the in-your-face déclassé scene of the dance hall that was bothering Lorna. All night long she'd been radiating an obscure anger, starting at the bowling alley and getting worse as the night wore on. She was also drinking more heavily than usual. It just didn't make sense: Lorna was on her first date with a man she'd been after for months and was acting like a spoiled teenager.

Suddenly the music stopped, and Jake joined the other dancers in boisterous applause. "What did you think?" he said over his shoulder, leading her back to the table.

Verdi was still trying to catch her breath. "I feel like I'd been waiting all my life for that moment. So tell me, where did you learn to dance like that?"

Jake laughed. "Neighborhood I grew up in, in Fort Wayne. Lots of ethnic families—Poles, Slavs, Armenians. My mother did all the women's hair there, working out of our kitchen, and she got invited to lots of weddings, birthdays, things like that. Guess who was dragged along, having to watch the old ladies dancing with each other."

"Ah." *A hair salon in his mother's kitchen?* Jake Wheeler was full of surprises, Verdi was learning. It also felt good being close to him while they danced.

They joined Lorna and Jonathan, who were ringed by empty beer pitchers and greasy cartons of french fries and pretzels. Verdi frowned at Lorna, who was staring vacantly into space as she finished off another beer. Jonathan was clearly relieved to have them back at the table even though disgust was still obvious on his face. Verdi wasn't sure if it was due to Lorna's moodiness, Blob's Park, or a combination of the two.

"You two haven't danced once." Verdi chided them, trying to keep things light. "It's really fun once you get into it."

"Thanks," Lorna growled, searching pitchers for more beer. "I'm ready to go."

Jake, the driver of the lead car, hemmed and hawed for a moment and said, "Well, if you'll excuse me for a minute." Verdi felt sorry for him, having to endure Lorna's sullenness. The oompah band started up again, and he had to plow his way through the crowd toward the rest rooms.

As Kate sat down and began nibbling on a cold pretzel, Jonathan Rashford leaned toward her. "So, Kate," he said, his voice honed to upper-crust distinction by many a Harvard seminar, "Lorna and I were talking a few minutes ago—"

"Oh, really? I must've blinked when that happened."

"—and we both agreed that you should have a go at a new assignment. Something overseas, like you've wanted."

Verdi crunched down on a chunk of salt. "Jonathan," she said, "I've been in CEC a little over three months now. And it's been a less than distinguished three months, believe me. Except for a miracle, I would have no more chance at a new assignment than—"

"But, Kate," he said, pressing closer. His pink button-down Polo shirt, heavily starched even for a Saturday night, seemed to crackle as he moved. "We've been hearing about what's happening at the embassies. There are shortages everywhere. Consular officers are in demand. You'd have an excellent shot."

"At what? Sarajevo or Mogadishu? Come on, Jonathan." Verdi looked at Lorna, but she was no help, gazing into her beer mug. What *was* it with her anyway?

"Kate"—he went on—"there are slots in some terrific posts, European capitals. But it's late, you'd have to get your application in immediately. Chalmers could pull some strings for you."

"What have *you* heard, Lorna?" Verdi asked, determined to get her into the conversation.

Lorna shrugged. "It's like Jonathan said. You'd probably have your pick of posts."

Verdi gave up on her pretzel. "This is insane. I'm lucky to still have a job, with what I've been through lately. A European post seems totally . . . farfetched."

"What's farfetched?" It was Jake, suddenly at her side.

"That Lorna and Jonathan would get out on the dance floor."

"If it'll make you happy," Lorna said sullenly, "I'll cross the dance floor on my way out."

Jonathan Rashford shrugged sheepishly at Verdi as he stood up to leave. Lorna and he went on ahead as Jake and Verdi followed. Verdi watched them, especially Lorna, who was weaving unsteadily and coldly refusing Jonathan's offer to help. She was surprised to see Jonathan Rashford whisper fiercely into Lorna's ear.

Verdi strained to hear what it was, but his words were drowned out by the off-key blare of the oompah band.

"Now, how does it go?" Verdi mused out loud as she set two wineglasses between Jake and her on the living room floor of her apartment. " 'Beer before wine, everything's fine. Wine before beer, something to fear'? Or is it: 'Wine *after* beer, something to fear'?"

"I think," Jake said, steadying his glass as Verdi poured, "that one could adjust the order to fit whichever beverage one consumed first."

"Ah, you mean as a rationalization?"

He smiled in agreement. "During my tour in Manila I shared an apartment with a guy, a gone-to-seed civil engineer with Bechtel. You know the type."

"No, I'm afraid I don't."

"This guy was amazing. He had beer with everything. With lunch, dinner, even in his cereal for breakfast. Anytime we went out to a site—he designed hydroelectric power plants—he brought along a cooler stocked with beer."

"Sounds like he had a problem."

"But the thing was, he was an artist. I mean, like a visionary, you know? He did things with plant design most people never dreamed of. I used to think that the beer did it, gave him some kind of edge. Guess what he's doing now."

"Drying out, I hope."

"Designing breweries in Belarus. Isn't that a hoot?" Jake suddenly became serious. "So," he intoned in mock severity, "what should we drink to?"

Verdi held up her glass. "To rationalizations."

They clinked glasses and drank. "Mmm, that's good," Jake said. "Washes out the taste of those french fries."

Verdi laughed. "Yeah, well, listen. I'm sorry about Lorna. I don't know what got into her tonight."

Jake shrugged. "First-date jitters. I know how it can be."

"Oh, do you? Somehow I can't picture you burdened with self-doubt."

He looked at her. "What do you mean?"

"Hey, all I meant was that you seem the essence of self-confidence."

Verdi clenched her jaw, feeling the pressure of the moment. She felt comfortable with Jake but didn't want to slip into speaking to him in the wise-ass joaning fashion she was used to with her brothers. What was going on here between them? she wondered. What would happen tonight? Did she really want— need—someone in her life now? Does anyone ever really plan it anyway?

"Sorry," he said. "I've been a little tense lately myself."

"Oh? Why?"

"I'm up for reassignment. They're due out any day now."

Verdi shifted uneasily on the floor. She jogged her wineglass but caught it before it could do any serious damage to her carpet. "But you, I thought you were just starting your rotation here. The course at FSI—"

"Oh, right. That was a Spanish course I was taking.

I've put in for Spanish-speaking Latin America and Spain. Watch, they'll send me to Italy or someplace."

A shudder went up Verdi's back as she imagined Jake in the same city as Antonio. What would *that* be like? Not that it mattered much. Once Jake left, Verdi would probably never hear from him again. Disappointment mixed with mild shock began washing over her at the thought of Jake's soon becoming a memory even before anything could happen between them. Her limbs felt heavy, like a statue's, and she felt vaguely sick to her stomach.

"So," Jake said brightly, "you didn't answer my question in the car."

"What question was that?"

"What's it like being a blackjack dealer in Atlantic City?"

Verdi gulped her wine. "Ever see *Atlantic City*, the movie?"

"Yeah. The one with Burt Lancaster and—what was her name?"

"Susan Sarandon. She was a blackjack trainee. They actually make you go through that, if you can believe it. Anyway, remember how she'd come home at night and rub lemons all over herself? She worked in an oyster bar to support herself while she was in training."

"Sure. And Lancaster would watch her from across the way."

Verdi nodded. "That was exactly how I felt every night I got home. Or day, depending on which shift I was on. I felt like taking the hottest shower I could stand just to wash the place off me. The drunks, the losers. It's a sad place, really, once you scratch the surface."

"So why did you do it?"

She shrugged. "The money, I guess. I was maxed out on student loans. I managed to pay them all off in three years. And I met a guy when I was waitressing here, he was director of security for one of the big casinos. Nice guy. I learned a lot about surveillance hanging around him: hidden cameras, telephone taps, the whole thing. He got me a job through a friend of his. It sounded interesting at the time."

She looked at Jake as he nodded and took a sip of wine. For a second she wondered what he'd be like in bed. "So tell me," she said, squashing the thought, "what was the worst job *you* ever had?"

He threw his head back and laughed. "Oooh, that's a tough one. Let's see. It's between sweeping hair in my mother's kitchen, busing tables at the Village Green in Fort Wayne during high school, and playing Zoltan the Star Fighter at video arcade openings, the first thing I did with my architecture degree."

"Zoltan the Star Fighter?"

"Yeah, Zoltan was the hero of this new video game they were promoting. Part human, part robot, he rescues nubile space maidens from the clutches of the evil Lord Kazil. What a zoo. These jaded little kids, mall rats, would come up to me and ask if I could get them dope. And the costume I had to wear. It was this silvery rayon suit that was so hot—"

Jake was interrupted by Verdi, who seized him by the shoulders and kissed him hard on the mouth. It

CHAPTER
★ TWENTY ★

"**Y**ou mean to say that you put in for an overseas assignment two and a half *years* ahead of schedule and didn't make a single post selection? Not even a *first* one?"

Kate Verdi lifted her eyes from her shrimp salad to Jonathan Rashford, giving him a bored heavy-lidded look that told him he was pressing his case a little too much here. From behind his tortoiseshell glasses, Rashford had the rabid look of a zealot hell-bent on converting an apostate. Verdi now wished she hadn't let it slip during their conversation that she'd put in her application three days ago.

"No, Jonathan," she finally said, unintentionally imitating his Boston Brahmin nasal drone. "I don't have to say that. I *do* say it."

"Amazing," he continued, not getting the sar

took him all of four seconds to overcome his surprise and kiss back. Sitting on her legs and trying to get comfortable, she leaned forward and fell on top of him. She used the opportunity to work her way down his cheek, chin, throat and was having trouble getting to his chest, his sweater and shirt in the way. Jake made a move for his clothes.

"In here," she whispered, pulling him up and toward the bedroom. She turned off the floor lamp, the only light on, and led him through the darkness.

"Where are you?" His voice sounded distant, unconnected to the moment.

"Be right back," she answered as she escaped into the bathroom and closed the door behind her. Verdi looked at herself in the mirror but could make out only her outline in the faint light filtering through the frosted windowpane. She held on to the sink, supporting herself.

What the hell are you doing? You hardly know this guy. You want to get burned all over again? She felt as if she were about to hurtle over a waterfall and wondered whether there would be a raging river or placid pool at the bottom of it.

A fine time to be having doubts, she lectured herself. Especially when it was she who made the first move back there in the living room. Swiftly she kicked off her jeans and pulled her sweater over her head. Leaving her bra and panties on, she stole into the bedroom and slid under the covers.

Jake edged up against her, his breath warm on her shoulder. "It was getting lonely in here."

"I was giving you a chance to warm up the bed."

"Mmm." This time it was Jake who kissed her. He was a good kisser, Verdi observed: slow, gentle, and he used his tongue creatively. A good sign. As it turned out, Jake was good at a lot of things. For a guy he displayed unusual facility in getting her bra off. That was significant. And there were other things, even more noteworthy, that revealed themselves as the night wore on.

Hours later the ubiquitous Adams-Morgan street noise had all but ceased when Verdi began to feel tired. But it was good tired, like the satisfying lassitude felt after vigorous athletic activity. The bedcovers were strewn over the floor, and one corner of the sheet had rolled back, exposing the mattress.

"You've done this before," she mumbled to Jake, her face in a pillow.

She rolled onto her back and was quiet for a long time, listening to him breathe. "Are you a raging river or a placid pool?" she whispered to him as she stared at the ceiling.

"Hmm?" He was almost asleep.

Verdi slowly raised her head, flipped her pillow over, and let her cheek sink into the cool cotton and down. She closed her eyes and let herself drift. At that calm moment she easily came to a decision she'd been wrestling with for days. Lorna Demeritte and Jonathan Rashford had brought it up earlier tonight. But it wasn't until now that she knew what she'd do.

"I'm gonna take them up on their offer," she whispered drowsily. "Lorna and Jonathan and the rest of

them. Put in for an overseas post. What do you th of that?"

She opened one eye and looked at Jake, but he w sound asleep.

"I don't think I've ever heard the likes of it before. It's either brilliant or insane."

In addition to Jonathan Rashford's inquisition, Verdi had to suffer the expressions of outrage from other Circle members around the cafeteria table who shared his astonishment at her heresy. Obviously it was beyond their comprehension that someone could be so trusting of the system as to allow it to decide where she should be posted. Verdi was aware of Rashford's eyes on her, studying her. She ignored him, keeping to her shrimp salad.

"Whoa, now," he said dramatically. "Maybe we're being too hasty in passing judgment here. Maybe there is method to Ambassador Verdi's madness. Could it be she has some kind of sweet deal worked out with Kendall? Enlighten us, Kate."

Verdi gave him a humorless smile and let it go at that. Actually he was closer to the truth than he realized. There was never any doubt in Verdi's mind that she wanted out of CEC and back into an overseas post, preferably in Europe. And since learning that Jake Wheeler was up for reassignment, Verdi was more willing than she'd been before to roll the dice and see what came up for her.

But something else spurred her into filing the application, especially with so many strikes against her: She wanted to test the Circle. All along she'd been hearing from Lorna, Jonathan, and Chalmers Mount that all she had to do was apply, and her first choice would be hers. Well, now was their chance to prove it.

Verdi's intention was to make it as difficult as possible for the Circle to find her a decent slot. First of all, the chance of her getting a new assignment while being a little more than three months into her current one was remote at best. Not only that, but she'd just gotten her application in a few days ago, well past the deadline. The panels would already have met and handed down their edicts. On top of it all, she didn't even bother to declare a first choice. No one in his right mind would award a cake European post to someone who hadn't even asked for it.

By applying, Verdi would be getting Lorna, Rashford, and the rest of them off her back. The next several days would be great, with Verdi having free license to declare self-righteously, "I told you so," to each and every one of them, once the assignment list was posted and her name wasn't on it.

Something occurred to Verdi, and she scanned the faces of the Circle members along the table. "Jonathan, where's Lorna?"

Rashford shrugged. "Haven't seen her."

Verdi checked with the others, but all she got were blank stares. "She hasn't been around for days. Is she all right?"

Rashford shrugged again. "She's probably out prowling the boutiques for a *costume* for the big affair this weekend."

"Affair?" Verdi asked, suddenly reminded of Jake Wheeler.

"Oh, I'm supposed to tell you. Kendall is hosting a black-tie this Saturday night in the Benjamin Franklin Room up on the eighth floor. He does this every year to celebrate the new assignments. Your attendance, I might as well divulge, is mandatory."

Even if I don't have anything to celebrate? Verdi quietly finished her salad. She checked her watch. It was time to get back to the office. Getting up to leave, she nearly ran into Alexandra Rhys-Shriver, who was joining the table with a man Verdi didn't recognize.

"Kate, hello," Rhys-Shriver said, as if they were old friends. It occurred to Verdi she hadn't seen much of her since her promotion. "I heard the news. I think it's terrific you put in for a new assignment."

Is there anyone who doesn't know? One more thing to puzzle over, Verdi thought.

"Kate, have you met Everett Wade, deputy chief of counterintelligence and special investigations? Everett and I are making the rounds. We're joining Kendall for lunch later on."

Verdi shook hands with Everett Wade, who then was introduced to Jonathan Rashford and everyone else at the table. His basic training haircut and stiff, formal manner more than suggested military to Verdi. He didn't seem the kind of person Alexandra would be chumming with. Verdi slipped off and made her way through the cafeteria. Glancing at her watch, she saw that she still had a little time before she had to get back to the office. Instead of taking the stairway to the fourth floor, she made a slight detour to another wing of the first floor, where she knew she would find Jake Wheeler.

"Kate, what a surprise!" Jake called out. He was leaning against the corridor wall, speaking with someone, when Verdi came around the corner. A long cardboard tube protruded from under his arm. "How did you know I'd be over here today?"

The man Jake was with moved off as Verdi approached. Jake worked in the Office of Foreign Buildings but was based in Arlington in one of the many State Department annex buildings scattered throughout the Washington area. But he'd mentioned to her that he would be over in Foggy Bottom today.

"You told me you'd be here. Hope I'm not disturbing you," she said. Looking at him, she felt her chest tighten. She wished they were someplace, anyplace, else. Alone.

"Are you kidding? Hey, I have to drop off these renderings up on the second floor. Walk with me?"

Verdi took him by the arm, and they strolled down the hall. "This is probably a stupid question," she said, "but do you own a tuxedo?"

"Huh?"

"I was just invited to a black-tie party for this Saturday, courtesy of Kendall Holmes. I want you to be my date." He was quiet for several seconds. "Uh, that is, if you don't have other plans," she added.

"Umm, no. The thing is, I may have to work through the weekend to get this project done to meet deadline. Some security enhancements on the ambassador's residence in Islamabad. They've been getting threats from the Islamic fundamentalists there. The renderings have to go out to Pakistan by Tuesday of next week."

"Jake, it's no problem. Listen, the reception is up on the eighth floor, in the Benjamin Franklin Room. You could rent a tux and bring it along, work here until nine, and we could go up for an hour. Whatever."

"We'll see."

Verdi felt a tinge of shame at Jake's reluctance. She didn't know if she should read anything into it, whether this could be the first stage in his pulling back from her. Silently she chastised herself for assuming too much, that he would be available to her for the party.

They were rounding a corner when Verdi sharply drew in a breath as she caught sight of a familiar face, one that she did not want to see right now. It belonged to Chester Lundquist, and he'd spotted her. He was even waving.

What do I do now? "Look," she said, pulling Jake toward a stairway. "Let's take this one. It'll put us close to my office."

Verdi yanked the door open and nearly pushed Jake through. As she did, she saw Chet approaching, an expectant look on his face. He was about to speak to her when the door slammed in his face.

"Man." Jake laughed, the sound echoing in the stairwell. "You Consular Affairs women mean business, don't you?"

But Verdi wasn't listening. Her cheeks were burning as she considered how incredibly manipulative and self-absorbed she was becoming, traits she'd despised in others. She'd just brushed Chet off like so much lint on a blazer. The incipient guilt she felt competed with her relief that Chet never caught up with them.

CHAPTER
★ TWENTY-ONE ★

A cloud of grim purposefulness hung over the office as Verdi walked in. Huddled in fevered discussion, death officers clotted the corridors. All the phones seemed to be ringing at once, and secretaries, their faces shrouded in pained expressions, scurried from office to office, depositing memos into in-boxes.

Verdi pieced together enough bits of conversation to understand that a catastrophe had taken place while she was at lunch. A jet carrying a congressional fact-finding mission to Brazil had crashed, leaving no survivors. No official word yet on the number of casualties, but everything pointed toward a major disaster.

The office was prepared for such an event. A task force was quickly gathering from around the department to handle the official deaths, while others were handling the unofficial ones. Press counselors were pouring in from around State and Capitol Hill. The story hadn't hit the networks, but it wouldn't stay under wraps for long. Press releases were being hammered out, official statements carefully crafted.

In the midst of the madness Verdi felt someone take her arm and pull her aside. It was Calamity John, a look of absolute concentration fixed on his face.

"Verdi," he whispered hoarsely, "you're to report to the seventh floor, the Secretary's office, to do liaison work with the congressional people. Get up there now and do what they tell you."

"But, Mr. Dietz, shouldn't you be doing that? I mean, this is sensitive stuff."

Dietz shrugged. "They asked for you by name. Go figure. Besides, there's plenty for me to do here. Now get moving."

Verdi did not go as he'd ordered. She gazed at Calamity John, who looked old and worn out. "A wet day," he said sadly, and walked off.

At her desk Verdi was aware of Parker Harrington's glare as she gathered up her things into her briefcase. Scattered over the desk were pink messages from Chet Lundquist, three in all. She shoveled them into the briefcase and zipped it up.

"So, this is what it's come to," Harrington said, sounding every bit the wounded animal. "*You* waltz up to the Secretary's office while *we* stay here, calling up hysterical relatives. Where's the equity in that, huh? Seniority. Shit, what a joke. All you have to be is a woman or a minority and the entire State Department falls down at your feet."

Verdi looked over at Harrington, framed by his

postcards of Morocco, his first choice as a next assignment. The generous thing to do would be to ignore him, but Verdi wasn't feeling particularly generous right now. She sidled up next to his desk, looking down at him.

"A suggestion," she said. "For your career, you might want to invest in a sex change operation." Parker Harrington's jaw dropped about twenty feet. Before he could manage a reply, Verdi was gone.

The Secretary's office was unnervingly calm as Verdi checked in for her assignment. An efficient, well-dressed secretary made a call after Verdi mentioned that she'd been sent there for the airplane disaster. Within moments a short, thin man emerged, his shirt sleeves rolled up, tie loose. It was unusual for Verdi to feel older than someone at the department, but the man gave the appearance of a high school junior here on a summer internship. She discreetly checked out his creaseless khaki pants, undistinguished tie, and boat shoes. Visibly nervous, he quickly brought her down a hallway marked "Corridor 5" and through a door he opened by sliding his ID card through it and then entering a code.

Verdi stepped into a room straight out of a James Bond movie. It was vast, with no windows, and every space seemed to be occupied by a computer. But these were like no computers she'd recognized from the fourth floor. They had large screens and were hooked up to TV screens suspended from tracks around the room. People in headsets stared into the screens, speaking softly into mini-mikes. Telephones trilled softly from consoles built into the floor. This was the Operations Center, one of two major installations in the State Department for monitoring incoming cable traffic from around the world. This one handled unclassified traffic. Verdi had heard about this place but had never been here.

"You'll be over there," the young man said, pointing to a vacant station off to the side of the room. Verdi noticed he didn't look her in the eye. "It should be quiet for what you'll be doing."

Verdi was about to ask: What exactly will I be doing? before the man gave her a piece of paper with names printed on it. She knew what it was before he explained it to her.

"This is the flight manifest. As the cables come in from the embassy in Brasília, check off the names and call the appropriate office on Capitol Hill. They'll call the families, you don't have to worry about that. A copy of the *Congressional Directory*'s been provided for you. Any questions?"

Verdi shook her head and took her place at the console. No sooner had she sat down than a cable came in, confirming the name of one of the congressional aides who died in the crash. Running her finger up the manifest list, Verdi found the name, Anne Devereaux, and crossed it off. She called Devereaux's office and was forwarded to an aide who gave Verdi the home number.

You'd think they'd have the decency to call the family, thought Verdi. But she called them anyway, as she did for thirteen other victims, including two members of Congress whose staffs were gone for the day. The afternoon was wearing on when Verdi checked her watch. She was shocked to see it was past eighty-thirty. Where had the time gone?

Verdi stood and stretched. She looked around the Operations Center, nearly empty except for a few scattered souls. She craved a cup of coffee. Suddenly someone appeared at her side. It was the young man who had ushered her in. He stood there, waiting. Verdi wasn't quite sure what he wanted.

"Everything OK?" he finally said.

"Yeah, I've gotten confirmations on everyone on the manifest. Cables are still dribbling in, but nothing very substantial at this point. I thought you said the congressional offices would call the families."

"Did they make you do it? You should've told me. They were supposed to do it."

"No problem. Listen, is there a coffee machine around here?"

"Oh, sure, back there. In the pantry."

"The pantry. Right." It occurred to Verdi that she didn't know his name. She asked him for it.

He almost blushed. "Oh, it's Mudd. Winthrop Mudd."

Verdi had to think for a moment. She knew she'd heard that name somewhere. First she thought of Calamity John, and then she remembered Winthrop Mudd was Dietz's contact in the Secretary's office, the one who told Dietz that the Van Slyke investigation was over. Something else began to dawn on her. She moved a step closer to him.

"Are you with the Circle?" she whispered.

Mudd's eyebrows went up, and his head swiveled

on his neck, surveying the room. "No, but I hope to be," he whispered back. "You should know that."

"Who told you to call me up for this assignment?"

"Chalmers. Chalmers Mount."

Verdi nodded. "Why did you say I should know if you're in the Circle?"

Mudd looked at her quizzically. "Because you're in it."

Verdi tried to stay cool, to keep her surprise from registering on her face. She felt a sudden urge to get out of the op center and head back down to her office to see what was going on there. Winthrop Mudd stayed with her as she made her way out of the center. Before opening the door to the hallway, he glanced around furtively and leaned close to her. "Listen," he said softly, "put in a word for me, would you? With Mount, I mean."

Verdi nodded dumbly and passed through the door into complete darkness. "Hey, what happened to the lights?" she said.

Mudd chuckled. "Didn't you know? The corridor lights go out at eight. Energy conservation. Take two steps to your left."

Verdi hesitated. "Go on," Mudd urged her.

She rolled her eyes and stepped into the dark. Suddenly the corridor lit up in a blaze of harsh fluorescence. She blinked twice, trying to adjust her vision.

"Photosensitive cells built into the walls," Mudd said, pointing at a panel about thigh high on the wall. "There's one every ten feet or so. They detect motion."

"How long do they stay on?"

"About a minute. But you'll be in the elevator by the time they go off."

"You bet," Verdi said, turning away from him and heading down the hall. At the Citizens Emergency Center on the fourth floor things were quiet when she arrived. A couple of death officers and press counsels prowled around, but the lights were out in Calamity John's office. As she passed an office, she overheard someone saying that the American death toll in the accident was up to forty-six, including the fourteen members of Congress or staffers.

Checking her desk, Verdi was surprised to find a phone message from Lorna Demeritte. Verdi had been trying to reach her for days, but she hadn't called her back until now. Odd, the message had Lorna's home number on it. Why would she be calling from there?

Verdi rubbed her eyes and began wandering aimlessly around the dark office, still stretching her legs after her long stay at the op center. She thought about Winthrop Mudd, wishing she'd asked him what he knew about the lawsuit from Patricia Van Slyke's family. Maybe she'd get around to it later. Strolling along, she found herself in front of the office bulletin board and on it the eagerly awaited postings for new assignments.

She stepped up close to the list and began reading. There were several names on it she recognized, mostly from the Circle. Their assignments—London, Tel Aviv, Singapore—looked good. As she read down, her heart nearly jumped out of her throat when she saw "Verdi, Katherine" toward the bottom. Following a shaking finger, she scanned across the list to the posting, Paris.

Verdi's hand dropped to her side. She felt rubber-legged and light-headed. A wave of electricity rippled over her skin as she realized she'd gotten exactly what she wanted. She was going to Paris. But how was this possible? How could the Circle have managed this? It was absolutely stunning. They'd called her bluff, in spades.

She read down a bit farther and found "Wheeler, John." Her hand trembled as she searched out his assignment. There it was. Madrid. Jake was going to Madrid! This was incredible. Her mind raced. How far was Madrid from Paris? They couldn't be more than a few hours apart by air. That meant weekends, holidays together, vacations.

Verdi had trouble holding her thoughts, she was so beside herself with joy. She had to call Nonno, Jake. As she turned to leave, she accidentally spied "Harrington III, Parker" on the list. Had he gotten Morocco as he wanted? Verdi wondered. She scanned across. Dacca. Imagine that, Harrington was on his way to Bangladesh. Verdi couldn't help laughing out loud. No wonder he'd been in such a foul mood that afternoon.

In a daze she returned to her desk and sat down. Alone in the darkness, she relished the moment, the improbably wonderful set of events. Whom to call first? What to say?

Then Verdi remembered the message from Lorna. She searched her desk, found the message under her briefcase, and began dialing.

CHAPTER
★ TWENTY-TWO ★

In the afternoon of the next day, Verdi was prowling the hallways of the Dumbarton Oaks Museum, searching for Lorna Demeritte. According to the brochure she picked up at the door, the old Federal style building had been a secret site of planning for the atomic bomb during World War II. There were rumors that spies and refugee German scientists had been constantly spirited in and out of the place. Dumbarton Oaks was the birthplace of the United Nations, as the Allied nations quietly gathered in its great music room in 1944 to decide the balance of global power. The place had a long, distinguished history of intrigue, Verdi thought.

She'd already checked the exquisite labyrinthine gardens that encircled the mansion and sloped down a hillside toward Rock Creek Park in Georgetown. She was sure that Lorna said to meet in the gardens. But after winding through them and seeing only tourists, Verdi gave up and went inside the building.

It was no wonder they'd gotten their signals crossed. Last night on the phone Lorna was borderline hysterical. Even after nearly an hour on the phone with her, trying to calm her down, Verdi hadn't a clue what was going on or why she was so upset. At first she'd thought Lorna had been blown off by Jonathan Rashford—not that she could blame him, considering the way Lorna had acted the other night—but it quickly became clear that something else, something serious, was troubling her.

Lorna was almost rabid in refusing Verdi's offer to drop by her place. Instead she begged Verdi to meet her the next day at Dumbarton Oaks, where she would explain everything, she said. She made Verdi promise not to tell a soul they were meeting there. Verdi had to keep herself from lecturing Lorna on how ridiculous this was getting.

Inside the museum Verdi made a quick pass through the pre-Columbian collection before spying Lorna sitting on a bench in the Byzantine section, her face in her hands. Verdi approached slowly, past a guard's desk and then magnificent silver liturgical relics and gem-encrusted gold jewelry enclosed in glass cases. As she drew closer, she realized that it wasn't a bench Lorna was sitting on, but a massive marble sarcophagus carved with Roman figures.

Lorna was sobbing softly into her hands, tears leaking through her fingers. Verdi stood next to her for several seconds before Lorna realized she was there.

"Oh, Katie," she whispered, fumbling through her

purse for a handkerchief, "I thought you weren't coming."

"I—I didn't know where you were. I was outside looking for you." Verdi, who had consoled more grief-stricken people than she could remember since starting in CEC, felt awkward and tongue-tied in Lorna's presence.

Lorna was obviously feeling the same. "How are you, Kate?" she asked. Verdi almost stepped back as Lorna looked up at her with shockingly red eyes. Her skin was parched and devoid of makeup. It occurred to Verdi that she had lived with Lorna for two years in college and never seen her without makeup. She wondered how long Lorna had been crying and how much sleep she was getting.

"I'm fine," Verdi said, declining to mention that her office was in turmoil over the plane disaster and she was taking a chance, sneaking out to come here. "Lorna, tell me what's wrong."

Lorna suppressed a sob and began coughing violently. Verdi's head shot up at the sound of the wooden floor creaking nearby. A tall man in a black suit emerged at the doorway. Verdi let out a breath when she realized he was just the museum guard. He glared at Lorna, who was clearly breaking a rule by sitting on the sarcophagus. Verdi took her by the shoulders and led her past the guard and out the door onto the bright Georgetown street.

They sat down on a ledge built into the stone wall ringing the museum. The sun was powerful, the heat oppressive. Verdi kept her arm on Lorna's shoulder, which occasionally shuddered as she lapsed into crying. She stroked Lorna's hair, giving her time to calm herself.

"This was a mistake," Lorna said finally.

Verdi stopped her stroking and looked at her. "What was?"

"This, the whole thing. Your coming here. I shouldn't have asked you."

"Well, you did, and here I am. So now you have to tell me what's going on."

"I should let you get back to work." She made a move to leave.

"Lorna, look at me," Verdi insisted. "I'm here, for you. I've been trying to get you for days, and I couldn't get to sleep last night worrying about you after we talked. Now stop all this crap and tell me what it is that's bothering you."

Lorna dabbed the handkerchief at the corner of her eye. "I'm glad you can write it off as just crap." She began twisting the handkerchief with her hands. "It's— it's gone too far. I had no idea. It's like getting hooked on some kind of drug."

"What is?" Verdi demanded, shaking Lorna by the shoulders. "What are you talking about?"

Lorna buried her face in her hands and shook her head. "You should take a vacation, Kate. Somewhere far away. And then forget about the Circle."

"Come on, Lorna. You got me into this, with the Circle. You owe me an explanation. Is it Holmes, Mount? What are they up to?"

Lorna stood up and began walking away. Verdi followed her, trailing like a terrier.

"What *is* it, Lorna?" Verdi said angrily, pulling at her sleeve. "How deep are you into this?"

"Go away, Kate," Lorna said, her hand shaking and keys rattling as she tried to open her car. "Get out while you can. Before they start following you too."

"Following me?" Verdi said just as Lorna slammed the door in her face. She tried to open it, but Lorna started up the car and left Verdi in a cloud of exhaust.

"What the hell—" Verdi muttered, and turned to go back down Thirty-second Street toward her Camaro. She felt completely disconcerted by Lorna. What was she talking about? Who would be following her? It was crazy. Verdi would call her later.

As Verdi approached the Camaro, she noticed a man in a maroon Taurus, his face hidden by the newspaper open in front of him. All the way back to Foggy Bottom she kept an eye out for him in her rearview mirror, but he never reappeared.

CHAPTER
★ TWENTY-THREE ★

"You're *sure* that's him?" Clarence Witherspoon said, squinting through the darkness at the group of young men gathered at a busy corner of Benning Road, almost a block away. He turned around in the unmarked police cruiser to face a heavy black man sporting a goatee and sunglasses. "Absolutely sure?"

"Hey," the heavy man protested, "I know what I know. You asked for Stray, and that's the dude calls himself that."

The man at the wheel—an undercover narcotics detective—hissed through his teeth. "Just remember, Dexter, you gave us the wrong dude last time," he said with more than a little menace in his voice. "Cost us a bust and my cover in LeDroit Park. You gotta make amends, my man."

"That's a shame, about your cover," Dexter said,

running his mouth too much, Witherspoon thought. "But Stray is easy, he's high profile."

"I see what you mean about that," said the other narc, a white guy sitting next to Dexter. "Looks like a Dennis Rodman wannabe."

Witherspoon knew what he meant. Stray, who was black, dyed his hair bright yellow like Rodman, the flashy forward with the San Antonio Spurs basketball team. He even wore San Antonio sweats with a hood, to complete the look. Probably had tattoos all over his arms too, Witherspoon thought.

"Just better be the right man, all's I'm sayin'," said the narc at the wheel.

"Yo, check it out. You got your man."

"All right, let's get this moving," Witherspoon said. "Take a walk, Dexter."

"Always a pleasure," Dexter said, and hopped out.

The narc at the wheel spoke softly into a microphone hidden in his denim jacket. He waited until a car with two narcs inside passed them and rolled into a line of cars idling along the curb, all waiting to score crack. Business was brisk tonight, Witherspoon observed. He looked back at the car edging up behind them. Two of his people, homicide detectives, were inside that one. As the narc started up the car, Witherspoon touched his Glock 17, standard D.C. police issue, under his jacket at the belt.

"Stray won't be holding," said the narc in the back. "He'll take our money and send us on to one of his men, either there or there." He pointed at two figures Witherspoon hadn't noticed in alleyways past the corner.

"Just remember," said Witherspoon, "that Stray is the reason we're doing this."

"Here we go," said the one at the wheel as they slowed to let a dealer approach the driver's side. Witherspoon didn't follow the conversation next to him. He focused all his attention on Stray, who was busy bargaining with the narc in the front car. He hoped that Rico was right about this guy, that he knew something about the Porter murder. This was the only real lead he had right now.

Witherspoon felt the adrenaline rise as he tried to prepare himself for the bust. He reminded himself of one of Tom Galvin's sayings: It's when you don't get nervous that you should get out of police work. He moved his eyes from Stray to the detective talking easily with the dealer at his side. The narc—with earrings, a blue bandanna covering his head, and heavy gold jewelry—looked exactly like the kind of punk Witherspoon was used to locking up. The car ahead of them moved off toward one of the dealers in the alley. Unobtrusively Witherspoon moved his hand to the door handle. This was it.

Just as the dealer in the alley pulled a plastic bag from his jacket pocket, the entire intersection seemed to explode as cops brandishing pistols and shotguns jumped from cars and dealers took off running. Witherspoon was two seconds late joining the others. He pulled his gun and yanked open the door right into the knees of one of the dealers running past, who screamed and crumpled to the ground in front of the door.

Witherspoon pushed at the door but couldn't get it open with the dealer lying there in his way. He watched in horror as Stray ripped free of a narc holding another dealer.

"Hey," he shouted through the window, "get that dude."

But the narc was still hung up with the other dealer. Witherspoon squeezed through the narrow door opening and stepped over the still-writhing punk on the ground. Looking up, he saw Stray's yellow head as it seemed to bounce down the street and melt into the blackness of an alley.

"God *damn* it," Witherspoon muttered, and set off after him.

He raced through the street and into the alley, around trash cans and piles of garbage. He slowed down, adjusting his eyes to the darkness. Aware that Stray could be hiding anywhere and holding a gun, Witherspoon moved carefully, two hands on the pistol he held out in front of him. He checked stairwells and around the piles of debris. Backup cruisers, their sirens howling, were pulling up into the intersection behind him.

Finally, after picking his way through the alley, Witherspoon came to a service road that ran behind the apartment buildings on either side of him. Across the road was a high chain-link fence barring access to the yards on the other side. Witherspoon swallowed hard and concentrated. Stray was young and fast and probably knew the neighborhood. He could have gone either right or left on the service road. By going right, he'd be heading back in the direction of the market, where the police were now mopping up. Left would have been a better move.

Witherspoon went left, trotting in the shadows cast by the apartments. He passed a line of Dumpsters but didn't stop to check them. A half block up the road he came to another, bigger street. He crouched behind a car and scanned the area. If Stray had come out of the service road from here, he could be two or three blocks away by now. But he could still be back on the service road somewhere, hiding among the Dumpsters. And there was still the distinct possibility that he'd gone right coming from the alley.

Witherspoon wiped his forehead and waited for what seemed an eternity. Desperation began setting in. Here he was, squatting in the dark next to trash, while his best lead in a case that had been a burr up his ass for a week was slipping away from him. Getting this close to being busted would keep Stray off the streets for a while or make him disappear forever. Witherspoon needed him now. What else did he have on this case? Nothing, that's what.

A few lights had come on in the houses beyond the chain-link fence. Witherspoon heard a dog barking in one of the yards. He drew in a breath and crouched lower as he saw someone moving in the shadows behind him, coming up the service road the same way he'd just come. Keeping his body still, Witherspoon lifted the gun with both hands up even with his shoulder.

Careful, Clarence, he warned himself, still holding

the breath. *Be easy. Could be one of your own. Or someone walking his dog.*

The figure in the shadows was coming closer. Witherspoon had an unobstructed view of the road. In a few seconds the person would be there, right on top of him.

The first thing Witherspoon saw was the San Antonio Spurs sweat jacket. Then he saw the yellow hair. He sprang up and swung the gun around, its barrel pointed right at the surprised face of Stray, whose hands shot up in the air, almost as a reflex.

Witherspoon finally let out the breath he'd been holding. "You should've gone right," he said, almost smiling.

Witherspoon was right: Stray had tattoos on his arms. And just about every kind of ring he could get on his face. When Witherspoon patted him down, he found a Blaupunkt handheld cellular phone, a Motorola beeper, and all the major credit cards in his wallet, as well as the numbers for his lawyer and stockbroker. The lawyer was on his way down from a party up in Chevy Chase, Maryland, so Witherspoon and the others had some time with Stray before he arrived.

Partly out of courtesy, partly out of strategy, Witherspoon let the narcs have the first crack at Stray. Witherspoon watched from behind a two-way mirror as the narcs got nowhere with him, questioning him about the drug operation of which he was no more than middle management. Stray, whose real name was Arthur Lamont Dixon and who had a string of JD raps and two drug busts, was a pro at this. He sat impassively as the narcs played their game, describing what was in store for him as a three-time offender. Witherspoon slipped quietly into the room behind Stray, and the narcs left.

Deciding to remain behind Stray, who was handcuffed to the chair, Witherspoon began speaking softly. "So, you been briefed on where you stand. That's good. It's always good to know where you stand."

Stray let out a long, slow, hissing sound to show how bored he was. Witherspoon went on, unfazed. "What would *not* be good is not to know where you stand. Especially out on the street."

Stray shook his head. "Man, I got no idea what you're talking about."

Witherspoon came up close behind Stray, to where he could see the black roots of his yellow hair. "Let me explain then," he said. "What would happen if you were suddenly back out on the street tonight, being seen in a police car dropping you off at your momma's house? Meanwhile, your business associates, the ones we caught, are still here, getting booked, posting bail. Then word gets out through our people that you helped set up that whole bust. We have lots of people, Stray, who'd say you're our informer."

"No one would believe it," Stray said.

"Man, I hope you're right. 'Cause all you need is one dude who *does* believe it, hear what I'm saying? You'd never know who he was. Might be in your crew, brother of one of the dudes who gets sent up from this bust. Word could get out in the joint too that you're working for us. I can hear the phone calls now, coming out of the place. You'd have to go around never knowing who it was who was gonna pop you."

Witherspoon saw the perspiration trickling down Stray's forehead. He left the room, letting Stray sit for a few minutes. He came back with a cup of water and put it on the table in front of Stray.

"So what is it you want?" Stray said, his eyes on the water.

"You help me out, you'll be arraigned and held over for three days until you see a judge who gives you probation before judgment. One other dude we busted gets the same, so it don't look like you been singled out. Nobody knows anything. You don't do any time, and everything's cool on the street."

"Like I said, what is it you want?"

Witherspoon paused for a moment and unlocked the handcuffs. Stray went right for the water, downing it in one gulp.

"A week ago," Witherspoon said, "you were on your way home from the crack market when you passed through the intersection at Orren and Simms, in Trinidad. Something went down in that intersection I want to know about. A body was found there: a white man. I know you were in that intersection, Stray. You saw what went down."

"Man, how do you know this? I never go that way."

"All right," Witherspoon said, waving at the two-way mirror. "Cut him loose."

The narcs came in and began leading Stray out of the room. Panic flashed on his face. "Now hold on," he screamed. "Let me think here."

"Think fast, Stray," Witherspoon said.

"OK, all right. I remember. Orren and Simms, right. I saw the car go through—"

"Car?" Witherspoon said, nodding at the narcs to let Stray sit. "What did it look like?"

"Uh, sedan, American-made. Black. Nothing special about it."

"All right, let's back up. Tell me exactly where you were when you saw the car."

Stray held out his hands. "Man, this was a *week* ago."

"Make an effort, Stray."

"I was . . . in the side street coming in, not the intersection. The car was coming up Orren; its lights were off, I remember. And the streetlights, they were off too. The car slowed down, stopped, and something fell out."

"Which door?"

"Back door. Passenger side. The thing fell in the garbage. Lots of that shit there."

Witherspoon nodded, studying Stray. So far everything he said checked out. "Did you look at it? Did you know it was a body?"

"No way, man. You learn to mind your own business in that part of town."

"You weren't even a little bit curious? You didn't check it out, maybe lift the dude's wallet and ring?"

Stray shook his head casually, getting back into his nonchalant routine. "Uh-uh."

"You get a license number?"

"Man, I told you. The intersection was dark. Even the car's lights were out."

Witherspoon slid forward in his seat. "But you said you weren't in the intersection. I've been there. All the lights in the side streets work fine. They're out only in the intersection. That car would've passed right by you, going out."

Stray took in a breath. "It was a funny license."

"Funny how?"

Stray shrugged. "Not like D.C. tags. I don't know."

"District plates have two sets of three numbers on them. Could it've been out of state? Or Maryland or Virginia?"

"Man, don't you think I know what they look like? Most of my customers at the market come from Maryland and Virginia. These were . . . different. Like, there was more space in the tag."

"More space," Witherspoon repeated, thinking. "You see any numbers on it?"

Stray nodded. "Just the first three."

Witherspoon waited. "So what were they?"

"I'm thinking. Let's see. The first one was an *S*. The other two were eight and four."

Witherspoon's eyes narrowed. "You use any of your product, Stray? Were you using that night?"

"Fuck, no. I just sell the shit."

Witherspoon rubbed his chin. "All right," he said, looking up at the narcs still standing by the door. "He kept his side of the deal. We'll do the same."

Stray and the narcs were at the door when Witherspoon said, "Stray." They all stopped and turned. "This deal's good only once. These guys catch you out there again, you belong to them."

Stray snickered through his teeth, and the detectives pushed him out the door. Witherspoon stayed behind at the table, pulled his notepad from his pocket, and began writing furiously.

CHAPTER
★ TWENTY-FOUR ★

Kate Verdi raised the wax-coated paper cup to her lips and sipped beer foam. Except for perhaps a fine cabernet, nothing tasted as good as this, ballpark beer. She bit into the underdone hot dog on a mushy roll slathered with mustard. It was perfect. These were the vivid associations of some of her most treasured memories: baseball, her childhood, Nonno.

"You think they'll strike?" said Nonno, sitting next to her, his Orioles cap pulled down over his brow.

Verdi unconsciously glanced over her shoulder toward the crowd. "I don't see how they can avoid it. The owners and players have staked out their territory too firmly. It's like George Bush and Saddam Hussein. Backing down would come at too great a cost."

Behind her the sellout Camden Yards crowd roared its approval as Cal Ripken stepped into the batter's box. The Orioles had a late rally going, with two on and one out in the bottom of the seventh. They were behind the Red Sox by a run.

"What I'm hoping," Nonno said, "is that the strikers will be quick to realize how much they'll be losing at the gate in the pennant stretch, play-offs, World Series. So, if the Orioles can keep their streak going, they'll at least be in a position to make the play-offs when the strike is over. But they gotta get that bull pen in shape. Nobody wins anymore without a bull pen."

Verdi nodded at Nonno's words, but she was barely listening to them. Instead she was scanning the faces in the crowd around her, trying to spot a familiar face or one that was taking too much interest in her. As best she could tell, no one had followed her here. But she was certain that she was being followed. She had even taken to leaving her apartment through the delivery entrance.

Nonno looked at her as Ripken took a ball, low and away. "You see that guy yet, the one in the bleachers?"

She turned quickly to him. "What guy? Did you see someone?"

Nonno chuckled and raised his open hands. "I meant whoever it was you were flirting with just now, looking around."

Verdi laughed, suddenly realizing the extent of her paranoia. Seeing Lorna at Dumbarton Oaks had really spooked her, making her see goblins in the dark.

"So, you haven't said much about your love life," Nonno said. "How's what's his name in Rome?"

Verdi waved her hand dismissively at the reference to Antonio. "*Una cosa passata,*" she said in a tone Nonno recognized as one discouraging further inquiry.

"I'm seeing someone else, a guy at the State Department. Name's Jake Wheeler."

"When you gonna bring him by the house?"

Verdi shrugged. It seemed a bit early for her to unleash something like her family on Jake. "I didn't mention it on the way here, but he's going to be in Spain while I'm in France."

"Sounds very romantic," Nonno said. "I hope you'll come back here for the wedding."

She laughed. "Don't rush it, Nonno."

They both looked up at the crowd rising around them as Ripken lined a shot that hooked just foul down the left-field line.

"Looked fair to me," Nonno muttered as the stadium settled back down. A fan behind them loudly whistled his displeasure at the call.

"Hey, that reminds me," Nonno said. "Something I been meaning to ask you. You having trouble with your phones where you work?"

"Phone trouble? At State? None I know of. Why?"

Nonno made a face. "Probably nothing. Last time I talked to you there I got a whistling noise on the line just after you hung up. I never heard that before."

Gooseflesh prickled Verdi's arms and legs as she prodded her memory, trying to salvage something from the distant past. She remembered Jerry Gale, the guy she'd dated in Atlantic City who worked security for the Trump Taj Mahal there. Jerry's specialty was high-tech security: video monitoring of gamblers and the hired help, computer fraud prevention, that sort of thing. Verdi had learned a lot from him about surveillance. One way to find out if your phone is tapped,

Jerry once explained, is to have someone pick up your phone when you call your own number and then listen for a whistling noise on the line after the person's hung up. Just like the one Nonno described.

Verdi sat up straight at the sharp crack of the bat as Ripken drilled the ball past the diving third baseman into left field for extra bases. All around her people were leaping to their feet, cheering wildly. Everyone except for Verdi, who stayed in her seat, paralyzed with the realization that her worst fears might already have come true.

All the way back to Seat Pleasant and then into Washington, Verdi kept one eye on her rearview mirror. If anyone was following her, he was damn good because she never saw him. She even put her Camaro through its paces by going through a couple of maneuvers she'd learned from her overseas training course, trying to lose a tail.

But it was almost impossible to keep a low profile. Her Camaro was fading on her in a bad way. Not only was the car leaving a trail of smoking oil behind it, but its muffler was going, sounding like the death groans of some large jungle beast. She was relieved to park it on Virginia Avenue, a block from the State Department building. She checked her watch. It was 11:25 P.M.

As Verdi walked briskly toward the building, odd bits of trivia about the neighborhood from her FSI course came back to her. She remembered that George Washington and Thomas Jefferson first chose Foggy Bottom as the site of the U.S. Capitol but went elsewhere to avoid the smog and swarms of mosquitoes.

The area, first known as Hamburg, was a swamp into the eighteenth century but was later drained, filled, and settled by slaughter houses, a brewery, and gasworks that gave it its name. Through the twentieth century Foggy Bottom grew in prestige, and today it is home to such illustrious residents as the Kennedy Center, World Bank, and Watergate.

Foggy Bottom. It occurred to Verdi how wonderfully appropriate the name was: obfuscation, intrigue, and infestation, all rolled up in one. Not to mention a nod to her employer's increasingly anal nature.

Inside the building Verdi flashed her badge to the guard on duty and took the stairwell to the second floor, where she navigated her way through the deserted corridors toward the Career Development and Assignments office. She was still disconcerted by the weird photosensitive light system that announced her presence by illuminating a corridor just as she was entering it.

Coming up on Career Development and Assignments, Verdi spied a large gray trash can on rollers, festooned with mops and squeegees. Cleaning people were still around. She slipped through the door to the outer office and dived beneath the same temporary tables she'd hidden under with Chester Lundquist two nights ago.

From under a table Verdi watched as the cleaning people did the obvious: emptying trash cans and hauling boxes. She picked up some of the Spanish they spoke. There was a party after work for one of the cleaners who was getting married. They would be in a hurry to leave. *Good.*

After hearing the office door lock, Verdi slipped out and made a beeline to Chet's office. There was just enough light around the exits for her to see where she was going. Inside Chet's office she switched on his computer. While it was warming up, she drew the Tabard Inn coaster from her pocket and tried to read the commands she'd scribbled down the other night after watching Chet. It was hard, the bad light and her shaky penmanship combining to make reading almost impossible. She waited until the monitor shimmered on, then sat down on Chet's chair and studied the commands on the coaster.

Verdi carefully entered the commands, but nothing happened. Had the codes been changed? She knew that some classified codes at State were changed every day. Chet had never mentioned if these particular ones were changed as well. At two places in the command protocol Verdi had drawn lines on the coaster, indicating she wasn't sure of the codes. She tried the whole sequence again, more slowly this time.

Again, nothing. Panic set in, fear that she was butting up against a wall. Verdi stared at the power switch, debating whether to flip it and get the hell out of here.

Come on now. Concentrate. Put ice water in your veins. Think of this as that one ass-kicking question in the math section of your Graduate Record Exam. You can hump it.

She started once more, making intuitive leaps from the sequence of commands she had. She noticed that each level of the code seemed to contain elements— letters or numbers—from the previous level.

Painstakingly she tried and retried combinations of

numbers and letters. With each attempt she grew more anxious, more aware of the occasional sounds from the office. Finally, after eight more tries, she rang up straight cherries: The State Department's entire personnel program—classified information and all—lit up the screen.

Verdi knew she wasn't out of the woods yet. She still had to feel her way through the search protocol and was fearful that an incorrect command might set off an alarm somewhere in the system. Finally, after several tentative clicks on the keyboard, she reached a point where she decided to execute a search. Her choice: Chalmers Mount.

Long seconds went by before Mount's file came up on the screen. She skimmed the file, impressed as anyone would be with Mount's remarkable career trajectory. A third-generation Foreign Service officer, he had picked up economics degrees from the University of Chicago and Princeton and a law degree from Harvard. He entered the Foreign Service straight out of law school and jumped from one high-profile assignment to another: London, Paris, Moscow, Beijing. Back at State he was with the undersecretary for political affairs and had positions on the Russia desk. Clearly a rising star.

Verdi puzzled over why Mount would now end up in Career Development and Assignments. It wasn't a bad posting, but it hardly made use of his talents and experience. He should have been at a major embassy in a sensitive position. It just didn't figure.

She tried Alexandra Rhys-Shriver, who also had a Foreign Service pedigree, her father having retired as the U.S. ambassador to Switzerland. Like Chalmers Mount, she had impeccable credentials: B.A. from the School of Advanced International Studies at Johns Hopkins, law degree from Columbia, and all-but-dissertation in Chinese at NYU. Verdi scrolled through the records, which showed that Rhys-Shriver was certified fluent in Mandarin and Cantonese. Tours in Seoul and Beijing. Nothing but top-notch positions.

"Good Lord," Verdi whispered as she came to the salary history portion of the file. Alexandra Rhys-Shriver had been stretched—jumped in responsibility and subsequently salary grade—not once or twice but three times in her relatively young career, almost unheard of in the State Department. Verdi was getting depressed.

Finally Verdi came to Kendall Holmes's file. It was twice as long as Mount's and Rhys-Shriver's combined. Verdi marveled at the range of positions he'd held throughout his career, including deputy chief of mission, the number two slot, at a host of big embassies. It didn't escape her attention that Holmes had been assigned to several of his posts during the same tour as Mount or Rhys-Shriver.

The only thing missing from Holmes's résumé was the plum on top of a distinguished Foreign Service career, an ambassadorship. Hell, thought Verdi, presidents handed out ambassadorships like candy to corporate executives and old money types who supported them in their campaigns. Most presidential appointments were jokes at best and disasters at worst. But the Foreign Service always got a handful of career ambassadorial appointments each year. With his record Holmes seemed like a shoo-in for one, even to some third-rate banana republic.

Verdi heard a noise from the outer office and sat silently for several minutes before keying in a print command for the files she'd read. It took awhile for all of them to print out. As she waited, she listened to the hum of the printer in the darkness of Chet's office, pondering the bizarre direction events were taking.

She wondered: What *was* the Circle? Was it simply the twenty-four-carat professional network Lorna and the rest of them claimed it was? Or was it something more, some kind of evil alliance? Just a cursory look at the three personnel files revealed all kinds of connections among them, interlocking directorates. Verdi suspected she would find many more when she studied the files closely.

There's nothing sinister *going on here.*

Where was Lorna anyway? Verdi had been trying to reach her for days, leaving messages everywhere. Maybe tomorrow she would stop by Lorna's office and buttonhole someone, find out where she was hiding.

Verdi froze as she heard keys jangling in the door to the outer office. The cleaning people, had they come back? Not taking any chances, she logged off the computer and turned it off. She quickly gathered up all the personnel files she'd printed out, then dived under Chet's desk.

She heard men's voices, muffled, coming closer. Shifting slightly under the desk, Verdi looked up in horror as she saw that she'd left the printer on, its green lights winking in the otherwise dark office. It was too late to try to turn it off. The men were almost upon her, their soles crunching softly on the carpet. Flashlight beams played over the floors. Verdi held her breath as a pair of Adidas appeared at her eye level, just visible in the weak light.

A deep gruff voice came from off somewhere. "What's up?" it growled.

Carpet crunching, and then the man with the gruff voice drew up next to the man in the Adidas. His shoes were scuffed black oxfords, heavy and functional. Neither man had the striped pants of a guard.

"I saw a light when we first came in," the man in the Adidas whispered. He had an accent that sounded Asian to her.

"Where?"

"I don't know. Around here somewhere."

The men were silent as they listened. "They told us no one would be here," whispered the gruff voice. "What kind of light was it?"

"Office light," said the other man.

"Ah, here it is," gruff voice said, and he stepped inside Chet's office. Verdi saw a hand reach down and switch off the printer. He lingered for several seconds and then left.

"Don't forget to pick up her file," he said. Who was she? Verdi wondered.

She heard file drawers being opened and closed and then keys locking the outer door. They were gone. Verdi waited ten minutes under the desk. She thought about the personnel audit reports she held against her chest. Remembering her earlier visit here with Chester Lundquist, Verdi knew the PARs contained only

234   Stephen Kimball

limited information about the employees. What she really needed was a copy of their official personnel files from the drawers against the outer office wall.

But Verdi's biggest worry was the door; if it was standard issue, like the one in the Citizens Emergency Center, there would be a dead bolt on it she could throw open from the inside. If it was anything else, she could be locked in here all night. After crawling from under the desk, she felt her way through the darkness to the outer office door. She expelled a long sigh of relief as she found the dead bolt.

Verdi turned back to the photocopy machine in the corner and flipped its switch. She raced to the file drawers against the wall, pulled them open, and dug through them as the searched for the Circle's files. She yanked one file after another and took them back to the machine, into which she fed thick stacks of paper. Perspiration drooled over her neck and shoulders as she copied the files in turn. *Hurry up*, she commanded the machine.

Finally done, she carefully returned the files to their places in the drawers. Then it occurred to Verdi that she was missing one file: Lorna Demeritte's. Verdi assumed it had been misplaced. *Oh, well*, she thought, *I've heard enough about Lorna's wonderful career over the years. I can fill in the blanks.*

Out in the hallway, trying to look as nonchalant as possible, Verdi realized she could get nailed for a security violation or worse if she were caught with the files she was carrying. She decided to head up to her office on the fourth floor, where she could hide them in her desk until tomorrow, when she could slip them out in her briefcase.

Deciding against the elevator, she took the stairs up, shielding her eyes from the bright fluorescent light in the stairwell. CEC was dark when Verdi entered. *Like a morgue at midnight*, she thought.

It was easy to find her desk and ditch the files beneath papers at the bottom of a drawer. They'd be safe there until tomorrow.

"I should be so safe," Verdi said softly, and turned to go. As she did, she let out a small shriek as she ran straight into someone. Backpedaling, she looked into the face of Boris Kubanyi hovering above her.

"I'm very sorry," he said. "I heard something and came out."

Verdi tried to compose herself, to keep her legs from shaking. "What are you doing here?"

Kubanyi smiled, showing dentures. His dark suit, like an undertaker's, seemed to breathe gin at her. "I was finishing report for task force I'm assigned to. Terrible thing, this plane crash. But I'm nearly done. May I escort you out of the building?"

Verdi backed off from him by two steps. Her heartbeat was beginning to slow down. "No, no. I'm OK. Thank you."

"I was very sorry to hear about Patricia Van Slyke's untimely death," he said, his Eastern European accent thick, stretching out his vowels. "I worked with her years ago, at embassy in Tokyo. She was good officer, very intelligent and good to staff."

Verdi's first inclination was to ask him how he knew

she was handling Van Slyke's death. Instead she said, "What do you think happened to her?"

His eyes widened, and he shrugged narrow shoulders. "Was an accident, no? Something about hotel shower. Terrible thing." Then Kubanyi did something totally unexpected: He bowed.

Verdi didn't take her eyes off him as he turned and strode toward the exit, melting into the darkness.

CHAPTER
★ TWENTY-FIVE ★

Clarence Witherspoon had a choice between cold coffee and warm Mountain Dew. A cup of one and a can of the other sat on top of his desk, sweating rings into the reams of MVA printouts accumulating there. He rubbed his throbbing eyes and looked up from the printout he was studying, considering his options. Neither was very appealing, so he returned to his reading.

It wasn't easy concentrating with all the commotion going on out in the main booking area of the station house. The heat wave was bringing out the worst in Washington. People's fuses were shorter, and violent crime was way up. An endless parade of hookers, gangsters, and victims was streaming through the station. Witherspoon shook his head and rubbed his eyes.

"You want me to tell them to be quiet out there?" said Jolene Myers, computer specialist with the Fifth

District police. She was sitting next to him at a makeshift desk, outfitted with two computers and a noisy dot matrix printer. The computers were old hand-me-downs, whose keys, Witherspoon noticed, were coated with a layer of grime from use. One of the most capable people in the Fifth District—or any district, Witherspoon thought—Jolene on her own had souped them up into high-performance number crunchers.

Witherspoon smiled and nodded. Jolene was doing him a favor, staying late to help him out with his search for the mysterious license plate number Stray had given him. So far it had been nothing more than a process of elimination, going through all the likely possibilities: Washington, Maryland, and Virginia personal and business tags. It was late, past eleven.

He stretched his arms. "Has this ever worked for you before?" he asked Jolene.

She folded her arms across her bright red silk blouse. He noticed that her fingernails and lipstick were the same shade of red. "Lots of things work for me," she said, looking off into space. "What are you talking about exactly?"

"This," he said, pointing at the printouts. "What we're doing. I got *part* of a license number from a crack dealer who *may* have seen this car dumping my John Doe. Now let's assume he wasn't high on crack or something else when he saw this car and that the light where he was standing was sufficient for him to see a tag. Let's also assume his memory isn't shot and that he at least got the numbers right. I am not assuming he got them in correct sequence, but the computer will adjust for that, right?"

"Mmm," Jolene said, looking at him.

"So now I'm checking the addresses of the names you're giving me of people with *S*, 8, and 4 *somewhere* in their license numbers. I'm getting a pretty long list, but nothing on it is jumping out at me, no address that tells me: 'Yes, Clarence, there's your carjacker.' "

"You're assuming it's a carjacker."

Witherspoon scratched under his collar. "No, not particularly. I'm just using that as an illustration."

"An illustration," she repeated, typing something on her keyboard. "I'm beginning to believe what they say about you, Clarence."

"Who? What?"

She held up a hand and leaned toward her computer screen. "Don't tell me," she said under her breath. "What is this? Now I'm getting attitude from my autoexec.bat program. I replaced a couple of new boards in my main disk drive this morning, just for the occasion. That might be causing it. Hold on, I'm going in."

She whipped a small tool kit from her purse, pulled out the thinnest screwdriver Witherspoon had ever seen, and jumped up. With two twists of her wrist, she had the back of the computer open and was fiddling around in there. As she worked, Witherspoon watched water from the window unit oozing over the side of a steel bookshelf, collecting into a gritty pool on the linoleum floor.

"There," she said triumphantly, "let's see how it does now." She typed in another series of commands, and lines of data sprang up on the screen. "OK, Clarence, what next?"

Witherspoon leaned back, his swivel chair squealing ferociously. "Something Stray said still bothers me. He said they were funny license plates. When I asked him what he meant, he said there was a lot of space in them."

Jolene frowned. "Hmm. Lots of possibilities. Truck and van tags could look funny to someone."

Witherspoon cocked his head. "Stray said sedan."

"OK, temporaries then. Or vanity plates."

"What about them? Can we check?"

"We did. They'd be included on these lists of unofficial licenses we're running."

Witherspoon sat back, mulling things over. He looked at Jolene. "Something you just said. *Unofficial* licenses. What are the official ones?"

Jolene shrugged. "In Washington there must be umpteen kinds of them: diplomatic, congressional, military, federal, city government. Most are issued by the General Services Administration. Hey, you got an oil can for that chair of yours? I might, somewhere."

"Jolene, can you run all the official license numbers together?"

"I think I can manage it. You know we're talking about half a million vehicles in the federal fleet: cars, trucks, buses, jeeps. Anything else you wanted?"

"That should do it."

Jolene flipped through a manual and, finding the page she was looking for, propped it up against the computer screen she wasn't using. "Haven't searched official tags for a long time," she said. "They have special entry sequences. I did one a few years ago for the FBI when they were investigating somebody over in Housing and Urban Development. Turned out she had four cars she'd procured with government money, including two registered with the city. For *official* business, she claimed. Can you believe it?"

She began keying in commands from the manual. "My first husband was a detective, you know," she said as she worked.

"No, I didn't know that," Witherspoon said, amused that she would be talking about it.

"Life just hasn't been as exciting since he left. Not that I'm complaining, mind you."

"What happened to him?" Witherspoon asked, not sure if he really wanted to know.

"Oh, he got another job," Jolene said. "Furniture outlet chain in North Carolina wanted him to come down and run security for their stores. Too many of their dinette sets were walking out of the showrooms. It's a black-owned company and wanted a black security director."

"But you didn't go?"

"Mmm, you got that right. Me in North Carolina? No way. I grew up here. I just couldn't picture it, me in some small southern town, baking for the local church."

Witherspoon chuckled and looked at Jolene. She was a good-looking woman: fine features, nice figure, and smooth skin a deep shade of brown, almost black. They'd always gotten along together, and he knew if he asked her out, she'd probably accept. But he just couldn't bring himself to do it. Dating was something he wasn't ready for, even though some of his friends were telling him: "Clarence, you got a lot of good years left. You got to get out there again. Yvette would want you to."

Witherspoon knew they meant well, even agreeing with them that Yvette would have wanted him to find someone else. She was never the possessive type, even though she would give him a hard look if he made a remark about some curvaceous woman on TV, or some such thing. But Yvette wasn't the issue for Witherspoon. She was gone, and he was dealing with it. What was holding him back was having to get out there, to start all over again with someone else. It just didn't feel right. Not yet anyway.

"Hey, Clarence," Jolene said, "your data's coming up now. Why don't you sit over here and show me how you want it printed out?"

Just then the phone rang, and Witherspoon scooped it up. "Homicide, Witherspoon."

There was a pause on the other end of the line and then a quavering voice. "Clarence?"

"Yes? Ruthie, is that you?"

"Clarence, I wanted you to know. Tom died an hour ago. He died in his sleep."

Witherspoon closed his eyes and took a deep breath. "Thanks, Ruthie. Thanks for letting me know. How're you doing? The kids?"

"We're—we're fine. Everyone's here at the hospital. They're going home now, and I'll be staying here with Tom a little longer."

Witherspoon nodded, knowing what her conversa-

tion with Tom would be like, alone in a room together
for the last time.

"Clarence?"

"Yes, Ruthie?"

"I'd like for you to be a pallbearer at the funeral.
Tom asked me to ask you."

"Of course, of course. You have a time yet?"

"No, one of our boys is handling it. George. He'll
call you."

"Fine."

"Thank you, Clarence."

Temporarily disoriented, Witherspoon had to scour
his cluttered desk for the telephone. He felt clammy
and was aware of his clothes sticking to his skin.
"Why doesn't somebody do something about the goddamn heat in here?" he grumbled, slamming down
the receiver.

He drew in a breath and turned to Jolene. "Tom
Galvin died earlier this evening," he said quietly.

Jolene sat still for a moment. "I'm sorry," she said. "I
always liked Tom. You and he were partners, weren't
you?"

Witherspoon nodded. "What you got on your
computer?"

"You sure you want to do this now?"

"It's OK."

"I went ahead and formatted it myself, by agency.
The GSA allocates blocks of license numbers to all the
agencies. According to the regulations, each agency
has its own letter prefix. Then the numbers follow, depending on how many vehicles the agency has. See,

look here. Department of Agriculture's begins with *A*, Army with *W*, and so on.

"Then I did a search for an *S* and *84*. It's called a Boolean search when you stick 'and' in there. But look, nothing comes up with that particular sequence. Maybe it's not federal."

Witherspoon clicked his tongue in frustration. He would have bet his pension that the federal government lead was right. But even that was slipping away. What did he have now? Out-of-state tags? That was a long shot.

Jolene grabbed the manual and paged through it. "Hold on, now, something's coming to me. I'm trying to remember something about that HUD investigation, how that crooked woman managed to keep her scam going for as long as she did. Ah."

Witherspoon did not say what was on his mind. Instead he was silent, watching Jolene.

"OK, right," she said, her face in the book. "Says here federal agencies can issue their own tag numbers that don't have to follow the GSA sequences."

"What's that mean?"

"It means that Agriculture can cut its own tags for vehicles in its fleet. All it has to do is inform GSA."

"So they can do whatever they want?"

"You didn't let me finish. The numbers Agriculture issues have to use the prefix assigned to them, but they can go outside of sequence if they want to."

"So what we have to do is find out which agency has been allotted the *S* prefix and then dig around for *84*, right?"

"You got it."

Witherspoon stood up and began pacing nervously as Jolene typed in more commands on her keyboard. "Answer me this, Jolene: How do the agencies get their tags if they issue them themselves? I mean, who makes them?"

Jolene shrugged. "Same place as makes all the rest of them. Lorton Reformatory's industrial division. Big business out there, I hear. Maybe you know somebody in the shop, someone you put away."

Witherspoon chuckled, despite himself. He rubbed his tired eyes.

"All right," she said, "here we are. The prefix part was easy, but the plate number itself took some searching. See, I'm getting a tag with *S* and then *8404*."

Witherspoon hustled over to the seat next to her. "Where?"

"Here," she said, pointing at a line of symbols on her computer screen. "Don't mind that stuff next to it. It's code. I haven't converted it from ASCII."

Witherspoon felt his pulse quicken. "Who's the tag registered to?"

"Hold on," she said, seizing her manual and flipping through it. "OK, let me see here. Um, appears to be . . . Department of State. They have the *S* prefix."

It was as if all the tension had suddenly drained from Witherspoon's body in a rush. He sat still, his eyes half closed, feeling oddly peaceful. "You sure now?"

"That's what the book says. Want me to do the conversion out of ASCII?"

But Witherspoon was gazing off, thinking. "Yeah, you do that," he finally said, almost to himself.

CHAPTER
★ TWENTY-SIX ★

Chalmers Mount squinted down the barrel of his Swiss-made Hämmerli 162 free pistol and lined up his target through the gun's rear sight notch and foresight post. He lightly rested his finger on the trigger, set for electronic action. The gun had an odd, futuristic look to it: ergonomically designed hand grip and bifurcated steel barrel with switches that activated the electronic trigger. He drew in a breath, clenched his teeth, and squeezed the trigger.

Even though the Hämmerli was virtually recoilless, it jumped slightly in Mount's hand as he fired at the human silhouette target with the bull's-eye between the eyes. The shot flared off from the target's head and grazed its right shoulder.

"Fuck," he said, yanking off his soundproof headphones. He scowled at his weapon like a tennis player studying his racket after blowing a volley. He folded his arms across his T-shirt that read: "Gun Control Means Using Two Hands."

"If that was an intruder, you'd be dead right now."

Mount turned toward Kendall Holmes, whose patronizing chuckle stuck in Mount's ego like a needle. Holmes had fitted a six-shot cartridge into his pistol and was adjusting his headphones.

Mount wished he'd had an excuse for staying away from the target range today. For him, shooting was about as appealing as a case of malaria. He could find no physical or intellectual enjoyment in it. Every time he went shooting, he felt as if he were compromising a part of himself, not the least of which was his will. It was Holmes who'd made Mount a Christmas gift of the expensive imported pistol, given him lessons, and dragged him to the range.

When Holmes called him this morning to go out to the range in Virginia, Mount couldn't bring himself to say no. Even if he'd manufactured an excuse, Holmes would have seen through it, and things would be worse. This was a particularly bad time for Mount to be traipsing off to the range with Holmes. He'd been under so much pressure lately, what with the new assignments just coming out and the added complications of managing the Circle.

Holmes had no idea how much Mount had done for him behind the scenes, all those difficult personalities he had to handle. Now there was trouble in the Circle he had to deal with, a dangerous breach in security, just as Holmes was moving closer to an important new relationship for the Circle. There'd been times when Mount thought he might explode from the pressure, from the overwhelming strain of keeping all the pieces in place for the thankless Kendall Holmes.

"Let me show you how it's done," Holmes said, sliding one hand into the pocket of his shorts and, with the other, raising his Hämmerli. Mount watched as Holmes's arm began quivering slightly and then worked up to a full-blown shake. His face stretched in a grimace as he tried to control the shaking, which worsened with each moment. Mount couldn't stand to watch and looked away.

Finally, Holmes steadied his arm with his other hand and snapped off three quick shots, each a small explosion ricocheting around the range. The smell of spent gunpowder lingered in the air. Holmes slammed the pistol down on the loading table in front of him, abruptly turned, and stalked away.

Chalmers Mount briefly considered saying something to Holmes, the verbal equivalent of a pat on the back, but thought better of it. Instead he silently packed both pistols in their cases. Before joining Holmes, Mount peered at the target through the telescope mounted on a tripod next to him. He gasped at the sight of all three shots drilled straight through the bull's-eye, as if made by a single large-caliber bullet.

Mount found Holmes fuming in a corner of the lounge. Despite the soundproofing in the lounge's walls and ceiling, the sound of gunfire reverberated in Mount's chest cavity. Carefully he took a seat next to Holmes and watched a waitress deliver a pitcher of beer to a table on the other side of the lounge. In a nearby glass case were displayed various holsters, hunting knives, and laser scopes.

Kendall Holmes broke the heavy silence between them. "So, did you get what you were supposed to last night?"

The waitress approached their table, but Holmes waved her off just before Mount could order a drink. He needed something strong. "We got it, yes," Mount said. "But there's something else." He paused, wanting to appear reluctant to continue.

"Well, get on with it," Holmes ordered.

"Two things. The first is Andreen. I'm concerned about him, Kendall. From my conversations with him, I'd say he's seeing himself increasingly as a free agent." Mount paused for effect. "I don't think he . . . respects your authority."

Holmes gazed off into the distance. "Andreen has been with me a long time. We go back to my Southeast Asia days. He's proven himself to be unusually competent in what he does. I've seen nothing to indicate that his role should be changed. Why do you raise this now?"

Mount folded his hands together tightly. "I've seen repeated insubordination, lack of regard for the chain of command. The people he brings on for special assignments report only to him. We have nothing to say about them."

Holmes dismissed him with a wave of his hand. "Right now there's no one else to replace him, even if he were a problem. His special talents are still of use to us. No, Andreen stays. Now, you said there were two things. . . ."

Mount nodded, trying to hide his anger. "Last night

Andreen found a light on in the office. A computer printer had been left on."

"So?"

"It bothered me, so I ran a check on the computer this morning. Turned out it had been used to enter the OPF database just shortly before Andreen arrived. They must've missed whoever it was by minutes. Not only that, but the same computer accessed the same database files two nights ago. The files that were entered are those of the Circle. Yours too."

Mount could see that he now had Kendall Holmes's attention. "Who was it?" Holmes said.

"The new guy, Chester Lundquist. I checked into his background. He's clean."

Holmes sat quietly as a fresh wave of gunfire erupted behind them. "How did you investigate these intrusions?"

"I had somebody from Information Management come in, a bright young guy. I have my eye on him as a possible recruit for the Circle. Anyway, I told him we were doing a routine survey of computer usage for the past seventy-two-hour period. He bought it. Then I had him put the information on diskette with the names on it, but he never saw them."

"Did he have any suspicions, ask any questions?"

"No questions," Mount answered. His lips were dry, and he scanned the lounge for the waitress.

"So," Holmes said. "Do you believe Lundquist is behind all this snooping?"

Mount shrugged. "Could be. I have someone on him around the clock." He paused for a moment. "But there's another possibility I'm exploring."

"Which is?"

Mount glanced over his shoulder. "Her."

Holmes nodded once. "Why isn't she being watched?"

"She is. Andreen's people are supposed to be on it. But none of them saw her go out the nights of the computer break-ins. By the way, just one example of Andreen's insubordination: When I pressed him on which computer was left on in the office, he said—and I quote—'Want me to come over there and wipe your ass for you?' "

Mount began to squirm as Holmes's dark stare focused on him. "We're at a very delicate stage of our negotiations right now," Holmes said. "The slightest problem or flare-up could be disastrous. I've worked too long and hard to let anyone disturb this process. Am I clear?"

Mount clenched his jaw and nodded, trying to look as if he shared his boss's worries. "I'll get on it right away," he said, and stirred to stand up.

Mount stood, but Holmes seized him by the wrist and pulled him back down. "Just remember," he whispered, "I will countenance no more mistakes like the one we had before. This time I will hold you directly responsible."

Mount nodded weakly as gunfire cracked in the range behind him.

CHAPTER
★ TWENTY-SEVEN ★

Kate Verdi, on State Department's seventh floor, searched for Lorna Demeritte's office, the Bureau of Legislative Affairs. Passing the corridor to the Operations Center, she soon came up on the Secretary's suite of offices and slowed down. She knew Legislative Affairs was near; Lorna always bragged how she worked next to the Secretary.

Verdi found a sign for the Office of Legislative Operations, where Lorna was director. She opened the door and came upon a group of staffers huddled around a receptionist's desk, whispering. *While the cat's away,* Verdi thought. They looked up in surprise at her and scattered, heading back to their cubicles.

"I'm looking for Lorna Demeritte's office," Verdi said to the receptionist.

"I'm afraid she's not in," said the receptionist, who seemed genuinely indignant at the imposition.

Verdi stood her ground. "Where is she?"

"And you are?"

"Katherine Verdi. A friend of Ms. Demeritte's. Will you tell me where she is please?" Heads popped out from behind cubicles.

"Ms. Demeritte is on extended personal leave. She's left instructions not to be disturbed."

"Where is her secretary?"

"She's not in either."

Verdi's stare bored into the receptionist's icy face. The woman began to squirm, and Verdi, feeling as if she'd gotten an ounce of blood, turned and left.

As Verdi headed toward the elevators, an awful feeling of life spinning out of control began to settle over her, insinuating itself into her consciousness like a virus. It was a sensation she'd had too much lately. She needed to talk with someone, to hear a familiar voice, but felt she was running out of people she could trust. Stepping into an elevator, she was about to push the button for the fourth floor but paused and pressed two.

She wanted to see Chester Lundquist, to apologize to him and invite him to lunch. So what if he worked in the same office as Holmes and Mount? Let them say something to her. They could stick Paris in their ears, for all she cared right now.

A chill seeped over Verdi's skin as she entered Career Development and Assignments, knowing that she'd been in this office last night, ransacking it like a thief. The place was quiet, with no sign of the bosses. A woman in a navy suit was collecting piles of papers from the tables Verdi had hidden under last night. She turned, eyeing Verdi suspiciously.

"May I help you?" she said.

"Uh, yes, I'm here for a meeting with a Mr. Lundquist," Verdi lied.

Her eyes flickered when Verdi said his name. "Chester? Why, he's not in today."

"But we had an appointment," she said. "Did he say where he'd be?"

"No, he didn't say anything. He's taken a vacation, I believe."

A sound, like high-pitched violins, rose in Verdi's ears. *Chet. Lorna. This can't be happening.* She tried to control her trembling by squeezing her fists. She forced herself to speak, to stay composed.

"A vacation. Would you know when he's due back?"

The woman began studying Verdi in a way she didn't care for. "I'm sorry. Perhaps you can tell me what it's about, and I can find someone else to help you. Mr. Lundquist doesn't handle grievances, you know."

Verdi took a step forward. "Listen," she said, aware her voice had risen an octave, "I don't have a grievance. I just want to *talk* with him. Can you understand that?"

The woman began backing away, her eyes on Verdi's fists. With one hand she felt her way along a table in the direction of a desk with a phone. Verdi turned and slipped out of the office just as the woman pounced on the phone.

Hurrying down the corridor but trying to avoid attention, Verdi felt predatory eyes fixing on her as she passed. The walls seemed to tilt and close in on her. Whispered conversations, fragments of dark, cryptic phrases echoed in her head.

Teeth clenched tight, legs pumping, Verdi kept moving. Who was an enemy here? Which one of these people lurking around her was after her? Up ahead two security guards wheeled around the corner, and Verdi pushed through a door into a stairwell. She ran up the stairs two at a time and burst through another door into a fourth-floor hallway.

Verdi wasn't sure how she found her way back to her desk. No one in the office seemed to take note of her arrival. Good. No sign of Calamity John. Even better. She sat down low in her seat, pretending to fiddle with her computer while sucking in air with great gulps.

She wanted desperately to be calm right now, to think clearly. All she could think about was Lorna and Chet: Lorna pitiful and frightened at Dumbarton Oaks, Chet pained and confused in the corridor, Verdi coldly snubbing him. The last time she saw them. The last time she'd ever see them.

Verdi closed her eyes to gather her thoughts. Why would anyone want Lorna and Chet dead? What had they done? At Dumbarton Oaks Lorna said that someone was following her, that she was into something too deep. Something like a drug. Then she told Verdi to forget about the Circle and take a vacation.

A vacation, the explanation for Chet's disappearance. Why Chet? Had someone discovered that Verdi had used his computer to access the personnel files? Someone willing to kill him for it? If that was the case, then Verdi was the reason Chet was murdered. And since Verdi was still alive, the murderer didn't know it was she who had used his computer.

Verdi felt utterly and terribly alone. Where could she turn for help? Who would believe her? She had to tell someone even if it meant professional embarrassment or censure. She thought of Jake. He would listen, try to understand. She called his office but was told he was out of the building.

Verdi found her State Department telephone directory in a drawer and turned to the office listing she was looking for: Counterintelligence and Special Investigations. She stopped when she came to Wade, Everett, deputy chief. She had met Everett Wade just a few days ago, in the cafeteria with Alexandra Rhys-Shriver. "Everett and I are making the rounds," Alexandra said. "We're joining Kendall for lunch later on."

Had the Circle gotten to Wade already? Was *he* in on it now, whatever "it" was? Verdi knew she couldn't call Counterintelligence. It would be like calling Kendall Holmes. Doors were slamming in her face, options narrowing. Disgusted, she threw the directory down on her desk, scattering papers.

Then something on the desk caught her eye, a slip of paper she'd overlooked. A telephone message. She picked it up and read it, her hand trembling. It was from Lorna! Verdi checked the time of the call: three-thirty, an hour ago. Could she still be alive?

Verdi punched Lorna's number on her phone. Someone picked up after the eighth ring, but no voice came on.

"Lorna?" Verdi said.

"Kate? Is that you?"

"Lorna." Fearful and elated all at once, Verdi groped for words. She cupped her hand over the receiver and whispered, "Are you all right? I've been worried sick about—"

"Kate, listen. Someone's been calling and not saying anything when I pick up. I thought you were them. I almost didn't answer this time. I'm really scared, Kate. I think they're—"

"Who, Lorna? Who's been calling you?"

"I don't know. I've been hearing things outside at night. I haven't been able to sleep. Someone's been here."

"All right, listen. Keep the doors locked. Don't let anyone in. I'm coming over. Do you hear me, Lorna?"

"Yes. Just hurry, Kate."

"I'm on my way." Just as she was about to hang up, Verdi felt her heart jump as she heard a whistling noise through the phone. She quickly gathered her jacket, purse, and briefcase. She thought of the personnel files still at the bottom of her desk drawer. Glancing around furtively, she pulled out the files and slid them into her briefcase. No one noticed her as she was leaving, except for Boris Kubanyi, who feigned interest in a file open on his lap as his eyes tracked her out.

For the first time since feeling as if she were being followed, Verdi spotted the car tailing her. It took her a while but she picked it up on Constitution Avenue on her way to Capitol Hill; a gray Ford hanging back by a block. She kept her speed the same as the traffic around her, not letting on she knew he was there.

After passing the Capitol Building and Union Station, Verdi was into a residential and small-business area on Maryland Avenue. She drove by the turnoff she would have taken to Lorna's block, A Street—and looked up at the mirror. The gray sedan was still there, moving closer.

"OK, you fucker," she said, and jammed her foot down on the accelerator, horns blaring around her as she ran a red light.

In the small square mirror Verdi watched as the sedan weaved through the intersection, hanging with her. *Damn it.* Darting around traffic, Verdi picked up speed, the old Camaro roaring in protest. Smoke billowed from beneath the hood. Row houses whipped past in a blur. Verdi screamed as she just missed slamming into a delivery truck pulling off the curb. Lunging into her brake, she pulled the Camaro into a residential street, too late in seeing the one-way sign pointing the other direction.

Strangling the steering wheel, Verdi chanted, "Oh, God, oh, God" as she floored it down the street. Suddenly a white van rushed straight up at her and she swerved out of its way just in time. From behind, she heard brakes shrieking and horns blaring as the van jammed up the gray sedan.

"Yesss," she shouted, punching the air. She beat on the steering wheel, more as a relief from tension than as celebration. In the rearview mirror she saw a cloud of blue tire smoke settling over the street.

Verdi didn't let up, tearing down three more blocks before hanging a right and doubling back in the direction she'd just come. She knew she was in a tricky part of town, where four sections of the city converged, each with its own address sequence. On Capitol Hill, addresses on the same street could be numbered several different ways. She tried to catch sight of a street sign, at least to tell her if she was in Southwest or Southeast Washington.

"Where the hell am I?" she muttered.

She drove on, searching for something familiar, a landmark. The Camaro bucked and knocked beneath her, its growl becoming urgent. Oil smell filled her nostrils, making her gag.

Up ahead she spied the lemon-and-turquoise awning of a bar, some southwestern place she'd been in when she first got back to D.C. She'd seen it going to Lorna's. She knew she wasn't far from there. Two blocks up and then a right, she was on A Street.

With her Camaro almost DOA, Verdi decided to park it in the first space she found. Out of habit, she took her purse and briefcase as she left the car. On her way up the street she nearly ran into an old man walking his dog, she'd been so preoccupied looking over her shoulder.

Verdi slowed her pace as she came upon Lorna's town house, her senses on full alert. If there had been an intruder lurking around, she didn't see him. Lorna's place was dark, Verdi noticed as she slowly approached on the front walk. She pushed the bell and stepped back, waiting for Lorna's face to appear in the window. But it never did, even after two more rings.

Where are you, Lorna? Verdi circled the walk, went through the wrought-iron gate to the back deck, and peered into the kitchen. No sign of anyone. She thought for a moment and rolled back the massive geranium planter, as she'd seen Lorna do before. The key was there, just as it was supposed to be.

"Lorna?" Verdi called out, stepping gingerly through the door, into the kitchen. She gasped at the unwashed dishes, empty cans, and boxes littering the table and counters. What had happened to Lorna? she wondered. She was the biggest clean freak Verdi had even known. How could she have tolerated this mess?

The living room was the same way. On her way toward the stairs Verdi stepped over piles of clothes and plastic dry cleaner bags. It looked as if Lorna were packing for a trip. Verdi reached into her purse for a can of Mace she'd gotten a few days ago, shortly after she knew she was being followed.

"Lorna?" Verdi called from the foot of the stairs.

Training her ears, she heard what sounded at first like voices coming from upstairs. Slowly climbing the steps, she realized it was music, sounding oddly familiar. Deep bass voices, frenzied, one on top of the other. Rising in rage, almost bellowing. Orchestra thundering, crashing. Fearful music.

Verdi reached the dark foyer at the top of the stairs. *Yes, of course,* she thought. It was opera, one she knew almost by heart:

> *Da qual tremore insolito sento assalir gli spiriti!*
> *Dond'escono quei vortici di foco pien d'orror?*

It was *Don Giovanni,* second act, final scene: Don Giovanni's descent into hell.

Verdi moved carefully down a hall, the only light

coming from an open guest room. Suddenly she jumped back as she felt something heavy against her leg. Instinctively she aimed the Mace can at it. Looking down, she saw a leather suitcase, packed and standing upright.

She slowly approached Lorna's bedroom, peered around the half-closed door. The music was coming from a clock radio on the nightstand. On the bed was Lorna, stretched out facedown on the bed in shorts and T-shirt. Poor thing was probably exhausted. *I haven't been able to sleep.* Verdi stepped in quietly, not wanting to wake her.

Verdi stood over the bed, the voice of Don Giovanni screaming in terror as the ghostly statue pulls him into the underworld. Holding her breath, Verdi peered at Lorna, who looked like a sleeping child, curled up in a fetal ball, her face turned away. Verdi looked closer, narrowing her eyes at a sliver of light glinting at Lorna's neck. Verdi moved her hand to Lorna's head, touched it gently with her fingertips.

A current of electricity seemed to crackle through Verdi's hand, up her arm, as Lorna's head rolled back, mouth open, eyes staring blankly. At that moment Verdi saw the needle impaled in Lorna's neck, blood streaming from it. Verdi felt the air sucked from her lungs as fear raged through her. She stumbled backward, knocking over a lamp.

From the corner of her eye she spied movement near the closet and, turning, saw a man with what looked like a baton. For one crazy moment she imagined him to be the conductor for *Don Giovanni.* But then she knew what it was, a blowgun. He was trying to line up a shot at her in the tight space.

Faster than she could react, he leveled the blowgun at her head and fired. At the last possible moment she raised her briefcase, and the dart sank into it with a sharp *thwack*. Her first instinct was to turn and run. No, he'd get her in the hallway, on the stairs. As he reloaded the blowgun, Verdi bolted straight at him. She saw the heavy eyebrows, the twisted nose. Their eyes locked in recognition just as she drew up the can of Mace and sprayed it in his face, sending him reeling.

He doubled over, the heels of his hands digging at his eyes. Verdi kicked him hard in the shins, and he cried out, falling to the floor. She raced down the stairs, barely hearing the screams of pain behind her.

She ran through the front door and up the street before ducking into a line of parked cars. Her chest heaving, she raised her head just enough to see through the back window of an Acura. Within seconds the killer came out of the town house and up the front walk, frantically rubbing the Mace from his eyes. He looked up and down the street.

Verdi stayed still until he turned and ran into Lorna's backyard. Staying in a crouch behind the cars, she hurried up the street. She didn't stop until she reached the Capitol Hill Metro station, where she was just another yuppie with a suit and a briefcase streaming through the turnstiles on her way home.

CHAPTER
★ TWENTY-EIGHT ★

After a transfer Verdi took the red line three stops to Dupont Circle, the station closest to her apartment. Her instincts told her to stay off the main drags, to cut back through side streets and up Florida Avenue. She came up on her street, Mintwood, from an alley directly across from her building.

Before stepping out onto Mintwood, Verdi stopped and studied the street. At first everything looked normal. The block was choked with the parked cars of kids hitting the trendy bars along Eighteenth Street. The streetlight at the eastern corner was flickering, almost out. But something was wrong. At first she wasn't sure what. She waited several minutes, and she spied a man in a car parked in front of her building. Moments later she noticed a woman strolling aimlessly up at the corner, where Mintwood met Columbia Road.

Then it hit Verdi: She couldn't go home. She couldn't return to her office or pick up her car. In fact, she couldn't do anything she'd normally do. She began to realize how big this was, how quickly these people could move within thirty minutes or less to block her apartment. Hell, she probably couldn't even call her family or friends without "Their" knowing about it. If everything wasn't bugged already, it surely was now.

How many of "Them" were there? How far did their influence extend? She could only assume they would go to any lengths to protect themselves and their interests. Beyond that she could assume nothing else.

Verdi backed into the alley, keeping her eyes on the street in front of her. Staying to the back streets, she made her way down to the Farragut West Metro station. Watchful for a tail, she rode the subway west into Virginia. Randomly she picked the Pentagon City station and hopped out. It wasn't long before she found an automatic teller machine that accepted her card. She would need cash, lots of it. She withdrew the maximum amount she could from the machine and returned to the Metro, which she took two stops back toward Washington. She exited the Metro and found another two machines, which she hit for the max.

That should just about do it for her checking account, she thought as she returned to the Metro for her longest ride yet. She took the blue line all the way east, toward Addison Road, the end station and the one nearest her parents' home. As the subway doors opened at Capitol Heights, the stop just before Addison, Verdi realized her pursuers might have guessed she'd try to escape to her parents. They also knew she had no car. They could very well be waiting for her at the stop ahead. Just as a bell sounded, signaling the doors were closing, she jumped out.

Verdi found a bench in the shadows of the station and sat down as trains rumbled in and out. She had to think. What options did she have? The way she saw it, there were at least three. The first was to run, to get out of town as fast and far as possible. The second was to go to the police, FBI, or Witherspoon. The third was to act as if nothing had happened and hope these people would forget the whole thing and leave her alone. She'd ruled out getting in touch with Jake; no doubt they were watching him. There was no way she was going to put him in danger.

She felt her body shake as trains rolled through the station, wind blowing her hair into her face. The last option was too ludicrous to consider. She was marked for killing. There was probably some financial incentive, a bonus, among these people for putting a bullet through her head. The first option, running, was probably what her pursuers were expecting. What would that achieve? Where would she go? For how long? Calling the police might be the best option of the three. But what could she give them as evidence? Maybe they would bring in Holmes, Mount, and the rest of them, but could they hold them? Probably not. Once they were out, they'd come after her for sure. Holmes might even have high-level connections with the police or the FBI, for all she knew.

Verdi trusted Witherspoon, but she knew he had to report to someone, who reported to someone else.

How far could she trust the system? She needed solid evidence, something they couldn't buy or sleaze their way out of. What could she do?

Feeling the tension building in her neck, Verdi rolled her head from side to side. She closed her eyes, wishing for peace, but images of Lorna's lifeless face—and the face of her killer—rose and assaulted her consciousness. She saw the killer in Lorna's house, the dark end of his blowgun leveled at her face. Then she imagined him cleaning his prints from the house to pin the murder on Verdi. Or he might try to take the body somewhere, make it look like an accident.

Verdi sat up straight on the bench, suddenly thinking of Witherspoon. Could he be bugged too, being the lead investigator in the Brian Porter case? She couldn't be sure. Digging in her purse, she found his card with his home number written on the back. She found a phone near the Metro elevators and dialed.

Two rings. "Hello?" said a young woman. Witherspoon's daughter, Verdi guessed.

"Um, is Clarence there?" she said.

"Uh, just a second." Verdi counted each second she waited. Jerry Gale, her security director boyfriend in Atlantic City, once told her it took seventy seconds for a call to be traced, given the right conditions. She would give Witherspoon no more than sixty.

She counted to fifty-four and hung up.

Then she called directory assistance and asked for the number of Pockets, a billiards bar in District Heights. She called the number and had Billy Verdi paged. Less than a minute later Billy was on the line.

With a finger stuck in one ear to block out the noise,

Verdi shouted into the phone. "Billy, it's Kate. Listen, I need your help."

"Kate?" Billy shouted back. "Where the hell are you?"

"Billy, listen. I'm at the Capitol Heights Metro. Can you come right away?"

"What's up, Kate? You sound like you're—"

"No questions, Billy. Can you come?"

"Damn, you know what you sound like? Like a hard-timer in the joint, talking to his lawyer. Yeah, I'll come. Give me ten minutes."

"Billy, thanks. Only, not a word about this to anybody. Promise?"

"Whatever."

Verdi dialed another number. "Witherspoon," said a strong voice after the first ring.

Verdi paused. "This is ... the person who visited you last week in your office. We spoke, and you gave me your card."

"I remember. Where are you now?"

"That's not important. Listen, there's been ... a murder. Go to 502 A Street. On Capitol Hill. You have to hurry."

"Listen to me. Were you there? Did you see anyone?"

Verdi kept her eyes on her watch. "Yes. Lorna Demeritte. She's been killed. A man was there. He might have made it look like an accident. You have to hurry."

"Now, hold on. I can meet you. Just tell me where."

Sixty seconds were almost up. "I can't. I'm somewhere else. I have to go."

"Wait. Call me later. I'll be at this number or at—"

Verdi, already at sixty-two seconds, hung up. She

took the escalator down to the dropoff area and waited. She kept to the shadows, studying everyone coming through the station. People who noticed her eyed her curiously, a lone white woman lurking in the darkness in a black part of town. Gripping the Mace can firmly, she prayed for Billy to hurry. She found it difficult to keep her thoughts together, to concentrate on the present moment. The minutes crawled by. *Come on, Billy.*

Twenty minutes later a boxy-looking beige step van pulled up to the entrance. Verdi stayed back until she recognized Billy at the wheel, beckoning her in. She pulled the sliding door on the passenger side and stepped inside. There was no seat.

"Sit there," Billy said, pointing at a blanket covering a toolbox. "Where to?"

"Anywhere but here," she said, dropping her purse and briefcase on the floor.

He drove two blocks before pulling into the parking lot of a Popeye's. "Now, you wanna tell me what's so important you make me leave a nine-ball game when I'm behind?"

Verdi rubbed her eyes. She knew he would press her for an answer, and she was ready. "I need your van, Billy."

"What?"

"Just for a couple of days. Look, I know you need it. I'll pay you to get a rental."

"Can I ask why?"

She paused, not wanting to appear too eager with her lie. "A friend of mine wants to move out on her boyfriend. You don't need to know why. But she doesn't want him to know she's doing it. I'm taking a couple days off, to be ready to go when she calls me. It would mean a lot, Billy."

Billy looked at her with an expression that told her he didn't buy her story. "You know how to drive this thing? See here, it's got a floor shift with—"

"No problem. In Indonesia I drove things they wouldn't even let on the street here."

"That's what worries me."

Despite herself, she laughed. He started up the van. "Where're we going?" she asked, checking the side mirror.

"You gonna make me hitch home from here?"

"Oh, right," she said, suddenly worried about showing up at her parents' house. She was sure it was being watched. "Hey, let me drive. I could use the practice."

They traded places, and Verdi drove home, only a couple of miles away.

"There's a cot in the back I use sometimes," Billy said, watching her as she worked the gears. "You need the room, just fold it up and move it out of the way."

"You mean you *sleep* in this thing?"

He frowned at her. "Another thing," he said, opening the glove compartment. "A cop stops you and you need to show him registration, just be careful of this." He pulled a handgun from the compartment.

"That's a service-issue .38 Special," she said, appraising it.

"How'd you know that?"

"Friends of mine in the Marine Security Guard in

Jakarta used a .38 to teach me to shoot. I learned a lot from them. So why do you carry it?"

"Protection. Lot of times I have to carry cash for the hardware store."

"You know you're flirting with a parole violation, keeping that thing."

"Yeah, yeah," he said, returning the gun to the compartment. "Just don't think about it and you'll be fine."

They were into the neighborhood, only a couple of blocks from their parents'. Verdi took out a small roll of bills and stuffed them into Billy's shirt pocket.

"What's this?" he said, trying his best to sound indignant.

"Just keep it, Billy. Least I can do."

He took out the money and jammed it back into the side pocket of her jacket. "Save it," he said.

Verdi began slowing down and then pulled over.

Billy looked at her. "What's wrong? Why are you stopping here?"

She looked into the side mirror. "You hear that noise from the back?"

"What noise?"

"Sounded like the muffler dragging. Or maybe we caught a stick."

"Can't be the muffler," he said.

"I don't know, Billy. Sounded big to me."

"Hold on," he grumbled, opening the door and hopping out. He walked around to the back and squatted. "Nothing here," he said. "Start it up a minute."

Verdi started the van, put it in gear, and stepped on

the accelerator. "Hey," Billy shouted, his protests fading as she rolled down the street, picking up speed. She avoided looking into the mirror until she was back on Addison, Seat Pleasant's main drag. She drove for miles, heading deeper into Washington's southeastern suburbs.

CHAPTER
★ TWENTY-NINE ★

A sound beating against Kate Verdi's skull roused her from sleep the next morning. Her eyes snapped open, and she stared up at a small square ceiling that looked much lower than the one in her apartment. Something was drumming on the ceiling, a tinny staccato sound. Slowly she rolled her eyes, taking in her surroundings.

"Where the hell am I?" she muttered. Then it came back to her: Lorna, her killer, Billy. Remembering was no great consolation.

Stiffly she swung her legs over Billy's cot and stood on the cold steel floor of the van, cluttered with pieces of her brother's chaotic life. Piles of oil rags, tools, and truck repair manuals were strewn about. Was that a cash register in the corner, wedged against the rear doors?

Verdi peered through the passenger window. A hard

rain pelted the van and everything else in the parking lot outside. Joylessly she remembered this was Penn-Mar Shopping Center in Forestville, Maryland, about ten miles from her parents' place. The van was parked behind a row of tractor trailers, now huddled together in the morning storm.

Verdi checked her watch. It was 9:57 A.M. How could she have slept so long, especially on Billy's Korean War cot? Her stomach growled as she grimly appraised her work clothes, rumpled and limp from the night in the van. Drafty air seeped in through the riveted joints of the walls, chilling her skin. What she would have given for a hot shower.

Careful to keep her face from view, she looked out the driver's window at the line of stores across the lot. Many were beginning to open. There were the usual maternity shops, record and tape stores. Detached from the mall, near the road, was a 7-Eleven. She saw other stores that could be useful to her.

Verdi sat back in the driver's seat and tried to put herself in her pursuers' heads, to imagine what they were looking for and where. She assumed there were many of them, judging by how well they covered her apartment, and that a photograph and general description had been circulated. Her apartment would still be watched, as would her car, office, and parents' house. They might even be watching her acquaintances and places she frequented. They would be looking for a dark, medium-build female yuppie in her mid-twenties.

Verdi knew she had to lose her current wardrobe, not only because it felt terrible but because it fitted the description. She needed an entirely new identity, and she had to find it here at the Penn-Mar Shopping Center.

She checked her purse for her roll of cash, all the money she'd withdrawn from her checking account. Then she yanked back the driver's side door and jumped out. She imagined herself dodging bullets as she ran through the rain, all the way to the shopping center.

Her first stop was an army surplus store. Inside the store Verdi passed by the larger items at the front—life rafts, tents—and found the racks of clothing in the back. There was the predictable yuppie casual—big shorts, pastel T-shirts—but Verdi went further back to the hard-core military stuff. She picked out boots, camouflage fatigue pants, olive drab T-shirts, and a brown irregular-size sweater. The clerk let her wear the outfit out of the store after she paid for it in cash.

Next stop was the drugstore. There she bought toiletries for the road, spending time in the hair care section, studying coloring. Which one did she want? A Courtney Love blond seemed appropriate. She bought White Cornsilk by Clairol, a pair of scissors, and some towels.

In the women's room Verdi stayed inside a stall until two clerks at the mirrors finished their conversation about the manager they despised and the new stockroom boy they wanted to screw and left. Verdi came out and immediately began cutting her hair. Since she had recently had a cut—a professional one—it didn't take as long as she'd expected. Then she dyed it quickly, anxious someone would find her and raise a fuss. She slipped back into the stall, waited for the color to take, and then inspected her work in the mirror.

"Dio mio!" she groaned, taking in the sight. Dripping wet, her hair rose in small spikes that shot off her head in all directions. The cut was not quite even, and Verdi could see dark roots she'd missed. Her new hair and guerrilla clothes combined to give her a look like something out of a second-tier punk band.

Her hair was still wet and spiky when she hit her third spot, the 7-Eleven. The checkout clerk watched her like a hawk as she made her way around the store, but he never looked her in the eye as she paid for her coffee, fruit, roll, *Washington Post,* and *Washington Times.*

Back in the van, eating her breakfast, Verdi scoured the papers for a story on Lorna's murder. She also had the radio on, tuned to the all-news station. But there was nothing, not a mention of the murder.

Witherspoon. He must have smothered the story. Verdi couldn't imagine it being overlooked by the press. Something else occurred to her: The killer could have covered up the murder, getting Lorna's body out of the apartment and cleaning up before the police arrived. He certainly had enough time to do it before Witherspoon could get police there. That would explain why the murder wasn't being reported anywhere. If that was the case, then she truly had nothing to offer Witherspoon as evidence. She might as well not even bother to call him.

As Verdi finished the last of her coffee, an eerie

feeling of unreality passed over her. What if she'd imagined the whole thing: Lorna, the killer, the people watching her apartment building? It certainly was plausible. All this was just too incredible, especially without a shred of evidence to support any of Verdi's suspicions. And now, the day after Lorna's supposed murder, there was nothing in the papers about it, not a word. Why couldn't this just be an awful dream, a hallucination brought on by something someone had slipped her?

The horrible memory of Lorna's dead eyes snapped Verdi back into reality. She certainly hadn't imagined *that*. No, this was the world at its most real. She'd have to be tough and smart to get through it, smarter than the people after her.

Verdi had enough of the radio, so she cut the engine. She leaned back on the cot, concentrating, trying again to focus on her pursuers. She was thinking: What would she do if she were they? Assume she was as far away from Washington as she could get, that's what. So that was precisely what she would *not* do.

Verdi knew she enjoyed some advantages over her pursuers right now. First, she had almost complete freedom, being able to come and go, and even sleep, in the van. As long as she could, she would stay here in Prince George's County, where she knew her way around. She wanted to keep them off-balance, spread them out thin. The long subway trip to her bank last night was a ruse to make them think she was hiding in Virginia. If they could tap phones, they probably could get into her bank records.

Second, she had money, at least enough to keep her

going for a few days, weeks if she had to. Third, her pursuers didn't know what she'd told the police. They would have to assume the police knew something, to have hushed up the story of Lorna's murder. That is, unless Lorna's killer had gotten back to her body, removed it, and cleaned up before Witherspoon could get the police there.

Verdi crawled from the cot to the driver's seat. She gazed out the rain-streaked window. *They* were out there now, combing the city for her. Who were they? What were they after?

It was a safe bet Kendall Holmes and Chalmers Mount were in on it. The rest of them—Jonathan Rashford, Alexandra Rhys-Shriver, and the others—probably had a role. But who was the killer? Verdi had recognized him as the man she'd seen at Patricia Van Slyke's funeral. Had he killed *her* as well? Or were there others? Verdi shifted in her seat, feeling vaguely sick to her stomach.

One thing she hoped was that the evil didn't go any higher than Holmes in the State Department. But she should be prepared for that, she realized, and not trust anyone at State. She wanted to call Witherspoon but decided that before she did, she'd have to come up with evidence against the Circle, something solid. But what?

Verdi wasn't sure, but she'd sensed that Mount might not be as careful as Holmes in covering his tracks. If she was going to get any evidence against them, her money was on Mount to give it to her. Maybe she could catch him in an unguarded moment meeting with Lorna's killer or passing money to Rashford or Rhys-Shriver. If she did, she had to be ready.

Her eyes drifted from the window back into the van. On the floor, half hidden by rags, was her briefcase. As she picked it up, she felt a knob of some kind. Turning over the briefcase, she gasped out loud as she saw the dart, a two-inch needle with a marble-size glass ball at the end of it, piercing the leather. Verdi studied the dart. Was it poisoned? It had to have been to have killed Lorna. She shuddered at the thought that it had been meant for her. She found a clean handkerchief in her purse and carefully withdrew the dart.

"At least I have some proof I wasn't hallucinating," she said dryly as she wrapped the dart with the handkerchief and nestled it in a pocket of the briefcase.

Inside the briefcase were the personnel files she'd copied. She riffled through them and pulled out the two thickest ones. She smiled as she looked at Chalmers Mount's file. The first page had been punctured by the dart. She began reading, searching for specific information. Kendall Holmes had a Potomac, Maryland, address. In the other file she found Mount's Washington address, but she didn't recognize the street name. She needed a map.

In the glove compartment, Billy kept several maps for his delivery business. She saw one for the District. Reaching in for it, she felt something hard and cold on her fingers. Billy's gun. Checking to make sure the safety was on, she pulled it out slowly. Damn thing was loaded, six rounds in the chambers. Carefully she stuffed it back into the glove compartment.

She glanced out the window one more time, to confirm something she'd noticed earlier. Three doors down from the army surplus store was a discount electronics outlet. Verdi drew her roll of bills from her purse and counted it. She had $727. She zipped it into a pocket of her fatigues and slowly stepped out of the van.

Watchful of strange faces, she moved off toward the shopping center, weaving her way through a maze of tractor trailers. As she reached the entrance to the electronics outlet, something made her turn back toward the van. She smiled when she caught sight of it, relishing the way it seemed to disappear in the parking lot.

CHAPTER
★ THIRTY ★

Wednesday is shark feeding day at Washington's National Aquarium, in the basement of the Department of Commerce building on Constitution Avenue. A popular attraction, the feeding usually draws crowds of tourists, schoolchildren, and an occasional government bureaucrat on a late lunch. But today the crowd was thin, accentuating the quiet gloom of the cavernous gallery.

Chalmers Mount kept his eyes forward as he searched for Kendall Holmes. Mount hated coming here. He found wild animals unsettling, even ones in tanks and cages.

Whenever Holmes was up on Capitol Hill—and that seemed to be frequently these days—and wanted to meet, he'd summon Mount here. Holmes said the aquarium was the perfect meeting place, not too public and not too private, and a visitor even remotely interested in a couple of men in casual conversation would quickly have his attention diverted to the dangerous creatures suspended in brightly lit tanks. Mount tried to suggest other, equally suitable places, like the Phillips Collection or the Willard Hotel lobby, but Holmes would just give him one of his baleful stares, and that would be the end of it.

Passing the electric eel tank, Mount could hear the sickening popping sounds of electrical discharges from the eel's body. He entered the main gallery and was suddenly surrounded by tanks of predatory fish. He was conscious of hundreds of eyes on him, of hostile animals appraising him.

A young couple looked at Mount, who quickly turned away toward a tank labeled "Alligator Snapping Turtle." As Mount looked up, a massive male turtle darted straight at him, its hideous mouth gaping open. Startled, Mount jumped back a foot.

Taking no notice of the trembling Chalmers Mount, the turtle swam off with a single stroke of its webbed feet. Then, from behind, came a familiar voice, gruff and mocking. "What's the matter? Turtle scare you?"

A chill went up Mount's back, and he spun around. Inches away, half hidden by a column, stood Dolph Andreen, his dark eyes riveted on Mount. Andreen never smiled, not even when he was ridiculing. Mount was always uneasy around him, sometimes even finding himself trembling in his company. He was certain Andreen sensed his fear and despised him for it.

"What a surprise!" Mount said, feigning insouciance. "Is it cleaning day for the piranha tank?"

Andreen scowled and shook his head. He pretended

to watch the snapping turtle. "You talk to the old man yet?"

Mount smiled, discerning the true nature of Andreen's question. "Yes, I did, as a matter of fact. He said your assignment last night was . . . less than successful. You let Kate Verdi see you at Demeritte's, and then you let her get away. Mr. Holmes did not seem pleased."

Andreen shot him a withering look. "Any word on Verdi?"

"You're asking *me*? That's your department, remember? Only, let's see how long you stay in charge of it."

Andreen took a step toward Mount. "Don't you talk to me about being in charge of anything. I wouldn't have had to hit Demeritte if you'd done your job right. I take the risks here, not you, shining your ass at your desk."

Mount's heart was beating faster, with Andreen moving so close to him. Emboldened by Andreen's recent misfortunes, Mount kept at him. "Risk? You call hiding in a woman's apartment and killing her when she's alone a risk? How could even you blow that? We could hire a street gang to do a better job. And what about that other debacle, the one with Brian Porter? Now we have the police poking around in our business."

Andreen's jaw muscles bubbled beneath his skin. "Let me tell you something, you little piece of shit. In Nam I saw eighteen-year-old cherries who showed more initiative than you. I'd give anything to see your pink ass in the jungle, water mites crawling up your dick and snipers shooting it off for you."

"Oh, is it Vietnam all over again? Can't you Special Forces guys ever stop fighting the war? That's where Holmes found you, wasn't it? Southeast Asia somewhere. You were an embassy regional security officer, right? Let me tell you something: This isn't Vietnam, and it isn't Southeast Asia. Why don't you get used to the idea that—"

"What's the meaning of this?" snapped a voice behind Mount, making him jump. He knew the voice at once, Kendall Holmes's.

"You dare to bicker at a time like this?" Holmes went on. "Maybe neither of you has any sense of the gravity of the situation we're in. We have a dangerous rogue on our hands, a time bomb that could go off in our faces at any time. And we're being asked to deliver on one of our most important, and lucrative, orders. Now I want answers. Dolph?"

"Nothing yet on Verdi. We have everything covered: her apartment, family, friends, even her favorite bar. If she's still in Washington, we'll get her."

Holmes's eyebrows went up. "You think she is?"

"Doubtful, but if she is, we'll get her. Best guess is she's on her way to a nearby large city, like New York or Philadelphia. Or maybe she'll think she's smart by legging it up to Baltimore. We have all those places covered: bus terminals, train stations, car rental agencies, the big hotels."

Mount shook his head impatiently. "What about airports? She's a Foreign Service officer, remember?"

Andreen didn't look at Mount. "All three local airports are covered. In case she did manage to get away, I made some calls last night and moved people into

O'Hare, La Guardia, LAX, and a few others. We're monitoring her credit cards and bank account. We found she made withdrawals last night from three Virginia automatic teller machines, so we're patrolling that area. And we're tracing all calls to the numbers she's likely to try."

Holmes nodded gravely. "Sounds as if you're spreading yourself rather thin. Take on more people if you need them."

"Yes, sir."

Holmes reached in his jacket, pulled out a photo, and handed it to Andreen. He gave him time to study it.

"Katherine Verdi," Andreen mumbled, nodding his head. "I have a photo I took from her apartment, but this one is more recent. OK if I make a copy of it, pass it out to my people?"

"That's why I brought it. Now, about last night. What happened with Demeritte? We have to assume Verdi called the police."

Mount grinned as Andreen looked at his shoes. "Yeah, she did," Andreen muttered. "We saw them arrive at Demeritte's about nine. I got the body out and cleaned up as much as I could. I wore gloves, so there shouldn't be anything connecting me to the murder."

"Except for Verdi," Mount said.

Andreen stared hard at Mount, but Mount didn't care. The pressure was now on Andreen to deliver Verdi.

Holmes looked up at the buzzing in the gallery as the shark feeding began. Chunks of smelt and squid were being dropped by unseen attendants from above into the tank. The small crowd pressed close to the glass.

"We don't know what Verdi has told the police," Holmes said, looking at Andreen. "Dolph, keep a low profile. The police are probably looking for you. Your new associate might be in a position to help us with Verdi."

Andreen nodded slowly. "Yeah, I got that covered."

"Be careful," Holmes said. "For all we know, the police may have believed her story and are setting a trap for us right now. I want to know immediately when anyone sees her before you move in. I'll be calling for reports every half hour."

Andreen nodded. "Verdi's an amateur. She has no idea what she's up against. It's only a matter of time before we nail her."

"See that you do," Holmes said sternly. "That's all." He turned to Mount. "Chalmers, I have some errands for you."

But Mount wasn't listening. He was hypnotized by the feral dance of the sharks as they attacked their food. Despite his distaste for wild animals, he found the sinuous movements of the sharks beautiful, even erotic.

"Chalmers," Holmes repeated, impatient. "Pay attention. I've some errands for you to run."

"Errands?"

Holmes took a quick look around him. "We're in the final stages of that important project I mentioned to you. As you know, it came up very quickly. I worked hard getting Alexandra her new job just so she could be in a position to help us on this. And we'll be taking a risk, exposing her as she's starting the job."

It took all of Mount's self-control to keep his lip buttoned as Kendall went on about how *he* had gotten Alexandra her big promotion. Mount had spent uncounted hours running interference for Holmes to line Alexandra up for the slot, talking her up to people in the East Asia Bureau, and writing up memos extolling Alexandra's qualifications to the career panels. Not that she appreciated any of it.

"So," Holmes said, "there are two important tasks you will perform. The first is to tighten security around the Circle. I want absolutely no loose lips or idle chatter, including cafeteria talk, to subvert this project. Am I clear?"

Mount nodded, understanding what Holmes meant. As part of his role as Holmes's lieutenant he randomly tapped the Circle members' phones, keeping tabs on whom they talked to and when. Now he would run a twenty-four-hour tap on each one.

"The second is to make a delivery tomorrow, the usual place in Maryland. I'll have the package for you tonight. I'll call you later with the exact time."

Mount felt his pores opening and the sweat weeping through them. "But why me, Kendall? I've never made a delivery before. We have people who do that. Besides, tomorrow I'll be—"

"The package will be in the car in the State garage," Holmes said, ignoring Mount's protests. "You can leave your car there until you're done. Get to bed early tonight. Delivery time is six A.M."

Mount swallowed hard, realizing it was useless to

argue. Behind Holmes the crowd around the shark tank oohed and aahed as the frenzied sharks thrashed through the water, devouring the last globs of gelatinous food tossed to them. The grand finale. Mount felt his lunch rising in his stomach.

"Oh, another thing," Holmes said. "Have you had the computer codes changed?"

"Uh, no. I was about to call someone today when I got your call to meet here."

"Do it immediately. I want all those loose ends tied up before the reception Saturday night. Everything has to be under control by then, especially Katherine Verdi."

Mount was about to answer when Holmes abruptly turned and stalked off, marching through the gallery, the electric eel crackling as he passed it.

CHAPTER
★ THIRTY-ONE ★

At five twenty-two the next morning Kate Verdi peered through the viewfinder of a video camera aimed through the rear window of the van at Chalmers Mount's house. She rubbed her arms and legs, which had been continually shivering since she woke up nearly an hour ago. It didn't help to watch as her breath turned immediately into wisps of white vapor on hitting the air. The smell of steel and damp wool clung to her skin, a further reminder that she hadn't bathed since going on the run thirty-six hours ago.

She'd been staked out here in front of Mount's house since picking up the camera at the electronics outlet yesterday. Through the afternoon and into the night she kept vigil, hoping to catch Mount on tape doing anything that might make her story more believable to Witherspoon. So far nothing. In fact, Mount had come home early from work and stayed in all night. Some bad guy. For her trouble she had sore muscles, burning eyes, and an intense desire for something warm to eat or drink.

To make matters worse, she had Jake on the brain again. All night long she'd been thinking about him, wishing she could talk to him, hear his voice. A couple of times she had to fight down the urge to go looking for a phone, if nothing else to find out if he was at his apartment. But she still feared for him, was worried that the Circle might go after him in the mistaken belief that he knew where she was. *Damn*, she thought, *why did I have to introduce him to Lorna and Jonathan?* They would probably never have known about him if she hadn't.

Verdi unwrapped a granola bar, her breakfast, and scanned the neighborhood, something she made a point to do every ten minutes or so. Mount lived in Cleveland Park, an old, genteel Washington community of gracious houses, tree-lined streets, and people who liked their privacy and could afford to keep it. Verdi vaguely remembered that the area was named for President Grover Cleveland, one of its early residents. Now its most important resident—at least to Verdi—was Chalmers Mount.

As she gnawed on the granola bar, Verdi thumbed through the personnel files again, her only entertainment during the long, slow afternoon yesterday. She'd had Mount's file almost committed to memory, and now she was going through Holmes's. She was searching for a dog-eared page she'd made in the file before it got too dark to read last night. It was a one-page memorandum going back to the seventies, when

Holmes was the ranking political officer at the embassy in Athens. Finally she found it and began reading it again.

> Confidential Memorandum, American Embassy, Athens, July 19, 1972 ... At an official embassy reception attended by the Prime Minister of Greece and Vice President and Mrs. Agnew, Kendall Holmes, first political officer, arrived clearly under the influence of alcohol and behaved in a grossly indecorous manner, inconsistent with the standards befitting an officer of the Foreign Service.... This report will remain a part of Mr. Holmes's permanent file.

"God," she whispered, "what did he do? Make a pass at Mrs. Agnew? No wonder he never made ambassador."

This memo must have hung around his neck like an albatross all these years. Why hadn't he had it pulled? He was director of the office. Then it occurred to Verdi that Holmes's name at State must have become synonymous with drunkenness, that his problem had become a wound all the higher-ups knew about and would reopen every time his name came up for an ambassadorship. Pulling the memo would have just made things worse for him. Sitting back in the passenger's seat, Verdi recalled something from Alexandra Rhys-Shriver's luncheon: Holmes never took a drink, not even to toast Alex.

It must have been crushing for someone of Holmes's stature and ego to have endured the Foreign

Service's equivalent of a tar and feathering. How could he have stayed on at State, having to face day in and day out the people who knew his dirty secret and were using it to hold him back from the very thing he coveted probably more than anything else? How could he face himself?

Verdi looked up when she heard a car door slam. She watched as a black sedan pulled out of a space next to Mount's house. She hadn't seen anyone come out of his house. Was it Mount? She had to decide fast what to do. The car was at the end of the block, beginning to disappear from sight.

Verdi started up the van and took off after the sedan. She caught up to it as it waited to turn north onto Connecticut Avenue. She eased off the accelerator and hung back, careful not to let the driver see her. As the sedan slid into traffic, Verdi followed, staying a half block behind as it continued eight miles up Connecticut into Maryland, until it turned east on the beltway.

Verdi always hated driving on the beltway, sixty-four miles and eight lanes of chaos that ring the nation's capital. Traffic here could range from zero to one hundred miles per hour, with drivers taking ridiculous chances as they defied laws of man and common sense. Driving a van didn't make it any easier.

Beltway traffic was light at 5:00 A.M., most of it tractor trailers that Verdi tried to stay behind while she kept the sedan in view. The sedan stayed within ten miles of the speed limit and hugged the right lane all the way. Before long Verdi was back in Prince George's County, passing exits she knew well. She was waiting for the sedan to spot her and make a fast move toward an exit. But it never did. She fought down a nagging doubt that the driver of the sedan was not Chalmers Mount. It *had* to be Mount.

If it was Mount, where was he going? She checked her watch; she'd been tailing him for twenty-five minutes now. They were now well past Seat Pleasant, halfway around the beltway from where they started. Traffic was thinning out, so Verdi slowed down even more, giving the sedan a half mile of slack. It was a calculated risk. If he'd made her, now would be his chance to get away. But out here on the open road she had to stay back because it was much easier for him to pick her out. She wished she could see into the car, to be sure it was Mount.

Verdi squinted hard at the sedan as what appeared to be its right blinker came on. *Damn, he's turning off.* She gunned the engine to come up on him, but she had to fall in line behind a car and a moving van. What exit was this anyway? She saw the sign just as she turned off: INDIAN HEAD HIGHWAY, SOUTH. She remembered this as the road to tobacco country. What would Chalmers Mount want way down here?

Verdi hung back behind the moving van, out of sight of the sedan. Suddenly she was climbing a hill, stuck behind the lumbering moving van and a car next to it, poking along at the same speed. For about three minutes she lost sight of the sedan and began to panic. Was he pulling away from her, heading down Indian Head and off into the woods somewhere? She'd never find him again out here.

The car alongside the moving van sped up, and

Verdi inched forward next to the van, trying to look around it. The sedan was gone, completely out of sight. Up ahead Verdi noticed a left-hand turn. Again an agonizing choice: Turn or keep going? She turned and stepped on the accelerator, heading deep into the country now. Weaving through back roads, passing towns with names like Welcome and Port Tobacco, she was beginning to give up hope she'd ever see the sedan again.

Then, as she rounded a long curve, she spotted the car up ahead, inching along the shoulder. For a second it looked as if the driver had something open in front of him, like a newspaper or a map. Verdi stayed with him until he veered off the road and abruptly stopped. She eased on the brakes and swung the van quickly onto the shoulder and behind a thicket, hiding it from the road.

Verdi sat for several seconds, watching to see what he would do. Was it a trick? Or worse, a trap? She remembered her can of Mace and Billy's revolver in the glove compartment. She thought of taking the gun out but decided against it. She had no reason to believe that the driver of the sedan knew she was there.

Verdi checked her watch: 5:47. No one had stirred in the sedan. She tried to make some sense of it. What would bring Chalmers Mount all this way out Indian Head Highway at six in the morning? What was around here, what government facility? None, as far as she knew. Certainly nothing related to the State Department. In fact, she was hard pressed to think of any place within a relatively short driving distance from

Washington that was this far removed from anything federal.

Maybe that was Mount's point: to be as far as possible from the eyes of official Washington. Maybe he came all the way out here to rural southern Maryland at the crack of dawn to do something no one was supposed to see.

Verdi slid out of her seat and rummaged around in the back of the van, searching for the black nylon bag loaded with the equipment she'd picked up yesterday at the discount electronics outlet. She found it where she'd hidden it, behind a stack of old automotive magazines. Careful to avoid loud noises, she left the van door open, slid the bag onto the roof, and climbed over the passenger-side mirror to the top.

The thicket was tall and dense, rising a foot above the top of the van. Keeping an eye on the sedan, Verdi unzipped the bag and removed a 35-millimeter automatic camera. She checked to make sure it was loaded and the lens cap was off and hung it around her neck. She then cradled out a video camcorder and tripod. She mounted the camcorder on the tripod, the way she practiced at least fifty times yesterday in the van while waiting for Chalmers Mount. It fitted perfectly.

Kneeling, she switched on the camcorder and aimed it at the sedan. She fiddled with the zoom and focus, just to get a feel for them. Her hands were damp from perspiration and the dew dripping from the trees above. She took deep breaths to steady herself.

Using the zoom lens, she tried to catch a glimpse of the driver's face, but all she could get was the back of his head. She could see him in the car, constantly raising his watch to his face. Verdi pulled the zoom lens back to a wide-angle shot.

Then the sedan door swung open, and a leg swung out, followed by another. Verdi heard her breath rush down her throat as Chalmers Mount's face came into her viewfinder. He looked terrible: unshaven, pasty white, and charcoal-colored rings under his eyes. Verdi left the camcorder running on the wide angle and snapped off six quick shots of Mount with the camera.

She shot several more as Mount began making his way along the road to a picnic bench Verdi hadn't noticed before. It was then that she spied the package in his hand. It was about the size of a stationery box. She lost her concentration for a moment and just sat and watched, stunned, as Mount lifted the cover of a trash can next to the bench and dropped in the package. He replaced the lid, and Verdi jumped back to the camcorder and zoomed in on Mount while he returned to the sedan. She panned the length of the sedan before Mount started it up again, turned it around, and drove back up the road.

Verdi was behind the thicket, flat on her belly, as he passed. The road was quiet. A crow cackled from the treetops. She counted to two hundred before sitting up again.

What the hell is going on here? And what's in that package?

Leaving the equipment on the roof, she slid down the side and carefully approached the trash can. She opened the cover, pulled out the package, and ran back to the van. Finding a knife in Billy's toolbox, she used it to split cleanly the heavy tape sealing the end of the package. Inside was a thick book of some kind. Slowly she pulled it out. The State Department seal on the cover was the first thing to catch her eye. The next were the letters TS—top secret—emblazoned across the top. She read the title: "Light-Water Reactors in North Korean Plutonium Development: A Status Report."

Her heart hammering in her chest, Verdi tried to focus, to decide the best course of action. She just couldn't leave this document here for whomever Mount had left it. On the other hand, if she took it with her, she might tip them off that someone had been here after Mount. They might look around here, even find her behind this thicket. She didn't want to leave right away; she wanted to capture Mount's playmates on videotape, for posterity.

In the back of the van she waded through Billy's pile of car magazines, but nothing was the right size. Finally, behind the cash register, she found a nice thick book—*Chilton's Guide to Brakes, Steering, and Suspension*—and stuffed it into Mount's package. In the toolbox she found duct tape. It wasn't the same as the tape on Mount's package, but it would have to do. Carefully she covered the slit she'd made and raced back to the trash can to hide the package.

Back up on the van's roof, Verdi fiddled with the video equipment, waiting for something to happen. She didn't have to wait long. In about three minutes—at exactly six o'clock—another car rolled up and stopped next to the picnic bench.

She trained the camcorder at the two men in the

front seats. The one on the passenger's side, an Asian, emerged from the car, his eyes casually scanning the area. He never looked down as he pulled the lid from the can and lifted out the package. She held her breath, hoping, praying, he wouldn't open it.

He didn't. He hopped into the car, which turned around and took off in the same direction as Chalmers Mount, toward Washington.

Back on the beltway Verdi was heading into Virginia, having just crossed the Potomac River on Wilson Bridge. As she drove, she emptied her pockets on the army blanket spread out next to her and counted her money. She was down to less than a hundred dollars. The video equipment and camera had set her back several hundred. And now she had to get the videotape reproduced and the film developed, not to mention pick up food and fill the van's big gas tank. She had to risk another withdrawal, this time from her savings account.

Where would be a good place to stop? she puzzled. Wherever it was, it had to be big and busy. She knew the perfect spot.

Tysons Corner was a huge sprawling shopping mall typical of the consumer-driven architecture of northern Virginia. As Verdi had expected, the place was deserted at this hour on a Saturday. Cruising the parking lot, she counted four automatic teller machines. She decided on one in a kiosk wedged between a multiplex and a Chi-Chi's restaurant.

She pulled up in front of the ATM, leaving the van's engine running. As she fed her card into the machine, a rent-a-cop car rolled slowly past her. She kept her eyes forward on the ATM as she waited. The car continued on its way.

Suddenly the teller machine began making strange chugging noises, and then her card disappeared into it. *What the hell*— Terror rippled over her skin as a transaction canceled message came up on the screen.

"Oh, shit," she muttered. How strong were these people chasing her that they could freeze her bank accounts just like that? How far did their reach extend? She was certain they would now know she was still in Washington. And it wouldn't be long before they would be all over Tysons Corner.

She looked back toward the van. Right now it felt like her best friend in the world.

CHAPTER
★ THIRTY-TWO ★

About an hour later Dolph Andreen, with his feet up on the couch in his Washington Circle Hotel efficiency, sipped tea and studied Kate Verdi's college yearbook. The room was one of three Andreen kept around Washington, each under a different assumed name. The Washington Circle, at the edge of Georgetown and Foggy Bottom, was convenient to restaurants, shopping, and his present client.

The yearbook was part of Andreen's folder on Verdi, consisting of her personnel file from work, desk papers, and odds and ends he had taken from her apartment. He'd scoured the yearbook in an effort to get to know Verdi, to understand the world she came from and possibly turn up a friend or acquaintance in the yearbook he hadn't known about yet.

But apart from learning that Verdi had been admitted into the Phi Beta Kappa honor society in her junior year, been elected an officer of the student government, and received a scholarship, Andreen had no more clues where she might be than when he started. He did come across Lorna Demeritte's photo, signed with the inscription "To a girl going places." It was the only signature in the book.

Andreen's head shot up at the sound of a soft knock on the door. He drew his Walther semiautomatic from a black nylon holster slung across the back of a chair and peered through the peephole. He grunted as he recognized Li Phan Ho, his most trusted associate, and swung the door open. Li stepped in, letting Andreen close the door before he spoke.

"She in Washington," he said, his excitement overpowering his usual command of English.

Andreen felt his skin tingling. "You mean Verdi?"

Li nodded. "She surfaced. We just picked up her trail, from ATM in Virginia. At 6:34 A.M. she tried to make withdrawal, but machine took her card, thanks to alert we posted."

"You have anyone out there?"

"Yeah, six people in two cars. But no sign of her. They were checking around ATM and found a private security guard who said he saw a woman there early this morning, about time Verdi was there. We passed him some money, and he said she was driving a delivery van, tan-colored."

"License number?"

"Didn't get one. But listen to this. When they showed him Verdi's picture, he said that wasn't woman he saw. This one had short blond hair, camouflage fatigue pants, and dark sweater. A punk, he said."

Andreen snorted. "She's disguised herself. And she can live out of the van. That's how she hasn't shown up in hotel check-ins or at any of her friends'."

Andreen crossed his arms and paced around the room, thinking hard. "OK, what do we know so far? She hasn't left the Washington area. And if she hasn't done so already, there's no reason to believe she will. So, what we need to do is shut down all the stakeouts outside Washington and bring those people here. Immediately. We'll need them to saturate the area.

"Verdi was trying to withdraw money from an ATM. She must have known that she'd be running the risk of exposing herself by doing that. What can we conclude? It's obvious: She needs money. So, now that she can't use an ATM, what we do is cover her bank's branches.

"Li, get our local people on it now. Don't wait for the others to get here. Make sure they're ready to move at a moment's notice. Keep in mind she needs money. She probably realizes by now her bank's branches are covered. She very well might go to her friends or family. Keep someone on them night and day. Got it?"

"Yes, sir," Li said, turning toward the door. "Will I be able to reach you here if I need to?"

Andreen shook his head. "I'll be out in the car, checking in with some of the stakeouts. And remember, tonight I'll be at State with Holmes and his crowd. I'll check in with you on the cellular."

Li nodded and left. One question bothered Andreen. Two days ago Katherine Verdi stopped at three Virginia automatic teller machines and withdrew $750 from her checking account. This morning she risked her cover, her life, to try to get more.

Either she needed more cash for something big, like a plane ticket, or she'd used up all or most of the cash she'd withdrawn in the space of two days. Since she hadn't yet left the Washington area, even with a van at her disposal, there was no reason to assume she was saving up for a ticket.

Andreen wondered: What had Verdi done with all her money?

He strapped on his holster, tightening it across his chest, and checked the magazine on the Walther. Eight rounds per clip, with extras in the holster. From a closet he brought out a gray case he opened with a combination. He drew out a steel cylinder and, with a few twists of his wrist, screwed it onto the Walther's muzzle. Even though it was usually called a silencer, he preferred the more precise British term, *muffler*. This was a Brausch, top of the line.

Andreen would have liked to have stayed with the blowgun, but it just wasn't practical in this situation. The Walther was faster, held more rounds, and was more accurate at a distance, even though he did sacrifice some accuracy with the Brausch. Also, he did not want Verdi's death, which he was sure would come at his hands, traceable to Lorna Demeritte's through the dart or poison.

He checked the time: 8:12. From a pocket he pulled out a palm-size telephone and punched in a series of numbers. One ring, two, and then a voice came on.

"Yeah," Andreen said, "it's me. I'm at the hotel. We just got word she's been sighted.... What? ... Northern Virginia, trying to withdraw from an ATM . . . No, she's got a delivery van of some kind, tan-colored. And she'd changed her appearance: dyed her hair blond, wearing Army surplus clothing. . . . I don't know. She obviously needs cash. Stick around where you are, she might drop in. . . . Yeah, you never know. Call me immediately if she does. . . . Yeah."

Andreen turned off the phone and moved toward the door. He lightly touched the Walther against his chest, switched off the lights, and went out the door. It felt good to be on the trail again.

CHAPTER
★ THIRTY-THREE ★

A little past noon Verdi was driving east on Route 66, returning from a photomat in Vienna, Virginia. Getting the film developed and videotape reproduced did not cost as much as she'd thought. She'd gotten it all done within a couple of hours, even managing to look at the video before it was retaped. She was pleased with the quality; Chalmers Mount turned up in destructively perfect focus. So now she had a little time to kill before heading back into Washington.

She had to assume that her pursuers knew she had tried to withdraw money at Tysons Corner this morning. She figured they would guess she'd try to get as far from Tysons as possible and would be looking for her in Maryland or Washington. For that reason she lingered in Virginia for a while after picking up the tape.

Verdi used the time to pick up a little battery-powered

radio that she now had on, tuned to the all-news station. Still no word on Lorna. As she drove, Verdi got the urge again to call Jake. Would one quick call *really* be so bad? The poor guy, he must have been agonizing over her. He'd *better* be agonizing over her, for all the worrying she'd done for him.

Verdi also toyed with the idea of calling her parents. She was sure they'd be worried about her. Hell, she'd already given away the fact that she was still in Washington. If she was careful, she could probably get away with one or two quick calls. Maybe three, just to make life interesting. If she wasn't careful, she knew these bastards would find her and kill her on the spot.

As she passed inside the beltway, a sign for St. Jude's Church caught Verdi's eye. Recalling that Jude was the patron saint of hopeless causes, Verdi turned the van into the church parking lot, which she circled twice before parking near the delivery entrance around back. She slipped into the church through a side door.

Inside, the church was dark and silent. A lone soul kneeling at the altar—man, woman, Verdi couldn't tell—turned around to look at her as she slid into the back pew. Whoever it was wore large black sun guards around his eyes. Alarms went off in Verdi's head: *Who was this person? Could it be one of "Them"?* She fought back the creeping paranoia, convincing herself even "They" couldn't have anticipated her stopping here.

She let the familiar sights and smells of the church comfort her, bringing back memories of a simpler, safer time in her life. Her hands trembling, Verdi said every prayer she knew. Phrases from the prayers jumped out at her, sticking in her head: "Lead us not into temptation . . . Deliver us from evil . . . Now and at the hour of our deaths." She concentrated hard and finished her prayers. She made a quick sign of the cross and left.

Behind the wheel again and feeling calmer, Verdi decided to call her answering machine. Up ahead on the left was a strip mall of five or six shops with a public telephone on the wall at the end of the sidewalk. The place looked deserted. Good. She pulled into the mall and parked behind the shops, away from the street. Before leaving the van, she flipped through the files in her briefcase and drew one out.

At the phone Verdi fed in a quarter she'd gotten from the photomat and dialed her answering machine, her eyes carefully tracking the second hand on her watch. She had four messages. To save time she listened to only the first few seconds of each one:

"John Dietz here, calling at 9:40 A.M. on Thursday—" *Click.*

"Kate, this is your mother. I've been worried sick about you. I called you at work, but they told me you weren't—" *Click.*

"Hey, Kate, it's Jake. So what's happening? I've been leaving messages all over the place. Hope everything's OK—" *Click.*

"This is Clarence. Call me when you can." *Click.*

Verdi hung up the phone and drew in a deep breath. Decision time again. Whom to call? In what order? None of the calls was a surprise except the last one. She recognized Witherspoon's voice. He was smart, identifying himself only by his first name.

She knew she'd have to think through what she wanted to say for each call before she made it. Sixty seconds each. That was it.

The first call was to her mother. Nonno answered.

"Hi, Nonno, it's Kate. Is Mom there?"

"No, you just missed her. She went over to St. Margaret's to drop off altar linens. You know we've been getting calls from your office, asking if you were here."

"My office?"

"Yeah, a Mr. Dietz. Your mother's been worried about you, calling around, leaving messages. I told her you were fine, probably shacked up with a nice guy somewhere."

"Nonno!"

"Just kidding. Listen, where are you?"

"Nonno, I've been busy, taking care of a friend who needs help. Tell Mom everything's fine. Gotta go now."

"Kate, just tell me—"

Sixty-two seconds. Verdi hung up. As she began dialing the next number, she felt her blood race as a car rumbled up alongside her. She turned to see a fire-engine red Trans Am idling four feet away, heavy metal music blaring from its radio. Custom-painted in swirly black script on the side were the words *Tawna's Toy*. Behind the wheel the ostensible Tawna glared at Verdi and impatiently drummed her orange-painted fingernails above the door.

Suddenly Jake's voice was on the line.

"Jake. Hi, it's Kate."

"Kate, hello. It's great to hear your voice. Where are you? How are you?"

"I'm fine, Jake," Verdi stammered, avoiding his first question. "I got your message and just wanted to call and let you know that."

"That's a relief. Listen, I called your office and left messages. I was even thinking of calling your parents, but I was afraid I'd worry them."

"No, you did the right thing. Jake, I wanted you to know everything's fine. I've been thinking about you. I'll explain everything when I see you."

Suddenly Tawna turned up the music on her radio. Verdi had to strain to hear above the thundering noise. "Kate, what's that music?"

"Nothing." She was nearly shouting. "I have to go."

"Are you in any trouble? Listen, tell me where you are and I'll come there."

"I'm OK, Jake. Really. I have to go. I'll call you tomorrow." The radio had thrown her off, making her lose track of the time. Reluctantly she hung up.

Verdi checked her watch. She had one more call to make and then could get out of here. She found Alexandra Rhys-Shriver's home phone number in her personnel file. Before dialing, she turned to the blonde in the Trans Am.

"Could you turn down your radio?" she shouted.

The woman sneered and gave her the finger.

"Listen, I have only one more call to make. It's important."

"Get the fuck off the phone, grunge," the woman said. "You've been on it too long and I need to use it."

Verdi plugged a finger into one ear and dialed Rhys-Shriver's number. It rang a long time. *Maybe she's in the office on Saturday,* Verdi thought. She hoped she was at home. The effect she intended would be a lot better.

Someone picked up the phone, and a woman's voice came on: deep-throated and cultured. Alexandra Rhys-Shriver.

"Hello?"

"Alex?"

"Yes. Who is this?"

"Alex, it's me. Listen, I can't talk long. I wanted to let you know that everything's set, just like you wanted. I have everything we need on Chalmers Mount."

"What?" Rhys-Shriver said testily. "Who *is* this? What are you talking about?"

"Is this a bad time to be calling?" Verdi said, sounding as innocent as she could manage, given the circumstances. "Tell you what, I'll call you later after I've made the delivery."

"Delivery of what? Is this some kind of joke?"

"I understand, Alex," Verdi said just before an orange fingernail came from behind and cut her connection.

"Hey," Verdi protested, turning to face the woman from the Trans Am, who stood inches away, right in Verdi's face, a menacing crowbar in her hand.

"Listen, grunge, my boyfriend is waiting to hear from me, and I told you to get the fuck off the phone," the woman said. She raised the crowbar. "Now get out of here before I use this on you."

Verdi dropped the phone, letting it dangle by its

cord. She walked away, up the line of stores. As she was about to turn the corner toward the back parking lot, Verdi heard tires squealing behind her. She ducked behind the corner and watched as a pair of black sedans roared into the lot and screeched to a stop behind Tawna, deep into her conversation on the phone.

Doors to the sedans swung open, and four big men in black suits jumped out. They rushed up behind Tawna, grabbed her by the arms, and began dragging her toward a sedan. The crowbar clanged on the cement. Kicking and screaming, Tawna was still no match for the men, who had now picked her up and forced her into the back of the car.

Seconds later one of the men emerged from the car with a pair of mules Tawna had been wearing. He tossed them into a trash can, picked up the crowbar, and climbed into the Trans Am. All three cars took off together.

Stunned, Verdi slumped against the wall. Her lungs felt paralyzed, and she struggled to draw a breath. If it weren't for the wall, she thought she would probably collapse.

"Gotta get out of here," she mumbled, trying to stir herself into motion. The men could come back any moment, looking for her. She commanded her legs to move, and they did, but as if they were filled with wet sand.

Finally she made it to the van and started it up. She roared out of the parking lot before closing the door.

CHAPTER
★ THIRTY-FOUR ★

"Tell me again," Kendall Holmes said slowly, his eyes dark with barely suppressed anger, "how a three-hundred-page report in a taped package could have been switched in the space of ten minutes."

Chalmers Mount ground the knuckles of one hand into the palm of another and squirmed in his seat. Normally Holmes and he would be having a conversation like this outside somewhere, beyond the reach of eavesdroppers. But Holmes was so enraged that the thought apparently never occurred to him. Mount tried very hard not to show his indignation at being hauled up like this.

What he *wanted* to say to Holmes was that he didn't care what happened to the fucking report, that he shouldn't have been made to drive around like some messenger to deliver the package in the first place. He also wanted to say how sick and tired he was of playing Holmes's lackey, not to mention nursemaid to a bunch of jaded pinheads.

Instead he kept his voice even and matter-of-fact. "I don't know what happened out there, Kendall. I did precisely as you instructed. I arrived at the picnic table at five forty-five and waited exactly five minutes before placing the package in the trash can."

Holmes hissed through his teeth. "You must have been followed. Did you have the presence of mind to watch for tails? Was anyone around when you made the delivery?"

"No one was around," he answered. "No cars passed by while I was waiting. On the way out there I had to divide my attention between driving and following the map."

"Ah, there. You weren't paying attention. Goddamn incompetence."

"But who would be following me, Kendall? Who knew I had the report?"

"Why don't you ask yourself that question?" Holmes sneered. "You must have been running your mouth, trying to impress someone. Well, I'm putting this squarely in your lap. Have you any concept of the damage you've done to our credibility? The Chinese have already told me they'll never do business with us again. All that effort and planning wasted, totally wasted."

Mount gritted his teeth. Paranoia washed over him like acid, shredding his already ragged demeanor. His mind raced with a flurry of questions. What was going on here? How had the report been switched? Someone had set him up, but who? How many of them were there? What did they want from him?

From a rack on his desk Holmes plucked a meerschaum pipe carved in the shape of a dragon. "I'm not through with this yet," he said ominously as he ran a finger over the dragon's snout. "I called Andreen. He'll be here later at the reception. He'll look into this for me, after he gets Katherine Verdi. You will cooperate with him in any way he asks."

Mount dared not even exhale. The thought of having to work under Andreen almost made him gag. And the reception. That was the last thing he needed right now, having to glad-hand a roomful of people he couldn't stand to be with. There was no way out of it, not with Holmes in the state he was in now. At least he'd already had his tux dry-cleaned and hanging in his office, so he wouldn't have to drag it down here tonight. Then something Holmes said struck him.

"Did you say Andreen has news on Verdi?"

"Yes, not that it's any concern of yours. She's in Washington, possibly northern Virginia. Andreen says he's closing in on her. With any luck, we'll have her before the weekend is over."

Holmes stood up, the sign that the spanking was over. *Finally*, Mount thought, relieved. He stood and turned to go.

"Not just yet," Holmes snapped. "I suppose I don't need to say how deeply disappointed I am in you, Chalmers," he said in his most solemn tone. "This lapse of yours is absolutely inexcusable. In fact, your entire performance lately has been careless, shabby."

He dropped the pipe back in the rack. "I think you

need a rest, Chalmers. Or, better yet, a change of scene. I'll make some calls on Monday, see what's open overseas. I think we can find you something suitable at some quiet post. That's all."

Dumbstruck, Mount felt his face grow hot, and an awful taste rose in his throat. He stumbled backward, feeling for the door. He turned around and frantically escaped from the office, managing to get out of Holmes's earshot before retching into a trash can.

CHAPTER
★ THIRTY-FIVE ★

Three blocks from the State Department building, in the gritty shadows of the Whitehurst Freeway, Chalmers Mount stood in the basement stairwell of an old apartment building. He did not want to be here on yet another errand for Kendall Holmes, but he knew things would be even worse for him if he didn't come. He rang the bell once and stepped back, giving the person inside a full view of himself through the peephole.

The door swung open, and a young man in jeans and ponytail, a technician, stood before him, his mouth full of a chocolate cream-filled doughnut, part of which was in his hand. Without speaking, he motioned for Mount to enter. Inside, the apartment was dark and cluttered, the paper remnants of someone's Burger King breakfast littering the floor.

Stacked high on a makeshift desk of unvarnished

boards and metal cabinets was sound equipment, lots of it. Mount recognized most of the instruments, although there were a few he hadn't seen before. There was a remote-access telephone supervisor, a cellular telephone interceptor, fax and computer intercept systems, and switching systems for tracing calls. He also recognized the digital audio enhancement system for analyzing sounds, and a high-quality Nagra reel-to-reel tape recorder.

"Who's your decorator, Eggers?" Mount asked the technician.

Eggers shrugged and crammed the last of the doughnut into his mouth. Then something occurred to Mount, and he quickly checked the bathroom in the back. The stink of the room hit him when he poked his head in, and he got out fast.

"Andreen been around?" he asked, coming back to the front room.

"Nope," Eggers said, rubbing the stubble on his pale cheek. "They're all out somewhere. Something must've gone down this morning."

"Oh? What?" said Mount. Eggers shrugged again. "And you haven't seen Andreen?"

The technician shook his head. "You know, I thought I just said I didn't. I must not have been specific enough."

Mount nodded, trying not to appear relieved at the news. Mount had never liked Eggers. Too much of Andreen's smart-assed arrogance had rubbed off on him. "I'm heading uptown for a while, getting cleaned up for tonight. I thought I'd check in. Got anything for me?"

Eggers shuffled over to the desk. "Busy morning, lots of action around here. For you, there were twelve calls since you last checked in. The times are all there on the transcripts. I just finished transcribing the last one maybe fifteen minutes ago."

He shoved aside a pile of newspapers and pulled a manila folder off the top of a computer. He handed the folder to Mount, who sat down in a chair and began reading the transcripts of the Circle members' calls, most of them meaningless, meandering conversations with family or friends. Eggers watched Mount as he read.

"You get to the weird one yet?" Eggers said.

"Huh?" Mount said, looking up from the folder.

"One call, short but weird. Not sure what to make of it. Even came with its own musical score."

"Well, play it."

Sighing loudly, Eggers turned to the Nagra and rewound a section of tape. "I had to doctor it a little," he said, "like turn down the music and ambient street noise, just to be able to hear the voices." He flipped a switch, and loud music came on, thumping in the background, and then women's voices. Mount strained to listen.

"Hello?"

"Alex?"

"Yes. Who is this?"

"Alex, it's me. Listen, I can't talk long. I wanted to let you know that everything's set, just like you wanted. I have everything we need on Chalmers Mount."

"What? Who *is* this? What are you talking about?"

"Is this a bad time to be calling? Tell you what, I'll call you later after I've made the delivery."

"Delivery of what? Is this some kind of joke?"

"I understand, Alex."

Silence followed. Eggers switched off the tape machine and looked at Mount, who was staring into space, his mind racing, trying to absorb the meaning of the conversation he'd just heard. There was no doubt that one of the voices, the person being called, was Alexandra Rhys-Shriver. He recognized it even before the caller spoke her name. And then he heard his own name mentioned, a reference to "having everything we need on him," or something like that.

He flipped through the transcripts until he found the one for the conversation. There it was again, his name. He checked the top of the transcript and saw that the call had been made to Alex's home earlier today, at 12:27.

"Play it again," Mount said.

Wearily, showing how much trouble it was for him, Eggers rewound the tape and played it over. Mount listened carefully. He wasn't so much interested in Alex as her caller. Who was she? The voice sounded familiar to him. Whoever she was, she was obviously calling from a pay phone, or maybe a car phone. The music in the background was hard rock, maybe from a radio. But who was the caller?

I understand, Alex.

"Kate Verdi," Mount said softly.

Eggers leaned closer. "What was that?"

Mount felt a nervous twitch above his right eyebrow, something he'd get sometimes when he was stressed. He stood up quickly. "Has anyone else heard this?"

"The tape? Just you."

"Give it to me, the whole thing."

Eggers looked at him. "Man, I don't know. Andreen ever finds out about it, my ass would be history."

"I'm telling you, there's no way he'd ever know."

"You'd be surprised what he knows."

Mount said nothing. He reached in his jacket and pulled out his wallet. Flipping through the bills, he pulled out two hundreds and held them up. Eggers shook his head, frowning, but then he turned back to the Nagra and pushed the rewind button. He removed the reel and handed it to Mount, who slid it into the folder.

"Are there any other copies?" Mount asked.

"That's it."

"OK," Mount said. "No one else is to know about this. Understand?"

"Hey, no problem there. You do the same, right?"

Mount held out the bills and muttered, "Go buy some dope."

"You bet," Eggers said brightly, snatching them from Mount's fingers.

Stepping out into the stairwell, Mount felt as he did when he'd emerge from a movie theater in the middle of the day: disoriented, slightly dazed. What had he stumbled onto here, a conspiracy against him? Rhys-Shriver and Verdi. Why hadn't he seen it coming? What did they want from him other than to destroy him? He had a terrible sense of forces mobilizing against him, circling him. Hostile forces.

He looked up at the sun, already approaching the horizon. Soon it would be time for Kendall's reception. Mount dreaded the prospect, and his eyebrow twitched wildly now. He climbed the stairs and went searching for his car.

CHAPTER
★ THIRTY-SIX ★

"Where the hell are you?" Kate Verdi whispered to Chalmers Mount from her perch in the step van. She'd been waiting there the better part of the afternoon, parked a half block away from his house on Macomb Street. The camcorder was set up on the tripod, with the zoom lens fixed right on Mount's front door. The constant waiting was getting old, especially now that she was expecting some action.

Verdi picked up the open can of tuna fish from the top of the toolbox and nibbled at it, one of the few necessities she'd picked up on the way here. On the floor the latest *Vogue*, another necessity, was open to a story she'd been reading about winter island escapes. The radio she'd bought was a godsend in breaking up the boredom. She'd given up on the all-news station and was now tuned in to her favorite, WHFS-FM, dedicated to alternative rock. Kim Deal and The Breeders were blasting away, doing "Saints."

The sun was going down, burning out over Virginia to the west. Verdi had been camped out on Macomb Street since coming straight over after her call to Alexandra earlier today. Seeing that woman dragged away by those goons added a new level of fear, giving her something else to think about while she waited for Mount to arrive. Who were they? Their speed was absolutely stunning; they fell on her like pigeons on popcorn. How had they found her? She wasn't sure. They must have been patrolling the area and traced one of her calls. She'd thought she was being so careful, timing herself. Obviously not careful enough.

Well into her third day of living underground, Verdi no longer minded the grunge. She didn't know what it was—*nostalgie de la boue,* or what—but she was enjoying the reactions she was getting, of respectable folks' eyebrows going up as she passed them the few times she'd gotten out of the van. Verdi felt she'd never had the luxury to rebel as a teenager, the constant pressure of having to earn money canceling out any inclination to pierce her nose or dye her hair green. So now was her chance to tromp around like a punk. It was small gratification for everything else she was going through.

Verdi's head popped up at the sound of a car approaching. A dark blue BMW slowed in front of Mount's house and slid into a space. She turned off the radio and swung the camera around toward the car and looked through the zoom lens. The man himself emerged, looking even worse than he had this morning. With her finger on the record button, she tracked him as he slowly made his way up his walk to the front door. Opening the screen door, he looked down and picked up the brown mailer leaning against the door.

"Attaboy," Verdi said, pulling back to a wider shot of Mount glancing around nervously. "Now go inside and enjoy the show."

As if on cue, Mount unlocked the door and went inside. Verdi released the record button and sat back. The videotape in the mailer—of Mount at his dropoff point this morning—wasn't long, no more than three or four minutes. She'd also enclosed a few photographs she'd taken, just to make him think he was the subject of a wider conspiracy. He could view the entire package in five minutes. Ready to capture the exit she hoped would come soon, she stayed by the camcorder.

Sitting there on Billy's toolbox, her finger poised near the record button, Verdi began to hum absently. She looked down at the top secret document in the briefcase, wedged between her army boots. She figured she probably had enough on Chalmers Mount with the document and videotape to get him arrested, at least enough to get her over her reluctance to call Witherspoon and surface from hiding. But Kendall Holmes was still out there free, as was the man with the blowgun, Lorna's killer. She had nothing on them yet, but she was hopeful.

If Verdi had succeeded in unhinging Mount just a little bit, he might be a cooperative little suspect. She was certain Holmes was behind Mount's treason and Holmes wouldn't be as easy to nail as Mount. No doubt he and the others in the Circle were well protected. And Lorna's killer, she might have his name, but she wasn't sure. Verdi wanted to get him too, as much as she wanted to bring down the others. Mount was the key. If he fell, the others would follow.

Verdi suddenly recognized the tune she'd been humming and started singing it softly:

> Round and round the mulberry bush
> The monkey chased the weasel
> The monkey thought it all in fun—

Suddenly the door to the house swung open and Mount burst through it. Verdi seized the camcorder and began taping. Mount slammed the door behind him, not bothering to lock it. Verdi kept the lens on wide angle, sacrificing a tight shot of Mount's face, contorted in terror, for a clean view of him running down the walk to his car, the brown mailer in hand. Fumbling with his keys, he got the car door open and jumped inside. The BMW roared off in a cloud of exhaust.

Verdi shut off the camcorder and leaned back against the wall of the van. She drew in a deep breath and let it out. "Pop goes the weasel," she said.

CHAPTER
★ THIRTY-SEVEN ★

The Fifth District police station looked even worse at night than during the day, Kate Verdi decided. Bare fluorescent lights cast ghastly shadows across the pocked walls and revealed shredded cobwebs dangling in corners. A wall clock with a film of grime across its face ticked loudly above the head of Detective Clarence Witherspoon, who sat across the desk from her, his eyes averted.

Witherspoon was playing with a corner of one of the Chalmers Mount photos Verdi had taken. He'd seen all the other pictures, watched the video, and made her go through the whole story with him, from beginning to end. Verdi had even shown him the classified report. But he was still skeptical of her story.

"One thing I don't understand," Witherspoon said, putting the photo down, "is why you didn't go to the FBI. They handle espionage. I'm a homicide detective."

Verdi shook her head. "I told you, I don't know who to trust. For all I know, these people have contacts in the FBI. They seem to have contacts everywhere else. Besides, there are at least three homicides here: Patricia Van Slyke, Brian Porter, and Lorna Demeritte. Then there are the mysterious disappearances."

Witherspoon read from a notepad in front of him. "The mother and daughter of Patricia Van Slyke, Chester Lundquist." He looked at her. "If they're dead too, these are some busy people we're dealing with. You think they might have gotten Jimmy Hoffa too?"

Verdi glared at him. "Don't ridicule me."

Witherspoon leaned forward, almost out of his chair. "But you haven't shown me one scrap of evidence that connects the people you're accusing to those murders. Miss Verdi, for days I've had cops all over this city looking for you. I didn't know what was going on. You drop out of sight, call me up at home, and hang up on me before you can tell me anything. And now you show up here, out of the blue—"

"I told you about Lorna Demeritte and the man there who tried to kill me. Didn't you find anything at her apartment?"

He shook his head slowly. "No, nothing. We found suitcases packed, a passport, and a plane ticket to Mexico City, but no sign of Demeritte. In fact, every indication is that she was fleeing the country, maybe putting her in with your friend Mount. She's been listed as a missing person. Tell you the truth, I'm this close to picking up the phone and calling the FBI."

"What about the killer?"

Witherspoon picked up a pen and began doodling.

"Andrea, you said his name was, right? Tell me again how you got it."

Verdi sat back in her chair and folded her arms. "About a week ago I was in Mount's and Holmes's office, after hours, looking up files on the Circle. Two men came in, and I hid under a desk. I never saw their faces, but one called the other by his name, Andrea, or something like that. I had the distinct impression they were bad guys working for Holmes."

Witherspoon exhaled loudly. " 'Distinct impression,' huh? Well, we're checking him on the computer. And you can give a description to a sketch artist. He'll be here in the morning."

"The *morning*? You're not going to do anything, are you?"

"Of course I will. But if I call the FBI, I want to have my ducks in a row. Plus, I'm not likely to see much more of you after they get into the act."

Verdi took in a breath. "About five days ago I was in the State cafeteria when one of the members of the Circle—"

"Those are the alleged conspirators, right?"

"Yeah, her name is Alexandra Rhys-Shriver, the one who replaced Patricia Van Slyke. She introduced me to someone, name of Wade, who is in our Office of Counterintelligence. Don't you see? They were recruiting him to the Circle. For all I know, he's a card-carrying member by now. And you can bet he has contacts at the FBI, people who'd call him right away if you were to turn me in."

Anger flashed on Witherspoon's face. "No one is turning you in, Miss Verdi. There are some very real jurisdictional issues here. If I were to follow this up with you, I could blow the case completely. I think this Mount person should be picked up. Maybe we can get him to corroborate your story."

"Fat chance," she muttered. The adrenaline was ebbing from Verdi's veins, and she felt tired, defeated. To have come all this way, risking so much . . .

Witherspoon saw the despair in her face and felt sorry for her. He didn't even need to see the desperation to feel sympathy toward her. Katherine Verdi, with her badly dyed hair and greasy combat clothes, looked pitiful enough.

"All right," he said. "Let's look at your video one more time."

Verdi looked at him. "Why?"

"To give me time to think of a reason not to call the FBI," he answered.

He rewound the tape and hit the play button. After ten seconds of static the tape began with Mount pulling up along the country road, a couple of yards in front of the picnic table. Using a remote, Witherspoon paused the tape.

"Now, where were you shooting this from?" he asked.

"About twenty yards up the road, from on top of the van."

"On top of it? How come he didn't see you?"

"I was behind a tall thicket."

Witherspoon was quiet for a moment. "Since we're on the subject, how is it he didn't see you tailing him? You said you followed him from Cleveland Park out to Indian Head Highway by way of the beltway, right? Have you had any training at State?"

Verdi almost laughed. "I was lucky. I almost lost him a couple times. I guess nobody suspects a step van."

Shaking his head, obviously dissatisfied at her answers, Witherspoon started the tape rolling again. Verdi rubbed her temples, trying to work some circulation to her brain. She needed it right now. She didn't know what else to tell Witherspoon except the truth. But she realized the more she tried to explain what had happened, the more fantastic her story sounded, even to her.

On the tape Mount was out of the sedan, walking toward the trash can with the package in his hands. He lifted the lid, dropped in the package, and put the lid back on. He trudged back to the sedan and got in. The camera panned over the car and back to Mount just as he drove away.

Verdi had forgotten to release the record button while she was taping, and the camcorder picked her up as she walked out to the trash can to retrieve the document. Watching herself on the tape, Verdi had a hard time believing she was really the punk with the spiky hair and combat fatigues. There was a jump in the tape before the next scene, the car arriving with the Asian men. As she followed the sequence of the man picking up the package, Verdi squinted, trying to determine his nationality. She was almost certain he was Chinese. The car drove off, and the screen turned to snow.

"Hmm," Witherspoon purred. "Hold on a second."

Using the remote, he rewound the tape, everyone moving backward in jerky motions, like Keystone Kops in reverse. When he got to the part where Mount dropped the package into the trash can, Witherspoon hit the play button again.

Verdi looked over as Witherspoon stood up and leaned over the desk, his face inches from the screen. He stared intently as Mount returned to the sedan and climbed back in, and the camera panned across the sedan from bumper to bumper.

"That's it," Witherspoon said abruptly, fumbling with the remote. He pressed the rewind button for a second, returning the tape to the point at which Mount climbed into his car. Then he pushed the super slow button, advancing the action frame by frame. It seemed to take forever for the camera to make its way from one end of the car to the other. When it reached the rear bumper, Witherspoon was ready with the remote and pressed pause, freezing the frame.

Verdi watched as Witherspoon's face came right up against the screen. His eyes narrowed, and his mouth came up in a faint smile.

"Come here," he whispered. Verdi inched up next to him on the desk. "Read that license plate to me."

Verdi had to focus her eyes, the frozen frame jittery on the TV monitor. "Um, looks like official District tags, number S-8-4-0-4. Hmm, I never noticed that before. Is it important?"

Witherspoon kept his eyes fixed on the screen. "It is now," he said.

* * *

Having showered and changed into an outfit a female detective lent her, Verdi felt almost human again. She didn't have a chance to dye her hair back, but at least it was clean. She joined Witherspoon back at his desk, where four other detectives were milling around, obviously discussing her case.

"The consensus here," Witherspoon said, spotting her coming, "is that it's a miracle you're still alive."

"Is that right?" Verdi said, smiling. "How nice to be the subject of public discussion."

The detectives chuckled. One of them, a slender young black man named Abernathy who was sitting on top of a desk, said, "You know, if you hadn't been so clever in losing me that night, we would have Lorna Demeritte's killer in custody."

Verdi looked at him. "You mean that was *you* in the gray car?" she said, indignant. "And at Dumbarton Oaks as well?"

"Dumbarton Oaks was me," said a white detective in a maroon Washington Redskins jacket.

"I don't believe this," Verdi said. "Here I am trying to convince you of this story when all along you've been following me like a bunch of—"

Witherspoon held up his hands. "Wait, wait. Miss Verdi, let me ask you something. Has anyone else besides us seen this tape?"

Verdi shrugged. "I'm not sure."

"Come again?"

"I forgot to tell you. I put a copy in Chalmers Mount's door this afternoon. While I watched from the van, he picked it up, went inside, and came charging out a few minutes later with the package. I assume *he* saw it, but beyond him, I don't know. I have some footage of him I took from the van, if you're interested."

Witherspoon and the detectives were staring at her. "Why?" was all Witherspoon could say.

"Why did I give him the tape? To flush him out, get him to make a mistake by believing that others in the Circle were out to get him. He also heard I was plotting against him on the phone. Detective, he's our best shot at nailing these people."

"Do you have any idea how dangerous that was? What if he'd seen you in that van? He could have—"

"But he didn't. It was a calculated risk."

Witherspoon stepped toward her, a stern look on his face. She imagined he used it on his daughter when she brought home somebody he didn't approve of. "Miss Verdi, your detective days are over as of this minute. With that license plate we have enough probable cause to bring in Mount for questioning. You can go home if you wish or enter protective custody."

Verdi groaned. "Don't you see? The big fish, Kendall Holmes, will get away if you drag Mount in now. Holmes is untouchable unless you come up with solid evidence on him."

"This Chalmers Mount sounds like an easy mark," Witherspoon said. "If we bring him in here, shake him up, he'll give us your Kendall Holmes and all the rest of them."

"No, he won't talk," Verdi protested. "He's more

afraid of them than of you. They murder people, re-member? And for all you know, he didn't order any of those murders. Oh, he probably was in on them, but all he has to do is clam up and you end up with zip."

"But—"

"Why *should* he talk? With good lawyers behind him, Mount will plead down on the espionage charge. And you can bet money the Circle will have closed ranks, even scattered to the four winds. That'll leave Kendall Holmes and the rest of them free, Mount in some country club prison for a few months, and you're still with how many unsolved murders on your hands? And just wait until Lorna Demeritte's wealthy, influential parents demand a full investigation of their daughter's disappearance."

Witherspoon and the other detectives stood quietly, subdued. Witherspoon scowled, clearly unhappy with losing the upper hand. "So what do you suggest?"

Verdi took a step toward him. "Let me call Mount, arrange a meeting with him tonight. Put a wire on me and let me meet him. The state he's in right now, he'll divulge something you can get him on later. All we need for him to do is implicate Kendall Holmes in the espionage, if not the murders."

Abernathy, the slender detective, spoke up. "This Mount, he knows you videotaped him, right?"

"He'll assume that," Verdi said.

"So what's to stop him from trying to kill you?"

"I frankly don't believe he's capable," she said.

"Anyone is capable," Witherspoon said. "Especially this crowd you're running with."

Verdi remembered something she'd brought in from the van. It was the dart Lorna's killer had shot at her, still in the handkerchief she'd put it in after pulling it from the briefcase. She placed it on Witherspoon's desk.

"What's this?" he said, unfolding the handkerchief.

"Be careful with it," she said. "It's evidence, and there might still be poison on it."

Witherspoon studied the dart, holding it carefully with the handkerchief. "This is what you claim the killer shot at you?"

Holding her temper at Witherspoon's persistent skepticism, Verdi said nothing. He handed the dart to the detective in the Redskins jacket. "All right," he said. "Boyko, run this down to the lab and come right back."

Boyko left, and Witherspoon began pacing. "What choices do I have here? Not many. The Brian Porter case was nowhere until you came along. Now I'm looking at multiple homicides, espionage, and God knows what else. Before this goes any further, I have to talk to my captain."

Verdi nodded. At that moment something came back to her: the incident that morning with the woman in the red Trans Am. Verdi wondered what had happened to her, whether the goons had ever let her go once they realized their mistake. As nasty as the woman was, she didn't deserve to be abducted like that. Verdi had forgotten to tell Witherspoon about her. What was her name?

"Tawna," Verdi mumbled. "Shit."

Witherspoon cocked his ear toward her. "What was that?"

"Uh, there's one other thing I didn't tell you about."

Witherspoon rolled his eyes. "Do I want to hear this?"

CHAPTER
★ THIRTY-EIGHT ★

One hour later Verdi was seated in a swivel chair bolted into the floor of a D.C. police van, parked at the corner of Twenty-first Street and Virginia Avenue, in sight of the State Department building. The van was used for surveillance, mostly for drug investigations. Listening and recording equipment was built into a console on the walls, green and red lights winking in the dim light.

Verdi sat patiently as a police technician named Myers fixed a wire inside the jacket, part of the ensemble on loan to her by a female detective. Across from her in another seat, Clarence Witherspoon was restless, adjusting and readjusting the settings on his walkie-talkie.

"I would keep the jacket buttoned," Myers said, sliding back on one knee and examining his work. "That will keep the wire more stable."

"Is it ready?" Witherspoon asked.

"Go ahead," Myers said, flipping a switch on the console.

"How's it sound out there?" Witherspoon said quietly, testing the wire for pickup.

A voice crackled through the walkie-talkie. "Loud and clear."

"Same here," said another.

Witherspoon turned back to Verdi, his face intense with concentration. "You have any idea why Mount insisted you meet in the State Department?"

Verdi shook his head. Her telephone conversation with Mount at his office had not left much room for questions. He spoke rapidly and sometimes unintelligibly, and his tone swung sharply from accusatory to hostile to enraged. When Verdi meekly suggested they meet, Mount laid into her, calling her every name in the book, including traitor, which she found ironic. Suddenly out of nowhere his manner changed to a disquieting calm, and he was almost civil in agreeing to see her at eight.

Witherspoon cleared his throat, obviously intending to snap Verdi out of her thoughts. "It's too bad the meeting's inside the building. Apart from the jurisdictional conflicts in entering a federal facility, we won't be able to cover you there. We'll have to wait outside unless you run into any problems."

Witherspoon drew in a breath. "OK, this is it. There are two unmarked police vehicles parked within fifty feet of the D Street entrance. Six plainclothes detectives, including me, will be standing by. I also had one detective suit up in a D.C. police uniform, in case we have to rush the building and identify ourselves to the guard.

"While you're inside, we'll hear everything you and Mount say and record it as evidence. But remember we won't be able to communicate with you. In the event we have to go in, I will notify the assistant district attorney, who will immediately call State Department security. He will also call the FBI.

"One other thing: There are to be no heroics here. You just go in, meet with Mount, and do what you can to get him to implicate Holmes and anyone else. If Mount doesn't talk, you leave. Got it?"

Verdi nodded gamely, trying her best to hide her shaking hands. She picked up a briefcase Witherspoon had lent her to make her look businesslike and hid her hands behind it. The jacket felt funny, as if it were riding up in the back, and Verdi moved a hand around to adjust it. She almost gasped out loud when she discovered that the .38 Special she'd hidden inside her belt was showing. She casually pulled down the jacket and turned toward Witherspoon.

"So your captain bought my story?" she said, a little too brightly, she thought.

Witherspoon looked at her. "Not until we sent detectives over to your apartment and saw the people waiting outside it, like you said."

"When did you do that?"

"While you were on the phone with Mount and later when you went to the van to get your purse."

Verdi nodded and, thinking of something else, asked, "Did you find anything on Andrea, or whatever his name is?"

Witherspoon shook his head. "We have a line on all federal employees. His name never came up."

An uncomfortable silence fell over the van. Verdi moved toward the edge of her seat. "Is it time yet?" she said.

Witherspoon glanced at his watch. "It's a little early. Whenever you're ready."

"I'm ready," she said. Witherspoon unlocked the door and pushed it open. She was almost out the door when Witherspoon's hand gently encircled her forearm, stopping her in her tracks. His face was inches from hers.

"No funny business, now, Kate," he said softly. "If he doesn't talk, you leave. Right?"

Verdi looked at him, feeling his strength and integrity washing over her like a warm shower. For a second she thought of Nonno. "Right," she said.

The night air was a tonic on her skin as she stepped out onto the sidewalk. She took in a deep breath and let it out, dragon's breath dissolving into the black sky. Looking up, Verdi felt her breath catch in her throat. The State Department building seemed right on top of her, looming massively and forbiddingly like a fortress across two full city blocks. Somewhere in there Chalmers Mount was waiting for her. Verdi hurried on toward the entrance, her hand tight around the handle of the briefcase.

Entering the vast D Street entrance, Verdi felt waves of anxiety rolling over her. The place seemed dead, the sound of her heels ringing off the marble walls. The lone guard on duty, a young black man stuck with the late shift, stood up as she approached. She handed him her State Department badge and hoisted her briefcase up under her arm, subtly communicating to him she was here for business. He studied the badge for an unusually long time, glancing up at her and back again to the ID photo.

Perspiration began to form above her lip. Her thoughts riveted on the revolver now digging into her back. She'd remembered there were no metal detectors on the employee entrances, only those for visitors. But maybe the guard would see the gun as she went through, or there were other detectors concealed somewhere else the gun would set off.

Something about her conversation with Chalmers Mount—his sudden change of demeanor in agreeing to meet—had troubled her, prompting her to bring the gun. Verdi feared a trap, so she'd slipped out of the police station under the pretense of getting her purse to retrieve the gun from the step van. Now she was beginning to regret bringing the damn thing; it could very well end up getting her into even more trouble than she was already in.

Finally, after what seemed like hours, the guard handed Verdi her badge. "You changed your hair," he said. "Makes you look different."

"Thanks," was all she could think of to say, and hurried into the building. She turned a corner toward an elevator bank but thought better of it. She didn't want to be seen now, especially by anyone she knew.

She saw an exit sign at the end of the corridor. As she walked toward it, she spoke softly into the hidden microphone. "I'm inside the building, heading up to

Career Development and Assignments. Hope you can hear this." She opened the door to the stairwell and began to climb the steps to the second floor, where she would wait for Chalmers Mount.

Outside in the van Witherspoon nodded silently as he heard Verdi's first communication directly for him. He was mildly comforted by the fact that she was thinking about him while she was in there. He hoped she would keep it that way, even if it meant only telegraphic messages to him while she was with Mount.

Verdi was smart, he thought, but was she smart enough to stay out of trouble? Her record in that department wasn't great so far. She'd been lucky not to get herself killed while collecting evidence against Mount. The whole bunch of them, including experienced professionals, were out looking for her now. Had been for days. She'd slipped past all of them, but just barely.

Witherspoon, who didn't care for most people he met, especially on the job, liked Katherine Verdi. He liked her from the first minute he met her. Sure, she was a head turner without making any big deal about it, and she was intelligent, well mannered. But there was also a toughness he recognized—not the showy bravado of the street punks he saw—but a strength of character. It had been that way with Rico. Witherspoon had seen something in him and trusted it.

For Witherspoon, it wasn't just that he had such meager alternatives in the Brian Porter case that he had to go along with Verdi's plan to trap Mount. He had to know that Verdi could pull it off. There were detectives he'd worked with he wouldn't trust as much as he trusted her. It might very well be his career he was putting on the line here. But Verdi was putting her life on the line in trusting him. He never forgot that.

Listening through the walkie-talkie, Witherspoon could hear Verdi's footsteps as she ascended the stairs. That was smart of her, using the stairs. The footsteps stopped, and he heard a door opening.

Without being aware of it, he reached inside his jacket and touched the holstered TEC-9 automatic he'd borrowed from another detective. He rarely used a TEC, a weapon of choice of the drug dealers and gang bangers. But tonight he didn't know what he was dealing with inside the State Department building. He hoped he wouldn't need it.

Before entering the dark second-floor corridor, Verdi used the stairwell light to check her watch: 7:38. Her appointment with Mount was for eight. She'd gotten what she hoped for, an opportunity to get inside the building, to poke around a bit before having to deal with him. Now all she needed was for Mount and Witherspoon to stay out of the way for a while. Witherspoon would be easier to handle than Mount.

Verdi took two tentative steps before crossing the path of a photoelectric cell built into the wall. She jumped as the corridor was suddenly bathed in light, blinding her momentarily. At least now she could find the Career Development and Assignments office, she thought.

Verdi followed the corridor, designated with a red stripe, and recalled the four-number sequence on the doors: The first digit is the floor, the second the corridor, and the third and fourth are the room numbers. She was looking for room 2328. Turning left into one corridor, and then right into another, Verdi noticed that the light switched on ahead of her, allowing just enough time for her to reach the next corridor, about one minute.

The door to the Foreign Service Career Development and Assignments office was unlocked when Verdi finally found it. She spoke into the microphone. "OK, I'm in the office, but there's no sign of him. I'll just sit tight here until he shows up."

Inside the office everything was dark except for a light in a corner office. Chalmers Mount. Using the dim red light from the exit sign, Verdi pulled open the drawer files built into the wall until she came to the alphabetical listings beginning with "AN." Flipping through, she found two files with the name "Andreas." One was a consular officer in Nairobi, the other a Foreign Service secretary in Uzbekistan.

Maybe he's not Foreign Service, Verdi almost said aloud.

She snatched up the briefcase and carefully picked her way around desks and cubicles to Chester Lundquist's office. His computer made noises when she started it up. Fearful Mount might hear her, Verdi counted to one hundred before continuing. From the briefcase she drew the Tabard Inn coaster with the entry commands, as well as the Foreign Service personnel audit reports for Kendall Holmes and Chalmers Mount she'd printed out.

In observing Chet call up Patricia Van Slyke's file,

Verdi learned how to search the personnel file. It was fairly simple to do, requiring only two commands. She noticed that when Chet searched Van Slyke's name, the computer went to a list of all the State employees' names similar to hers. She tried the same thing, this time using the name Andrea.

Within seconds a row of names, beginning with Andreas, flashed on the computer monitor. Verdi recognized the names of the two Foreign Service personnel she had found in the drawer files. She skipped those and scrolled down, checking the files for each similar name. She scanned through each one, but none seemed right. Where was the killer's résumé?

Verdi got all the way down to Atherton before giving up. She sat back, rubbing her eyes, commanding her brain to work harder. There was something she'd seen in one of the early command screens, a prompt for active or inactive files. She'd always hit active when entering the system. What if she tried inactive?

She went back to the command screen and called up the inactive file. She said a little prayer of thanks that the search commands were the same for the inactive files as for the active ones and called up Andrea. Again she got a list, and again she scrolled down, checking the file for each name that was remotely similar. Five names down the list she came to one for Andreen, Dolph. She called up the file.

The first thing she checked was the current and past assignments section, listing positions in reverse chronological order. Andreen had been a regional security officer, assigned to protect embassies and other foreign federal installations. His first job was in Vientiane, Laos, in 1972, followed by a slew of Asian postings, interspersed with the usual Washington tours. His last post was Manila, 1989.

Something about Andreen's assignment history gnawed at her, but she couldn't fathom what it could be. It was a little odd that he resigned before reaching retirement age. Maybe he went into corporate security, trying to make a little money while he still could. Or maybe he found some other source of income.

Reading further, she saw that Andreen was single with no dependents, and his legal residence was given as Topeka, Kansas. He'd graduated from Kansas State in 1965, had served in the military, and had additional special agent training during his Washington tours. He'd been awarded several citations and was rated as having native ability, the highest tested level, in French and Vietnamese.

Native-speaking Vietnamese. Verdi looked again but didn't see any postings in Vietnam. How would he achieve native fluency without spending time there? Then she realized: Andreen must have seen military duty there during the war. The PAR didn't give his branch of the military, but Verdi guessed Green Berets or some other part of the Special Forces that required a command of the local language. She thought of the many skills he'd have picked up in the Special Forces: warfare, demolition, sabotage.

Verdi's head went up when she heard what she thought was a sound from the outer office. Checking her watch, she saw she still had ten minutes before her meeting with Mount. She sat silently for many seconds before taking out the performance audit reports she'd printed out for Kendall Holmes and Chalmers Mount.

She held up Holmes's PAR to Andreen's on the computer screen, clicking down his many assignments. *Look at that.* There were no fewer than three matches in tours and posts where Holmes and Andreen served together: Washington, Tokyo, Beijing. Each time the overlap was for exactly the same period. Next, she held up Mount's PAR and checked his assignments against Andreen's. The blood in her veins surged as she read. *Mount, Holmes, and Andreen were in three embassy postings at exactly the same times.*

Verdi sat back in the chair and folded her arms, staring at the computer screen shimmering in the darkness. She thought of Lorna Demeritte's killer, the same man she'd seen at Patricia Van Slyke's funeral. She thought of his dark, menacing eyes, misshapen nose, and large hands. Dolph Andreen.

"The hit man," she whispered.

Verdi could not enjoy her discovery. Something nagged at her, a small reference in Dolph Andreen's assignments list. His last posting was Manila, from 1989 to 1991. Why was that important? She quickly printed Andreen's PAR, shut off the computer, and tucked all her papers into the briefcase. She stood up and quietly left Lundquist's office, heading back to the drawer files in the outer office. Everything she needed to know would be right there.

Clarence Witherspoon strained to hear from his walkie-talkie. Verdi had said something, her first words since telling him she was on her way to the office. But it was spoken so softly, and had come and gone so quickly, he wasn't sure if he'd heard right.

He spoke into the walkie-talkie to the other detectives. "Anyone hear what she just said?"

"Sounded like 'shit, man,' " one of them answered. Witherspoon recognized Abernathy's voice.

"No," Witherspoon growled. "I heard 'hit man.' "

"Maybe," Boyko said from the other car, "but what are those noises I keep hearing?"

Witherspoon shook his head. "I don't know." He'd been hearing the beeps and clicks and had assumed they were office noises. Now he wasn't so sure.

"Detective," said Myers, sitting at the console, "they sound like someone's operating a computer."

"Operating a computer? Now why would she be doing that?" Witherspoon held the walkie-talkie close to his mouth. "All right, stand by and be ready to go in at my signal. Keep your sidearms holstered. Myrick in the uniform goes in first. We'll have to give the guard a chance to talk to his commanding officer before letting us in. And remember to keep those floor plans of the building handy, in case we need to get somewhere fast."

Witherspoon sat back, the tension making his neck itch. *What was Kate Verdi doing in there? Why was she taking so long?* He checked his watch and turned toward Myers, the technician. "Get the assistant district attorney on the line," he said.

CHAPTER
★ THIRTY-NINE ★

Leaning on a personnel file drawer in the outer office, Kate Verdi felt her cheeks burn, and she blinked back tears. The faint light of the exit sign above her cast a crimson glow on Dolph Andreen's folder, which Verdi had left on top of the open files. Next to Andreen's folder was one labeled "Wheeler, J. Harcourt, IV."

Verdi heard breathing behind her and spun around to see the crooked smile of Chalmers Mount, a gun in his hand that was pointed at her eyes. He raised a finger to his lips, gesturing with his head toward the door. Verdi heard a shuffling noise in the corridor outside—a guard—and then watched as the doorknob turned slowly. Mount slowly brought his free hand up to the gun, ready should the guard come in. But he didn't, and Mount gestured with his gun toward his office. As Verdi moved in that direction, he picked up the two folders on top of the files and pushed the drawer shut.

"Find what you're looking for?" Mount said, closing the door behind him. Verdi looked at him. He was all dressed up in black tie. Then she remembered tonight was the big reception to which Jonathan Rashford had invited her. She'd completely forgotten about it in all the chaos.

He grabbed the briefcase out of her hand and rifled through it. "Where's the report, the one you took from the trash can?"

"I didn't bring it."

He tossed the briefcase into a corner. Verdi scanned the office for the first time. Knickknacks from Mount's travels cluttered the shelf-lined walls: Chinese figurines, minutely painted lacquered Palekh boxes, and wooden nested dolls. Verdi noticed that the faces on the nested dolls had been painted to Mount's likeness. Behind her, on the back of the door, hung a samurai sword with an elaborately carved ivory handle. On the desk, prominently displayed, was a photo of Mount with Kendall Holmes in front of St. Basil's Cathedral.

"A shame," Mount said, rudely appraising her. "You changed your hair color, but you didn't dress for the occasion."

"Black seems to be the right color for the Circle," she snapped back. "You must have to attend a lot of funerals."

Mount shook his head and sat down behind his desk. He looked shaky, distracted. Verdi tried to look through his window to see if the police vans were out there but realized they were parked at the other end of the building.

"So, what do you think you know about the Circle?" he asked.

Verdi studied his gun for the first time. She'd never seen one like it before. The barrel seemed to be split into two, with switches and colored lights on the lower stem. The top stem, where the bullet would come out, was silvery and narrow. She had no doubt the gun could kill her. It was pointed straight at her face.

"I don't know much," she said, "only what Lorna and you told me about it."

Mount slowly waved the gun back and forth, as if he were shaking his head in disbelief. "Oh, come now, Kate. Obviously you know a great deal. But I don't think you're able to put it together."

Verdi shrugged, wanting to appear nonchalant. Through her fear and anger, she tried to think straight, to coax information out of Mount for Witherspoon. "Well, I sure would be interested to know what the Circle had in mind for me."

"Katherine Verdi. A small fish in a very, very large pond. You flatter yourself even wondering about it. You were nothing more than a hedge, an insurance policy, in case other ventures fell through.

"Think of the Circle as a corporation in the service sector. It must diversify to survive. You represented diversification, Kate, nothing more. Your role was to sell entry visas, green cards—access to America—to wealthy foreigners in Europe. Paris, where you were headed, is ideal. It's steady income for the Circle."

"So it's all about money," Verdi said scornfully, hoping he would divulge more.

"Come, come, Kate. Were *you* in it for the money? Think about it. You and everyone else who comes to Washington, do you come here for money? Of course not. Power is the currency here, access. Kendall Holmes gives power in exchange for information. It's that simple."

"They sell their souls for their careers," Verdi said softly. "What does Holmes do with the information?"

"Peddles it to the highest bidder. Or he provides it on spec. Either way, everyone gets what he wants. Like you, for instance. The minute I met you I knew you were made to order for the Circle. A greedy little climber, someone who'd give anything for a crack at the top. Am I right?"

"You're wrong, Chalmers."

"Oh, am I? Then why did you leave that videotape in my door? Ah, you thought I wouldn't find out it was you and Alexandra? You joined the wrong side, Kate."

Verdi decided to take a chance. "It must've been hard for you," she said.

"Huh? What?"

"Helping everyone else—Alexandra, Jonathan—get promotions while you stayed put, doing chores for Kendall Holmes." She could see Mount's eyes darting this way and that, the sweat drooling down the side of his face.

"Someone of your stature reduced to a courier. Did it ever occur to you why Holmes would want to tear down the State Department, the very organization he professed to love?"

Verdi had clearly touched a nerve. "It won't work," Mount said, vainly trying to recover his composure. "Whatever you're trying to do."

"Think about it, Chalmers. Holmes has held nearly every important job a Foreign Service officer could have. Except for one, an ambassadorship. All because he showed up drunk at some reception in Athens way back in the seventies, made a scene in front of the Vice President. Is that fair?"

Verdi watched Mount's eyes as he stared at her in disbelief, trying to focus as he parsed her accusations. The gun quivered in his grip. *Come on*, she thought, *say something that'll put the whole damn bunch of them away*. She wondered if she had enough on the Circle now. Her mind raced, trying to figure a way to tip off Witherspoon about Mount's gun without arousing suspicion. She shivered as she wished Witherspoon were on the way.

In the van Witherspoon hung up the phone and fumbled for his walkie-talkie. It had taken him a while to get the assistant DA on the line, this being a busy Saturday night on his social calendar. Witherspoon did not like having to break off from listening to Verdi, even for a minute. At least he had a full clearance to move on Mount and a call on the way from the DA to State Department security to warn them.

He mashed the walkie-talkie to his ear and listened as Kate Verdi worked on Mount, now beginning to unravel. Witherspoon would give Verdi a little more time before he went inside. Verdi had told him he could get to the second floor in under five minutes, once he was inside. Witherspoon was aware that by rushing inside to Verdi, he might push Mount to do something stupid. If all went well, Verdi would get out of there before Mount pulled anything.

There were a few things Witherspoon heard through the walkie-talkie that gave him pause. Like, what was Mount doing in black tie? Did he have an engagement of some kind this evening? It was possible. Another thing was Verdi's voice. It sounded tight, strained. She was keeping cool, playing Mount for information, but Witherspoon listened carefully, reading between her words for any indication she was in trouble.

"So," Verdi said, gamely trying to keep the conversation going, "Holmes's revenge is to screw over the Foreign Service, to sell off secrets in exchange for good jobs to power-hungry yuppies. It sure doesn't hurt that he pads his pension with the proceeds.

"Correct me if I'm wrong, but Alex helps Mount with the Chinese, giving them whatever information they want. And Jonathan Rashford, he helps out by feeding info to the old KGB factions in the Russian government and maybe the Russian Mafia.

"But sometimes the Circle can't deliver on a client's request. Like when someone stands between the Circle and the information it wants. Someone like Patricia Van Slyke or Brian Porter. Then the Circle bumps them off. Except Andreen got sloppy with Porter, didn't he?"

By the look on Mount's face Verdi knew she was

getting closer to the truth. She also knew the only thing keeping the conversation going was her playing to Mount's arrogance. He stood and came toward her.

"You're not as smart as you think you are," he said, pulling her toward the door and grinding the gun into her back. "In fact, I'm going to tell you how wrong you are. Maybe Patricia Van Slyke did stand between us and that report you stole. Holmes needed it immediately to sell to the Chinese. It was unfortunate, two deaths so close to each other. We worried a lot about that. But Porter was an entirely different situation. You misjudged that completely.

"Porter was one of ours, part of the Circle. But he refused two direct orders from Kendall for information. His death was a mistake. He wasn't supposed to have been killed, only scared into submission."

They were nearing the door to the outer office. Verdi frantically looked around at the desks and files around her for something to distract Mount's attention. She thought about the gun under her jacket. She'd never be able to draw and fire it in time. Her best bet was to buy time, to keep Mount talking.

"And what about Van Slyke? Why did you have her case assigned to me?"

"You still haven't figured it out, have you? That was Lorna's idea. We called her Lorna Doom after that. She was the one assigned to recruit you and was a failure at it. Since Van Slyke was assigned to be killed anyway, Lorna's plan was to set up the cremation as your fault. You would look bad and come to the Circle for help."

Verdi felt sick to her stomach as the whole scheme

became clear to her. "Van Slyke's mother never did call to complain or threaten a lawsuit, did she? That was all done by Winthrop Mudd, that little Circle wannabe. So why did you have Lorna killed?"

Mount's skin looked like dough; his hair was matted with sweat. "Lorna was cracking. Kendall and I even thought it was she who was hacking into the computerized personnel files. But that was you all the time, wasn't it? Lorna was becoming a liability, even a potential traitor to the Circle. Her death was supposed to look like an accident until you came along."

"Lorna a traitor," Verdi spit at him. "That's real good. Ever read Dante, Chalmers, the *Divine Comedy*? He reserved the bottom circle of hell for traitors like you, to be buried over their heads in ice."

"You'll be the first to find out," he said. "And Alex will be right behind you."

Verdi watched as Mount tried to steady the gun and open the door with his free hand. *He's losing it. He could snap at any second. She had to warn Witherspoon.*

"Chalmers, please be careful with that gun. It could go off any—"

Verdi's head snapped back as Mount slapped her with the back of his hand. As she rubbed the sting from her face, he shoved her through the door.

"Let's go to the party," he said.

CHAPTER
★ FORTY ★

Outside in the police van Clarence Witherspoon was sliding open the door and barking orders through his walkie-talkie. "Get Myrick up in front. I want them to see that uniform. The DA's already called State security. Keep your weapons holstered. I want to hear that back."

"Holstered," Abernathy replied.

"Ditto," said Boyko.

Hopping out of the van, Witherspoon saw the detectives scrambling, moving toward the D Street entrance. He kept his walkie-talkie on Kate Verdi's frequency, hoping to find out what was going on and where Chalmers Mount was taking her. By mentioning a gun, Kate Verdi had set everything in motion.

Witherspoon turned back to Myers, the technician, who lifted up one of his headphones to hear him. "When the SWAT team gets here, give them the floor plan and our frequency on the walkie-talkie. This looks like a floating crap game, so I don't know where to tell them to go. Just call me inside and I'll report."

Myers nodded and disappeared behind the steel door as Witherspoon pulled it closed. He quickly joined the other detectives gathered in the shadows around the entrance. "Shields out?" he said. They nodded. "All right, let's go."

With Detective Myrick in uniform leading the way, they entered the building together. The security guard on duty looked up as the six men approached him, his hand moving toward his sidearm. Witherspoon held up his shield. At that moment the guard station telephone rang.

Witherspoon shouted above the ringing. "Clarence Witherspoon, D.C. Homicide. That call is for you, from your commanding officer authorizing us to enter the building and pursue a homicide suspect inside."

"Stay right there," the guard said, and picked up the phone.

Witherspoon held up a hand for the other detectives to stop. Watching as the guard spoke rapidly into the phone, Witherspoon pressed the walkie-talkie to his ear, listening for a clue to where Kate Verdi was going. But there was nothing. He could have missed something, a word from Verdi, while he was scrambling the detectives. He squeezed the walkie-talkie, hoping something would come out.

"All right, you can pass," said the guard.

"Listen," said Witherspoon, rushing up to the guard's desk. "Does your log show a reception or party anywhere in the building for a Chalmers Mount or Kendall Holmes?"

The guard picked up a clipboard and studied it. "No, I don't see anything with those names. I've got to call building security now. Where is your suspect?"

"Second floor," Witherspoon said. "But he may be moving. Where are parties held here?"

The guard shrugged. "Could be almost anywhere. Seventh, eighth floor. And people have parties in conference rooms all over the building."

"Shit," Witherspoon grimaced, and waved for the other detectives to follow. They would have to start at the second floor, at Chalmers Mount's office. Maybe they would find something written down, the location of the party. As he ran for the elevator, Witherspoon glanced over his shoulder at the security guard calling for backup.

CHAPTER
★ FORTY-ONE ★

Up on the eighth floor no one noticed as Chalmers Mount and Kate Verdi inched their way into the huge Benjamin Franklin Room, where the reception was in full swing. Verdi held her breath, believing somehow that breathing might endanger her further. Perspiration stung her eyes, and the unyielding muzzle of Mount's pistol pressed into her back.

As if in a dream, Verdi took in the swirl of tuxedos, gowns, and sparkling jewelry sweeping past her field of vision. She passed tables set with beautiful food, fresh-cut flowers, and champagne. Bright chandelier light blazed in her eyes. She remembered she had been here once before, with Lorna. From somewhere far off she heard piano music: Chopin. She stayed in front of Mount, who pressed her forward with the gun. She fought panic as his hand gripped her arm.

Verdi managed to spot some familiar faces—

Jonathan Rashford, Alexandra Rhys-Shriver, Kendall Holmes—who seemed to float past as if on a merry-go-round. There too were at least fifty other people, many she didn't recognize. Someone screamed, and the music and all conversations stopped as Mount thrust Verdi in front of the face she least wanted to see, Jake Wheeler's.

The color seemed to drain from Wheeler's face into the champagne glass he'd been holding to his lips. Verdi locked her eyes onto his, sickened by his fearful expression.

"Katherine Verdi," Mount said. "Meet J. Harcourt Wheeler the Fourth."

Wheeler stared at her, unable to speak.

Verdi glared back, her rage and shame competing with her will to stay focused on letting Witherspoon know where she was. "I wonder, Jake, what you're the fourth of in your family. The fourth lying little prick? Where did you learn the polka, at Exeter? Now, is that anywhere near Fort Wayne and your mother's hair parlor?"

"Kate, let me—"

"I saw your PAR. How does one work his way through Purdue while attending Harvard, huh? And what did you have to do to work your way up to the Benjamin Franklin Room on the eighth floor, go to bed with me?" She hoped Witherspoon heard that last part.

Mount's voice was in Verdi's ear. "Jake didn't *have* to go to bed with you, but if it helped us recruit you to the Circle when Lorna Demeritte failed, so be it."

All around Verdi, faces were frozen in fear. Kendall Holmes emerged from the crowd and took two cautious steps toward Mount. "Chalmers," he said in a soothing voice, "you did well, bringing Verdi in. Give her to me, and I'll take care of the rest."

Verdi turned toward him. "Oh, sure you will, Holmes. You'll take care of me like you did Brian Porter and Patricia Van Slyke. Did you really believe your bullshit about saving the Foreign Service while you were busy destroying it? Was it all because you showed up drunk at that reception in Athens and never made ambassador? I wonder, will Mount be docked for not getting that secret report to the Chinese?"

The crowd, silent until now, began to buzz nervously. "That was you?" Holmes said, moving toward her.

Mount yanked her back by her hair. "Not just yet, Kendall," he said. "You'll get her. But first there are a few things you need to know. It's Alexandra who's really the traitor. Verdi and she were in on the whole thing from the beginning. They tried to set me up. Down in my office I have proof, a tape of their conversation. Verdi videotaped everything, the dropoff at the picnic table, the pickup by the Chinese. She left it at my—"

"Shut up, Chalmers," Holmes said, stepping closer.

Holmes's voice was quavering, Verdi noticed. She also noticed Alexandra and the others slowly backing away from Mount, who was talking rapidly and wildly waving his gun. She braced herself for a gunshot.

"How could you let her come between us after all these years, all I've done for you? *I'm* the one who has to coddle these idiots and deal with their petty problems. *I'm* the one who wipes their asses. And where were *you*? Fucking Alex in your office? Where is she? I want her to admit it."

"Give me the gun, Chalmers," Holmes said weakly, his face ashen. "Let's talk about it." Verdi watched Holmes's eyes as they jumped from Mount's face to somewhere off behind him.

Verdi felt Mount let go of her as he scanned the room for Alex, his gun out in front of him. Guests screamed and dropped to the floor. Verdi spied Holmes's face again, his eyes twitching, looking past Mount and her. At what? She turned her head slightly, trying to see behind her but afraid to incite the manic Mount.

Suddenly Mount was screaming horribly into Verdi's ear just before something—his elbow, the gun, she didn't know what—cracked her on the base of her skull, sending a shower of stars across her field of vision. The room seemed to pitch, the chandeliers tilting. People were scattering, some rolling on the floor.

Verdi staggered and tried to turn around just as Mount's body fell past her, crashing into a table and a tureen of red caviar. She screamed and jumped back at the sight of Mount, a red-black hole behind his ear. Paralyzed, her eyes fixed on Mount, Verdi tried to think, to decide what to do. She turned to see a face she'd seen before—dark eyes, gnarled nose—two feet away. Dolph Andreen. He was holding a gun on Mount, one with a silencer at the end of it. Verdi moved her hand around her back, under her jacket.

Andreen raised the gun toward Verdi but froze as he looked into the black muzzle of her .38 Special revolver.

"Drop it," Verdi commanded. She was behind Kendall Holmes, her left arm locked around his throat.

Holmes nodded at Andreen, who slowly placed the gun on the floor. As Andreen backed away, Verdi kicked his gun and the Hämmerli under the table where Mount had collapsed. She pointed the .38 at Holmes's temple.

"All right," she said, her eyes sweeping the room, looking for exits. "I'll use this gun if I have to, understand?" Andreen and Holmes nodded. "Good. First, I want some questions answered. Mr. Holmes, I want you to tell me who ordered the murders of Patricia Van Slyke, Brian Porter, and Lorna Demeritte. I also want you to tell me who carried out those orders."

His forehead gleaming with sweat, Holmes scanned the room for help. Except for Andreen, everyone was cowering on the floor. He looked at Alexandra Rhys-Shriver, sobbing uncontrollably into the carpet.

Verdi pressed the muzzle of the .38 into his ear. "For whatever good it will do you," he said, "I ordered the deaths of Van Slyke and Demeritte. Andreen executed those orders. But Brian Porter's death was not my doing. You should have asked Chalmers about him."

"But I'm asking *you*," Verdi snarled, screwing the muzzle into the loose skin below his right eye. She knew she had enough evidence on all of them now. Pretty soon she'd have to figure a way out of here. She thought of Witherspoon. Where the hell *was* he?

Witherspoon and his men were less than twenty yards away in another wing of the eighth floor, racing through the corridors as they desperately tried to find their way to the Benjamin Franklin Room. They were trapped in a maze of hallways that dead-ended into small dining rooms or doors that didn't open.

Witherspoon kept his walkie-talkie pressed to his ear. He listened closely, trying to follow the heated conversation in the Benjamin Franklin Room. Then he realized that *Verdi had a gun on Holmes*. He stopped in front of a floor plan bolted on the wall, and the other detectives rushed up to join him.

"You hearing this?" Witherspoon said, catching his breath. He studied the floor plan, tracing his finger from the You Are Here arrow to the Benjamin Franklin Room. It seemed he'd tried every route already.

Abernathy pressed close. "What the hell is going on?"

"Listen," said Witherspoon. The detectives held their walkie-talkies to their ears. They heard screaming and shouting, some of it Verdi.

"Sounds like she has a gun," Witherspoon said.

Detective Boyko drew the Glock from his shoulder holster. "Where'd she get a gun from?"

"Hell if I know," said Witherspoon.

"Damn," said Abernathy. "Where the fuck is she?"

Witherspoon shook his head. "Right there," he said, his finger on a box on the floor plan.

"But how do we get there?"

"I'm open to suggestions," Witherspoon said dryly. He wished he'd brought someone from State security with him. Maybe he'd run into someone patrolling this floor. But he just couldn't stand around here waiting for one to show up.

"Hey, down here," Myrick, the uniformed detective,

shouted from the other end of the corridor. "I got a door open."

Witherspoon followed the others as they ran after him.

In the ballroom Holmes was holding forth at Verdi's insistence. "Porter wasn't doing his share for the Circle," he said, trembling in Verdi's arm. "Chalmers decided to make a lesson of him, in case anyone else decided to renege. Porter wasn't supposed to be killed, just frightened. But Andreen didn't do it. It was Wheeler. He volunteered. Tell her, Wheeler."

Verdi turned toward Wheeler, who was near the table where Mount lay, his arms covering his head. "He doesn't seem to be his usual witty self," she said. She turned toward Holmes and felt her head throb where Mount had struck her. "Why don't you finish the story?"

"Wheeler was supposed to take Porter out into the country somewhere, down past the dropoff point in southern Maryland. That's where Wheeler was to stage his execution. Porter was sedated—phenobarbital—but he woke up from it before they got out of town. He attacked Wheeler, who shot him and dumped the body."

Verdi kept an eye on Andreen, who was watching her like a cobra. She felt Holmes breathing heavily against her. The revolver was heavy in her hand. "So," she said, "did that little act of bravery earn Jake his membership in the Circle, like some street gang?"

"N-no. He would have been inducted if he'd turned you."

Verdi shook her head, using the chance to check out the service doors in the back of the room. There seemed to be a kitchen back there. Maybe stairs as well. She needled him. "Aw, did I mess things up for you, Jake? You must have had your hopes up for joining the Circle ever since you met Andreen in Manila."

Wheeler kept his face covered.

"I compliment you on your acumen, Kate," Holmes said. "If you'd just put down your gun, maybe we could work things out to our mutual satisfaction."

"Yeah, just like you worked things out with Mount. No, the only talking you're going to do is with the police, who'll be here any minute."

Verdi glanced over her shoulder. The piano player, curled up under the baby grand, was the only person behind her. Beyond him, next to a white marble fireplace, was the door to the kitchen. The waiters were in the back with the kitchen staff. Had they called security? she wondered.

Hearing a sound, Verdi whirled around to see Jake Wheeler lunging for Mount's Hämmerli. "Stop," she screamed. Wheeler ignored her and fumbled with the gun under the table. She fired, splintering a table leg inches from his head. There was screaming all around her. Holmes passed out in her arms and dropped to the floor. From the corner of her eye she saw Andreen rolling over the carpet, reaching for his gun.

Verdi turned and sprinted for the service doors. She was almost there when someone behind her shouted, "Freeze," and a bullet ricocheted off the fireplace. Verdi pushed through the door as another bullet split an oak panel with a loud crack.

She burst into a kitchen—industrial-size refrigerators, ovens, cupboards, all stainless. She tried to think quickly. Could she hide in here and hope they'd pass over her? No, she had to get out. Where? How?

Hearing footsteps rushing up behind her, Verdi ducked down a narrow corridor. Utensils hung overhead; knife handles presented themselves. She kept moving, praying for a door. She looked around for help from the waiters and cooks, but they were all gone. A red exit sign was up ahead, tucked in an alcove. She threw herself at the door, tried to grip the greasy handle.

Verdi heard Jake Wheeler shout, "There she is," just as the door jumped open and she went through it.

Witherspoon listened grimly as the scene in the ballroom played out. He had come to another dead end and had shot the lock off the door, only to end up in a broom closet. He had his men split up and try different routes. He heard gunshots as they blew off locks whenever they dead-ended.

Witherspoon didn't want to be around his detectives as they shot down doors. He stayed in front of the broom closet, listening to the walkie-talkie. He heard Verdi shout, "Stop," and a shot ring out. He guessed it was a .38. Other sounds followed, tinny echoes, as Verdi's high heels clicked rapidly over tile.

More heel clicks over tile and then a man shouting, "There she is." Then a long silence.

"Come on, Kate," Witherspoon urged. "Tell us where you are."

He heard footsteps, different this time. Had she

taken off her shoes? he wondered. Then, like sweet water to Witherspoon's dry lips, he heard Kate Verdi's voice speaking to him.

"Witherspoon," she whispered, the sounds of doors opening and closing filtering through the wire. "I'm in a stairwell, heading down to the fourth floor. Citizens Emergency Center. I don't know what corridor that is, but I know the area. Mount's dead, but I'm OK. Andreen and Wheeler have guns. They're right behind—"

Through the wire, the sound of a door slamming from far away, then another one opening. Then silence. "Fourth floor," Witherspoon shouted as he raced to the elevators. He hoped the others heard him.

CHAPTER
★ FORTY-TWO ★

After giving the message to Witherspoon, Verdi raced down the stairwell, her heels in one hand, the .38 in the other. On the way down she'd opened the door to the seventh floor in the hope that Andreen and Wheeler would take the bait and look for her there.

No such luck. Reaching the fifth floor, she heard the door open on the seventh floor and two sets of heavy footsteps behind her. How did they know so quickly she hadn't entered that floor? There must have been miles of corridors on it. Had she left some clue to tip them off or forgotten to do something that would have kept them there?

Padding down the stairs, almost to the fourth floor, she cocked an ear into the stairwell. Maybe her pursuers would split up or get out on the wrong floor. She found it hard to hear over the sound of blood thumping in her veins. Then she heard a door swing open two floors above her, and the relentless footsteps continued. *Dammit, how do they know?*

Verdi pushed through the fourth-floor fire door and sprinted down the dark corridor. Less than ten yards later the hallway suddenly exploded in white light. Verdi stopped in her tracks. What was going on here?

She turned to see the stairwell door open, and she darted left down a dark corridor. She pulled up almost immediately as she heard a man's voice. Andreen. She crouched in a doorway. Maybe he would leave, she thought, go to another floor.

"All right," she heard him whisper. "She's here somewhere. You go that way, to the end of the hall."

Verdi grimaced and shook her head. *Shit, how did he know? He couldn't have seen me come in here.*

Footsteps approached slowly. Verdi jammed the high heels she'd been carrying into her jacket pockets. She forced herself to concentrate. Andreen knew within seconds that she wasn't on the other two floors, and he knew just as quickly she *was* on this one. What had she done to tip him off?

Light footsteps were coming closer. Verdi held the .38 out in front of her toward the lighted corridor, readying herself. *The lighted corridor.* A thought flew into her head and she tried to capture it. *Of course. He knew I was here because I tripped the corridor light.*

Verdi pressed her back against the door as Jake Wheeler in his black tie suddenly appeared in the light, both hands on Mount's gun in front of him. She held her breath as he peered down the corridor in her direction. She slowly raised her gun until Wheeler was in her sights. He stood there for several seconds and then moved forward down the corridor.

Verdi studied the walls around her, trying to find the photosensitive monitors that activated the lights. She remembered Winthrop Mudd showing them to her up on the seventh floor. They were about waist high, that much she knew. What she didn't know was how far apart they were placed. It was too dark to see anything. The only way to avoid them was to crawl.

On her belly she made her way as quickly as she could over the floor, keeping close to the wall. If Wheeler caught her this way—vulnerable, her back to him—she'd have no chance. From behind her she heard Andreen say, "Check the doors," and then the sound of doorknobs being tested. She knew they would be checking the dark corridors once they'd tried all the doors. She had to get out of here. She tried to get her bearings from the room numbers on the office doors, but it was too dark to see them.

She was looking for another stairwell that led down to the guard station on the first floor. She'd discarded the idea of taking an elevator out of fear the bell would be a signal to Andreen and Wheeler hovering nearby. She thought of speaking to Witherspoon through the wire but couldn't risk it. Her pursuers were too close.

Reaching the end of the corridor, she could only go left. She counted three red exit signs down the left-hand side of the corridor. She kept crawling. One of them had to be a stairwell.

* * *

Andreen and Wheeler had finished checking all the doors on the lighted corridor, not one of them open. They met in the middle of the corridor. "OK," Andreen said, shuffling and reshuffling options in his head. "She probably knows how we're tracking her. We'll split up and cover more ground. She's on this floor, I'm sure of it."

Jake Wheeler was puffing, out of breath. "She said something about the police coming. Maybe we should get out of here."

Andreen shook his head impatiently. "I called the guard station from the eighth floor and told them there was a disturbance on floors one and two—a man with a gun. By now they've sealed off those floors and are searching them. I estimate we have about ten minutes before security or D.C. SWAT gets here, even if Verdi came with the police. We'll shoot her and ditch her body. There must be hundreds of places to hide it on this floor."

"Verdi's office is on this floor," Wheeler said. "You think she's hiding there?"

"Check it out," Andreen said. "Stay alert."

Flat on her belly, her cheek sliding on the cold granite floor, Verdi was coming up on the second of the three exit signs. The first had been an elevator. She was hoping, praying the next one would be a stairwell. Once inside, she could tell Witherspoon where she was.

Three feet from the sign she had to keep herself from screaming when the lights came on in the corridor. On all fours, she scrambled into the elevator bank alcove. She stood and peered out of the alcove at the corridor behind her. No one. Who tripped the light? Whoever it was would soon be on her.

Across the corridor Verdi saw "4813" on the door. It was an entrance to the Citizens Emergency Center, her office! She felt her pockets for her keys and remembered they were in her purse, in Mount's office. *Damn.* She looked again and saw that the door was ajar. Why would it be open? She checked the corridor one more time and dashed through the door into her office.

Verdi felt her way through the outer office suite, past Calamity John's office, his secretary's desk. She moved quickly toward her own office and a phone. She had to reach Witherspoon, find out where he was. He needed to know where she was as well. A sound from behind her, and Verdi whirled, the .38 out in front.

"Miss Verdi?" said a figure in the darkness.

"Who is it?" she said, the words sticking in her throat.

"Boris Kubanyi, your colleague." He stepped forward, and Verdi could make out the gaunt outline and then the cadaverous face. "What's wrong, Miss Verdi? Why do you have a gun?"

She raised the .38 at his head. She would shoot him if she had to. "Don't come any closer."

"But what is wrong?" he asked, spreading his arms as if to declare his innocence. "I mean you no harm."

"Just stay back, Mr. Kubanyi. I'm warning you."

"Everything's fine, I assure you." He took a step toward her and held out his hand. "Why do you—"

"No!" Verdi heard herself shout as gunfire cracked

from the shadows behind him. Kubanyi's chest seemed to explode, drenching Verdi in a shower of warm blood and bits of flesh. Kubanyi fell onto her, blood gushing from his chest. She pushed him away and saw yellow flare in the darkness, another shot. She saw Jake Wheeler running in a crouch toward the outer door and fired at him but missed.

Crawling on hands and knees, Verdi inched her way through the shadows, searching for cover from Jake; a file cabinet, a desk. She ducked into an open office and pulled herself up onto her knees. Training her ears for any sound, Verdi heard nothing. And then, from somewhere far off, gunshots. Three of them, two and then one. Witherspoon.

Decision time, Katherine. Stay here, trapped near a dead man, or keep moving? A dead man. How many were there now?

She slid along the wall and found a doorway to the corridor, now dark again. What had happened to Wheeler? Gone, but where? Verdi wanted to find a safe place to talk to Witherspoon, to let him bring her in. She knew there was a stairwell near here—she used it all the time—but she was too disoriented to find it. The smell of blood in her hair and on her skin was beginning to sicken her.

Back into her belly crawl, Verdi could hear distant shouts but didn't recognize the voices. She was at a corner. Where could she go from here? How close was the stairwell? She heard footsteps in the dark behind her, and she jumped around the corner just before the lights came on again. Looking up, Verdi saw signs for men's and women's rest rooms. She burst into the women's room and went immediately into the last stall, closing the door behind her. She stood up on the toilet seat, balancing on her stocking feet and keeping her head below the top of the door.

Seconds later she heard the rest room door open and someone enter. Verdi gritted her teeth at the sounds of footsteps approaching, someone yanking open the stall doors one by one. She eased back the hammer on the .38 and aimed it at the door. *Come through and you're history.* The stall door next to hers swung open, and shoe leather slid over tile, closer.

She heard the rest room door open again and someone else enter and say, "Frank, let's move. Bokyo just saw someone running down the hall."

They left, and Verdi tried to catch her breath. Boyko: She knew that name. One of Witherspoon's detectives. Then she realized she'd come that close to shooting a cop.

Verdi began to speak into the wire, to give Witherspoon her location. Suddenly more shots were fired, much closer this time. Then complete silence. *What is going on out there?*

Verdi cleared her throat and spoke down into the wire. "Witherspoon, it's Verdi. I'm in the women's bathroom on corridor 4300, right in front of the Citizens Emergency Center. Your detectives were just here. I'll be in the last stall, waiting."

Relieved to have sent the message, Verdi nestled her chin on her knees and listened intently. Outside in the corridor it was deathly still. She tried to recall how many shots had just been fired but couldn't. This didn't feel right to her: the exchange of gunfire and then lingering silence. Where was the SWAT team, the FBI? *Why is it so goddamn quiet out there?*

Perched on top of the toilet seat, Verdi began rocking nervously on the balls of her feet, her mind racing. A thought was forming, one so terrible that she wanted to suppress it before it became any more real.

CHAPTER
★ FORTY-THREE ★

In a stairwell about twenty yards away from where Verdi was hiding, Jake Wheeler stood triumphantly over Clarence Witherspoon, pointing the detective's TEC-9 at his chest. "Any more of these you got on you?" Wheeler said.

Witherspoon said nothing, looking away and clutching at his arm as blood leaked through his fingers. Wheeler had clipped him back in the corridor, grazing him with a shot as he came around a dark corner. On the floor next to Witherspoon lay Detective Abernathy, unconscious with two rounds in his chest where Andreen had shot him. Blood from Witherspoon and Abernathy mingled on the stairwell platform and seeped down the stairs in steady drips.

"Check him," said Andreen, who was pointing his Walther at Witherspoon's face.

Wheeler knelt over Witherspoon and patted him

down at the ankles, inseam, and belt line. Wheeler
smiled and pulled out a Glock 17 holstered behind
Witherspoon's back. "Just lost your insurance policy,"
Wheeler said.

Andreen held up a hand for Wheeler to be quiet and
pointed at the walkie-talkie propped up against a wall
next to him. "Witherspoon," said the voice from the
walkie-talkie, "it's Verdi. I'm in the women's bathroom on corridor 4300, right in front of the Citizens
Emergency Center. Your detectives were just here. I'll
be in the last stall, waiting."

Wheeler smiled again. "You called that one right,
Dolph."

Andreen nodded once, his eyes fixed on Witherspoon, who was staring back. "You see her, shoot her,"
Andreen said.

"Right," said Wheeler, sliding the Glock into his belt
and checking the magazine on Witherspoon's TEC-9.
"How many rounds this carry?"

"Thirty-two, nine millimeter."

"More than plenty."

Wheeler slipped through the steel fire door and
moved soundlessly down the hall. He was careful,
alert for anything. It didn't worry him that he was trip-
ping the corridor lights. He wanted to see what was
going on around him. There were still some policemen
on the floor, and Kate Verdi had already shown her
ability with a gun. If anything moved, he'd shoot it on
sight.

As he worked his way, Wheeler checked the signs
posted on the walls. He was on corridor 4, a yellow
stripe running along its length. The women's room

Kate Verdi was in was straight ahead on corridor 3, marked with a red stripe.

Checking blind corners both ways, Wheeler entered the red corridor, already seeing the women's and men's rooms up ahead. Silently he came up on the door to the women's and lightly rested an ear against it. No sound. He prepared himself to go in. He would kill Verdi even if she tried to surrender. There were no plans even to give her the chance.

His shoulder against the door, Wheeler pushed his way in, both hands on the TEC-9. Bright light reflected off tile and chrome. Mirrors on his right, his reflection aiming the gun back at him. He charged the last stall and squeezed the trigger on the TEC-9, spraying the door with fire, peppering it with lines of bullet holes. The sound was deafening, ringing off the tile, like a pneumatic drill in a cave. The magazine was spent in seconds.

Wheeler stuffed the TEC-9 into his belt and drew the Glock. He kicked in the shredded stall door, which clattered to the floor. *Empty.*

"Son of a ..." His voice trailed off to stunned silence. Holding the Glock out in front, he kicked open the rest of the stall doors one by one. Still no one.

"Damn bitch," he muttered, and stomped to the outer door, angrily shoving it open. He was determined to find her, to kill her wherever she—

"Aaah," Wheeler screamed as the steel muzzle of a gun appeared out of nowhere and was savagely thrust up his nose. He stiffened and blinked twice as he looked into the face of Kate Verdi, her brown eyes fixed on him like an eagle on a mouse.

"Hiya, Jake," she whispered. "Looking for me?"

"Wha—Where did you come from?"

Keeping her eyes on his, Verdi took the Glock from Wheeler's hand. Then she took the TEC-9. "The men's room, across the hall. I saw you go in here. You think I'd be waiting around for you? Where's Andreen?" Wheeler nodded his head slightly in the direction of the stairwell. "Take me," she said.

Feeling Verdi's revolver in his back, Wheeler, trembling, led her down corridor 3. He knew that this was it for him, that Andreen would never be taken alive. Wheeler would be killed in the crossfire with Verdi. If he tried anything with Verdi, she'd shoot him in the spine. He could lead her somewhere else, away from the stairwell. But she'd still probably kill him. He had to take her to the stairwell. Unless.

Unless Andreen knew he was coming. Andreen must have heard them just now on the cop's walkie-talkie through Verdi's wire, just as they'd heard her before. He'd let Andreen know they were coming and who was leading whom.

Verdi pulled Wheeler by his collar as they came to an intersection in the corridor. "Which way?" she said.

"Down this one," he said, indicating corridor 4. "Andreen's in the stairwell up ahead. He's got your friend Witherspoon, a gun to his head."

"Get moving," she ordered, pressing the .38 into one of his vertebrae. "And keep your hands up."

As Verdi prodded Wheeler forward, his mind worked to come up with the right plan to save his ass while burning hers. He took a breath, mustering all his sincerity. "Kate, listen," he said. "Andreen's in that

stairwell with a gun on Witherspoon. If I go through
that door first, without any warning, he'll blow me
away."

"And what a tragedy that would be," she said. "It's
a chance we'll have to take."

Wheeler could see the stairwell door up ahead. He
now had to think through how this would go down.
Andreen, hearing Wheeler's instructions, would probably be waiting behind the door, leaving Witherspoon in
the line of Verdi's fire. As soon as Verdi opened the
door, Wheeler would get down fast and let Andreen
pop her from the back. The most important thing for
him to do would be to get to the floor quickly. He'd
have to be careful not to go tumbling down the stairs
and hurt himself.

They were now two feet from the door. "Don't do it,
Kate," he pleaded, preparing to jump as the door
opened.

Verdi put her hand on the doorknob and moved the
gun up to his neck. She leaned close to his ear and
whispered, "It's OK, Jake. I took off the wire. Andreen
hasn't heard a word you've said."

Verdi raised her knee to his back and booted him,
screaming, through the door. She hit the floor just as
Andreen began firing, peeling off shot after shot
muffled by the silencer. He emptied his gun point-
blank into Wheeler, who, arms flailing, toppled forward
and slammed into Andreen. Together they tumbled
backward down the stairs.

Witherspoon, who'd been covering his head, looked
up when the shooting stopped. Seeing Andreen's
Walther on the floor, Witherspoon picked it up with

his good hand. Looking up, he saw Verdi standing over the stunned Andreen, the .38 in her trembling hands, aimed at his head.

"Kate," Witherspoon said softly, "it's over. Put the gun down."

Witherspoon waited a moment, but Verdi didn't respond. "Kate?" he said, more firmly this time. "I'm going to take the gun now, OK?"

Verdi kept glaring at Andreen, even as Witherspoon reached out and gently lifted the revolver from her hands.

★ EPILOGUE ★

Kate Verdi barely heard the minister's words as he called on the small congregation gathered in the Grace Memorial Garden chapel to say a final prayer for Lorna Demeritte. It was all she could do to raise her eyes from the floor toward the white casket at the front of the chapel. In the pews to the left of the casket, Lorna Demeritte's parents and family had locked arms together, weeping quietly. Verdi had heard that the family had gone to great expense in hiring security to make sure no TV cameras or reporters were at the funeral.

A week had passed since Kendall Holmes confessed to ordering Lorna's murder. He told the police that Andreen had hidden her body in a Capitol Hill Dumpster a few blocks from her house. It took the police a while to recover the body from a dump site in

Northeast Washington. Verdi was spared the details of the search.

That seemed to be the only thing she'd been spared. The shootings at the State Department and the Circle had stirred up a media feeding frenzy. Reporters hounded Verdi wherever she went—even her parents' house, where she'd been staying—until she secretly checked into a hotel and slept for three days.

At the front of the chapel the prayer ended, and the family slowly began filing out. Verdi kept her eyes down as they passed, looking up only as Lorna's parents reached out and patted her on the shoulder. She could see the agony and disbelief on their faces as they prepared to bury their daughter, the girl who had everything.

Verdi was the last to leave, hoping that the family would be in their cars by the time she got outside. She didn't want to see them, had no idea what to say to them. She wasn't even sure why she'd come here. At the entrance to the chapel a solitary figure lingered by the door. Verdi smiled when she recognized Clarence Witherspoon, dignified in black, a hat in one hand, his other arm in a sling. When she approached him, he offered her his good arm, which she took.

They began strolling through the parking lot. The air was cool, dry. "How are you?" she asked. "Your arm?"

"Oh, fine," he said, looking off. "I guess I'm going to have to work for my pension."

"And Detective Abernathy? I heard he had more surgery. How is he?"

"Abernathy is doing well. He had a punctured lung, which the doctors repaired. He lost a lot of blood in that stairwell, but I talked with him this morning. He'll be getting out of the hospital next week sometime."

"That's good."

"And you, Kate? How are you doing?"

Verdi was quiet for several seconds. "Still numb, I guess. My doctor wants me to 'see somebody,' as she puts it. But I'll be all right. I *am* tired of going to funerals."

A breeze started up, blowing strands of hair across Verdi's face. "I feel like I've talked to every lawyer in Washington, if that's possible. Appears all of them in the Circle have their own attorneys to defend them. I've been deposed by four already and have a two o'clock appointment today to meet with Kendall Holmes's attorneys. Can you believe it? He'll probably walk."

"Oh, I don't know about that," Witherspoon said. "It's a good thing there're a lot of them. The Circle, I mean. I hear they're falling over themselves to turn state's witness, testify against one another. The FBI's beginning to run everything down, finding out how extensive that espionage operation really was. Looks like they'd been dealing in millions of dollars' worth of secrets way before you ever came on the scene. They did a lot of damage. Holmes won't be walking away from this one."

They walked in silence over a yellowing lawn and into the parking lot. Verdi stopped and looked at Witherspoon. "It's still amazing to me the Circle went on as long as it did. I mean, what did Holmes really offer them besides career advancement? Is that enough for you to sell your soul?"

"Seems like it was," Witherspoon said.

Verdi shook her head. "This is my car," she said, nodding at her Camaro. "I was thinking of going into the office before seeing the lawyers. My boss told me I could take off as long as I wanted. I'm not sure I'm ready to go back there just yet."

Witherspoon shrugged and smiled. "So don't. Give yourself time. You're young; you have a long, illustrious career in front of you."

"Career." Verdi sighed. "Yeah, that's what got me into this to begin with."

Witherspoon tucked his hat under his arm and held out his hand. "Kate," he said softly as she shook it.

She smiled, blinking back tears. "You take care of yourself."

Witherspoon stood stiffly next to the Camaro as Verdi slid into it. He smiled when she started it up, the roar of the failing engine in open defiance of the morbid cemetery stillness. He kept smiling while she waved and rumbled out of the parking lot, turning in the direction of Washington.

Walking through the empty hallways at the State Department, Verdi found returning more difficult than she'd expected. This was the first time she'd been back since the shootings. The place was quiet, even for a Saturday afternoon. Twice she caught herself glancing over her shoulder to see no one there. She was beginning to wish she'd done this on a weekday, with people milling in the halls.